TITLES BY JO SEGURA

• • • • • • • • • •

Raiders of the Lost Heart
Temple of Swoon
The Lust Crusade

PRAISE FOR JO SEGURA

"*Romancing the Stone* meets *Indiana Jones* in this thrilling adventure romance."

—Entertainment Weekly

"Nail-biting adventure and steamy chemistry."

—*People*

"Heartbreak, redemption, and steamy narrative drive a true enemies-to-lovers tale."

—*The Seattle Times*

"A thrilling, page-turning story that will take readers for a wild ride: *Raiders of the Lost Heart* is as unique as it is compelling—a dash of academic rivals, a pinch of second-chance romance, a sprinkle of intrigue, a most badass female lead, and a whole lot of archaeological shenanigans in a beautiful Mexican setting! Jo Segura delivered the ultimate enemies-to-lovers adventure rom-com!"

—#1 *New York Times* bestselling author Ali Hazelwood

"It was everything I wanted: riotous fun, heart-clenching romance, and pitch-perfect characters!"

—*New York Times* bestselling author Christina Lauren

"*Temple of Swoon* is a true adventure rom-com—filled with snappy banter, heart-pounding twists and turns, and a romance between two people who were lost until they found each other. Jo Segura has such a talent for writing cinematic prose and chemistry between characters that will absolutely sweep you away. No one in romance is doing exactly what she is—no one!"

—*USA Today* bestselling author Alicia Thompson

"*Temple of Swoon* is the fast-paced romp I didn't know I needed. Jo Segura has a gift for the snappy banter and sizzling tension in an enemies-to-lovers romance. From the first page, you will be transported into Miri and Rafa's lush world, and you won't put it down until the end."

—*USA Today* bestselling author Adriana Herrera

"Jo Segura has done it again! *Temple of Swoon* is everything I'm looking for in an adventure romance. It's full of humor and heart-pounding action, and is steamier than the Amazon itself. I was riveted from beginning to end!"

—*USA Today* bestselling author Jenna Levine

"Adventure, intrigue, and steamy romance! Jo Segura skillfully weaves all three—and more—in this delightful debut!"

—*USA Today* bestselling author Priscilla Oliveras

"This book has it all! Passion, adventure, and so much swoon! Perfect novel for anyone who grew up wishing they could accompany Harrison Ford on a quest! Obsessed!"

—Alana Quintana Albertson, author of *My Fair Señor*

"An adventure romance so steamy you'll need to rinse off in a sexy jungle waterfall after reading."

—Jen Comfort, author of *What Is Love?*

"Segura's rip-roaring debut is sure to put her on the map."

—*Publishers Weekly*

"Unputdownable. Perfect for readers who enjoy a slow burn, witty banter, and plot twists and turns."

—*Library Journal* (starred review)

"Segura balances action-packed adventure with enjoyable romance tropes: Instead of 'just one bed,' there's 'just one tent.' Corrie is a likable heroine, and she and Ford have enough chemistry to keep readers turning the pages. A fun, fast-paced adventure rom-com with plenty of steamy scenes."

—*Kirkus Reviews*

"It's a hopeful sign of good things to come, both by Segura and possibly the genre as a whole: There's been a dearth of adventure romance novels for far too long, and *Raiders of the Lost Heart* is a thrilling addition to the canon that will hopefully kick off a new wave of the subgenre." —*BookPage*

"Readers looking for a thrilling romance with a nerdy heroine, a sensitive hero, and lots of bad guys will enjoy watching Miri become a badass, and maybe, just maybe, fall in love, too."

—*Booklist*

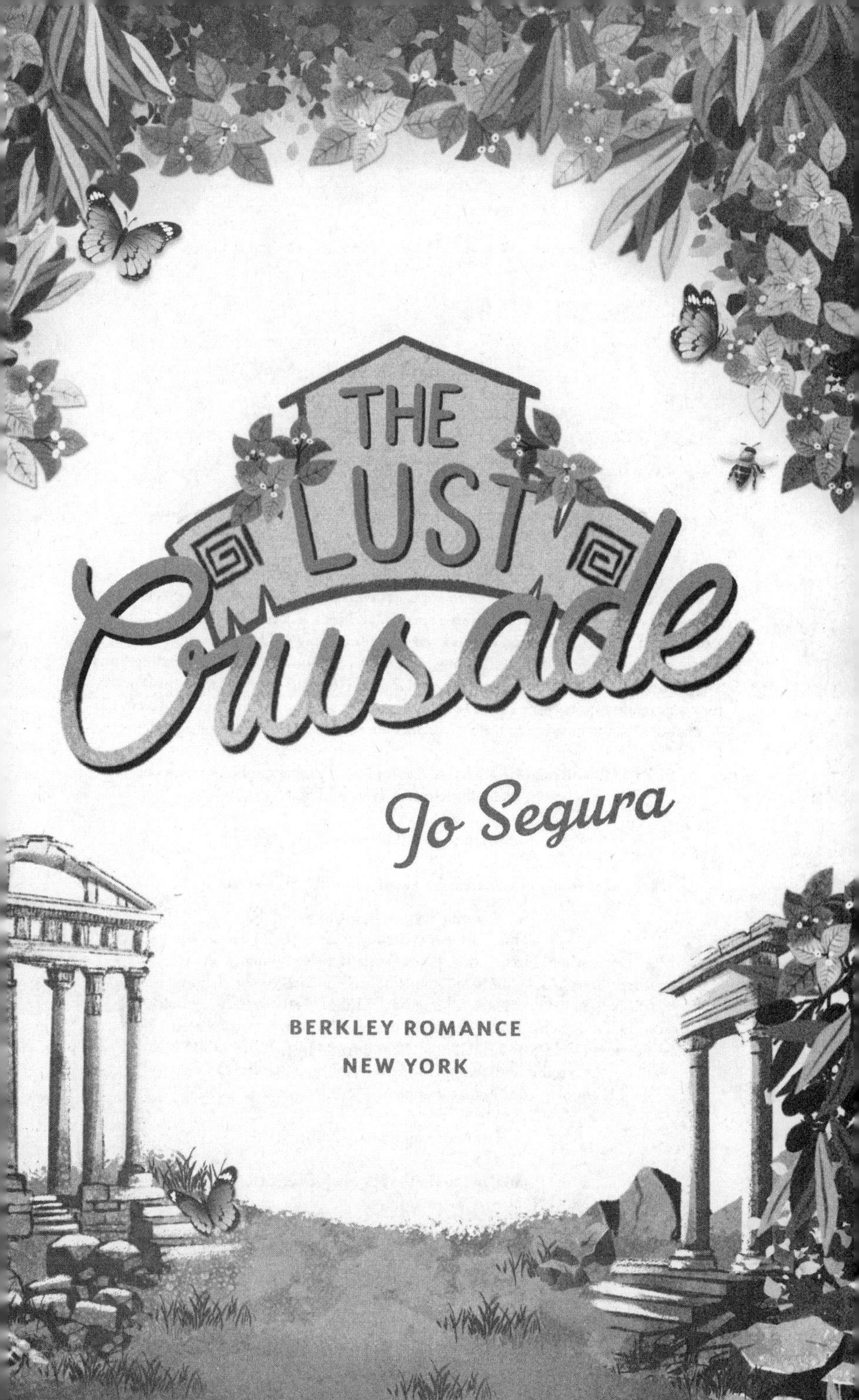
THE LUST Crusade
Jo Segura
BERKLEY ROMANCE
NEW YORK

BERKLEY ROMANCE
Published by Berkley
An imprint of Penguin Random House LLC
1745 Broadway, New York, NY 10019
penguinrandomhouse.com

Book design by Daniel Brount

Library of Congress Cataloging-in-Publication Data

Names: Segura, Jo author
Title: The lust crusade / Jo Segura.
Description: First edition. | New York: Berkley Romance, 2026.
Identifiers: LCCN 2025025256 (print) | LCCN 2025025257 (ebook) |
ISBN 9780593953280 trade paperback | ISBN 9780593953297 ebook
Subjects: LCGFT: Romance fiction | Action and adventure fiction | Novels | Fiction
Classification: LCC PS3619.E4158 L87 2026 (print) | LCC PS3619.E4158 (ebook)
LC record available at https://lccn.loc.gov/2025025256
LC ebook record available at https://lccn.loc.gov/2025025257

First Edition: January 2026

Printed in the United States of America
1st Printing

The authorized representative in the EU for product safety and compliance is Penguin Random House Ireland, Morrison Chambers, 32 Nassau Street, Dublin D02 YH68, Ireland, https://eu-contact.penguin.ie.

This one's for me.

THE
LUST
Crusade

CHAPTER One

Dani

GREECE: BIRTHPLACE OF MANY OF DANIELA GUITERREZ'S FAvorite things. Libraries. Gyros. Democracy. Cheesecake. And Dr. Theo Galanis.

His name had played on repeat in her head ever since she'd landed in Crete three days ago. *Theo. Theo. Theo.* This trip wasn't supposed to be about him. This was supposed to be her opportunity to finally see the world. Meet new people. Maybe meet a guy. Someone who might allow her to forget about Theo.

Dani laughed to herself at the idea as she stared out the window of the tour bus on its way to the palace of Knossos. The sparkling, crystal-blue water as they pulled away from the harbor reminded her of his eyes. A moment later, they passed a stand selling dolmades, tangy stuffed grape leaves—Theo's favorite food. And then, a local bar with a poster-size advertisement for raki, a celebratory drink at every one of Theo's family gatherings.

Forget about Theo? Who was she kidding?

She'd come to Greece, of all places. If there was anyplace in the world that could remind her of Theo, this was it. Place of his birth.

And of his death.

Are you gonna get busy living or keep busying yourself with dying? Her dad's question, butchering his favorite movie quote, echoed in her ears. As did her mom's follow-up: *What he's saying, mija, is it's time for you to get a life.*

Ouch.

It was some thanks after dedicating the last sixteen years of her life—ever since her dad's work accident—helping them out by taking her dad to his doctor's appointments, doing their grocery shopping, and picking up their prescriptions only for them to tell her a month ago that they were packing their bags and finally moving to Florida like they'd threatened to do so many times. Forgive Dani for thinking they'd never go through with it, seeing as they'd lived in Grand Rapids, Michigan, for the entirety of their lives. Yet there they were, kicking her out of her childhood home so they could sell it to some young family looking to put down roots.

Okay, so maybe they *did* offer to sell it to Dani first, but the price they needed to be able to put down the deposit on their new place in Florida was *not* in her librarian's-salary budget and she wasn't going to ask them for a deal. Especially not after they'd apparently considered the last sixteen years as *their* favor to *her*, when she'd been over there naively thinking it had been the other way around. They didn't even seem to remember that her brother, Eddie, hadn't offered to lift a finger when her dad first got in the accident whereas she was packed and moved out of her dorm at the University of Michigan the minute her mom muttered the words, *I don't know how I'll be able to take care of your papa alone.*

Okay, okay! So maybe Eddie *offered*, but come on. Not only did he not have a single nurturing bone in his body, but he and Theo, his BFF since the second grade, had just left for a non-refundable study-abroad program in Spain. Dani, on the other hand, was only a little over a hundred miles away and one (miserable) semester into her undergrad at Michigan. It made sense for Dani to be the one to help.

Right? She furrowed her brow as she watched Heraklion passing by out the bus window, thinking back to that pivotal time in her life all those years ago.

She'd always planned to return to U of M. Helping out her parents was supposed to be temporary. At least, that's what she'd been telling herself for the last decade and a half. It was better than admitting that Daniela Guiterrez, former high school daredevil and talker of big dreams, was too scared to go out on her own and eventually got comfortable living above her parents' garage and gave up on all those things she'd said she was going to do. She got comfortable never having ventured from Grand Rapids other than that short stint in Ann Arbor.

But now what? Her parents were moving a thousand miles away, Eddie was in Chicago living the bachelor life, and Theo's family, who'd been like an extension of her own, had all left the area. There was no one left to call Grand Rapids home. Her parents' suggestion that maybe it was time for her to start her *own* family, to settle down and find a husband, begged the question: With whom?

God, I need a date.

"Well, I'll go out on a date with you tonight, little missy. Happy to oblige," a voice said to her left.

Dani spun her head around to her tour bus seatmate, Harold, and blinked. Had she really said that out loud? The old man smiled, cheery as always, and she actually pondered his invitation for a moment. As she'd come to discover over the last couple of days, Harold *was* pretty funny. But ignoring for a moment that he was old enough to be her abuelo, in no universe did the term of endearment *little missy* ever result in someone agreeing to go on a date, and it certainly wouldn't be starting today.

But as her *actual* abuelo had always said: *Respect your elders.*

"I don't know why I said that," she responded. "I was thinking about something else. Besides I think we'll be too tired after today's excursion, don't you think?"

"Bah!" Harold said, waving his hand dismissively. "Ain't nothing but a bit of walking around at Knossos. Wait 'til we get to the Acropolis. Glad I got that knee replacement surgery taken care of last year." He made a fist and knocked on his knee, clearly proud of his mobility.

"But I get it," he resumed. "If I were a beautiful young lady like you, I wouldn't want to hang out with an old fogey like me, either." He winked and smiled, and Dani couldn't help but smile in return.

She was used to old men hitting on her—or really, men of all ages hitting on her, especially whenever she came out from behind the counter at her job at the Grand Rapids Public Library and they got one look at her . . . *generous* hips and ass—but she didn't get that sort of vibe from Harold. After only three days with him, he gave off more *You're the only person I can stand on this group tour* than *Hubba-hubba.*

"But," Harold continued, "if you want to check out the

nightlife and need a wingman, I'm your guy. I'm the only one in this crew who can stay up past five p.m., after all."

Harold gave her another wink, and she snickered. At thirty-five, Dani was the youngest person on the tour bus by *at least* thirty years, and, in most cases, more like forty. On the first day when Harold had joked he must have been twice her age, it had turned out he wasn't wrong. But how was Dani supposed to have known that Silver Sunset Singles Tours, LLC, catered to the sixty-plus crowd?

Okay, so maybe *silver* should have been a hint. And sure, there *were* a lot of photos on Silver Sunset's website of happy retirement-age individuals. But it was the only Greek singles tour with last-minute availability she could find within her budget. It wasn't her fault that some sort of internet form snafu didn't catch that she was "underage," something she hadn't been in quite some time. So when she'd arrived in Crete for the start of the tour and the guide, Cosmo, had gone to check her in, they decided to honor the reservation.

What were they going to do? Cancel it and leave her stranded, alone, in Greece? She was just glad there was *someone* on this bus who was interested in talking with her.

Though becoming besties with a septuagenarian wasn't exactly what she'd envisioned for the trip when she'd booked it a few weeks ago. Right after her parents told her they were selling the house two days after . . . Theo's memorial service.

Seriously, could they have picked a worse time to break the news?

Her entire world had been turned upside down in a matter of forty-eight hours, her parents' announcement being the final nail in the proverbial (and in Theo's case, nonexistent) coffin.

Seemed like as good a time as any to take a last-minute midlife crisis vacation to a foreign country.

"Penny for your thoughts?" Harold asked.

"Oh, I was thinking about a friend."

"A friend?" Harold raised his brow. "What sort of friend?"

"Not that kind of friend," she said with a bit of a laugh and then waved her arms around their surroundings. "I mean, look at me. I'm by myself. On a seniors' singles tour."

"Why is that, exactly?" he asked, folding his hands in his lap and turning in his seat to face her. "What brings a gal like you on a tour like this?"

Dani sighed and leaned back against the headrest. "I didn't know it was a sixty-plus tour, if that's what you're wondering."

"I figured as much. Been meaning to ask you, but I didn't want to be rude by asking what in the golly heck brought you here. Thought maybe you were Cosmo's girlfriend at first."

Dani scrunched her face at the idea. Cosmo may have been a young whippersnapper when compared to Harold, but he was still at least twenty years her senior.

"So maybe Cosmo's not your type," Harold said with a chuckle. "But alone? Don't you have someone special—or maybe even that friend of yours you're thinking about—who could have gone on a trip with you?"

Oof.

"Well, when you put it *that* way . . ." Dani said, and let her voice trail off.

Because what was she supposed to say? That, no, she didn't have someone special because for the last decade she'd dated only casually so she could be available if and when her parents needed her? Or perhaps that her only real friend nowadays, her coworker Beau, preferred sand and mojitos over crumbling ruins and ouzo. In his words, he *wouldn't be caught dead in hideous hiking boots.*

Poor word choice, Beau. Too soon. Much too soon.

Of course, there was always Eddie, but *she'd* be caught dead before taking a trip like this with him. Nothing was worse than when people asked if *they* were dating. Gross. Besides, they got along fine—she might even consider them "friends" given how much time they hung out together with Theo—but things were different now that Theo was gone. It was almost as if his absence was an elephant in the room whenever they got together and they didn't know how to act around each other without him there.

Most of Dani's other friends had left Grand Rapids straight after high school, and those who hadn't, well, there was nothing like showing her face again after moving back home only a few weeks into college. Sure, Dani, the dutiful daughter that she was, could point to her dad's accident as the justification for her return to Grand Rapids. But she'd heard the rumors:

Did you hear Daniela Guiterrez couldn't hack it at the University of Michigan?

I heard she flunked out.

I knew she was nothing but talk.

She thought she was so much better than us, and look at her now.

Ah yes, look at her now. Single. Midthirties. And working in the library, of all places. Served her right for that stunt she pulled in tenth grade, reshelving all the books in their high school library by "vibes" rather than author name and genre. Back then, she'd never been one to turn down a dare.

But that was then.

Once voted "most likely to bungie jump off the Eiffel Tower," now Dani would probably be more accurately described as "most likely to die of *actual* boredom." The only times she felt like her old self were the times when Theo visited.

We figured you *needed* us, her parents had explained, sitting her down at the dinner table to break the news about their impending move. *You seemed so unhappy and sad all the time. We thought you* wanted *to come home.* It was difficult to recall the discussion surrounding her return home all these years later. She remembered saying she'd come home without hesitation when her mom first told her about her dad falling down a manhole working for the city's public works department during a storm event and how he'd be out of work for at least a few months. She'd volunteered because they'd asked. Hadn't they?

The conversation was a little hazy now.

Her return had nothing to do with the fact that she was homesick. Or that she didn't get into all the classes she'd wanted. Or that she and her new roommate weren't getting along. Or that she missed her old friends and family.

Home made sense. At least it did back then.

Could she even call it that anymore, though, when her home was literally being taken from her?

"I'm sorry. There I go, being nosy again," Harold said.

Dani smiled and put her hand on his arm. "It's fine. Really. My life right now . . . it's . . . it's complicated."

That was one way to put it. Definitely too complicated to get into in the last ten minutes of their bus ride to the palace of Knossos where soon they'd be crawling around ten square kilometers of sprawling ruins, learning about the lives of the Minoan civilization with thousands of other tourists. At least they were going in the latter half of the day after the crowds had hopefully thinned out.

"Well, then, you can tell me all about it over dinner tonight," Harold said with a wink. "Only as friends. I promise."

Dani smiled. "Okay. Friends."

"I was only teasing about the date thing earlier, you know. I know I'm here on this whole single seniors' thing, but ever since my Patricia passed away five years ago, I haven't been able to imagine life with someone else." There was a crack in his voice, and suddenly he stopped talking, pulling his lip in to keep it from trembling. "I'm sorry. I don't mean to get morose. You probably came here to enjoy an adventure, not think about dead people."

Dead.

The word thumped in her chest. Suddenly the words that she still refused to accept flashed through her mind:

GREEK AMERICAN ARCHAEOLOGIST PRESUMED DEAD

By the time the newspapers printed that headline, the story of Dr. Theo Galanis's disappearance had already been blasted all over the news and social media. When Dani had first learned that he'd gone missing, his last known whereabouts being a marina where he'd chartered a boat for a journey off the coast of Neapoli, she hadn't been able to breathe. Theo had arrived in Greece one week earlier. He was supposed to have been there for only a couple of months, six tops, having been contacted by his old friend on behalf of some archaeological society to assist with a dig on the Peloponnesian peninsula given his expertise in ancient Greek archaeology. The details were a little fuzzy, as was any paper trail with the specifics.

In the weeks that followed, they'd come to find out that his friend hadn't actually contacted him and the alleged archaeological society didn't actually exist. The supposed Peloponnesian dig site, unheard of. So after he'd been missing for four months and the boat was found beaten up and washed ashore on Kythira—without any sign of survivors—well, everyone had assumed the worst.

Dr. Theo Galanis, the love of Dani's life, was dead.

And she'd never even told him how she'd felt.

A solid thirteen months had passed since he'd vanished. At the one-year anniversary, his family held a memorial service, even though it was too early to declare him legally dead. The family had intended the service to give them all closure, but the only thing it had done was make Dani restless. She still couldn't picture life without Theo in it, even *if* only in his role as Eddie's best friend. Maybe she and Harold had more in common than she thought, being unable to imagine life without that one special person. But this trip was supposed to be her opportunity to get out and finally see the world. To do all the things she'd planned to do after high school.

And if the memorial couldn't give her closure, hopefully this trip would.

She'd go to Greece, the country of Theo's heart. See the sights. Taste the food. Soak in that Mediterranean air. Go to all the places he'd talked about from his travels. And then she'd say goodbye to him forever. Finally get busy living *her* life, instead of someone else's.

The singles thing was supposed to be an added bonus. *Maybe* she'd meet someone on the trip who could make her stomach swirl the way Theo could. Wouldn't that be fitting, after all? To meet a new man of her dreams in the very place she'd lost her first love?

Okay, maybe not actual love. They'd never even kissed. But she felt something for Theo she'd never felt with anyone else. And now, she'd never know what it could have been.

"Attention, Silvers!" Cosmo called out on the bus PA system. "We're arriving at Knossos. We've got two hours here before closing. Now, let me take you back in time," he said, waving his hands in the air like a mystic and hunkering down as he lowered his voice, "to the seventeenth century BC, when the Minoans ruled the region. We'll traverse the ruins and picture our lives behind the walls, with creatures lurking in the depths of the palace. But don't get lost, or the *BEAST* might get you!" he said, bringing up his hands like a grizzly bear attacking its prey.

Plenty of oohs and aahs from the group accompanied his description.

"Or," he said, matter-of-factly, standing straight and dropping his arms along with the mysticism, "there is a self-guided tour available at the ticket office that you can listen to on your phone at your own leisure. Either way, we'll meet back at the bus at sixteen forty-five to depart at seventeen hundred on the dot. Do not be late."

With that, the bus lurched to a stop and the group of fifteen unloaded, shuffling their way in a wad toward the entrance gates after Cosmo scanned the tour group through.

The grounds appeared unassuming as they first passed through the ticket turnstiles. The site was much more tree covered than Dani had imagined based on the research she'd done before the trip. It honestly wasn't at all the grand castle that she'd pictured in her head. There were some giant pits called kouloures at the entrance of the West Court, which Cosmo explained may have been used to store grains. A processional corridor. But as they followed a pathway to the right and then finally rounded a corner, the palace and all its glory came into view.

A giant courtyard at least the size of four football fields sat in the center with partially reconstructed limestone buildings on either side. Some were still in a state of repair and excavation. Others were reimaginings of explorers who'd come before. Painted frescoes with depictions of Minoan life lined the walls—re-creations, Cosmo explained, of Sir Arthur Evans, the British archaeologist who staked claim to the discovery of Knossos. There was an air of disdain in Cosmo's voice—apparently, Evans had taken some liberties in his reconstructions—but the paintings were works of art, nonetheless.

They climbed stairs. Snapped pictures of giant jugs. Squeezed into the "throne room," even though the worn slab apparently might not have been a throne at all. But it made for a better story.

Dani absorbed everything around her, from the structures to the cypress and olive trees, and even the mountainside behind them, trying to imagine what it must have been like to live here thousands of years ago. There was still much excavation work to be done, as evidenced by the actual archaeologists still working in areas roped off from the public. To think, what more could be found? She was starting to understand the thrill Theo got when he was on a dig, a similar rush to that feeling from her younger, more adventurous days.

"And here we have the Minotaur," Cosmo said as they sidled up to a fresco on the far side of the grounds. "I'm sure you've all heard the tale of the Minotaur, yes?"

Dani's travel companions all seemed to nod in unison. She remembered the gist of it—a bull-like man trapped in a labyrinth—but she couldn't tell you much more than that. Theo would be thoroughly disappointed.

"Ah, good. Now, let me tell you the *real* story," Cosmo continued. "King Minos, ruler of Knossos, was said to have built a labyrinth underneath the palace to hide the creature that had been born out of the love his wife had for a majestic white bull. Trapped in the center of the labyrinth, half man, half bull, the Minotaur was a beast unlike any other. Its strength, unmatched. Its ferocity, unimaginable. Terrifying eyes that glowed red, like rubies on fire. Teeth that could tear apart a body in a single, gnashing bite. Only the bravest even dared challenge it, but none succeeded. Some say the Minotaur is still hidden in the depths of this palace to this day. Others believe it is simply another Greek myth. But it hasn't stopped explorers from trying to find it."

Cosmo was using his spooky voice again, and Dani had to admit he was a talented showman. And she loved a good story, always surrounding herself with half a dozen books at any one time—and those were only the ones on her immediate TBR list. Working at a library made it difficult for her master TBR to be anything other than a mile long, and it was full of fantastical tales.

But that's clearly all that this beast was—a tale. If no one survived an encounter with the Minotaur, how would they even know? Did anyone actually believe this as anything other than fiction?

A hand shot up in the crowd. "How big was the monster?" a lady wearing a wide-brimmed visor, a linen sundress, and hiking sandals asked.

"Well, Roberta, it would be huge," Cosmo responded. "Picture the Minotaur, eight—no, ten feet tall," he said, lifting his hand and standing on his tippy-toes to demonstrate the height of the monster. "Its head, this big." He shifted and held his hands out wide in a half circle, letting their imaginations fill in the rest. "Now picture the size of an eye on a creature that large. It must be the size of a football!"

A few people gasped. Roberta clutched her chest.

"How old was it?" Roberta then asked.

"Thirty—no, one hundred years old!"

More murmurs.

"How many people did it kill?" she continued.

"At least a thousand!"

A few sharp inhales and more pearl clutching followed.

"If you'd like," Cosmo said, lowering his voice to a whisper and huddling toward the group, "tomorrow, instead of visiting the archaeology museum in Heraklion, I can take you to a cave where it's rumored they did religious rituals to worship the Minotaur. Though it will cost each of you another thirty euros. Sixty-five if you want a traditional Greek lunch prepared by my uncle Vasilios."

Immediately, Roberta's hand shot up again, and the group started clamoring for this little side venture. Something told Dani this sudden, unexpected side journey was part of Cosmo's normal shtick. She had to hand it to him, though—he knew how to sell it to his audience.

Dani stood there for a moment as Cosmo went over the details—cave tour and lunch for those who wanted, or they could visit the Heraklion Archaeological Museum, which they'd already paid for as part of the overall tour package—but once Roberta persisted down the path of twenty questions, Dani slinked away from the group, hoping to catch a bit more of the grounds before they had to start making their way back toward the bus in another thirty minutes.

So while Cosmo and the others pressed on to check out the ramp that was supposedly used to cart in goods to the palace grounds, Dani wandered to the east side of the site, the area where it looked as though the excavation was still in progress. But as Dani drifted aimlessly, a figure caught her eye in the distance, climbing over the railing down into the restricted area below the palace.

A man.

She couldn't make him out from the one hundred or so yards away other than that he had a beard and dark hair sticking out from under a baseball cap. But something looked familiar in his movements. The way he walked. The long length of his stride. He appeared in a hurry—and even though he walked with purpose, he clearly didn't want to get caught.

A tourist going off the path? A thief?

Someone looking for the Minotaur?

Dani shook Cosmo's voice out of her head. *Don't be ridiculous.*

But something was definitely off. She'd witnessed enough people trying to sneak behind the stacks or into the private collections areas at the library to know when someone was up to no good.

Hell, she used to be one of those people.

Dani spun around looking for an employee, someone she could tell, before realizing she didn't really even know *what* she saw. What if the man worked here? Wouldn't that be embarrassing? Tattling on an employee?

If thirty-five years as a little sister taught her anything, it was that nobody liked a tattletale—though she'd argue Eddie was the bigger snitch between the two of them anyway. And this really wasn't any of her business. She didn't come on this trip so she could play Nancy Drew.

But . . . maybe she needed a closer look.

Dani picked up her pace and headed toward the area where the man had disappeared. Once she got to the railing, she crouched behind a placard, slowly peeking over the edge. There he was, now with two other guys dressed in all black carrying shovels.

Uh-oh. A sinking feeling filled Dani's stomach. She couldn't be sure, but whatever these guys were doing didn't seem above-board.

Right then, the man with the beard turned around as if double-checking that he hadn't been followed, and she dropped into a crouch. But when Dani saw the logo on his dark blue hat—a white Old English *D*—she immediately fell backward, bracing herself with her hands behind her in the dirt.

The Detroit Tigers. Theo's team.

Not only that, Theo's lucky hat.

No, no, no. Dani shook her head. She had to have been seeing things. Harold's prodding had her mind playing tricks on her. She had Theo on the brain, that was all. Besides, Theo had never sported a beard.

Oh yeah, and he was dead. Right?

But what if . . . ?

As her heart pounded, Dani scrambled to get back up, peering over the railing again, but the men were gone. She glanced at her watch. 4:32 p.m. She had less than fifteen minutes to make it back to the bus.

But what if?

No, this is absurd. It didn't make any sense. If there was anyone who loved their family as much as she loved hers, it was Theo. There was no way he'd ghost them like that if he were alive. She brushed her hands on the front of her olive-colored linen shorts then turned away from the railing and headed back toward the exit.

He's dead, remember? Let him go.

But that *D* flashed in her mind again, along with the thought one more time: *But what if?*

Like, what if he had amnesia?

She looked at her watch once more: 4:33.

Walking away meant she'd have a new question weighing on her: *What if?* One that she could very well get the answer to if she only dared to . . .

Without another second of hesitation, Dani rushed back to the railing, and once she determined the coast was clear, she scaled the metal barrier, dropping down to the pathway below with a dull *thud* that was no match for the pounding in her chest.

A rush of adrenaline whooshed through her. A reminder of her old life. Back before she turned into the sort of person who shushed people in the library when they were too loud.

She missed this feeling—taking risks, breaking rules.

Before she knew it, her feet were carrying her in the direction of the men, snaking their way along the palace perimeter until she came to a doorway with a set of stairs descending underneath the ground. She followed the staircase to a tunnel, eventually needing her cell phone flashlight to see. Who knew if the men even went this way, but something pulled her farther down the corridor. Eventually she came to an active work area with lighting and tables set up, but clearly the archaeologists had gone home for the day. She kept going until it appeared she'd hit a dead end.

But then she heard the voices.

"We don't have the tools for this," someone said.

Dani spun around, looking for the direction the voices had come from, when she noticed a sliver of light between the stones.

A passageway.

She turned off her flashlight and tiptoed over to the glow, putting her face up to the crack where the light shined through. The three men were about thirty feet away, huddled over another smaller opening in the stone wall.

"Use this," the stockier of the men in black said to the guy in the Detroit Tigers ball cap, handing him a shovel. But Detroit didn't take it.

"That's not going to work," Detroit said, pushing the shovel away.

Was that voice familiar? Dani couldn't tell with the echo of the tunnel. She also couldn't see him with his back to her. *Turn around. Please, let me see you.*

"Make it work. We've got all night," the other taller man responded.

"Listen, I need my tools. I've told you before, I can't work under these conditions," Detroit said. "If you'd let me go to a hardware store—"

"So you can run off again?" Stocky interrupted.

"Why are you acting like you make the rules here? I shouldn't have to keep reminding you who's in charge. Get to it," Tall Guy said, now tossing the shovel at Detroit's chest.

Detroit caught the shovel, turning ever so slightly in Dani's direction, but not far enough. Dammit. She still couldn't see him, not with the shadows and the poor lighting.

"And what are you going to do while I try to cut through stone with this?" Detroit asked.

"Don't worry about it," Tall Guy said, resting on the dirt and pulling a knife out from behind him along with a piece of fruit from his satchel. He started cutting off chunks of the fruit, bringing it up to his mouth with the knife. "Want a piece?" he offered.

"Only if you're finally trying to kill me," Detroit responded. "I'm allergic to apples."

Dani gasped and quickly put her hands over her mouth. *Theo.*

But it was too late. All three men's heads shot in the direction of the opening. She immediately backed away but tripped on a rock and came crashing down on her ass.

"Someone's out there!" one of the men yelled. "Get them!"

Dani scrambled to her feet and ran. Her hand trembled as she fumbled with her phone to turn the flashlight back on. She had been right: these men were up to no good, and she didn't need to find out any more than that.

As she made her way through the tunnel, she heard the grinding of stone behind her, likely them pushing open the doorway to the room they'd been in. Moving as quickly as she could, she ran through the underbelly of the palace and all its twists and turns, not stopping for even a moment to look behind her.

She didn't miss *this* part of taking risks and breaking rules.

The light from the outside was ahead, signaling she was almost out of danger. When she emerged from the tunnel, she stopped for a moment, shielding her eyes from the sun's rays, and a brief wave of relief washed over her.

"There she is!" one of the men called from behind her. "We can catch her."

Forget about that relief. Her heartbeat pounded in her ears. This was it. This was how she was going to die. But at least she wasn't going to go without a fight.

Thankfully, she'd gained a bit of distance in the tunnel even though her short legs weren't exactly doing her any favors. Especially when she had to climb back over the railing. She pulled herself up, damning herself for quitting that CrossFit class that might have earned her the upper-body strength to do a pull-up. But she dug her toes into the side of the wall, using all her might to scale the six-foot embankment. As she was about to swing her leg up over the side, however, something grabbed her ankle.

No, not something. Someone.

"Not so fast," Stocky said.

But where Dani failed in upper-body strength, she excelled in leg power. She may have been small in stature, but that didn't keep her brother from teasing her about her "tree trunks." So, with as much force as she could muster, she jerked her leg like a bucking horse.

"Get . . . your . . . hands . . . off!" she growled in sync with her kicks.

The bottom of her hiking shoe connected with what she could only assume was the man's face—she didn't bother looking—which was followed by a grunt and a string of profanities as she pulled herself the rest of the way over the ledge. The dry, pebbly dirt scraped against her skin as she skirted away from the edge, stirring up a cloud of dust around her. As she rose to her feet, she kicked as much of the dirt as she could, hoping it would get in the man's eyes. Then, like a bat out of hell, she booked it across the courtyard, down the pathway toward the exit, out the gates, and straight for the tour bus.

"Ticktock, missy," Cosmo called out from fifty feet away, tapping his clipboard on his watch. "Just because we bent the age requirement for you, doesn't mean the rest of the rules don't apply."

Now wasn't the time to say *Fuck off*, but the words *were* on the tip of her tongue. But she didn't need to piss Cosmo off when the only thing standing between her and those guys was (hopefully) the bus.

"Noted!" she called out as she ran up to him. "Now please, let's go!"

She yanked on Cosmo's arm, pulling him into the bus behind her and shouted, "Go, go, go," to the driver.

Cosmo smoothed out his shirt, apparently oblivious to the fact that Dani had been running for her dear life, then told the driver to get them on their way. The *whoosh* of the bus exhaust and release of the brakes signaled they were getting ready to pull out as Dani made her way to the back beside Harold. He scanned her filthy clothes, then furrowed his brow.

"Looks like you've been off having some fun," he said, suspiciously.

"'Fun' isn't how I would put it."

Right as the bus started to drive off, however, the three men ran up to the side, right to the window where she sat looking over Harold.

Detroit took off his ball cap as he eased up his running and he looked straight at her. Dani's heart skipped a beat. Beard or not, she'd recognize those cerulean eyes from behind those dark-framed glasses anywhere.

It was Theo. And he was back from the dead.

CHAPTER
Two

Dani

STOP THE BUS!" DANI YELLED, RUNNING TO THE BACK WINDOW to try to catch one more glimpse of the man her brain could only impossibly process as being Theo.

But the bus didn't stop, and soon the man was nothing but a tiny speck in the distance.

The rest of the Silvers gawked at her as she ran down the aisle toward Cosmo in the front, a few of them casting her judging glances like she was some ridiculous, overly dramatic youngster on what should be their calm, relaxing vacation.

"I said stop the bus," she said again, rushing down the walkway.

"No, I believe you said 'Go, go, go,'" Cosmo said.

Dani found it difficult to keep from rolling her eyes. Now wasn't the time to be literal and hold her to her words.

"I know. But that man back there," she said, tossing her

thumb behind her. "I didn't realize who that was earlier. He's dead. We need to stop."

Cosmo raised a brow. "I'm sorry, did you say 'dead'?"

Dani waved her hands, dipping her head as she tried to catch her breath. "That's not what I meant. I mean, people *think* he's dead. But he's clearly not."

"And how do you know that?"

"Because he's right there!" Dani said, pointing back toward Knossos. "We have to go back."

"Can't," Cosmo said, flipping a page on his clipboard without looking at her. "We have a tight schedule."

Dani braced herself with her hands on the back of one of the bench seats and took a deep breath. *Relax. Relax and explain what you saw.*

"Cosmo?" she said, using her most pleasant voice. The voice she used whenever she approached a group of rowdy teens in the YA section *not* studying or reading quietly despite the abundance of signs demanding silence throughout the library.

"Yes?"

"We have to go back," she said, calmly.

Cosmo sighed and brought his clipboard in front of his waist, folding his arms atop it. "And I told you. Not. Possible."

"Why not?!" She dropped the calmness.

"Tell me, Miss . . . ?"

"It's Dani."

"Miss Dani—"

"No, it's Dani Guiterrez, but—"

"Okay, Miss Guiterrez, then—"

"I mean, you can call me Dani."

"Fine. Dani, tell me what exactly the reason is we need to turn around."

How to explain this in a way that would make sense?

"Have you heard of the missing American archaeologist, Dr. Theo Galanis?" she asked.

"No," he responded, pointed and direct. He then lifted the clipboard and returned to his notes, but Dani put her hand over the page to stop him.

"Dr. Theo Galanis went missing over a year ago, and he was just there. At Knossos," she said.

"So then he *isn't* missing, is he?"

Dani brought her hands into an upside-down V in front of her face, placing the apex of her index fingers at the bridge of her nose. "You're not listening to me."

"No, I'm listening. But you're not hearing me. We can't make any changes to the schedule."

"Oh really? What about lunch at your uncle Vasilios's tomorrow?"

Cosmo's gaze narrowed at her, but as he opened his mouth again, the driver called out over his shoulder.

"Galanis? I remember him. The archaeologist. He was Greek, too, no?"

Dani pushed past Cosmo and knelt beside the driver. "Yes! Theo Galanis. He is Greek American."

"Yes. His boat capsized, right? There was a huge reward for any information surrounding his disappearance," the driver said.

Dani looked up at Cosmo, whose eyebrow ticked up half an inch. This bit of information piqued his interest.

"Fine," he said.

Dani clasped her hand around his forearm, relief washing over her. "Fine, we'll go back?"

"No. Fine, I'll call the authorities and let them know what you think you saw."

She didn't like the way he said *think*, but it was better than nothing.

"Should I pull over to wait?" the driver said. They hadn't gone *too* far, but probably farther than Dani would like to walk on a busy, sidewalk-less road.

"No," Cosmo responded. "We have a schedule."

• • • • • • • • • •

"SO EXPLAIN IT TO ME ONE MORE TIME. I THOUGHT I HEARD YOU say he's dead?" Harold asked, chomping on the crunchy bread in his Cretan salad in the outdoor seating area at a restaurant in the square near their hotel later that evening for dinner. It may have been well after nine p.m., but Dani wouldn't have guessed it based on the number of people mingling about the brick plaza, eating, drinking, and socializing under string lights and neon restaurant signs.

"Well, clearly he's not. Or at least, I don't think he is," Dani said, staring at the table trying to make sense of things. Hell, she had no idea *what* she'd seen.

"You think it was a ghost?"

Dani's eyes flashed up to Harold's and she furrowed her brow. "No, Harold, it wasn't a ghost. I'm telling you, it was Theo. I know it."

Harold shrugged and scanned their shared plates full of gyro meat, salads, and fries, planning his next bite. "How can you be so sure? If there was ever a place for ghosts to be lurking, I bet the lair of the Minotaur would be prime real estate."

Because, she thought, *I'd never forget his eyes.*

The same eyes had stared down at her during senior prom after her date stood her up. He'd been a sophomore in college, so it was patently *uncool* to go to high school dances at his age. Not that Theo had ever have been considered cool even when he was in high school anyway. He was the guy who was constantly (and annoyingly) over at their house all the time, built his own clay replicas of stills from the movie *Clash of the Titans*, and talked about Zeus like he was a real person. But when he showed up at the Guiterrezes' doorstep wearing a suit and holding a bouquet of flowers after Dani had already changed into her pajamas thinking she'd have to miss the prom, well, that night she no longer saw him as Eddie's dorky best friend. And on the dance floor when he spoke the words, *Whenever you need me, I'll always be here for you, Dani*, well, those words were the dawn of Dani's epic, decades-long crush on Theo Galanis.

The funny thing was that Theo was decidedly *not* her type. Up until then, and even after, Dani went for the bad boys. The risky options. Men who broke her heart without a second thought. Theo, on the other hand, dated nice girls. *Good* girls. Most importantly, good *Greek* girls. Triple Gs, as the Galanises all called them. Women who sat politely and quietly at Thanksgiving dinner, unlike Dani, whose M.O. was to be loud and brash, leading her father to call her "cochina" all too often at the dining table.

But over the years, she sometimes caught those blue irises staring at her. At a summer pool party. At Eddie's college graduation. Then again at Theo's parents' thirtieth-anniversary celebration after the words *When you know, you know* were spoken. And, of course, that last night they'd spent together a few weeks before Theo had left for Greece, a night that seemed to change things between the two of them. Those two cerulean seas trapped her in their depths time and time again, threatening to never release their hold on her.

That's how she could be so sure. Those eyes. Not even a thick, dark beard and his glasses that he'd abandoned sometime during college could disguise him from her.

"His body was never found," she said. "And the guy down there was wearing a Detroit Tigers' hat and said he was allergic to apples. Theo is allergic to apples. Those can't all be random coincidences."

"Hmm," Harold murmured as he looked off to the side as if he found those facts particularly curious. "So then what happened? Tell me again—my old brain doesn't retain things so great nowadays. And pass the pita, if you don't mind."

Dani handed the bread basket across the table and then recounted the events leading up to the news of his death and the details thereafter—the mysterious dig, the harbormaster's eyewitness report, weeks without a single sighting. No calls. No texts. No tracking on his phone. And then finding the boat waterlogged and mangled on the shore months later. She left out the parts about the devastation the news caused Theo's family and her own. Theo had been a staple in their lives. Even after he'd moved away for college and eventually landed in Chicago to take a job at the National Hellenic Museum, he'd still managed to pop on home to Grand Rapids every few months between his travels to Greece, though he'd all but stopped participating in actual digs in recent years since the new gig had him either behind a desk, on the phone, or rubbing elbows with museum donors.

But each and every time he visited home, Dani would be there. Not specifically waiting for him—whereas he spent his adult life traveling and seeing the world, her biggest adventures nowadays involved little more than altering her grocery store routine or trekking over to another county for a library-book exchange. A pathetic change from her younger days of river-rafting excursions and backcountry camping at Pictured Rocks.

She didn't have time for those things anymore. Her parents needed her.

Or at least, she'd thought they did.

But she remembered Theo once saying that one of his favorite things about coming home was knowing she'd be there.

Not his parents. Not Eddie. Her.

You're the one thing I can always count on, he'd told her over a couple of micheladas and fries in their midtwenties, which had started somewhat of a tradition. Even though he wasn't always there physically, she felt the same.

Like how he always left her a book when he visited. It was subtle at first, going back all the way to when they were kids. Dani used to think he was simply forgetful, often leaving behind a book when he came over. Then in high school, he'd talk about books he was reading, and whenever she said it sounded interesting or asked the name, he'd give her his copy to borrow. By the time they were in their twenties, it became unspoken again. Sometimes he'd show up at a party and hand her a book when saying hello to someone else. Or he'd leave a book inside the garage door, so it would be waiting for her when she got home.

Like the last time he'd been home before he left on that final fateful trip to Greece. She hadn't even seen him that time despite the fact he'd texted a few days before saying there was something he wanted to talk to her about and that he'd be coming to town soon. That talk never happened. Instead, after a late night at karaoke with Beau, waiting for her in the garage was a first edition of *The Wonderful Wizard of Oz*, her favorite book of all time.

She'd never even gotten the chance to thank him. By the

time she found the book and realized he'd stopped by, he was apparently long gone. He wouldn't even answer her texts.

"So what were those men doing under the palace?" Harold asked, tearing her thoughts from Theo.

Dani grabbed a stuffed grape leaf and popped it in her mouth. "I have no idea, but it didn't look legit."

Right then, Cosmo walked up to them, and Dani sat straighter in her chair. She'd been waiting to hear back since he helped her call the police about the men sneaking around Knossos (though she omitted the part about her climbing over the railing and instead said she'd only seen *them* emerging from the stairway beneath the palace).

"Have you heard anything?" she asked.

"I just got off the phone with the police. There was no one back at Knossos. The gates are locked for the evening and the attendant checked the area beneath the palace himself," Cosmo explained, seeming perturbed to have to explain this to her.

"They didn't find the secret passageway?"

"What secret passageway?" he asked, his gaze narrowing in on her.

Shit. She hadn't told him about the secret room.

She stabbed another stuffed grape leaf with her fork and waved it around, nonchalantly. "Oh . . . I . . . I mean, I assumed there must be something under the palace . . . lair of the Minotaur and all . . . otherwise what were they even doing there?" she asked.

Cosmo eyed her skeptically, like he didn't believe her. Dani stared at him, willing her face to maintain composure while her mind screamed at her for trying to blow her cover. Once he finally deemed her innocent, he answered. "No. They didn't find anything. Nor did they find any men dressed like burglars."

Phew.

"What about the man in the baseball hat?" she asked. "Did they say anything about him?"

"Again, they didn't see anyone."

"But you saw him, didn't you?" She set down her fork and turned in her seat to face Cosmo head on. "The men who were chasing me when I hopped on the bus?" Dani's voice pleaded.

"I don't know what you are talking about."

Dani's mouth gaped open. How? How could he have missed them? "You saw them, Harold, right?" she asked, turning to him.

He shrugged. "I'm sorry. I was looking at you, remember?"

She couldn't believe it. No, she wasn't making things up in her head. He was there. Theo was there.

"Maybe you can ask the rest of the group if they noticed them. Maybe they—" she started, but Cosmo cut her off.

"I'm sorry, miss, but I think you should probably let this go. These people came here for vacation—to get *away* from their troubles, not to get into some. Besides, it looked like you had fallen, perhaps? You were covered in dirt when you arrived back at the bus. Maybe you hit your head?"

Dani blinked several times before answering. "You think I'm making this up? Did you explain again that it was Theo Galanis?"

Cosmo nodded, his face turning morose. "Yes, they confirmed he's dead—"

"He's not dead!" Dani said, slamming her fists on the table and raising her voice loud enough to garner a few stares from guests at other tables.

But, God, she really wished everyone would stop saying that.

"Listen, I understand that you knew him. A lover, perhaps?"

Cosmo said, almost sympathetically but with a slight air of disbelief. "Maybe that's why you came on this trip, no? To say goodbye? It's only natural that your eyes might play tricks on you. Greece is a mystical place, full of ancient tales and mythologies."

"I wasn't seeing things," she said, leaning back in her seat and folding her arms.

"I know you may not think that, but with jet lag and the time difference—"

"Okay, thanks, Cosmo. I think I'm good," she said, waving him off and turning her head away. She didn't care to hear any more of Cosmo's pity.

She watched from the corner of her eye until Cosmo finally walked away, leaving her alone with Harold once again. When she turned back to face him, his mouth was twisted, as if trying to assess how to fill the silence.

"I'm sorry I didn't see them," he finally said. "My eyesight's not so good anyway."

"But you believe me, right?" she asked.

"Sure, I do."

"And you don't think I'm crazy?"

"Nah," Harold said, swatting his hand in front of his chest. "Maybe a little kooky for wanting to hang around an old fart like me, but I know crazy when I see it. Like that Roberta, for instance."

Dani snickered. Glad she wasn't the only one who thought so.

But then she sighed. "What if Cosmo was right?" she asked.

"Right about what?"

"About me making him up in my mind because I *wanted* to see him?"

"Do you?"

"Of course I do. I wish nothing more than that he was still alive."

"Because you love him?"

Dani shot her gaze to Harold's. His question threw her off guard. How could he possibly know that? She hadn't told him about her feelings toward Theo. She'd never told *anyone* how she truly felt about him. Not even Beau.

"I mean, of course I love him," she said. "He's been in my life since I was six years old. He's practically family."

"Okay," Harold said, "if you say so." He reached across the table and patted her hand.

Dani tilted her head, now full-on staring at Harold. "What's that supposed to mean?"

"My eyesight might not be good anymore, but my hearing is still impeccable," he said, tapping on his ear.

She eyed him, curiously.

"The way you've been talking about him," he continued. "I'd been in love with my Patty for fifty years. You talk about Theo the same way I do her. You've got an airiness to your voice when you say his name. Like even now, he takes your breath away."

Oh God. She'd never realized she spoke about him that way. Hopefully no one else—such as Eddie—had ever realized it, either.

"I . . . I . . ." she stuttered.

"It's okay. You don't have to explain. Sometimes there's no explaining to do. Love is love. It is what it is."

"But we were . . . we weren't together," she explained.

"Doesn't matter. Did he know how you felt?"

Dani shook her head.

"And why not?"

"He's my brother's best friend. I think he pictured me as his own kid sister, nothing more."

Harold chuckled to himself.

"What's so funny?" she asked.

"Oh, nothing. Just an old man who ain't got nothing better to do than laugh to himself."

She pursed her lips at him and folded her arms. "If we're gonna be friends, Harold, you'd better tell me what you're laughing about."

"All right," he said, taking his napkin from his lap, wiping his mouth, plopping it on the table, and then leaning forward. "Since I'm guessing you look about the same now as you did last time you saw your Theo, I can guarantee he did *not* picture you as his kid sister. Now, I don't know the fella so I can't say whether he felt the way about you that you do him, but sister? Uh-uh." Harold wagged his finger.

Heat washed over Dani's cheeks.

"And don't you go thinking I'm being a creepy old geezer," he continued, putting up his hand. "Just being honest, is all. Maybe now's the time I should mention that Patty was my friend's sister, so I think I'm a bit of an expert on the topic. Though older sister, I should add."

"So what you're saying is I'm not your type?" Dani asked, with a smile.

Harold let out a full belly laugh. "Exactly. I like my women like I like my wine and my cheese: aged to perfection." He brought his fingers to his mouth and gave a chef's kiss.

"You know, Harold," Dani said, smiling while she nibbled on the last of the grape leaves, "you aren't the travel companion I envisioned, but you're better."

He placed his hand on his chest and gave a little bow from his seat. "Just keeping it for real life. That's what the young 'uns say nowadays, right?"

Dani snickered. "Something like that."

"So besides the fact that he was your brother's best friend, give me some other reasons why nothing ever happened between the two of you."

She smiled and eyed him curiously. "What for?"

"I want to poke holes in your reasoning."

"Oh, I don't know." Dani sighed. "He was too good for me."

"Poppycock!" Harold called out about two volumes louder than anything else he'd said all night.

A few passersby turned to look, and Dani sank a bit into her chair and put her hand up to her forehead to cover her face. Harold sat confidently in his seat, even more confident in his words. But he knew nothing about Dani's real life. He didn't know that all the things Dani boasted about accomplishing in the future, all the places she said she'd go, yet none of them ever happened. She was stuck. Her old classmates had been right. She *was* all talk. She *couldn't* hack living on her own.

Theo, on the other hand, was out there. Doing things. Traveling the world. Being someone. It wouldn't have been fair of her to expect him to give all that up for her. Not when he had a whole sea of possibilities in Chicago. And plenty of Triple Gs in the dating pool.

It wasn't that Grand Rapids was small. Or without opportunity. But moving back home out of fear? That was the sort of thing only failures did. People who were scared to spread their wings.

"What makes you think he was so much better than you?" Harold asked. "I've only known you for a few days, but you seem like a right catch to me. Any man—or woman, if you're into that sort of thing—would be lucky to be with a smart, caring, funny, beautiful woman like you."

Dani smiled. "Well, thank you, Harold. I only mean that he

had a lot going for him, and I'm literally living in a studio apartment behind my parents' house."

"So?"

"*So*," she continued, "I'm not exactly a model of success. He's the director of research for a museum."

"Pfft," he spit, waving his hand. "Love doesn't give a rat's patootie about job titles and 'success,'" he said, using air quotes.

Where was Harold when Dani could have used this pep talk years ago, back before it was too late?

"You're right," she said.

"I know I am. I'm just sayin', don't go letting love pass you by again. You never know if it might be your last opportunity."

His words hit her in the heart like a ton of bricks, as did the memories from her last night with Theo. The ones she could remember, anyway.

"So, you doing this cave thing tomorrow?" Harold asked, changing the subject. "Can't say I liked Cosmo's upsell, but I'm not one to turn down an authentic meal." He patted his stomach as if he hadn't already eaten a plate of gyros, salad, grape leaves, and fries.

She shook her head. "I'm not too keen on spending more time with Cosmo at the moment. Not when he thinks I'm over here seeing things."

"Then I might tell him you're coming anyway so they make extra food, and maybe I can bring you back some leftovers."

"Sure, that would be great."

"What do you think you'll do instead? Go to that archaeology museum?"

"I don't know," Dani said with a shrug.

But she knew. She'd already made alternate arrangements in her head.

She knew she'd seen Theo.

And if Cosmo and the police weren't going to help her, she'd confirm it herself.

• • • • • • • • •

APPARENTLY, HAROLD WASN'T THE ONLY ONE WHO COULDN'T PASS up a home-cooked meal. The following day, the entire Silver crew embarked on the excursion with Cosmo to this alleged "Minotaur cave" (aka, tourist trap), except for Dani. She had other ideas.

To return to the scene of the crime.

Well, okay, maybe nothing *that* dramatic. But she needed to know. She needed to confirm that her mind hadn't been playing tricks on her.

Her plan had been set: She found a cheap bus that would take her all the way to Knossos around the same time as the day before, and then she'd wait. She'd focus her eyes on the railing. Watch the area that led underneath the palace. And if the men returned, she'd be ready for them.

She figured there was a reason they'd been there right before closing time. Probably entering the site hoping they wouldn't be spotted. There wasn't any guarantee that they'd be back again so soon, but she had to give it a shot, especially when her time on Crete was limited.

Now all she had to do was find something else to keep her busy in the hours leading up to it.

After grabbing a coffee and a crispy breakfast pastry filled with custard, she wandered around the streets of Heraklion. The shops and cafés were waking up in the seaside town, but soon the main town center was bustling with people. She stopped a few times to consult her tour book before eventually making her way to the archaeological museum. The building was full of Cretan artifacts: tools, bowls, statues, and frescoes. The diorama of the palace of Knossos was something to marvel at, a re-creation of what the palace might have looked like in its heyday.

Interestingly, however, it didn't include the hidden chamber she'd spotted the men in.

She weaved through the exhibits, coming upon a room dedicated to the Minotaur. The description of the myth on the placard next to an artist's rendition of a man fighting the Minotaur with a spear was largely the same as Cosmo's, minus anything related to caves or Minotaur worshippers.

Another display included a drawing depicting the labyrinth, a complex system of walls and dead ends intended to trap those who'd dared to challenge the Minotaur. King Minos had purportedly had Daedalus construct the labyrinth. Although no such labyrinth had ever been discovered at Knossos, the tale of the labyrinth persisted in Greek mythology.

Dani moved through the room from one artifact to the next, taking each one in. Now she understood why Theo went into this field. Sure, it was always cool to see old buildings and artifacts, but to picture the lives of ancient Greeks was almost magical. So much history in one place.

She came up to a clay vessel set under a glass case, likely used for water or some other liquid—wine perhaps—with an elaborately painted scene on the side: the Minotaur's head being held up by a man standing outside a cave set in a wall of stone with a crowd of people bowing to him. And on top of the wall, a structure with columns, but the painting had begun to wear off, so it was unclear. On the chest of the man holding the head was a medallion with the Greek letter μ atop what appeared to be an eye. She felt like she'd seen that symbol somewhere before.

Hmm. Maybe there was something to Cosmo's "Minotaur worshipper" story after all.

She read the placard on the stand holding the vessel:

Clay wine vessel depicting the beheaded Minotaur.
Circa 225 BC Peloponnesian peninsula.

That was odd. The date of the piece was much later than the others, and the origin of its discovery was placed on the mainland, not Crete.

Shit. Maybe she *should* have gone on the cave excursion.

She wished she'd gotten Harold's phone number so she could have called or texted him to find out where exactly they were, though when she looked at the time, she realized they were probably already over at Cosmo's uncle's house enjoying their lunchtime feast. Dammit. She needed to find them so she could ask Cosmo more about these worshipper theories.

Fortunately, there was always a research librarian's best friend: Google.

She stood in front of a large glass display case that sat in the center of one of the exhibition rooms with an eight-foot-tall model Minotaur as she furiously searched "Minotaur worship cave Crete" on her phone. A bunch of hits came up, but none of the places seemed close enough for the Silvers to visit *and* get back in time for lunch.

From the corner of her eye, she glimpsed someone on the other side of the display case. She looked up from her phone for a split second, glancing quickly at the person standing in front of her, then returned her gaze to her phone screen before their identity registered in her mind.

She looked back up, and there he was, staring at her with cerulean eyes once more.

"Hey, Juicy," he said, placing his hand on the glass.

Dani sucked in a breath—and passed out.

CHAPTER Three

Theo

WELL . . . THAT DIDN'T GO AS EXPECTED.

Theo rushed to the other side of the museum display case in the exhibition room, empty except for the two of them, and dove to his knees, lifting Dani's limp body in his arms. The warmth of her soft skin and her sweet vanilla scent released a flood of hope and memories.

She was here.

God, Dani was a sight for sore eyes.

Though based on her reaction, maybe the same couldn't be said for him. Seeing as he'd envisioned Dani running into his arms for a hug, the fact that she'd looked at him like she'd seen a ghost didn't give him much confidence in what people probably thought of his fate back home, even though he already assumed they imagined the worst.

"Dani," he said, cradling her in his arms and jostling her body. Nothing.

He lowered his ear to her face, listening for breathing. The light air from her breaths tickled the hair on the back of his neck, and he turned his head ever so slightly, their noses now almost touching. Theo scanned her face, taking in each feature that he could probably recite from memory. Her long, thick eyelashes. The tiny scar on her left temple from the time she fell out of the boat and hit a rock when they went white-water rafting. Her full, wide lips, which Theo had stared at more times than he could count and more often than her brother's best friend should have.

He brushed a few wisps of hair from her forehead and whispered again. "Juicy?" he said this time.

Still nothing. *Shit.* He needed to figure something out and fast. It was only a matter of time before Maurice and Louis came looking for him.

After his last couple of paltry escape attempts, it wouldn't take long for them to realize Theo *wasn't* in the bathroom where he said he'd be five minutes earlier before he slipped around the corner when their backs were turned. But he had to try one more time. Because this time was different. This time he might actually have a chance.

What had it been? Seven months? Ten since he'd gone missing? He'd lost track of time. Counting the days, weeks, and months only increased Theo's anxiety and hopelessness. He didn't need anything else keeping him awake at night. After all, being held captive by unknown criminals and being forced to search for an artifact that Theo had absolutely no clue how to find didn't exactly make for a peaceful night's sleep.

By that point, he'd given up expecting that someone would recognize him as the Greek American archaeologist who'd disappeared after a boat accident. Crete was miles away from the area where he'd gone missing. No one would be looking for him here. And even though his picture had been plastered all over the news and the papers for the few months after his disappearance, apparently his beard—something he'd never sported before—was as good as a fake nose-glasses-mustache Halloween getup. By now people had mostly stopped searching. So a few months ago, once his handlers, Maurice and Louis, deemed the coast clear, they set him to work searching for the Minotaur at the behest of "the boss." Neither they nor Theo presumed anyone would recognize him all the way over in Heraklion.

When he lay awake at night for all this time, he liked to think about how he'd react if he saw someone he knew in the rare circumstances that Maurice and Louis allowed him to be seen in public. Would he scream for help? Would he merely pray that they reported the sighting to the authorities? Or, after his last attempt to escape left him with a broken nose and a black eye, would he pretend he was someone else, too afraid of what Maurice and Louis might do if he tried to get away again? Up to this point, he'd survived by playing dumb, hoping his failure to make any discoveries would eventually lead to his release.

He honestly never thought he'd have the opportunity to find out how he'd react, until he saw Dani at Knossos the day before. Had he been dreaming? Because seeing her face? Seeing her beautiful brown eyes seemed almost impossible. And not only because he didn't think he would ever see *any* of his friends and family ever again.

Because it was her. Daniela Guiterrez, the woman he'd always wanted but could never have. Not after making that ridiculous teenage pact with Eddie twenty years ago after what they'd termed Operation Juicy-Gate.

We can never, under any circumstances, date each other's sisters. EVER. Deal?

Of course, the odds of Theo's sister, Ophelia, taking an interest in Eddie were about a thousand to one. By the time they'd made that agreement, Ophelia was already out of the house, finished with college, dating her future husband, and referred to Eddie as "Edweirdo." And according to Theo's parents, he was supposed to marry a Triple G: a "Good Greek Girl." Plus, Theo was only seventeen at the time. He was *not* interested in Eddie's fifteen-year-old sister.

But after he'd taken Dani to her prom a few years later, something had changed. Theo would never forget the first time he got that flutter in his stomach that night. The feeling only grew more intense in the years after—and so did the echo of Eddie's words in his head whenever she was near.

Even now as Dani lay passed out on the cold marble museum floor, the flutter had returned, and Theo had to tamp it down.

Though primarily because he didn't have *time* for those feelings right now. Not with Maurice and Louis soon to be hot on his trail. With the two of them determined to find the woman who'd spotted them at Knossos and after they'd been following her all morning from her hotel through the streets of Heraklion and finally into the museum, he needed to get her out of there and as far away from them as possible so they could get to the US consulate.

Theo shook Dani once more, and when she didn't flinch, he gathered her in his arms and lifted her from the ground. "Okay, Juicy," he said to her even though she was out cold, "we've got to get you out of here."

Without further hesitation, Theo exited the room and high-tailed it through the museum, moving as fast as he could without causing Dani to flop around too much.

"Sir, is she okay?" an older woman asked in English, clearly a tourist, as he whizzed by.

"Yep! Just needs some fresh air," he assured her, continuing toward the emergency exits in the back.

"Are you sure you don't want me to call for some help?" the woman insisted, following him. "Ma'am? Ma'am? Are you all right?" the woman then called out to Dani.

Shit. This didn't look good.

When Theo didn't stop, the woman yelled at full volume, "Young man! Stop right there! Someone, stop him! He's taking that woman!"

Goddamn tourists! Mind your own business!

The woman was now jogging toward him, creating a commotion. This was the *last* thing he needed. Maurice and Louis were surely going to hear. He may have wanted to get rescued, but not at the expense of potentially putting Dani in danger.

"Lady!" Theo said, spinning on his heels to confront the woman. "This is my fiancée, and I'm taking her to get some air. Now, please. Stop following us. You're making a scene." His words were forceful, but he needed this woman to back off.

But the woman didn't. She put her hand on Dani's wrist and tugged. "I'm not letting you take her. How do I know you're not some sort of kidnapping creep?!"

Theo wanted to laugh. Kidnapping creep. If only she knew.

Dani started to stir in his arms. *Yes. Please wake up.*

"Dani? Baby?" The endearment slipped out without warning. Where had *that* come from? "Dani, I need you to wake up," he said.

Her eyes fluttered open for the briefest of seconds. Long enough for her to see his face. "Theo?" she whispered, before closing her eyes again.

"See?" Theo said to the old woman. "Now if you don't mind," he said, nodding his head at the woman's hand on Dani's wrist.

The woman finally let go, and Theo turned and ran out the back door. Once in the alley, he booked it down the street to a small hillside park. Hopefully Maurice and Louis were still searching the museum for Dani and wouldn't look for him in the deserted park. After setting Dani down on a bench, he scanned his surroundings, noticing a few locals sitting near the side of the road a short distance away. He ran over and asked if they had any water for his friend, pointing to Dani in the distance. They'd offered to call a medic, but he quickly waved them off, explaining she'd overheated and would be okay in a few moments. One of the men called out to someone in the house to grab a water, and a moment later, a child ran out with a bottle of water, handing it to Theo. He thanked them profusely, then ran back to Dani, slumped over on the bench. He brushed the long black hairs that had come loose from her braid away from her face.

"Dani," he said, rubbing her face and putting the bottle of water to her lips. "Dani, please. Wake up."

She opened her mouth, drinking from the bottle, and her eyes started to flicker open, taking a moment to focus.

"Theo?" she said a little more confidently this time. "Is it really you?"

"Yes, it's me."

Upon hearing his words, her eyes flew open all the way and she flung her arms around his shoulders causing him to spill the water over her back. But she clearly didn't mind, pulling him in tightly as she pressed her face against his chest.

He held firm, not wanting to let go for fear that she'd vanish. She was real. He could feel her enveloped in his arms. Smell her vanilla cream lotion. He couldn't believe he was touching someone from home—and not anyone, but Dani.

The woman he thought he'd lost forever.

Slowly, Dani pulled back and stared up at him with her hands on both sides of his face, sending an aching in his stomach. He'd seen that look many times. There was a hopefulness to her eyes. A questioning. But it never lasted, primarily because Theo always had a knack for killing the mood.

"Hey, Juicy," he said, smiling down at her.

"I can't believe it. You're here. You're really here."

"So are you."

"Everyone thinks you're dead," she said with worried eyes.

"I know."

She drew back and knit her brows together. "You know?"

Before he could respond, Dani cross-jabbed him in the shoulder.

Damn. That hurt. He brought his hand up to the spot where she'd hit him and rubbed it.

"What the hell was that for?" he asked, massaging his shoulder with the opposite hand.

"What the hell? What the *hell*?" she growled back at him. "Did you not hear me? Everyone thinks you're fucking *dead*, Theo. Capital D-E-A-D, dead! Yet apparently, you're . . . living in Greece?" she said, waving her arms at their surroundings.

"Okay," he said, trying to stop her, "I'm not over here on vacation or something."

"Oh really? You've been missing for over *a year.*"

Shit. Had it been that long?

But she didn't stop there.

"The boat you were allegedly sailing on was found capsized. The papers all reported that you were presumed dead. You may not be on vacation, but you didn't think to, oh, I don't know, maybe call your parents to let them know you're alive? They've been worried *sick* about you. We all have."

"It's not what you think," he tried to explain, but she put her hand up to his face to stop him from talking, clearly not having it.

"We had a fucking *funeral* for you, Theo. There's a gravestone for you in Cedar Memorial Cemetery that says something like, 'Dr. Theo Galanis, lost at sea but never lost in our hearts.' Your mom was devastated. *Is* devastated. They even moved away from Grand Rapids a few months ago because they said they don't want to be in a place that reminds them of you."

His stomach roiled.

"I think I'm going to be sick," he said, leaning over and resting his elbows on his knees and his head in his hands.

This was worse than he ever imagined. Of course he'd seen the newspaper article about himself that Louis left sitting in the bathroom, and he imagined his family would be concerned. But in his desperation for escape, he'd never let himself consider the full extent of that pain. They'd moved from their home? From the place his parents had immigrated to over thirty years ago? And a funeral? It pained him to picture his mom and dad dressed in all black, standing over a headstone with an empty grave underneath.

"Good!" she snapped. "You should be. If everyone knew you were over here galivanting around Greece and doing Lord knows what with those shady-ass men over at Knossos—"

Her words snapped him back to reality. Maurice and Louis. He took her hands in his to stop her from talking.

"Listen, we need to get going."

"Going where?"

"To the US consulate," he said, standing and attempting to pull her up by her hand. But Dani resisted.

"Theo, you need to tell me what's going on."

"We can talk about it at the consulate."

She folded her arms and sneered at him. "No. I'm done with being left in the dark with you. I want you to tell me now. I want you to tell me to my face."

He blew out his breath. God, she always was stubborn. "We don't have time for that."

She threw her head back and laughed. "Oh, this is unbelievable. You've been gone for a year with no communication whatsoever, but you don't have five minutes to spare to tell me what the fuck is going on? Who are you and what did you do with Theo?"

"Look, Juicy—"

"Don't call me that."

The anger in her voice couldn't be masked. Sure, the nickname was silly, but he'd called her that for years. Once the initial annoyance of the nickname had worn off back when they were teenagers, she hadn't seemed to mind. It was so second nature that sometimes he wondered if she even remembered its origin. Not that he could ever forget Operation Juicy-Gate. Clearly, things had changed between them.

Hence why he up and ran away to Greece in the first place.

But they didn't have time for explanations.

"Fine. Look, I get that you are mad. And confused. And probably a whole slew of other emotions right now, but I need you to trust me. When have I ever let you down?"

"Um, well, for starters, how about the last time you were home?"

The punch she'd given him in the arm a few moments earlier was no match for the figurative punch in the gut he felt now.

She had no idea. No idea what it had been like the last time he'd been home. Spotting her out with someone new, singing, drinking, and dancing, after doing all those same things a few weeks earlier with him.

No—after *saying* all those . . . *things* to him.

It's always been you.

Clearly everything she'd said to Theo had meant nothing.

She sure had a lot of audacity acting like he let *her* down. She wouldn't have even known he'd stopped by one last time had he not left that book. Forgive him for treating it like some sort of parting gift to mark the end of their nonexistent relationship.

After all those years, all that time waiting for the "right" moment, none of it made a lick of difference. Because when it came to him and Dani, there was no right moment.

It was easy to blame things on timing. Or on being in other relationships. Or his parents' insistence that he find a Good Greek Girl. Or even that absolutely *ridiculous* juvenile pact. All those things were easier than admitting that maybe he and Dani simply weren't meant to be.

Instead of accepting that, however, he'd run. Taken the first opportunity that came to him and gotten the hell out of Dodge. That was it. No more torturing himself with fantasies of what would never be. So he dropped the book off at her apartment—the last, he vowed, he'd ever give her—and he boarded a plane back to Greece, hoping a couple of months of digging in the dirt would finally get her out of his system.

"I didn't think you'd miss me," he said.

"What's that supposed to mean? Of *course* I missed you."

She did? He looked her straight in the eyes, and she quickly added, "We all did."

Of course. She missed him like any other of his friends and family missed him.

"I know you were there, Theo. I found the book."

He hadn't exactly tried hiding the fact that he'd stopped by. Leaving the book in the garage was a dead giveaway. An unspoken love note. And that time, not any book. Her favorite book. A reminder that there was no place like home.

Home meant they were together. Even when everything else in his life piled on him—the weight of the pressure to succeed at the museum, the anxiety of hiding his true passions from his family, the strain on his relationships when he could never give other women his full heart no matter how hard he tried, the burden to fulfill his parents' American dream—Dani never let him down. Being with her eased his mind. They could hike and kayak like carefree kids again. Sit quietly beside each other reading, Dani always tucking her perpetually cold feet under his thigh. Take a drive to nowhere. Laugh together over a basket of fries and micheladas, though for the life of him he didn't know how she could drink the ones with Clamato.

He liked to joke that she'd be pretty cool if not for her love of clam water, which always earned him a playful ribbing. Or as he saw it, a jolt of electricity from her touch.

It was time to let those things go, though. Childish things, as his parents frequently told him.

It was time to let *her* go.

"Dani, we don't have time for this," he started to explain, but she wasn't having it.

"No, you can't say shit like that, act like it was okay for you to disappear for a year and not give a shit that we were worried sick about you, and then brush it off like it's nothing. Or like it's not important enough to spend, oh, I don't know, more than two minutes telling me what the fuck is going on? After everything you've put me through, after I cried over your *grave*, you owe me more than that," she said, pushing him back on the bench.

She might as well have thrown a brick at his chest. Yes, he knew everyone had probably been worried about him. Scared, even. But this? This wasn't sadness or fear.

This was anger.

She was right. He owed her more than that.

"I've been kidnapped," he said. Hearing those words aloud for the first time from his mouth made his skin crawl. He was a thirty-seven-year-old man, for fuck's sake. How does an adult man even *get* kidnapped and manage to stay held captive for an entire goddamn year?

Cowardice, that's how.

Dani blinked back her confusion. "Kidnapped?" She scrunched her face and looked around, obviously perplexed by the illusion of his freedom.

"Kidnapped, captured, held hostage, take your pick."

"Theo, what on earth are you talking about? You're standing right in front of me now, alone."

"I know it sounds absurd."

"Wow." Dani laughed, incredulously. "I can't believe you. You know, if you're in trouble or if you're running from something, maybe you could spare me the bullshit and come clean. Because this?" she said, twirling her hands in a circle in front of his face, "This is insulting."

His eyebrows drew together. What was insulting was the fact that she thought he would ever lie to her about something like this. Especially after the year he'd had.

"Daniela—" he started, but she laughed.

"Daniela?" She nodded her head and looked away. Her eyes bulged and she mouthed, *Wow*, exaggeratedly. With the limited time they had, he had no choice but to ignore her temper tantrum.

"Believe me or not, but it's the truth. And it's not safe for you to be here. To be seen with me. Those men you saw me with yesterday? They're probably looking for me right now. So I'm sorry, but we need to go."

Footsteps sounded in the distance, and Theo looked over his shoulder.

And his stomach sank. It was too late. Maurice and Louis crested the hill, staring down at them from atop.

"Fuck, fuck, fuck," he said, standing and pulling Dani up beside him. "Here, take this."

He reached for the letter in his back pocket that he'd written that morning on a piece of scrap paper just in case he didn't have more than an opportunity to slip her a note and shoved it in her hand. "It explains everything. Take it to the US consulate. But you've got to go now. Please," he pleaded, shifting his attention to Maurice and Louis heading straight toward them.

Dani followed Theo's gaze, her eyes going wide at the sight of Maurice and Louis barreling down the hill.

"Theo?" she said, her voice shaking, anger replaced with fear.

"Go!" he said, pushing her away.

She clutched the note in her hand and took off running, but Louis—a champion sprinter, as Theo had discovered the first time he tried to escape—quickly caught her by the arm.

"Let me go!" she said.

"Be quiet!" Louis snapped back at her with a force that would silence just about anyone into submission.

"Let her go," Theo said. "She doesn't know anything."

"Oh really?" Maurice asked. "Then what's this?" He plucked the letter Theo had written out of Dani's hands.

"It's nothing," Theo said, knowing Maurice and Louis weren't that stupid.

"Mm-hmm. We'll see about that," Maurice said, tucking the letter into his back pocket. "The boss thinks it's time to meet you."

The boss? In the last several months, Theo had yet to learn his name.

"Fine. Take me, but let her go. She's nobody," he said, catching a curious glance from Dani.

"Really? Because some old broad over at the museum said that a man took off running out the back with his *fiancée*," Louis said. "Don't you remember telling us about your fiancée when we first met?"

Dani and Theo flashed each other a look. The only way Theo could describe Dani's face was with one word: *hurt*. God, he wished he could explain. *Fuck, fuck, fuck. Not now.*

"So nice to finally meet her," Maurice said.

"She's not her. Not my fiancée, I mean. She's just some nosy woman. I've never seen her before in my life. Aside from yesterday."

"Then why give her this?" Maurice asked, pointing to the letter in his pocket.

Theo shrugged. "She seemed curious. Figured I'd take my chances?"

Maurice scoffed. "You think we're stupid? Yesterday I

thought she was just some snooping tourist we needed to make sure wasn't going to head to the police, but now I'm not so sure. She's coming with us."

"I'm not going anywhere with you," Dani said, wriggling to free herself from Louis's grasp. "I don't know what you three are up to, but I'm going to call the cops as soon as—"

"Call them with what?" Maurice asked. "With this?"

He held up what Theo could only presume was Dani's phone based on her wide-eyed look. *Crap.* It must have fallen out of her pocket when he was carrying her through the museum.

"Who *are* you people?" Dani asked.

"You'll find out soon enough," Maurice said. "Come on. The dock's thataway. And don't even *think* about trying to scream or run."

Maurice flashed the handle of something metal out of the pocket of his pants—some sort of weapon—and Theo hung his head. He'd brought Dani into this. Brought her into this hellscape that he'd been living in for the last year since these two captured him on the boat and destroyed the ship to make it look like he'd been lost at sea.

No communication with his friends and family. No real communication with the outside world. He may have been walking around like a free man, but he was essentially their prisoner, and they controlled his every move. Save for trips to the bathroom and his handful of pathetic attempts to escape, they hadn't let him out of their sight. And after they'd threatened to go after his loved ones, he stopped even trying.

If only he hadn't lied when he told them about *her.*

Fuck.

Dani may have given him hope, but now he'd do anything to

take the last ten minutes back. He'd forgo ever seeing her again if that meant she'd be safe and far away from this shitstorm.

Suddenly his strategy of dragging out the search for the Minotaur didn't seem like the best of ideas—not that he knew where to find it anyway. Theo wasn't sure the damn thing even existed.

But now? Now that they had Dani? Well, this game of "play dumb and they might give up" probably wasn't going to end well.

Because playing dead was easy.

But playing dumb was no longer an option.

CHAPTER Four

Dani

DANI WISHED SHE COULD SAY SHE WAS HAPPY TO SEE THEO.

Then again, as she was being ushered by a couple of men who looked straight out of an *Indiana Jones* movie onto a small white speedboat to God knows where, she wished a lot of things.

Such as that she'd gone on Cosmo's scam-scursion instead of to the museum.

Or that she'd minded her own business at Knossos.

Or that she'd stayed home and never come to Greece in the first place. Home was safe. Predictable. Boring. And maybe she needed to appreciate that a little bit more.

Dani glanced around the marina, wishing she could get someone's attention, but their boat was docked at the end far away from anyone else, and, really, they probably just looked like a group of people going out on a boat ride.

Why? Why hadn't she walked away when she'd had the chance?

Oh right, because she was a stubborn brat who wanted an explanation instead of trusting Theo like he'd asked.

But she couldn't help it that after a year of not seeing him she didn't want to let him out of her sight again. She'd found him. She couldn't let him go now.

Plus, she needed answers, dammit!

Dani and Theo, not having spoken a word to each other since these two goons found them, were directed to the white leather bench at the back of the speedboat. Based on Theo's body language and what she could translate only as distress in his voice, whatever shit Theo had gotten himself into wasn't good.

And now Dani was in it, too.

The tall guy started the boat and quickly sped away from the marina. Dani spent enough time doing water activities to know that speeding was probably against marina rules even in Greece, but chastising a criminal for not following boating laws probably wasn't such a good idea. Not after the tall one flashed a knife in his waistband.

Her heart pounded. Was this it? Was this how she was going to die?

Dani started picking at the skin around her nails—the nervous habit that her abuela had always reprimanded her for that had only been exacerbated by her chronic dryness working at the library—when Theo took her hand and squeezed it.

For a few moments, all her fears quieted in her mind. She was with Theo. He'd keep her safe. He'd always kept her safe.

Dani glanced at him, and he mouthed, *I'm sorry*. The boat

was too loud for them to have any sort of real conversation, not without the goons hearing them.

Who are they? she mouthed back.

Bad.

A sinking feeling settled in her stomach. It wasn't as if she couldn't already tell these guys were bad news, but confirmation wasn't helping.

Theo looked away and then tipped his head to the side as if something caught his eye. The goons were standing at the controls, steering the boat, not paying them any attention. Slowly, Theo let go of her hand and stood up, though still crouching low as he inched his way toward the men. But Dani snatched his arm back. He glanced at her, and she shook her head, telling him no. Whatever he was planning to do, she wasn't in support. But he squeezed her hand again and pumped his hand downward, motioning for her to relax. How a simple hand squeeze could reassure her that everything would be okay was a mystery, but it worked. She settled back into the bench, watching as he crept closer to the goons, then he reached for the letter sticking out of the tall guy's back pocket and snatched it right as the other man noticed Theo.

The stocky guy lunged toward Theo, but Theo ducked away and quickly tore the envelope in half, tossing it over the side of the boat right as the man tackled him. The tall guy slowed down the boat, but it was too late. The letter was gone.

Stocky held Theo down by the collar as the other approached and pointed his finger in Theo's face. "Try something like that again, and I'll toss you overboard."

"Go ahead," Theo spat back. "You'd be doing me a favor. At least *I* can swim."

The man glowered at him. "You think tearing that piece of

paper up is going to save you?" the man asked. "Just because we can't see what you wrote doesn't mean we don't already know that you were going to rat us out."

He pushed hard at Theo's chest then returned to the ship controls.

"Think we should go back for it?" the other man asked. "What if he put our names in there?"

The driver glanced over his shoulder at Theo, then looked at the water. "So what? He doesn't know who we really are," he said.

The stocky man scrunched his face. "Well, what if he snitches on Pierre?"

Theo's body tensed, and he sucked in a breath. Theo clearly recognized the name Pierre. And it didn't seem like he was too excited to meet him.

The boat sped through the waters of the Mediterranean, weaving through the dozens of islands dotting the way. Some large. Some small. Some inhabited. Others looked to be no larger than a football field. Theo stared out to the sea, looking away almost as if avoiding her. He'd left home without a single word, though, so what difference did it make? So instead of getting those answers she so desperately wanted, she gazed out at the blue waters in the opposite direction. Nervous. Scared of what was awaiting them at their destination.

Finally, after traveling for what seemed like an hour, Tall Guy eased up on the throttle as they approached a luscious island of greens and blues. The terrain varied with rocks and gardens leading up from the beach to a glass-walled building sitting atop a hill. It looked like something straight out of a *James Bond* movie—the evil villain's lair.

Stocky hopped out of the boat, taking a rope to tie the vessel up to a pylon driven into the beach. Dani looked over at Theo, who was taking off his boots and rolling up the hems of his pants. Realizing they were docked in a solid two feet of water, Dani took off her shoes as well. No words were spoken between them and the men, but none were needed. The four of them had an understanding. And really, what were Dani and Theo going to do? Run off down the beach on this remote island in the middle of the sea? Dani highly doubted there'd be an emergency phone or spare boat to save them. So one by one, they jumped out of the boat and into the clear water, wading through the warm shallows before heading toward the house along a stone trail lined with all sorts of exotic plants.

They came to the modern white building with straight lines, walls of windows, and minimal furniture. Once over the threshold, they made their way through the structure toward the outside yet again, out to an infinity pool that rivaled a five-star resort.

Hmm . . . maybe this was a resort?

Dani scoffed at herself. *Yes, because that's what happens when you get kidnapped. You get taken to a resort for an all-inclusive vacation.*

She froze at the thought. *Kidnapped.* Oh God. That's what was happening, wasn't it? Acknowledging it made it feel more real.

And more terrifying.

"Wait here," Tall Guy said, walking away and leaving them with Stocky.

Now was her chance to ask some questions.

"Theo, what is going on?"

He glanced over at Stocky standing roughly ten feet away, and then turned to her. "Not now."

She looked at Theo. Seriously? He wasn't going to tell her why they'd been kidnapped because this pendejo was here?

"Do you know these people? Are you working with them?" she asked, ignoring his desire not to talk.

"Not exactly," another voice said from behind them.

Both Theo and Dani spun around to face a man in all-white linen sporting a matching white beard. His accent was French, but based on the tan he was sporting, he'd clearly been spending a significant amount of time out in the Grecian sun.

"Come, join me," he said, motioning toward the outdoor seating area near the pool. He moseyed over there, and they followed. What other choice did they have, really?

"Would you like anything to drink? Sparkling water? Wine? Ouzo, perhaps? Or maybe you're a raki man?" the man asked.

"What is this? Cocktail hour?" Theo said, sarcastically.

The man snickered. "Call it whatever you like. Maurice," he said, motioning with his hand overhead for the taller man to come over. "Can you please get us a bottle of the Dom Pérignon from the cellar?"

Dani didn't know much about wine—she was more of a michelada sort of chica, herself—but she knew enough to know Dom Pérignon wasn't something that would be sitting next to the Monarch vodka on the bottom shelf at the gas station.

"Yes, boss," Maurice said with a teensy bow before walking away.

"Are you hungry?" Frenchie then asked.

She was, actually. But what if he tried to poison them? When neither she nor Theo answered, Frenchie called over to Stocky. "And, Louis, bring us something to eat."

Once both Maurice and Louis were away, Frenchie settled into his chair and took in a deep breath, as if he was savoring a delightful moment.

"Who are you?" Dani finally asked.

"Do you really not know? Not even a guess?" the man responded.

Dani certainly had no clue, but Theo took him in, scanning his face and surroundings before saying, "You're Jean-Luc Monfils. Or should I say, Pierre Vautour?"

"Voilà!" he said with a flourish of his hand.

Well, that was easy.

"Um," Dani said, interrupting their moment and raising her hand. "I'm sorry, but should I know who you are?"

"He's a notorious artifact smuggler," Theo answered, not taking his eyes off Pierre.

"I prefer antiquities enthusiast," Pierre responded, looking smarmy and smug.

"Yeah, an *enthusiast* who tricks people into working for him and then steals the artifacts they uncover so he can sell them in the illicit trades," Theo said very matter-of-factly.

Pierre waved his hand in front of him and rolled his eyes. "I'm no different from the British Museum."

"At least the British Museum isn't in hiding," Theo retorted.

"You say that as if that's somehow better," Pierre said with an air of superiority.

He had a point.

"What are you doing here? I thought you were dead," Theo said to Pierre.

"Funny. I believe that many say the same about you."

"Yeah, except I'm sure you're the one responsible for people thinking I'm a goner. What about you? Rumor was that you'd died in the Amazon after that blown Moon City expedition."

Oh my God, he's THAT guy?

Dani remembered reading about that expedition in the news over a year ago. An expedition to a real lost city ending in deception and a scuffle in the Amazon rainforest. She wouldn't haven't been able to recall his name had she been asked earlier, but now that she heard it, yes, he was the man behind the whole thing. And the subject of an international manhunt thereafter.

Holy shit. This was wild!

Dani watched with fascination. Theo, Eddie, and Dani had had some fun adventures back in the day, but this was next level. She could picture their families together at the dining table, with everyone in stitches when they recounted the story of when they were on a school field trip to Chicago and somehow ended up in Milwaukee on their way home rather than Grand Rapids. Or the time they went on a kayaking trip and Eddie lost his bag so by the time they made it home, his chones were threadbare. How would they ever top this one?

If they got out of it, that was.

"Ah, yes. The Cidade da Lua," Pierre said. "One thing I've learned in all my years in this business is to never trust anyone and to always, and I mean always, have a plan B. I always plan for contingencies. Fortunately for me, I had a team waiting for me in Caracaraí who'd come to find me after I'd escaped."

"You mean, after you scurried away like a rat," Theo said, pointedly.

Pierre rolled his eyes. "What did you expect me to do? Let those glorified Amazonian equivalents of grail protectors lock me in jail? I don't think so, Dr. Galanis," he said, wagging his finger and shaking his head. "I'm not finished with my world travels. Besides, this is much better than a Brazilian prison cell, don't you think?" he said, holding his hands up and displaying his surroundings.

Dani scanned the luxurious estate that looked straight out of a Restoration Hardware Modern catalog. Yeah . . . she may not have known anything about jail, but this place was *definitely* better.

Pierre looked up toward the house and smiled as Maurice approached.

"Ah, Maurice. Thank you," he said reaching his arms up to take the bottle as Maurice set down three champagne flutes on the concrete coffee table.

Pierre popped the cork and filled their glasses moments before Louis returned with a tray of olives, dried fruits, cheeses, meats, and bread. Dani's mouth watered. Their kidnapping had put a damper on her lunch plans.

"Eat. It's not poisoned, I promise," Pierre said, motioning toward her.

"You first," Dani said.

Pierre's lips turned into a devilish grin, as if she amused him. He leaned forward, taking a few grapes and a handful of nuts, before popping them in his mouth and raising his eyebrow. "See, madame? Now please. Eat." He gestured toward the food again.

Good enough for me. She was never one to pass up good food.

Dani scooted forward and knelt at the coffee table, then dug in. Her first bite—pita dipped in some sort of eggplant mixture—made her groan with pleasure. She closed her eyes, savoring the flavors dancing along her taste buds. *My God, the food here . . .*

Dani opened her eyes to Theo and Pierre watching her, and she swallowed. "Did I say that out loud?" she mumbled, holding her hand over her mouth as she ran her tongue along her teeth to catch any bits stuck in between them.

"There's nothing to be ashamed of," Pierre said with a suaveness that shouldn't have been so charming for someone who had taken them as prisoner. "I agree—the food here is unmatched."

Dani glanced at an expressionless Theo—what was he thinking?—before returning to the snacks.

"Well, now that we got who I am out of the way," Pierre started again, "I must tell you how excited I am to finally meet you. I've been following your career for quite some time."

"Me? Really?" Dani said, looking up and pointing her finger at her chest. "How do you know who I am?"

"Pretty sure he's talking about me, Juicy," Theo interrupted.

Dani snapped her mouth shut. *Oh.* Heat rose from her stomach, up through her chest and neck, and eventually stopped at her cheeks. Of course he wouldn't know some random public librarian from Michigan. Though she wasn't sure why she was embarrassed by what this crook thought of her.

Or maybe it was Theo calling her "Juicy"—again—that got her all hot and bothered.

The day that had been the impetus for the nickname flashed in her head, as it did almost every time he said it, and she had to look away from him.

"I'm sorry, madame, but he is correct," Pierre said to her.

"So why have you been following me?" Theo said.

"Your studies of the Minoan civilization. It's quite fascinating."

"Lots of people study the Minoan civilization."

"Ah, yes, but few have written about the myth of the Minotaur with such depth."

Dani cocked her head to the side. Who hadn't heard of the Minotaur? She knew the mythical creature existed in all kinds of modern literature. It didn't seem all that unusual.

"You can cut to the chase, Pierre. I already know why I'm here. You want me to find the Minotaur."

Pierre wrinkled his brow and then looked over at Maurice and Louis standing behind him like statues. "Is that what you told him?"

Maurice and Louis looked at each other, obviously confused. "That's what you said. 'Find the Minotaur'?" Louis said like it was a question.

Pierre closed his eyes and sighed before turning back to Dani and Theo.

"So, you were saying?" Theo asked once Pierre took a sip of his drink.

"I want you to find the *eye* of the Minotaur. The ruby gemstone cut from its head."

Theo scrunched his face. Dani had seen that face many times, usually whenever Eddie said something particularly ridiculous.

"You've got to be joking," Theo said. "The eye of the Minotaur is a myth. A fable. In other words, it's not real."

"Then why did you write that piece five years ago with your theories on its whereabouts? 'The Mind of the Minotaur'?"

Theo burst out laughing. "My theories? *That's* why I'm here, why you've commandeered a year of my life? Because . . . because of a story I had published in a *children's* magazine?"

Pierre glared at him. "Children's magazine?"

Dani wondered the same thing. Theo had always been a great storyteller. She remembered finding a journal of his from when they were teens full of his own tales of Greek legends. His stories were always based in the original mythologies, but with his own spin. He'd been embarrassed when he'd caught her reading it back at the time, but she'd told him there wasn't anything to be embarrassed about. His stories were good. By the time they were adults, he freely shared his stories with her. She'd always thought he could have done something with them someday.

But he'd never told her that he published one of them.

"I wrote that for *Archaeology Kids* magazine, not a scientific journal," Theo said, "based on a story my grandfather used to tell me before bed."

"You based it on fact. You said it yourself in the article—it was founded on the account of a real person."

"Yeah, my grandfather. He told me a lot of things: rumors of cults, Minotaur worshippers, and treasure hunts. But I've never been able to confirm any of it. I've yet to see a single mention of the eye in any reference books. And that's beside the point," he said, waving his hands like they were getting off topic. "The *story* was made up, and it wasn't an article. It was something I wrote for fun."

"I don't understand this . . . this obsession with fiction and fairy tales," Pierre said, scowling and twirling his hand dismissively in the air. The deep-seated anger in his voice was palpable. "Why do people with so much potential waste their time on made-up nonsense? There is so much truth to discover."

Yikes. That seemed to be a personal problem.

"Sorry I didn't check with you before I pursued my hobby. I'll remember that next time," Theo said.

"You're quite impertinent."

I'll sure say. Typically, Dani was the one being snappy, not Theo. He usually followed orders. A GGB: Good Greek Boy. He didn't talk back. Or disobey. Which was why it was always so fun whenever she was able to get him to break the rules.

"Well, you're quite gullible," Theo responded.

Pierre's eyes narrowed on Theo with laser focus.

Uh-oh.

"You know, most people know better than to treat me with such disrespect," Pierre said.

"Well, fortunately I haven't had the pleasure of getting to know you better. So can we cut with the phony formalities and get to the point?"

Who *was* this Theo? It was sort of hot, the way he was being so . . . brazen.

"You're going to find the eye for me," Pierre said.

"No," Theo said definitively without flinching.

"No?"

"You heard me."

"Need I remind you of your current predicament? You don't exactly have much negotiating power here."

"Who said I'm negotiating?" Theo asked, glaring at Pierre. "I said no."

Dani stopped eating, her gaze ping-ponging between the two of them.

"You can't keep me here forever," Theo continued. "I've already been searching under Knossos for months, and we haven't found jack shit. It isn't like we found a giant ruby gemstone and tossed it aside because we thought you were looking for a mummified Minotaur instead. Keeping me here longer isn't going to change anything."

With the way Pierre's nostrils flared, she assumed the word *no* wasn't in his vocabulary. At least not when directed at him. Right then, at the worst possible time, Dani dropped the olive she'd been holding near her lips, the tiny fruit hitting the concrete coffee table with a dull *thud* before rolling down the patio and straight toward the pool.

Kerplunk.

Dani winced. But her embarrassment was washed away by the look Pierre gave her. A look that said he was only now remembering that she was even there.

"And who are you exactly?" he asked her.

Before she had a chance to respond, Theo cut in. "She's no one. A tourist I saw at the museum."

"Nice try," Maurice chimed in, catching Pierre's attention. "We already covered this. She's his fiancée, and he tried passing her a note."

Where was this fiancée idea coming from? The way Maurice had said it made it seem like he truly believed she and Theo were engaged.

Wait a minute. Theo's words from earlier echoed through her head: *She's not her.*

Oh my God. Theo . . . is engaged?

Dani looked at Theo, who, in turn, appeared to be trying desperately to avoid eye contact.

Engaged.

Theo.

Getting married.

To someone else.

The squeeze on Dani's heart almost took her breath away.

Apparently a lot had happened since they'd last seen each other, after their night of drunken debauchery. She wished she could remember everything that had happened.

They hadn't planned to spend the evening barhopping, but Dani was feeling like a night out after dumping her most recent pendejo of the month. "You can be my wingman," she'd told him.

Not that any other guy could even get close to her that night. She and Theo were thick as thieves. Doing shots. Playing pool.

Singing "I Got You Babe" at karaoke. Dancing. She remembered putting her hands on his hips, trying to teach him how to do a merengue even though the song playing was decidedly *not* a merengue.

Her recollection of them stumbling home was a bit fuzzy, though not as hazy as the whisper of a vision with his hand cradling her face and a vague memory of waking up in the middle of the night with the two of them sleeping beside each other on the couch. When she woke the next morning with the world's *worst* hangover but no Theo, she knew something wasn't right. Especially when he wouldn't answer her calls or texts a few days after.

So when he followed up a few weeks later with a text—*I have something I want to talk to you about. Fries and micheladas soon?*—she'd figured it had to have been related to something that had happened that night.

Apparently she had been wrong. Theo was getting married, and he'd planned to tell her . . . over french fries? He had to be joking.

She glared at Theo and finally got his attention, questioning him with her eyes. He furrowed his brow and gave her a slight shake of his head.

What was *that* supposed to mean?

The shake was likely imperceptible to someone like Pierre who didn't know every one of Theo's mannerisms, but Dani had studied his face enough times to know when something was off.

My God, what is going on? She wanted to scream. She wanted *answers.* Theo couldn't go and get engaged and then not tell her.

Even though an engagement didn't make sense. His family had talked to his long-term girlfriend, Giorgina, after Theo had disappeared, and she'd said they'd broken up a few weeks before he left for Greece.

Had he really already found someone else?

Oh God, that was it. He'd met someone else. While she was busy horsing around with Beau, Theo had met the love of his life and gotten engaged in a matter of weeks. That was what he wanted to tell her.

"Let me see the note," Pierre said, holding his hand out to Maurice but staring straight at Theo.

Now Dani was *really* wishing she knew what was written in that note.

"He tore it up and threw it in the water so we couldn't read it," Maurice offered.

Pierre's gaze homed in on Theo, like lasers boring into his pupils. "What did it say?" he demanded.

"None of your business," Theo spat back.

"A love letter to your sweetheart?" Pierre asked.

"I told you. I've never seen this woman in my life." Theo tossed his head in Dani's direction with disdain.

Pierre pursed his lips, shifting his eyes back and forth between the two of them, trying to read their expressions.

Funny. Dani was trying to read Theo's expression, too.

"Well, if she's truly no one to you, then I guess we don't have a need for her," Pierre said. Um, Dani didn't like the sound of that. "Maurice? Louis? Get rid of her."

The words turned Dani's blood to ice. *Oh God.* Forget what she thought earlier. *This is it. This is how I die.*

The air stilled, everyone's gaze shifting from one to another. But when Maurice took a single step forward, the patio broke out in a blur of commotion. Theo hopped out of his seat so quickly it skidded on the floor behind him, and he immediately backed up to shield Dani.

"Stay back," he said, holding his hands out wide.

"Out of our way," Maurice said, practically foaming at the mouth with delirious pleasure.

"Put your hands on her, and I swear to God I'll break them," Theo spat.

His right hand curled around Dani's waist, tucking her behind him, as his left hand remained outstretched, holding off Maurice and Louis. The surrealness of the situation caused her knees to buckle. So she gripped his broad shoulders, which blocked her view, and she pressed her forehead against his back between his shoulder blades. She'd always marveled at Theo's height compared to her own, but she'd never realized how perfectly built he was for protection until now.

He smelled of saltwater and the sun, or at least what Dani imagined the sun would smell like. She could bask in his glow all day, soaking in his scent like she took in the sun's rays, filling her with warmth. Closing her eyes, she allowed herself to consume him. To *be* with him.

If only he weren't with someone else.

And, oh, you know, if only her life weren't on the line.

"You are awfully protective over some tourist," Louis said.

"And it's quite interesting that you have a cozy nickname for her," Pierre said. "Juicy, was it?"

Dani felt Theo's muscles tense under her palms. That fucking nickname.

"Theo?" she whispered. Whatever was happening, his current approach wasn't working.

He craned his neck to look at her behind him, then reached around bringing her to his side. Dani stared into his eyes, searching for an explanation, but all he gave her was a half-hearted smile and a whisper back. "Trust me. It will be okay. I promise."

Theo then wrapped his arm around her waist and pulled her into his side. "Fine," he said to Pierre. "You're right. She is . . . she *is* my fiancée."

Warmth spread across Dani's cheeks, and she fought to keep her body from flexing under his touch.

"That's more like it. There's no reason to lie, Dr. Galanis. Things will be much easier if you don't try to play tricks on me," Pierre said.

"Just let her go. I'll do whatever you want, but don't hurt her," Theo pleaded.

"I find it fascinating the number of people who think I'm some sort of murderer," Pierre said to Maurice and Louis, amused. Then, turning to Theo, he continued, "I was never going to hurt her. I only needed to know whether I could use her as leverage. And it seems I can."

Theo's head hung a little as if realizing he'd put her in even greater danger than before.

"So, now, tell me, Miss . . . ?" Pierre said to her, waiting for her name.

"Daniela," she answered, immediately wishing she'd been quicker on her feet and given him a fake name.

"Daniela. Beautiful name. Tell me, what are you doing here? Had he found a way to communicate with you? I need to know what damage has been done, and please, please don't lie to me. I'm not in the mood."

"I . . ." She needed to think fast. "I came looking for him. For my . . . fiancé. I didn't believe the stories that he was dead. I would have known. I would have felt it."

"That's quite the bond you have."

It may not have been quite the truth, but the idea that he was dead never sat right in her stomach.

"And the letter?" he asked.

"I never even got the chance to read it before your goons over here found us."

Maurice and Louis glared. Good. She hoped she offended them.

Pierre eyed her curiously then turned his gaze toward Theo. "Well, now that she knows you are alive, my whereabouts, and what you're doing here, I'm sure you understand, Dr. Galanis, that I simply cannot let her go. She'll need to stay here with you in Greece."

"Please," Theo said, taking back his arm from Dani's waist and moving a few steps toward Pierre. "If you let her go, I'll do whatever you say. You don't need her here."

"She knows I am alive."

"She won't say anything," Theo assured him.

"I've trusted someone with that promise before, but I've learned my lesson. She's staying here."

"What about my family?" Dani asked, her voice trembling. "And the tour group I was with? People will know I'm missing."

"We'll handle that," Pierre said.

Dani pictured another headline: *American Tourist Missing in Greece.* After Theo had already disappeared, their families would be shattered. Even *if* their families put their disappearances together and sparked a manhunt, would that honestly be any better?

"Please," she pleaded. "Please, I don't want my family thinking I'm missing. Or dead. It will destroy them. We already lost so much after Theo . . ." Her voice cracked and her throat seized up.

Theo looked down at her, his worried eyes bouncing around trying to read her face. Dani's eyes welled with tears. Tears of fear. Of sadness. Of . . . she wasn't going to go there.

"I'll tell you what," Pierre said after a moment, tearing their attention from each other. "I'll make you a deal."

"What sort of deal?" Theo asked.

"How long was this tour to last?" Pierre asked Dani.

"Ten days," she said.

"And how many days in are you?"

"This is day four."

"All right. We'll deal with the tour company. Check you out of the hotel. Explain that you were homesick and returned to the United States."

Pierre seemed to know her better than he could have even imagined.

"Then, you'll spend the next six days searching for the eye. So long as you find it, I will let you return home, and your family will be none the wiser."

"Six days?!" Theo said, exasperated. "I've been looking with your men for over a year and now you're giving us six days?"

"Perhaps you should have been working a little harder."

"Harder? I didn't even know what I was supposed to be looking for!" Theo protested. "And even now that I do, I have no fucking clue where it might be. I told you it was just a story."

"You're a smart man," Pierre said matter-of-factly. "Like I said, I've been following your career. You've been quite successful at finding things. This should be no different."

"And what happens if we don't find it?" Dani asked.

"Then I make no guarantees," Pierre said, yet again turning Dani's blood ice-cold.

Pierre stood up. "You will stay here tonight as my guests. Please, feel free to enjoy my island. Eat my food. Raid my wine cellar. Swim in my pool. I've already had some clothing left for you in your room."

Um, creepy.

"Understand, however, that we're the only inhabitants on this island," he continued. "There is no phone, and Maurice has the only key to the boat, so please do not even bother with trying to steal it. I'd like to enjoy my evening without having to worry about the two of you trying something foolish."

"And tomorrow? After this little holiday getaway?" Theo asked.

"Tomorrow, you will return with Maurice and Louis to Crete to continue your search for the Minotaur. All of you."

"She doesn't know anything about this," Theo said. "She's not an archaeologist."

"Then I suggest she start learning." Pierre then turned his attention to Dani. "What is it that you do, Daniela?"

"I . . ." She paused for a moment, debating whether to lie. But what difference did it make? This man clearly had money. He already knew who Theo was, and it wouldn't be difficult to confirm who she was, too. "I'm a librarian."

Pierre clapped his hands together and smiled. "Seems your fiancée, Dr. Galanis, is your perfect complement."

CHAPTER Five

Theo

"WHEN ARE YOU GOING TO TELL ME WHAT THE HELL IS GOING on, Theo?" Dani asked as he brushed by her searching their—shared—bedroom for bugs.

The recording sort, that was. By the spotless look of this place and everything about Pierre Vautour's image, a bedbug wouldn't stand a chance on this island.

"I don't think it's safe to talk here," he finally answered softly, lifting a corner of the king mattress on the one—and only—bed in the room.

"What do you mean it's not safe to talk here?" she asked at full volume as he continued looking for microphones. Opening drawers. Looking in vents.

"What are you even doing?" Dani asked.

"Making sure no one is listening or watching," he said. He couldn't stop. Not until he knew the coast was clear.

"Theo? What sort of trouble are we in, exactly?"

"Enough that people think I'm dead," he said without looking at her as he turned over a lamp. "I think that probably explains enough."

"Will you stop for a minute? You're scaring me."

Her words stopped him in his tracks, and he stood up straight to face her head on. Her arms were wrapped tightly around her waist. She looked small, and not only in the literal sense. This wasn't the Dani he was used to. The tough, no-nonsense woman who stood up for herself. The woman who took care of business and never shied away from danger. She was never scared of anything.

It was one of the things he loved about her.

No. You can't say that. Theo quickly wiped the thought away.

It wasn't that Theo hadn't thought about Dani in that way. Oh, he'd thought about her in lots of ways over the years.

And now, there she was—his *fiancée.*

What the hell had he been thinking when he'd told Maurice and Louis months ago that he had a fiancée? Answer: he'd been trying to save his own ass.

But now? He wanted nothing more than to scoop her up in his arms. Repeat all the words she'd said to him that night back in Grand Rapids, the words that at the time he couldn't say back. Protect her from this mess he'd gotten himself in. Promise her everything would be okay.

But he couldn't do any of those things. Because the fact of the matter was, he *didn't* know if everything would be okay.

And those words—*It's always been you*—well, she clearly hadn't meant them.

"Juicy, I—" he said, taking a step toward her with his arms open to pull her into a hug.

But she put up her hand to stop him.

"You need to tell me what's going on," she said.

"I will. It's just—"

"The pool," she said.

He cocked his head to the side. "What about the pool?"

"We can talk there, right by the edge. It's huge. There probably aren't any recording devices. No Maurice and Louis. It's not like they're going to *swim* next to us."

Hmm . . . it wasn't a *bad* idea, especially since Maurice couldn't swim. Except . . .

"We don't have swimsuits," he said.

"Yes, we do. Right there," she said, pointing to a stack of men's and women's clothes on the dresser. And sure enough, swimwear right on top.

"Don't you think that's awfully convenient?" he asked. "Swimsuits? They probably *want* to get us in the water."

Dani narrowed her eyes to him, marched over to the piles of clothes, and snatched the suits. "I don't give a shit if it's convenient," she said, tossing a pair of trunks at Theo's face.

He pulled the shorts from his face, finding Dani staring at him with her hands on her hips.

There's the Dani I know.

"I want some answers. Meet me in the pool," she said before retreating to the bathroom to change.

• • • • • • • • • •

THEO WADED INTO THE POOL ALONE, WAITING FOR DANI. SOMEthing about swimming in the luxurious infinity pool of his captor felt a bit icky, but what other choice did he have? Dani was right. She needed answers. And since he couldn't be sure their room wasn't bugged—or that Maurice and Louis wouldn't follow them around the island if they tried to talk elsewhere—this would have to do.

The water was warm, heated by more than the sun's rays setting above them. He could get used to this—minus the whole kidnapping thing.

He stared out to the sea, watching other boats far off in the distance. Too far to be able to see him waving his arms for a rescue.

A flash of something shiny caught his attention behind him and he looked over his shoulder, spotting Dani approaching the edge of the pool and—

Holy fucking God, Pierre is taunting me.

The swimsuit she wore should have been fucking illegal. The shimmery teal fabric reminded him of the prom dress she wore back in high school the year she'd gotten stood up and he went in place of her date. But whereas that dress had merely accentuated her curves, this suit revealed them. It was technically a one-piece, but really that meant only that all the little pieces were connected, even if only by the thinnest of threads. The triangular bra area barely covered her full breasts, revealing a significant portion of her side-boob (the best part of the boob if you asked him). They plunged to her navel, creating the deepest V possible. He couldn't see the back, but based on how it looked from the front, he was sure it didn't cover her ass.

Juicy.

He couldn't believe he'd used that nickname in front of Vautour. God, how stupid could he have been?

She'd pulled her hair up into a messy bun with a few tendrils of hair loosely falling onto her neck. What Theo wouldn't do to sweep those loose pieces aside, grazing her neck with his fingers to make space for him to plant kisses along her honey-colored skin.

"Don't look," she said, crossing her arms over her chest. *Too late.* "This suit is absolutely ridiculous."

Ridiculously sexy.

Theo wanted to respond, but he could already feel his voice getting trapped in his throat, so he stayed quiet.

"It says it's my size, but I swear they made this at least two sizes too small," she said, tugging at the hem around her thighs.

Fits just right, he thought.

He cleared his throat and tried to clear his mind of dirty thoughts. God, looking at her was dangerous.

"I doubt they knew what sizes we wear," Theo tried to explain, ignoring the fact that *his* swimsuit fit him fine.

Dani descended into the water then sat on the stairs across the pool from him.

"You're going to need to get closer than that," Theo said from about twenty feet away. "Honey," he added, quirking an eyebrow.

"I'm fine right here . . . *babe*," she said, ticking her head to the side with attitude for emphasis.

"Sound carries over water," he then pointed out.

She let out a breath, then stood and pushed off from the stairs, gliding through the pool with minimal effort. Once she reached him, she leaned back against the edge of the pool, then turned to face him.

"Explain," she said, not wasting any time.

But Theo still hesitated, scanning their surroundings. "Did you see Maurice and Louis around?" he asked.

She narrowed her eyes at him, sending a chill over his skin despite the heated pool water. "Quit stalling," she said.

If looks could kill.

But she didn't understand. They may have been surrounded

in opulence, but his reality for the past year couldn't have been further from luxury.

"I'm not stalling. What if they're watching us?"

Dani sighed and rolled her eyes. She then inched closer to him, reaching her arms around his waist under the water and causing him to flinch.

"What are you doing?" he said under his breath, gazing down at the top of her head as she rested it on his shoulder.

"Pretending you're my babe," she whispered. "In case they're watching."

He let himself relax, then stretched one arm along the edge of the pool steadying their bodies and placed the other around her back, delicately resting his fingers on her bare skin. Surprisingly, she didn't recoil, seemingly unbothered by the fact that he was touching her so . . . intimately. Funny, seeing as the only thing *he* could focus on was the placement of their hands upon each other's bodies.

They stayed in place for a few moments, quiet save for the water spilling over the rim. For the first time in months, all the noise in his head—the fears, the what-ifs, the strategizing—subsided. He could have remained that way forever, even allowing his eyes to close briefly, when her soft, silky leg brushed against him, bringing him back to attention.

"Theo . . . please tell me what's going on," she pleaded, finally breaking the silence.

He blew out a breath. "I don't even know where to begin."

"Then start with Grand Rapids. When were you there? And why did you leave without saying anything? I thought you wanted—"

She stopped herself and pulled away. But he knew what she was going to say. *I thought you wanted to talk.*

Fries and micheladas. That was the plan. Until it wasn't.

No, he couldn't start there.

"I'd planned to stop by," he started, "but right when I arrived, I got an email from an old schoolmate, Dr. Ford Matthews. He was looking for someone to help with an expedition on the Peloponnesian peninsula, said that some Minoan artifacts had been discovered. Which didn't make any sense since the Minoan civilization was centered on Crete. Because of my expertise in Minoan antiquities, he asked if I could come to verify their find. I'll admit, I was fascinated. A cache of Minoan artifacts on the Peloponnese? I had to see it. And it had been a while since I went to a dig site."

Plus, it was a convenient excuse to get away.

"But," he continued, as his arms skated back and forth across the water, "when I got here, Ford was nowhere to be found. And when I got to the site where the expedition was supposedly taking place, no one knew what I was talking about. I emailed Ford using the address he'd sent the original request from, but I realized it was a fake. I eventually got ahold of Ford in Connecticut, but he said he'd never contacted me. It should have been a sign to go home."

"So why didn't you?" she asked, leaning over the side of the pool and resting her chin on her forearms.

"I wanted answers. I wanted to know who took the effort to trick me into coming to Greece and why. I couldn't let that go. I mean, would *you* have let it go?"

Dani tipped her head to the side. She didn't need to answer. He already knew what she'd say. She never let anything go.

"Then what happened?" she asked.

"Well, I tracked down the IP address from the email that had been posing as Ford to an island in the Cyclades, so I chartered a boat to take me there. It was only me and the captain—Maurice. And thirty minutes into our journey, we were joined by a man in a smaller boat—Louis. I immediately knew something wasn't right, and I tried to get them to take me back to the harbor, but, well, honestly, I don't even know what happened next. One second, I was arguing with Maurice to turn the boat around and the next I was lying in a bed on some remote farm on Crete with a goose egg on the back of my head. I don't know when or how I got there. I don't remember much of what happened over those next few days. Or, the hell if I know, maybe it was weeks. Then once I was back on my feet, Maurice and Louis filled me in on their plan—I was to help them find the Minotaur. Or else."

"I don't understand. Why didn't you try to get away?" Dani asked, lifting her arm and propping her head in her hand.

"You think I haven't tried?" he asked. "I did. Numerous times. The first time I tried running away in the middle of the night. But somehow, they found me. The next, I managed to steal Louis's car, but it literally ran out of gas. I thought it was a cruel joke the universe was playing on me. Though now that I've been around these goons for the last few months, I've learned this is a relatively common occurrence when it's Louis's turn to pay because he's too cheap for a fill-up. The last time, however, was when we were stopped at a gas station about thirty miles outside of Knossos. I saw a cop across the street; Louis was in the bathroom and Maurice was pumping gas this time, so I figured I had time. I ran up to the officer and told him I'd been kidnapped. He took me to a station, interrogated me for five hours, and then he released me—to Maurice. Apparently the local police were paid off. So I resigned myself to being stuck in this situation. Until I saw you at Knossos."

"So you're going along with it?" She wrinkled her nose.

Theo shrugged. "I thought they would have given up by now."

"What about that area where you were digging under Knossos?"

"It's nothing. A dead end. Like every other dead end I've taken them to," he said, leaning in toward her in case Maurice or Louis was nearby. "But they think the Minotaur is in the center of a labyrinth, and despite me telling them a thousand times that there *is* no labyrinth under the palace, they don't seem to believe me."

"Maybe that's because you keep tricking them, so they know not to trust you anymore," she whispered, giving him a look.

"Then why won't they let me go?"

She shrugged. "Maybe they think you know something you're not telling them . . . Do you?"

"Do I what? Know where the eye of the Minotaur is?" he asked.

She nodded.

"You heard me," he continued. "It was a story for kids."

He'd never told her—or anyone—about getting one of his stories published in a magazine, especially one geared toward children. She spent her days surrounded by books and journals written by prolific authors writing serious research for adults. And there Theo was *still* writing children's stories at thirty-seven.

Maybe on the outside he presented himself as an established professional with a grown-up job, a grown-up apartment, and grown-up aspirations. And also thankfully (according to his parents, at least), no longer "playing in sandboxes" on archaeological digs now that he had a respectable job as the director of research at the National Hellenic Museum. But deep down, he was still that giant dork who geeked out over fictional stories about Greek gods fighting mythical beings and human heroes saving beautiful young maidens from the wrath of angry deities. It didn't exactly fit his parents' vision for his future as a serious adult.

"But it must have been based on something," she said.

"My papou said there is a secret journal from some ancient old dude—Demetrios Papantonis—that talks about the eye, but I've never been able to confirm either he or the journal existed, which is why I didn't cite to any actual authority. Besides, my story was clearly marketed as a fictional tale in a children's magazine. I didn't think an *adult* would read it and assume it was true."

"Too bad for us then that someone *did* read it and now that person is holding you—holding *us*—hostage."

"It's not my problem he's a gullible fool."

"Well, it is now. It's *both* of our problems."

Theo hung his head. "I'm sorry I got you involved in this. I swear, had I known this was going to happen, I never would have tried slipping you that note."

"How did you even find me?"

"Maurice and Louis were set on finding you after what happened at Knossos. Said we couldn't let you get away. They looked up the name of the tour company on the bus and found where you were staying. So this morning, we were staking out the hotel, but we didn't see you when the rest of the group got on the bus, so we waited until you finally left the building and followed you to the museum. Once there, I pretended I had to go to the bathroom so I could sneak away and, well, you know the rest."

"They just let you walk away out of their sight?"

Theo shrugged. "I told you. Once I realized the cops were in on it, I stopped trying to escape. That garnered me a little trust, I suppose, though I don't know whether we can count on it any longer."

"What's the deal with them? I can't tell if they are idiots or just as bad as this Pierre guy."

"Maurice is bad news. He's given me a fat lip, a broken nose, and more bruises than I can count," he said.

"He broke your *nose*?" Dani exclaimed. "Didn't you have to go to the hospital?"

"It wasn't that bad. Though it did leave me with a little scar," he said, tipping his glasses down to expose the tiny mark on the bridge of his nose.

Dani leaned in to get a look, squinting to see the scar under the moonlight. Theo's heart kicked up a beat as he stared at her examining his face, sending a swirl through his stomach.

"Not your perfect Greek nose," she said, mimicking his mother and jokingly putting her hands on her cheeks.

He snickered and shook his head, recalling all the times his mom bragged about her children's perfect Greek noses.

"I know. My chances at becoming the next top nasal model are shot."

"Your mom will be devastated."

"Guess she'll have to find something else to boast about," he said, resituating his glasses.

"Too bad it was your best feature."

"You're just jealous," he teased.

"Of your schnoz? Please. I'm thoroughly satisfied with this sniffer, thank you," she said, brushing her fingertip across her nose in a display.

He couldn't help but smile. He'd always liked her beautiful Nubian shape much more than he liked his own.

"So then what's up with Louis?" she asked, pulling him back into reality.

"Louis?" Theo said, turning around and resting his arms atop the rim of the pool. "He's not *quite* as awful. He lets Maurice boss him around and he's a bit of a nitwit, but he doesn't seem to have any interest in hurting me. He actually seemed to feel a little sorry for me after we talked about our families one night and how worried I was about everyone back home thinking I was dead."

"Like your fiancée?" Dani stared at him pointedly, and his stomach sank like a bowling ball had been dropped into the center.

He'd been waiting for her to bring this up, even if he'd been unrealistically hopeful that she'd forgotten until now.

"About that . . ."

"Why didn't you tell me?"

Theo wrinkled his brow. *Shit.* Did she know how he felt about her?

"That . . . that you were engaged," she said, her voice cracking. She looked away and bit her bottom lip. "I mean, when did this even happen?"

Theo opened his mouth to explain, but the words "Giorgina said the two of you broke up" came out of her mouth and ripped like a record scratch through his brain.

"Wait . . . you talked to Giorgina?" he asked.

"Of course we did. We were looking for you everywhere, Theo. We had to tell her you were missing. She was your girlfriend."

The operative word being *was*.

"What did she say? Did she tell you why we broke up?"

Dear God, what had Giorgina told her?

"No, Theo, she didn't," Dani said, turning to face him and clearly a little pissed. "Though, oh, I don't know, I'm guessing maybe you having a new *fiancée* had something to do with it?"

"What? Wait, no, no, no," he said, pushing off the wall, waving his hands, and squaring his chest to hers. "Juicy, I'm not engaged."

She tipped her head to the side. "But you said—"

"I made it up," he said.

"Oh."

What kind of *oh* was that? A relieved *oh*? A confused *oh*?

"Why would you do that?" she asked, furrowing her brow.

"When they first caught me, I'd told them I was engaged for sympathy," he said, "so they'd think I had someone waiting back home for me. A fiancée had seemed more plausible than a wife—a wife could be looked up, but a fiancée? But now that you're here, and seeing as we clearly know each other, well, they put one and two together and assumed you're her. They obviously didn't believe us otherwise, so what was I supposed to do? It's not like I ever imagined that you—or anyone—would actually find me."

"Yeah, well, you and me both," she said, pushing a bug floating in the water over the edge of the pool.

They waded silently for a few moments, the chirps of the birds and lapping of the waves the only sounds around them, before Dani finally spoke again.

"God, Theo . . . what are we going to do?" she asked.

Great question. One that he'd been pondering since the minute Maurice and Louis took them on the boat.

"We've got to get you out of here."

She frowned. "We *both* need to get out of here."

"Let's worry about me once we get you out. Once you're gone, you can tell the authorities about what's happened to me. Tell my parents. Tell anyone who will listen. Here," he said, bringing his hands around to the back of his neck to unclasp the chain he always wore around his neck. "Show them this, then they'll know you found me."

But Dani put up her hands to stop him, wrapping them around him and twisting his hands away from the clasp. "No, that was your grandpa's. I can't take it."

She left her hands around his neck, kicking up the heat a few notches. She was so close. So beautiful.

"He's dead. I don't think he'll care."

"Well, I do," she said, taking her arms back and leaving Theo with an emptiness. "And what if this Pierre guy does something to you for letting me get away before we find you again?"

"I'll deal with it."

This time she didn't frown. This time she scowled. "Theo, I'm not leaving you here. What if I escape and they take it out on you? What then?" she asked.

"Dani," he said, taking her hands and getting closer. He noticed a hitch in her breath. "I need you to trust me. You're so worried about what's going to happen to me, but if I put your life in danger and something happens to *you*, Vautour is going to be the least of my worries when Eddie comes to murder me."

She laughed, and finally he felt like they were on the same page again. "He would murder you, wouldn't he?"

Seeing as Eddie threatened to kick his ass if Theo ever even dated Dani, death was definitely on the table.

"I mean, I don't really care to find out, but probably. How is Eddie, by the way?"

"Aside from missing his best friend?" She stared at him with those big, beautiful brown eyes full of sorrow.

Obviously, it wasn't Theo's fault that Eddie was left without a best friend, but it sure did hurt to hear it.

"Aside from that," Theo said.

"Oh, you know," Dani said in a singsong voice. "Living his bachelor life in his bachelor pad. Though he did bring someone to Thanksgiving last year."

"No way!"

"Way. You should have seen my mom when they walked in. She almost dropped the turkey."

Theo started laughing, picturing the scene in his head.

"Were my parents there?" he asked.

Dani nodded. "They hadn't moved yet."

That sickening sensation gurgled through his stomach again. "Where did they go?"

"Cleveland. To be closer to Ophelia's family. Since they no longer needed to be in the middle."

"I can't believe they left," he said aloud, but to himself.

"I know," Dani answered anyway. "My parents are leaving, too. Next month."

"What? Where are they going?"

"Florida."

"Wow, so they're finally going to do it, huh?"

"Mm-hmm."

There was a sullenness to her voice, which Theo understood full well. Once her parents were gone, no one would be left.

"What are you going to do?" he asked.

"Great question. Stay, I guess," she said, shrugging her shoulders. "Though they're selling the house."

"Are you serious?" he asked, raising his eyebrows.

"Yep," she said, with an emphasis on the *p*.

It was hard to imagine Grand Rapids without his parents *or* the Guiterrezes. Carlos and Maria were some of his parents' oldest and closest friends. They spent every holiday together. Every graduation. Every birthday. It was why Theo had initially viewed Dani as a little sister or cousin.

Until he didn't.

Dani sighed.

"I suppose I knew someday I'd have to move out of my parents' house. Spread my wings and all that shit," she said, demonstrating her arm span in the water. She sighed again and looked over her shoulder at the sea in front of them. "It really is beautiful, isn't it?"

Theo stared at her silhouette, illuminated by the moon's glow. It didn't really matter if Eddie would kill him—Theo would never forgive himself if he let anything happen to her.

"Sure is," he responded.

"I know you've seen it a million times, but is it always this beautiful?"

"Absolutely." His eyes remained transfixed on her.

She looked over at him, and he quickly turned his gaze to the Mediterranean. "How many times have you been to Greece?" she asked.

Theo ran a hand through his hair and thought back. "Oh, I don't know. Fifteen? Twenty? Something like that."

"Do you ever get bored seeing the same place over and over?"

"Nah. It's never the same trip, and I don't always go to the same spots. Sometimes I'm here for work. Sometimes to see family. Sometimes a stopover when I'm heading somewhere else. There are so many things to see in Greece. Stories to uncover. People to meet. Foods to eat."

"Oh my God, the food!" she said.

Theo could practically see her mouth watering. His was nearly watering, too, watching her in the moonlight.

"It felt dirty eating Pierre's food," she continued, "but it was so fucking good." She closed her eyes and licked her lips, bringing her hands up to her mouth, which had the unfortunate effect of pushing her breasts together. Unfortunate for him.

What felt dirty was thinking about all the different ways that swimsuit was turning him on despite the predicament they were in. He should *not* be thinking about those things right now.

"You never told me why *you're* here," he said, trying to change the subject. "In Greece, I mean."

She turned around so her back was against the edge of the pool, and she was facing the house.

"You talked about this place all the time," she explained. "It was special to you. So after everything that happened with thinking you were dead and all, I wanted to see it for myself. Plus, I'd never been to Europe. I mean, I've never been *anywhere.* I figured this was a good place to start."

He liked that she'd chosen to visit Greece because of him. As if it connected them in some way.

There'd always been a connection between the two of them, even though he was supposed to be Eddie's best friend, not Dani's. Dani was the one who forged his mom's signature on a sick note on the day he skipped school after his papou died. Dani showed up for his doctoral graduation. Dani sent him a handwritten copy of her favorite cookie recipe when he was craving a taste of home—along with a tin full of a batch she whipped up just because.

But his parents had told him, it was time to grow up. Settle down and find a wife. Stop trying to relive his youth by galivanting around Michigan with Daniela Guiterrez. How was he supposed to show commitment to someone else with little Dani always in the background?

Not that his parents didn't like Dani. They loved her. But she wasn't a Triple G. And her penchant for breaking the rules and brazen personality, while amusing for everyone at the dinner table, weren't exactly what his parents pictured for a future daughter-in-law. Plus, her tendencies leaned toward bad boys in leather jackets, not archaeology nerds like Theo.

But after that drunken Saturday, he couldn't dance around his feelings any longer. He also couldn't—no, *wouldn't*—continue dating Giorgina when his heart belonged to someone else. It wasn't fair to either of them. The problem was, however, that he didn't know if Dani had even meant those words. They'd both been smashed. The fact that moments later she'd thrown up on him didn't exactly instill confidence. But the way she held him that night . . . the way she'd brushed her finger over his skin . . . well, it *felt* real. He owed it to himself to take a chance.

So after giving himself some distance, he'd finally planned to tell Dani how he'd felt. Rip off the Band-Aid and put it out there. Fuck that stupid pact he'd made with Eddie. Fuck the Triple Gs. He was in his midthirties, goddammit. It was time to stop letting others dictate his love life.

It's always been you.

If only he hadn't been too late. If only she hadn't already moved on.

The vision of the last time he'd seen her in Grand Rapids flashed through his head. Dani at the bar with *him*.

She's with her beau at the brewpub, her father had told Theo when he'd called their house the night he'd pulled into town for a surprise visit.

Her beau.

Those two little words had gripped his heart and given it a tight squeeze.

Theo had needed to see for himself, though he regretted it the minute he showed up at the karaoke bar. There they were, singing on the small makeshift stage in the corner of the room, singing a duet and holding each other in their arms. Singing "I Got You Babe," the song Theo and Dani had sung only a few weeks earlier.

He'd felt like he'd been punched in the stomach by Sonny and Cher themselves.

The night they'd spent together had meant nothing.

It's always been you.

Dani would never settle down.

It's always been you.

There would always be someone else. Someone cooler. More exciting. Less nerdy. Better.

It's always been you.

Theo hadn't bothered going into the bar after that. Instead, he dropped off her book at her place, then drove straight back to Chicago, and less than a week later, he was on the plane to Greece.

So where was her boyfriend now? Why wasn't he with her on this trip?

"Why didn't you come with anybody?" he asked, looking at his hands gliding through the water, trying to be as nonchalant about it as he could.

"I wanted to do this alone. For myself, you know?"

He knew the feeling well. He'd been doing things like this on his own for the entirety of his adult life.

"Besides, who would I even bring with me?" she continued. "My mom? Eddie?"

Theo's stomach swirled. He had to know.

"What about your beau?" he said, mimicking the words of her father. God, that sounded so stupid coming out of his mouth. He'd never used the term *beau* before.

"*My beau*?" she said with a laugh. "Oh my God, I never call him that. He would die if he heard you refer to him that way. Who even told you about him?"

So he did exist. "Your dad."

"Well, this isn't really his sort of thing. He's much more of a beach vacation sort of guy. Plus, it's a pain in the ass when we're both gone from work at the same time."

"You work together?"

"Yeah, that's how we met. He started working with me a little over a year ago, and we hit it off right away."

A little over a year ago? Right around the time of their last night together?

The realization slapped him in the face. What would have happened had he not taken his time to get back home?

Theo was about to be sick.

"Do you travel together often?" he asked.

Theo didn't know why he was asking so many questions. To torture himself, apparently.

"No, not really. You know I'm not really a beach girl."

"That's because the only beaches you ever go to are the ones on the Great Lakes. You need to check out the beaches in Naxos. Best beaches in the world."

"I'll let him know. I'm sure he'd love it."

Sonny and Cher, kill me now.

"Does he . . . does he like micheladas?" he asked.

"God, no. He's like you," she said with a laugh. "He says the words 'clam' and 'juice' have no business being involved in his beverages. But what can I say? Opposites attract."

With each comment, another tiny piece of his heart broke off.

"And he's still around?"

"Yeah. I told him he's never allowed to leave, which is great because he said he's not going anywhere."

The hits kept coming, but it didn't quell Theo's curiosity.

"I wonder if there is anything to eat, here," Dani said, clearly not noticing how the discussion of her boyfriend was affecting him.

"Louis got that food earlier, so I'm sure there's more."

"Well, I'm going to look."

She started to push off from the edge, but something caught her attention in the corner of her eye, and she spun back around, facing the sea.

"Oh my God, Theo, there's a boat," she said, pointing out in the distance.

He shot his gaze toward the Mediterranean. "Where?" he asked.

"Right there!" She pointed, then stood on the ledge below the water, wide enough only for half a toe. With her torso now out of the water and her arms flailing about trying to get the boat's attention, Theo stared up at her. And he really shouldn't have. Because his gaze was bouncing all over Dani's body, Dani who was very much taken and unavailable, but he couldn't tear his eyes from her.

Suddenly, Dani lost her footing and came crashing back into the water. Without hesitating, Theo rushed underneath her, catching her body before she hit the edge. But now . . . now that he had her in his arms, he didn't want to let go. He hadn't ever touched Dani, not like this. Sure, a hug here and there. And of course there was the slow dancing at her prom when his hands were wrapped around her waist. But that was young Dani, who still wasn't comfortable in the body gifted to her by her parents' flawless genes. This? This was Dani, the woman. Dani who turned heads wherever she walked.

Dani who didn't turn Theo's head because he couldn't ever bring himself to look away whenever she was near.

Despite the pool around them, her skin was warm. And soft. With one arm underneath her thighs, the other wrapped around her back, reaching around under her armpit—with his fingers grazing ever so slightly below that spectacular side-boob.

"Shit," she said, wrapping her own arms around his neck and shoulders, seemingly oblivious to their skin-to-skin contact. "Do you think they saw me?"

Theo's mind went blank. What was she even talking about? Oh right . . . the boat. How could her mind be on anything other than what was happening between them in the pool?

"I doubt it," he said, more disappointed by the fact that she had a boyfriend than the fact that they'd missed a possible opportunity to get out of this mess.

"What's going on out here?" Maurice asked from the edge of the pool. How long had he been there? "I heard splashing."

"Oh, you know, two lovebirds taking an evening swim," Dani said. "Hey, know where we can get something to eat?" she asked, releasing her hold on Theo.

Physically speaking, at least.

"Kitchen's that way." Maurice pointed.

"Oh good. You coming, honey?" she asked Theo, swimming over to the stairs and slowly walking out of the pool like a Bond girl. Theo watched Maurice's eyes practically bulge out of his head, staring at Dani as she strutted over to her towel.

Theo rushed to join her, glaring at Maurice when they finally made eye contact. *Don't even think about it*, Theo's eyes told him.

But as his eyes fixated on Dani's swaying hips, Theo wondered if maybe he should be saying the same to himself.

CHAPTER *Six*

Dani

I TOLD YOU, THAT'S NEVER GOING TO WORK," DANI WHISPER- growled once they were back in the bedroom, frustrated by Theo's absurd insistence on what she was now referring to as "the bathroom bit."

Why didn't he want her help getting out of this mess? When had he become a solo strategist? They'd *always* hatched plans together.

"It will work," he said, whispering into her ear from behind, still irrationally worried about recording devices despite his already having turned over the entire room unsuccessfully searching for one. "All you have to do is say you're going to the restroom while they're docking the boat back in Heraklion, and then slip out the back of the terminal building and run to the consulate."

"You don't think they will have wised up? What if they follow me into the bathroom?"

"They're not going to follow *you* into the bathroom. Besides, everyone has to use the bathroom. They're not going to be too suspicious. Now maybe the *next* time I have to use the bathroom . . ." he joked.

She turned her head and glared at him. "This isn't funny, Theo," she said at full volume.

"Keep it down!" he commanded as forcefully as one could do at whisper-volume.

And Dani's body instantly succumbed to his tone, like her insides suddenly turned to Jell-O. Theo stood behind her as he spoke into her ear, sending a delightful titillating sensation down her neck to her chest, buzzing through her nipples, tingling her stomach, and ending straight in her core. He was so close.

Too close, to be honest.

Could he feel her body clench or see her fists tighten around the hem of her shirt? Did he notice the hitch in her breath at the tickle of his beard brushing against her ear?

His hands gripped her waist, reminding her of how his hands felt when he caught her in the pool. They'd been so much larger than she remembered, wrapping from her back around her side, with his fingers grazing dangerously close to her breasts.

Now that she knew what his hands felt like on her bare skin, well, fuck. How was she supposed to sleep in the same room with him all night?

"I'm only saying," she whispered, trying to steady her breath and fighting to keep from pressing her backside into him, "there has to be a better way. I can stay here and help."

"Stick with the plan, okay?" he said.

Dani closed her eyes, imagining her arms floating above her head and reaching around his neck, pulling him toward her own. She could almost feel his soft lips planting delicate kisses along her neck. For the slightest moment, she felt his fingers press into her hip bone and the pads of his thumbs graze the sliver of bare skin where her shirt rolled up at her midriff. How easy it would be for his palm to flatten against her stomach and dip below her waistline. Or for one hand to skirt between her skin and her panties, and the other glide up her shirt and cup her breast.

"Theo," she whispered, breathlessly, "what if I—"

"Please stop. You're leaving tomorrow, end of discussion," he said, and instantly released his hold on her, like a rip cord had been pulled, yanking him from her.

Breathe.

She filled her lungs and let out a long exhale, centering herself as he backed away. A technique she'd utilized for years whenever she felt herself wanting to take things a step too far, threatening to cross that invisible, unspoken line between the two of them. Because as much as she wanted Theo, his commitment to only dating Triple Gs made it patently clear he didn't want the same.

Once she'd gathered herself, she spun around, finding Theo arranging blankets and a pillow on the sofa at the foot of the bed.

"What are you doing?" she asked.

"I'm going to sleep," he said, fluffing up the pillow while looking in the opposite direction.

Dani turned toward the bed—the *king*-size bed—and then back at Theo again. "There's plenty of room," she said.

"I'll be fine," he grumbled.

"Quit being silly. You should sleep up here," she said.

Theo's gaze shifted from Dani to the bed and to Dani again.

"I don't think that's a good idea," he said. His words felt like a kick in the stomach.

"Why not? We're both adults. I think we know how to behave."

Theo's eyebrow raised. Something about the way she said *behave*, as if he maybe disputed that fact. That one look sent images of Theo cuddled up behind her through her mind. His big, wide hands splayed over her stomach, pulling her closer to his body. Her ass pressed against his firm abdomen, sensing his cock starting to stiffen as his lips pressed against her earlobe.

Sure, they *knew* how to behave, but did she really want to?

She allowed her eyes to travel to his groin for a moment, then quickly flicked her gaze back up.

"Look," she said, not waiting for him to respond and trying to wipe away the images in her head. "We're . . . *engaged*. That means, from here on out, we're only getting one room. One bed."

"I think I can handle the couch for a week."

"And if there *is* no couch?"

"Then I'll sleep on the floor."

"Why are you being so weird? It's a fucking bed. A *huge* one, at that. And it's not like we haven't slept beside each other before."

"Yeah, well, that probably shouldn't have happened, either."

She frowned and furrowed her brow. "What is *with* you? I haven't seen you in over a year and you're acting like I'm the *last* person you want to see right now. Like being next to me is the worst thing that could be happening to you."

He jerked his head in her direction and stood straight. "Because it *is* the worst thing that could be happening to me right now. I don't want you here!"

Dani blinked several times.

"I had things under control before you got arrived," he continued, returning to making up the couch, only now more aggressively.

"Please!" she snapped back. "You've been held hostage for *a year*, Theo. Nothing about that says 'control.'" She brought her hands up to form air quotes.

"Yeah, well, now I've got a deadline and *you* to worry about."

"You don't need to worry about me. I know how to handle myself."

"Oh really? This isn't like one of those silly stunts we pulled back in high school. This is real life. I mean, seriously, your first time out of the country and *this* happens? It's the kind of shit that would only happen to you."

His words smacked her in the face. Theo, the one person who she'd thought believed in her, was thinking the same thing as everyone else: she was a joke. All the times he'd visited. All the adventures they'd gone on. He was only humoring her.

Poor, pathetic Dani. Stuck living with her mom and dad in her thirties because she was too big a loser to try. Theo wasn't coming back to spend time with her in Grand Rapids because he had feelings for her. He felt *sorry* for her. His trips were nothing different from a big brother checking on his sister, trying to help her through her litany of tough times and silly bad breakups.

She pictured the two of them on the couch together that last night in her apartment, spooning with his arms around her waist, and she cringed. *That's* why he was gone the next morning. Things had gotten weird.

How had she not realized it before? How could she have been so foolish to carry on this childish little crush for all these years? He pitied her like everyone else.

"Wow, Theo. I didn't realize I was such a *burden* on you."

"Well, sorry, but I didn't exactly have taking care of you on my kidnapping bingo card."

"And I told you that I can handle myself. You don't need to take care of me."

"As if our parents would be okay with me leaving you on your own," he said, rolling his eyes. "I can't just wash my hands of any responsibility, here. You're practically my sister."

You're practically my sister.

The image of him pressed against her body evaporated like the wave of a wand.

Over the years, she thought she'd sensed a shift between them, but apparently she'd been wrong.

"Fine," she said, tearing the covers from the bed and getting in. "Be the hero. Have it your way."

She turned off the lamp beside her while Theo was still standing in the middle of the room.

"Can you turn that back on? I wasn't done," he said.

"Turn it on yourself. You don't need my help, remember?"

At least this trip wasn't a complete bust. She'd finally gotten what she'd been looking for.

Closure.

• • • • • • • • • •

IT WAS A CHILLY BOAT RIDE TO CRETE—AND IT HAD NOTHING TO DO with the air temperature.

Theo and Dani hadn't spoken a word to each other since she'd turned off the light the night before. But she didn't need to open her mouth to speak to him. Her icy glare and cold shoulder did plenty of talking for her.

Not that Theo tried smoothing things over, either. He carried with him an air of righteousness. Like he thought he knew better than she did and so his plan was the right plan.

It didn't matter that it was the only plan.

Dani tried to pay attention while they traveled back to Crete so hopefully she'd remember how to get to Pierre's island, taking note of unusual landmarks and the shapes and sizes of other islands, but Maurice and Louis might as well have blindfolded them. The ride back took detours and roundabout directions, obviously in an effort to confuse Dani and Theo. After an hour in, she couldn't make heads or tails of where they were. Any hopes of being able to find the island again were lost.

So what was she supposed to tell the authorities?

Pierre Vautour has a secret island lair somewhere in the Aegean Sea!

Yes, one island in a sea of over six thousand. They'd find it in no time.

For the briefest of moments, Dani wished she hadn't been such a stubborn brat all night so they could have at least firmed up the details of Theo's dumbass plan. But it was too late now. Finally, Heraklion appeared in the distance.

The puttering of the speedboat matched her heartbeat as they pulled into the harbor. She glanced over at Theo, seemingly deep in thought, looking out at the sea with his chin propped up in his hand resting on the side of boat. What was he thinking?

She looked at the bench seat between them where his other hand rested mere inches from hers. She wanted to take it and give it a squeeze. But as he turned his head slightly in her direction, she could have sworn she saw his eyes gaze downward, also noticing the closeness of their hands. And seconds later, he pulled his hand away. Things were worse between them than she thought.

As they eased toward the dock, Louis jumped out and Maurice tossed him a rope to tie up the boat. With Louis and Maurice distracted, Theo finally spoke to Dani.

"You're still set on the plan, right?" he whispered to her, though his eyes were focused on the guys.

"I guess," she answered, and his head snapped in her direction.

He wrinkled his brow, clearly wanting to rehash things like they'd done last night, but what did he expect her to say? It was a terrible idea.

She hated this plan. Sure, if everything went right, then she'd happily eat her words at the end of the day. But right now? Leaving him alone with these criminals didn't sit right with her. What if they were pissed that he'd helped her to escape? Or that he'd lied to them? What if they hurt him as a punishment? She wasn't going to sit there and pretend she was happy about this.

"Don't worry," she said before he could start lecturing her but not without rolling her eyes, "I know what I'm supposed to do."

His shoulders relaxed.

"All right, time to get out," Maurice said, and they turned their attention to him.

They climbed out and stood beside Louis as Maurice finished securing the boat. Dani looked at Theo and he tipped his head back and tossed a glance at the ferry terminal, signaling that it was time.

She nodded, then announced, "I need to use the bathroom."

Maurice glared at her. "Is this another one of your tricks?" he asked.

"Oh, I'm sorry, don't you ever have to take a shit? Or are you backed up all the time? Oh my God, is that why you're always so grumpy?" Dani said, placing her hand over her mouth in feigned shock. "Because you're in a constant state of constipation?"

Maurice glowered at her. "You think that's cute?" he asked.

"No, I think it's inhumane that you are depriving me of a basic human necessity," Dani said, folding her arms over her chest. "Come on. It's been over an hour since we left the island. Did you not see how much of that orange juice I had at breakfast?"

It *was* a remarkable amount.

Maurice stared at her for a solid beat then said, "Fine, but you stay here," directing himself at Theo. Dani breathed a sigh of relief, until Maurice then turned to Louis and said, "And you go with her."

Shit. Theo flashed a glance at Dani. So much for that trust. They started to walk toward the ferry terminal, and she was eyeing all the doors and exits when Theo took her hand and pulled her back into a hug.

"Be careful," he whispered, his lips brushing against her ear.

This was it.

What might be her final goodbye to Theo forever.

She wanted to take back all the bickering and the fighting from the prior evening. Tell Theo she didn't want to leave him. Even *if* he only thought of her like a sister. Except . . . he didn't want her to stay. He didn't need her.

No one did.

But it didn't stop the warm fuzzies from dancing across her skin. Or stop her from burying her face in his chest and squeezing her arms tightly around his waist, never wanting to let go. He returned the squeeze, and she allowed herself to be enveloped by him.

Funny how letting go felt more like holding on.

"It's a trip to the bathroom, you're not sailing out to sea for battle," Maurice said.

"Hurry up!" Louis followed.

Theo's grip loosened and he stepped back, but not before saying one last thing.

"Remember why you're Juicy." It wasn't a question. It was a statement.

As if she could ever forget how she earned the nickname that she'd loved-hated after all these years.

Dani looked back over at the terminal, searching for windows. There. It wouldn't be easy, but as she'd learned the day she became Juicy, she could squeeze her way out of almost anything.

With a subtle nod and an ache in her heart that this quite possibly might be the last time she ever saw Theo again, she headed toward the ferry terminal with Louis. The building was bustling with tourists and locals waiting for the next boat. It would take only one little scream to end this nightmare they were in. But then Dani thought about Theo, still at the boat with Maurice. She couldn't risk it.

"We've learned your fiancé's little tricks. I'll wait for you right here," Louis said, pointing at a spot right outside the bathroom door.

Of course he would wait.

"I might be a few minutes," she said.

"In five minutes, I'm coming in."

It didn't give Dani much time. Thankfully, she was skilled in the art of climbing in and out of windows. The instant the bathroom door clicked shut, she rushed toward the window high up on the wall. Not that she could reach it. Damn her short legs. She scanned the bathroom, eyeing a trash can in the corner, the only movable object in the room. Careful not to make too much noise, she tipped the round, three-foot-high bin on its side, rotating it in the direction of the window. It wasn't going to be easy, but she could do this. Once she situated the can directly underneath the window, Dani took a deep breath and placed both hands on either side of the bin. But right as she was about to lift herself onto the edge, she looked into the can and something caught her eye.

A grocery store sale paper advertising what appeared to be a bottle of something. She couldn't tell because the paper was torn in half. But it wasn't the prices or the realization that, sure, they had grocery store ads in Greece like in the US. It was what was on the bottle.

A μ with an eye. Like on that clay vessel in the museum.

She dug into the trash, pulling out the paper. What if this wasn't a coincidence? What if it *meant* something?

Then she couldn't leave Theo. Not now.

She tucked the paper in her pocket, and then resituated the trash can and washed her hands, right as Louis busted into the bathroom.

"I said I'd be a minute," Dani said, hoping Louis couldn't sense her anxiousness.

He looked around as if not fully trusting her—fair—before they made their way back to the dock, coming up behind Maurice and Theo. Maurice noticed her first, then said, "Okay, we can go," clearly not knowing that moments earlier, she'd been thirty seconds away from her escape.

But when Theo turned around and saw her, the color drained from his face and his eyes went wide. He shook his head as if asking what she was doing there.

She tried smiling, but he didn't seem to be in a smiling mood.

"What happened?" he whispered into her ear as they followed a few feet behind Maurice and Louis leading the way to the parking lot.

"I found something," she responded, staring straight ahead and trying her best not to make it seem like a big deal.

"In the *bathroom*?" he asked, unable to fathom any sort of great archaeological discovery lurking in the public toilet. Also fair. "Juicy, we had a plan." He sounded exhausted.

"No, *you* had a plan. I came up with another."

"This isn't the time for competition. That was our one shot to get you out of here. We're not going to get another opportunity like that."

"You mean, another opportunity to use the great crapper caper?" she joked.

"This isn't a game," he snarled, gently pulling her in tight by the back of her arm and stopping them in their tracks.

She snapped her face toward his so they were now nose to nose—or rather, her face to his chest—and they paused for a beat. His nostrils may have been flared and his brows wrinkled with frustration, but God, she'd missed his face.

"Yet you wanted me to climb out a bathroom window and thought *that* wasn't a game? I get that I'm not some *amazing* archaeologist like you," she said, waving her arms around and rolling her eyes, "but I'm not some dummy, either. Just because I've never been out of the country doesn't mean I don't have experience."

"I know that. And I never said you were a dummy."

"Then why won't you let me help you?"

Theo put his face in his hands and groaned. "I told you, I don't need your help."

"Oh really? Because it looks to me like you do. Whatever happened to 'I'll always be there for you'? It goes both ways,

Theo. We were never like this before. Why won't you talk to me?"

He put his hands on his hips, gazed up at the sky, and then blew out a long breath. She watched his Adam's apple bob as he took in his thoughts, now closing his eyes to shield them from the bright Grecian sun. The fight within him was obvious. Of course he knew at this point he had no choice but to work with her, but she didn't know when Theo became so . . . bossy. Growing up, she'd always been the bossy one. When had the tables turned?

"I know you don't want me here," she said, "but like it or not, I'm *still* here, so you might as well work with me instead of trying to push me away."

He took one more deep breath, then returned his gaze to her.

"Fine. What did you find?"

"Here. Look," she said, pulling the sale paper out of her pocket and handing it to him.

Theo unfolded the crumpled paper, turning it over, looking for an explanation. "You're kidding, right?" he said.

"No, look here," she said, pointing to the μ.

"And?"

"And I've seen this before!"

Theo furrowed his brow. "Of course, you have. Right here," he said, pulling the chain around his neck from under his shirt and showing her the pendant. There, etched into the gold, was the same μ and eye symbol.

Oh, so *that's* why it had looked familiar when she'd first seen it at the museum. She hadn't noticed last night when they were in the pool.

"What does it mean?" she asked.

"What do you mean, 'What does it mean'? It was my papou's. Something he'd had since he was in his early twenties, that's all. I don't think it *means* anything."

"Do you know where he got it?"

"I have no idea. He left it to me in his will, but it didn't say why."

"Well, I saw this symbol in the museum yesterday. In a painting on a clay pot of a man holding the Minotaur's head. He had this on a medallion around his neck."

Theo ticked his head to the side and blinked a few times.

Okay. Now they were getting somewhere. "What if this symbol has something to do with it?" she asked.

"A symbol . . . on a bottle of olive oil?"

So that's what it was. Olive oil.

She twisted her mouth. Of course, now that Theo was saying it out loud, she had to admit—it sounded a little ridiculous.

"And on your necklace!" she proclaimed, hoping that counted for something. "Don't you think that's an odd coincidence?"

"A coincidence? So that's what you're calling it now? Because a second ago you were only relying on a piece of paper you 'found' in the bathroom," he said, using air quotes.

"Didn't you hear what I said? Theo, the symbol that's on your necklace was on a vase from the second century BC. How can you be so easily dismissing this?" She couldn't conceal the exasperation in her voice. This was so unlike him.

He tossed back his head and groaned, dragging his hands over his face. "Yes, it's an intriguing coincidence, but we're focusing on the wrong thing at the moment. Jeez, Juicy. I don't understand why you wouldn't stick with the plan," he said, clearly frustrated and exhausted.

"Oh, I'm sorry that I didn't want to leave you here to *actually* die. Sorry that I thought you needed help."

"Help? How is this helping me? Now we're both in trouble."

"Yeah, no thanks to you."

"Me?" he said, pointing at his chest with the sale paper still in his hand.

"Yeah, you. If you hadn't gone and told them I was your fiancée—"

"Well, if *you* hadn't been snooping around Knossos—"

"And if *you* hadn't abandoned us in Michigan—"

"Abandoned you? Oh that's rich, coming from you," he said, laughing as if he found her comment doubtful.

"What the hell is that supposed to mean?" She folded her arms and glowered at him.

Now Theo was the one rolling his eyes. "Please."

Dani opened her mouth to protest, when Maurice yelled out to them, "Hurry up!"

"Come on," Theo said, turning to head toward Maurice and Louis.

"We're not done, here," Dani said, jogging to catch up to him and his unfairly long legs.

"Yes, we are. And if we don't come up with something more tangible than a label on a bottle of olive oil, we'll *really* be done, so please no more going rogue."

For supposedly being engaged, their body language certainly wasn't acting like it. Theo followed Maurice and Louis in a huff, keeping himself far from Dani. And her crossed arms weren't exactly screaming *I can't wait to marry you*. Luckily, neither man seemed to notice.

"Where are we going?" Dani asked once they got in a black SUV and started driving away from the harbor.

"To the farm," Maurice said.

The farm? Dani furrowed her brow and looked at Theo for answers.

"It's where we've been living," he told her.

"And then what?" she asked.

"Then Louis will go pick up your belongings at the hotel while we wait until closing time, and then we'll go back to Knossos," Maurice said.

"And do what?"

"Search for the eye," Louis said, though he might as well have said *Duh.*

"But it's not there," she said with matching duh-energy.

Maurice glared at her from the rearview mirror, and Louis spun around to look at her.

"What do you mean, it's not there?" Louis said.

"Tell them," she said to Theo. But he stayed silent. Verbally, that is. His wide eyes and subtle shake of the head told her plenty. So she answered for him. "The place you were searching at Knossos was a diversion. There's nothing there."

Theo closed his eyes and pinched the bridge of his nose above his glasses as he let out a long breath.

Maurice slammed on the brakes and pulled the car over. "Were you sending us on wild-goose chases?" he demanded of Theo.

Theo opened his eyes and glanced at Dani. "What did I say about going rogue?"

In her defense, he should have known better than to try to impose rules on her. Dani may have been a librarian, but stuffy rules were never her forte.

"We have *five* days, Theo. Sorry that I don't want to waste one of them poking around a bunch of rubble."

"Do you have any *better* ideas? Because maybe this will come as a shock to you, Juicy, but the *grocery store* isn't going to help us find an artifact that's been missing for thousands of years, and neither is this necklace."

"Grocery store? What are you talking about?" Maurice said.

"It's nothing," Theo spat back, looking away from Dani. "Just some silly idea she had."

"Silly?!" she guffawed. The *nerve* he had right now. Dani didn't care what Theo thought. At least she could make a correlation between her wild idea and the Minotaur, as outlandish as it may have seemed. It was better than his schemes.

"Yes, silly," he said, pointedly looking at her. "I mean, what, do you think an olive tree sprouted from the rotting corpse of the Minotaur? Or, I don't know, maybe the labyrinth is buried under an olive grove or something?"

The minute the words came out of his mouth, their bickering stopped. Like a light bulb went off in his head. In *both* of their heads. What if?

"You don't think?" she asked, turning in her seat, excitedly.

He shrugged. "It's not the most far-fetched thing I've ever heard in this job. I've certainly seen stranger things be true."

"Stranger than a giant Minotaur with glowing red eyes?"

"Glowing red eyes?" he asked, quirking his lips. It was the first time she'd seen him smile all day. A glimpse of the Theo she knew.

She loved that smile. Even on the coldest of cold Michigan winter days, that spark from Theo would warm her up. Raise her spirits. Make her believe anything was possible.

Except for a Minotaur with fiery eyes, that was.

"*I* didn't make it up," she said, pointing at her chest with a matching grin. "Cosmo did."

"Who's Cosmo?"

"The tour guide. Oh my God, you should have heard him spinning a yarn to the group." She laughed.

"Spinning a yarn like Ariadne did to help Theseus escape the labyrinth?" Theo joked.

"Enough!" Maurice called out, instantly silencing them. Theo playfully grimaced, like the teacher had caught them passing notes. "You need to explain and tell me where we're going."

"To the grocery store?" Theo asked, looking at Dani.

"To the grocery store."

CHAPTER
Seven

Theo

IN THEO'S TEN YEARS AS AN ARCHAEOLOGIST, HE'D NEVER ONCE taken his research to a grocery store. He'd also never considered the myth of the Minotaur was anything but that. A myth. Guess there was a first time for everything.

He still wasn't convinced there was a hidden labyrinth on Crete or an "eye" of the Minotaur, but Dani was right. They had only five days. Even if this olive oil excursion turned out to be a waste of time, at least they wouldn't be squandering energy chipping away at walls underneath Knossos that certainly wouldn't lead to any sort of relevant discovery.

He knew Knossos inside and out, having done an internship there back in graduate school and after spending six months there during a research stint once he got his doctorate, back in the days when he still went on digs. Sure, there were likely many more discoveries to be made at Knossos. But the Minotaur's eye wasn't one of them. If only his papou were still alive. Then he could ask him about the story he'd told him before bed when he was a kid.

Theo reached up and held the gold medallion hanging from the chain around his neck. *If only.*

He had to admit, his interest had been piqued.

Maybe this grocery store stop, however, could be an opportunity to get Dani the hell out of there. Grocery stores meant people. People meant unpredictability. Unpredictability that he might be able to use to his advantage.

If Dani insisted on going rogue, then he could go rogue, too.

Once they explained their olive oil theory to Maurice and Louis and figured out which market the torn sales paper belonged to, they made their way through town and pulled into the store parking lot. But as Theo started unbuckling his seat belt, Maurice reached back to stop him.

"You're staying here with me," he said.

What? No! How was he supposed to create a diversion to help Dani escape if he was stuck in the car with Maurice?

"But . . . but I need to go in with her," he said, trying to calm the panic in his voice.

"Uh-uh. I don't want the two of you trying any more of your tricks," Maurice said. "They'll go in and find what you're looking for," he said, motioning between Dani and Louis.

"But neither of them speak Greek," Theo protested.

"Well, that shouldn't be a problem since they have no reason to be speaking to anyone."

"What if they need help finding the olive oil? Or deciphering the label?"

Maurice rolled his eyes.

Theo was running out of excuses, then he looked at Dani, beautiful as always. Even though she belonged to someone else, his heart ached as he stared at her.

And that was reason enough.

"I'm sorry," he said, taking her palm in his. She stared at their hands, furrowing her brow, and then looked at him, wondering what he was up to. "But it's been over a year since I saw her, and I just . . . I don't want her out of my sight."

He stared into Dani's eyes, and he saw that look. That hopeful, questioning look he'd seen so many times. The look she'd given him that night in her apartment.

It's always been you.

"Aw, come on, Maurice," Louis said. "They're in love. What's the harm if we all go?"

Dani quickly looked away and tucked a loose strand of hair behind her ear. A light rosy color spread across her cheeks. He'd seen that look, too. Like the night of his parents' thirtieth-anniversary party when she caught him staring at her from across the room after his dad said, *When you know, you know.*

None of it mattered now that she was with someone else. But when she looked at him that way, he still heard those words.

When you know, you know.

"Fine," Maurice said. "But if you try anything, if you breathe one word to anyone about who you are, I swear to God you will regret it. And don't think I'm above hitting a woman."

"Got it," Theo said through gritted teeth.

They all got out of the SUV and headed toward the store, but Theo took Dani's hand in his. She snapped her attention to him and tried to pull her hand away, but he only gripped harder and gave her a slight tug back.

"What are you doing?" she muttered under her breath.

"I'm supposed to be unable to bear not having you by my side, remember?"

"Well, you're laying it on a little thick, don't you think? I could have found the oil on my own."

"I don't want to be separated. Besides, we need to be convincing."

"We *need* to find the oil. Come on, Casanova."

"Casanova was Italian."

"Okay, then who was the Greek god of love?" she asked.

"Eros. God of love and sex."

She shot a glance at him at the word *sex*. Those rosy cheeks had returned. Funny, he never pictured Dani the type to get bashful. She'd always been a casual dater, never with any guy for more than a month or two. They didn't necessarily talk about those sorts of things, but they had made plenty of jokes and innuendos over the years, especially whenever Eddie was around, since he *hated* the thought of his sister being a woman with needs. But Theo assumed Dani enjoyed sex, given how comfortable she was with the topic. Until now.

Fuck.

Theo shook the thoughts away. It wasn't the time for distractions.

They entered the store, and he scanned the space for opportunities. Exits. People who looked like they might be able to help. Any sort of commotion that could distract Maurice and Louis. The store wasn't much different from what they would've found in the United States. Even the layout was reminiscent of a supermarket chain back home.

They wandered through the store in a wad with Maurice and Louis following way too close for comfort, which in and of itself garnered a few curious glances. It also didn't help that

Maurice and Louis were dressed in black as though they were on a tactical ops team while Theo and Dani wore more of Vautour's Grecian resort wear—flowing linens in whites and blues. They were a bizarre foursome, to say the least. They weaved down the aisles, searching for the olive oil, even though Theo already had a good idea of where it would be. But he needed to figure out a plan. So he took his time, calculating potential moves in his head.

Finally they came to an aisle that had a display of various bottles of oil at the end, providing an entry to a wall and shelves of oils in bottles of all shapes and sizes.

"Holy shit," Dani said staring at the assortment.

An employee walked by right at that moment and Theo grabbed his attention, but not without Maurice sidling up to Theo, giving him a silent warning.

Theo took the sales paper from Dani's hand and showed it to the employee. "Do you know this bottle?" Theo asked the young store employee in Greek.

"No, I'm sorry," the boy responded.

"Thanks, anyway."

Theo ran his hands through his hair as Dani started going down the aisle, running her finger along each bottle so as not to miss it. There had to be an easier way, though. There were at least a hundred different varieties. In theory, he may have supported the olive oil farm idea, but really he was buying time.

Louis joined Dani in her search while Theo continued asking passersby about the sales ad, Maurice standing closely beside him. The idea that a person would recognize a brand based solely on a symbol was a bit of a stretch. It wasn't like Theo could remember what was on the label of oil he had back home.

He scanned the area when his eyes fixated on another employee restocking a tower of oils, and an idea popped into his head. What would it take to knock it over? A bump? A nudge?

Slowly, Theo backed up, pretending not to see the display, when he finally backed into the stack, knocking a few bottles from the top before an all-out cascade of bottles came crashing down, breaking into a million pieces. Bright greenish-yellow liquid spread over the floor as the bottles clattered and the employee called out, "Help, help!" trying to stop the entire display from falling.

Maurice and Louis rushed over to help, finally distracted, when Theo reached over to grab Dani's wrist so they could get the hell out of there. But she stopped him, completely oblivious to the commotion around them, and she reached onto her tippytoes to grab a bottle on the top shelf.

"I found it!" she called out, spinning to face Theo and holding the bottle high above her head. Her eyes went wide as she noticed the scene unfolding around them.

"Great, Juicy! Now, come on!" Theo said, taking her hand and pulling her away from the shelves. This was their chance to run.

But one step back and he skidded on the oil, his footing slipping out from under him. He went crashing to the ground, but not without taking Dani down with him. He landed on his back with a *thud*, then caught Dani on top of his chest in his arms.

"Oof," he winced when she cradled the olive oil between them, pushing it right into his abdomen.

"Oh God," she said, placing her hand on the ground alongside him to try to prop herself up, but her hand slipped out from under her, and she crashed atop him again, bracing herself on his shoulder.

He hissed in pain at the pressure. It was the same arm that Maurice had twisted behind his back a few months ago. The shoulder he'd fallen on while climbing down a cave on an expedition a few years ago. The one he'd injured back in college playing intramural softball. Thankfully, it hadn't popped out of the socket like the last time he'd injured it, but damn, it hurt.

"Ope," she said, falling again and again. Every time they tried getting up, they slid back into each other's arms. And each time, a searing pain shot through his shoulder. She eventually rolled off him and got on all fours as he slowly stood up and reached down to help her. He took both of her hands and pulled her up, and she wobbled on the slick liquid before finally making her way to standing in front of him.

"Sure could have used some of this slippery shit back at Ma Barker's," she said. They took one look at each other, and burst out laughing, recalling the day Dani got stuck in their neighbor's window.

Dani leaned into Theo's chest, burying her laugh in him. God, he loved her laugh. He'd heard it so many times, yet it still gave him warm fuzzies. He thought of their night at Palmer's, laughing and singing karaoke. What he wouldn't do to go back to that night. To say the fuck with it. To tell her how he'd really felt when she spoke those words.

It's always been you.

But his smile faded when Maurice walked over, glowering at them.

"We need to go," he said.

A crowd had gathered around them, people stopping and gawking. An older employee rushed over, holding his hands on his head.

"What happened?" he asked the stock boy.

The boy explained that Theo had bumped into the display, and the other man, presumably the store manager, started yelling that they needed to pay for all of the damaged bottles.

"Come on," Maurice said, brushing the man off and trying to pull Theo and Dani away.

"He says we need to pay," Theo told Maurice as the manager continued yelling at them in Greek.

"I don't give a fuck what he says. We're leaving," Maurice said.

"I'll call the police!" the manager said.

The police? Yes, please. This was it. This was their way out!

Theo spun around looking for security cameras. If they left and reviewed the footage, maybe they'd see his face. Recognize who he is.

"Maurice, I think he's saying something about the police," Louis said, tugging on his arm.

"So fucking what?"

"So, what if they go looking for . . . him?" Louis said, nodding his head in Theo's direction. "What if he's recognized?"

Fuck!

"Fine, pay them off," Maurice said to Louis, then turned to Dani and Theo and pointed. "And you two? You're coming with me."

Maurice marched them out of the store and straight to the SUV. But the minute Theo and Dani settled into the back seat, Maurice clicked the door locks, reached over the center console, and pulled Theo toward him by the collar.

"You little shit!" he growled.

Theo closed his eyes, bracing himself for impact with Maurice's fist. After a year together, Theo had grown accustomed to Maurice's mannerisms and reactions. One of his least favorites:

Maurice's fist's attraction to Theo's face. Growing up a nerd unfortunately resulted in Theo being on the receiving end of more than his fair share of punches, seeming to be the subject of bullies up until he moved schools and became best friends with Eddie.

Or rather, until he became best friends with Dani's brother. Dani was taking on thirteen-year-olds when she was ten, eighteen-year-olds when she was fifteen. Like that time Bobby Thomas and his buddies cornered him behind the school, and Theo threw a book at them while Dani picked up a fistful of dirt and tossed it in their faces so he could get away. Nobody messed with Dani or those she cared about.

So as he squeezed his eyes tight waiting for a fist-meets-face connection for longer than normal, he eked one eye open, unsurprised to see Dani beating on Maurice from over the headrest.

"Leave him alone," Dani called out as Theo struggled to break free from his grasp. "Let him go or I'll poke your eyes out. It was an accident!"

Glad to see she hadn't lost her spunk.

"Bullshit!" Maurice said, shoving Theo into the back seat and straightening himself in the front. Theo held his shoulder, trying not to let the pain show on his face. "I know you did that on purpose, trying to get away. Do I need to break your nose again? Because I'm getting really tired of having to put you in your place."

"I stumbled, that's all," Theo protested, though he wasn't sure how convincing he actually was. Stumbled into an entire pyramidic display of olive oil? Please. This wasn't the Three Stooges.

"And look," Dani said, holding up a dark glass bottle of oil, "I got it."

"Let me see that," Maurice said, snatching it from her hands. He turned the black bottle in his hands, inspecting it. "This is it?" he barked. "How the *fuck* is *this* supposed to help us find the eye?"

Theo barely caught the bottle when Maurice tossed it at his stomach, wincing as he lifted his arm to catch it before it hit him in the same spot where he got hit earlier. He grunted as he cushioned the bottle with his body—*that's gonna bruise*—and he rubbed his abdomen with one hand, while bringing the bottle up to inspect it with the other.

Like Maurice, he turned the bottle in his hand. But unlike Maurice, he actually knew what it said.

Δημητρίου

And beneath the word, a symbol. An eye with a μ. Okay. *Now* Theo was beginning to believe it wasn't a coincidence.

"What does it say?" Dani asked.

"Demetrios's."

As in Demetrios Papantonis, perhaps?

Her eyes lit up and a crack of a smile formed on her face, though it was obvious she fought not to appear too excited. Under normal circumstances, Theo would have been excited, too. Right now, though, all he wanted was to figure out what it all meant.

"Is there anything else?" she asked, scooting closer to him to get a better look. Their sides were flush together and her side-boob accidentally grazed his biceps. Or, at least, he assumed it was an accident.

He pushed the thought out of his mind and turned the bottle over to the back and read the short narrative aloud:

"Demetrios's olives are grown on the slopes of Chania,

Crete. There, our olive trees grow out of the soils made fertile by the watchful eye of our ancestors. We pay respect to Demetrios by making the finest, richest olive oil in all of Crete in the hopes that one day, our ancestors will return."

"Watchful eye?" Dani said. "Do you think that could be a reference to the eye of the Minotaur?"

"Possibly," Theo said. He had to admit, it was a pretty interesting word choice on a bottle of olive oil.

"One of you better start explaining what you're up to," Maurice said.

Theo had almost forgotten he was sitting in the front seat.

"Oh, just looking for somewhere we can find some souvenirs and gifts to take home to our family and friends, right, honey?" she responded, patting Theo on the leg and leaving her hand resting dangerously close to his inner thigh. His muscles strained, trying to remain still so she wouldn't notice his tightening adductors and how her touch affected him. "Think my mom will finally be willing to swap the lard for olive oil if we get her the good stuff?"

God, she was a smart aleck. Though, no, he didn't think Mrs. Guiterrez would ever willingly give up her lard.

"We're up to trying to find the eye so we can go home, Einstein," Dani said to Maurice, who glared at her. Clearly, he didn't find her so amusing.

"And how, pray tell, is that bottle of oil going to help you to do that? Explain it to me again like I'm an idiot," Maurice said.

Dani opened her mouth, likely to deliver another wave of insults, but Theo put his hand on hers, the one resting in his lap, to stop her. He knew from experience that Maurice had his limits. "Babe?" he said, tilting his head to the side and raising his eyebrows. "Let me explain this one."

He then leaned forward and held up the bottle to Maurice.

"See this symbol here?" he asked, using his thumb on the hand holding the bottle to tap on the μ symbol. "She saw this same symbol on some pieces at the archaeological museum. We think that maybe . . . maybe the secret to the eye's location has something to do with it."

Maurice looked back and forth between the two of them. "A symbol? On a bottle of olive oil?"

"And in the museum," Dani was quick to point out. Though they both left out the part about his necklace.

"So what are you saying? What are we supposed to do with this information?" Maurice asked.

"We need to go to Demetrios's Olive Mill in Chania," Theo said.

"First the grocery store and now an olive mill? What is this? A food tour? I thought you were supposed to be some sort of archaeological expert?" Maurice said.

Theo scanned his surroundings, covered in oil, taken hostage, and unable to undertake even the simplest of schemes to get Dani out of this mess.

Yeah, so did I.

CHAPTER Eight

Dani

THERE WAS NO POINT IN MAKING PLANS ANYMORE. IT SEEMED every hour, plans changed. Since they were no longer going back to Knossos, they first needed to stop by her hotel before they headed out of town to Chania. She'd wanted to leave Harold a note. They may have known each other for only a few days, but it didn't feel right not saying goodbye.

Of course, Maurice refused. Eye roll.

Sure, Dani understood that they weren't on vacation, but this guy seriously needed someone to love him because he was the most unpleasant person she'd ever met. Even Pierre Vautour wasn't this unbearably unlikable. Did someone piss in Maurice's Cheerios when he was a kid? Because for fuck's sake, he had a permanent scowl on his face. She hoped that someday she'd be able to locate Harold again to thank him for being a friend, even if for only three days.

By the time they made it to Chania, Demetrios's was closed,

so they'd have to wait until the next day to visit. So for now, they checked into a small hotel on the outskirts of town, and after Maurice and Louis set up remote sensors on the doors and windows that would alert their phones of any escape attempts, Dani and Theo were finally alone. In another room with only one bed.

They stared at the queen-size bed in the center of the small, standard room, both of them still coated in olive oil and in desperate need of a shower. The room was a far cry from the opulence of Vautour's guest room. The sickly sweet white lacy bedspread looked like the one her mom had gotten her for her fifteenth birthday—and that Dani had promptly taken to the bathtub to dye dark purple. The bedside lamps had matching lace shades. Aside from a dresser and nightstands, there wasn't much more to the room. But man, did it have a nice view out the window to the slopes of Chania.

"Well, at least we don't have to worry about the room being bugged like when we were at Pierre's," she said. "Now we can bicker like an old married couple in peace."

She tried to lighten the mood, but Theo just stood there, awkwardly holding his arm across his waist.

"I'll sleep on the floor," he finally said.

Guess he wasn't in a chatty mood. *Sigh.* They were already back to this. But fine. Normally Dani wasn't one for chivalrous gestures—which was a good thing since the casual relationships she usually engaged in left few opportunities for chivalry—but if he wanted to wake up with a stiff back and a crick in his neck, that was on him.

"Do you want to go ahead and shower first?" Theo asked.

"Oh yeah, sure," she said, reaching for her bag.

She wasn't used to being around Theo when they weren't

joking around and having fun. Not that their circumstances fostered that sort of environment, but still. Was this it? Was this how things were going to be between the two of them from now on?

There was no point in worrying about it now, so she dragged her suitcase into the bathroom and closed the door. For the size of the bedroom, the bathroom was quite large, with a sizable bathtub rather than a shower. It wasn't an ideal way to rid her body of the oil film, but it would have to do.

She tried not to take too long since Theo was still out there covered in oil and likely unable to sit down or do much of anything else. But the oil was stubborn, requiring multiple lathers and vigorous scrubbing. Eventually, she was oil-free enough, so she quickly got out, drained the tub, and threw on a pair of linen shorts and a tank top, then turned the faucet back on to refill the tub before returning to the bedroom.

"It's all yours," she announced. "There's only a bathtub, so I started refilling it for you."

"Okay, thanks," he said, grabbing his things and heading to the bathroom. But not even twenty seconds after the door closed, she heard something crash to the floor and Theo howl in pain. She rushed back to the bathroom and knocked on the door.

"Are you okay in there?" she asked.

"Yes . . . no . . ." he groaned.

"Okay, I'm coming in. Hope you're decent," she said.

Though she wouldn't have minded if he *wasn't.*

She opened the door and there he was, leaning against the vanity with his shirt pulled up on one side and cradling his arm on the other.

"What happened?!" she asked, hurrying over to him.

"It's my shoulder. I fell on it wrong in the store," he said, clearly frustrated by his slight incapacitation.

"Can you lift it at all?"

"No. Hence why I look like this," he said, motioning to his half-disrobed body.

"Do you need to go to the hospital?"

He cocked his head to the side. "They wouldn't take me to the hospital when they broke my nose, so I highly doubt they'd let me go for this. It will be fine, though. I just need to rest it for a couple of days. It's happened before."

"Well, let me help you," she said, putting her hands on the hem of his shirt.

"No, I've got it." He flinched at the brush of her fingertips, and she noticed bruising on his stomach.

"Oh my God, Theo!" she said, lifting his shirt to reveal his abs.

Oh my God was right. It had been several years since she saw Theo with his shirt off, and he certainly wasn't this ripped back then. Even last night in the pool, it had been hard to see his physique under the lapping water and the moonlight.

She blinked several times to focus on the bruising and not on the tautness of his body, running her hand along his skin.

"And how did *this* happen?" she asked. "Do I need to break out of this room so I can go kick Maurice's ass?"

Theo laughed. "Relax, it's from the oil bottle, Juicy. But please, feel free to kick Maurice's ass anytime."

"God, that guy is a real piece of work, isn't he?"

"You have no idea. Try spending a year with him."

"I'd rather not, thanks. Come on, let's get you out of this shirt."

Theo crouched to her level, and she peeled the shirt over his head, careful not to pull at his shoulder.

"Okay, there you go," she said, setting the shirt beside him on the vanity. She then noticed a bit of ink underneath his arm on his side right beneath his armpit. "What's that? Is that . . . is that a tattoo?" she gasped.

He looked down, realizing his ink was visible. "It's nothing."

"Oh, come on. You got a tattoo? Lemme see," she said, lifting his arm. Thankfully, his good arm.

His arm was limp in her hand, and he looked away as she inspected the tattoo.

Πάντα ήσουν εσύ

"When did you get this?" she asked, running her finger along the words. The letters were clean and crisp. It couldn't have been too old.

"Right before I left the States."

"Well, what does it say?"

"It's a Greek saying."

"Okay? And what does it mean?" God, he was being weird, again.

"It's . . . it's personal."

Dani's gaze shot to Theo's. Oh. Personal. In other words, none of her business.

"Sorry, I'm being nosy, aren't I?" she asked, ducking her head and tucking her wet hair behind her ear.

No response. Point taken. She felt like she'd been punched in the gut.

She slowly lowered his arm. "Well," she said, backing away, "need anything else?"

"No, I think I'm good."

"Okey dokey," she said, giving him a salute as she turned around. *Did you seriously salute him?* Dani's entire body recoiled, and she squeezed her eyes tight as she walked toward the door, waiting for him to tease her for it. But no teasing came.

She hated how awkward things were between the two of them. It never used to be like this. Normally, if she did something that cringey, he'd never let her live it down. And she wouldn't want him to because keeping each other in check was one of the things she appreciated about their connection. It didn't mean that they didn't still have their weird personality quirks and annoyances, but she sort of enjoyed his playful ribbings.

This boring-ass shell of their former relationship wouldn't do.

Dani spun back around right as he was untwisting the button on his pants. "Really?" she said.

He jumped and then froze with his hand on the fly of his pants.

"Jeez, Juicy! You startled me."

"Sorry, but are you really not going to say anything? I literally saluted you and nothing. Nada."

"Did you *want* me to comment on it?" He looked beyond confused.

Welcome to the club.

"Come on, Theo. That was Grade A cringe and you're giving me blasé. Give me some sort of emotion!" she said, throwing her hands up in the air.

"Is exhaustion not an emotion?" he asked, hanging his head to the side.

"No, Theo! It's not!"

"Well, can we pretend it is then?" he asked, his weariness palpable. "Because it's been a really long fucking year, and while

I'd love to make fun of you for being a gigantic dork, I also just really want to get this oil off me."

If Dani hadn't already gotten clean, she would have wrapped her arms around him and given him a hug. Being practically alone for a year surely did a number on him. Of course he wouldn't be joking around like the good ole times.

But at least he acknowledged the dorkiness of her salute.

"Thank you," she said.

He wrinkled his nose. "For what?"

"For calling me a dork."

He shook his head and smiled. For now, she'd consider that a win. But his smile was quickly replaced by a glower when he attempted to lift his arm again.

"You know, it was really hard to get all the oil out of my hair. You sure you don't want help?" she asked.

"Help with what?"

"With washing your hair. I don't think you're going to be able to do it with one hand."

Theo's eyes about popped out of the sockets. "You want to help me bathe?"

Did she?

Oh God, what in the holy fucking Pandora's box had she just opened?

Dani's gaze shot to Theo's groin, and then she blinked and straightened her body, quickly looking back at his face.

"Well, no, I think you can handle washing your naughty bits," she said, trying to play it off, "but you look like you might struggle with everything else."

He raised his brows.

"Oh, don't be weird about it," she said, waving her hand like it was nothing, despite feeling her palms starting to sweat. "It's a naked body. We've all seen them."

Sure, maybe if it was someone else's body.

"Yeah, but we haven't seen each other's." He was saying everything her brain was screaming. But as if she had to prove how unbothered she was—whether to Theo or to herself, she wasn't sure—she pressed on.

She shrugged, trying to play it cool. "There's a first for everything."

"Is there?" he asked, raising a single brow. "Because there are plenty of people in the world whose nude bodies neither of us will ever see."

Okay, why was he acting like seeing each other unclothed was the most ludicrous thing in the world? It wasn't *that* big of a deal. She was starting to feel a little offended that he was so put off by the suggestion.

She rolled her eyes and crossed her arms. "Okay, fine. Don't accept my help. But when you're lathering that oily mop of yours for the fifth time and your arm is aching, don't come crying to me about it."

Dani spun on her heel to leave again, pissed at herself for even making the suggestion, when Theo called out, "Wait." A teensy hint of a devilish smile started to form on her lips, but she quickly bit it back.

"Changed your mind?" she asked.

"Only because my shoulder really fucking hurts. No peeking, though," he said, putting his finger up as if giving her a rule.

"I promise I'll try not to."

"You'll *try*?"

"Well, I won't *sneak* a peek, but if I catch a glimpse of a dick in my periphery, I cannot guarantee that my reflexes won't give in to my body's carnal desires."

The words spilled out without hesitation. What had gotten *into* her? She'd never talked like this to Theo before.

But . . . she sort of liked it.

"Why do you say that like there might be dicks popping up left and right?"

"Hey, we're in Greece," she said, shrugging. "Maybe there's some mythical multi-dick creature lurking about."

He placed his free hand over his eyes and laughed. "My God, where do you come up with this stuff?"

"You should see some of the new monster romances that we've been getting at the library. It's some sexy shit," she said, relieved that he seemed to be relaxing a bit.

He shook his head, still smiling. "Okay, Juicy. Turn around for a second, would you?"

"Fiiiiiine," she said, rolling her eyes and smiling.

The sound of his pants hitting the floor was like a dinner bell, calling for her to come get a taste. What was she doing? Why was she tempting herself like this?

Sure, she could say it was because of his shoulder. But was that the only reason? Given how badly she wanted to turn around, she'd say not.

"Okay, I'm getting in," he announced.

The water sloshed as he climbed in.

"I'm in. You can turn around," he said.

She spun back around, and there he was, crouched in the tub with about a third of his torso out of the water. She came up behind him and knelt on the floor, sitting back slightly on her heels. It was the safest spot to avoid sneaking a peek.

"Want me to massage your shoulder?" she asked. "Take advantage of the natural massage oil?"

"Um . . ." he said, hesitating for a moment, "sure. But be gentle, okay?"

"No, Theo, I'm going to torture you," she said, and he snapped his head in her direction. "Relax, will you? You're like a feral child."

"Sorry," he said, dejected. "I've gotten used to being on my own."

"Well, I'm here now. Should I take this off?" she asked, reaching for the clasp on the gold chain around his neck.

"No," he said, holding the necklace in place. "You were right. I can't take it off."

She released the clasp and then placed her hands on his shoulder, lightly applying pressure.

He hissed.

"Is this okay?" she asked.

"Yeah. Maybe a tad lighter, though?"

She loosened her grip. "Better?"

"Mmm . . ."

His body instantly relaxed as she lightly worked on his shoulder, working her way across his back and neck. She'd never touched him like this before. So deliberately. So . . . consciously. Sure, they'd touched many times, though usually only a quick hug when saying hello and goodbye, an arm around the shoulder for a picture, or a playful slap on the knee at trivia night. This? This was *much* different. She was aware of every ripple of muscle as her fingers kneaded his flesh. Each placement of her hands was intentional and unhurried. She liked the way his muscles felt in her grasp. She liked touching him this way.

He propped his good arm up on the side of the tub and rested his head in his hand, allowing her to rub his bad shoulder. He was silent, which prior to this trip would have seemed odd, but it had become normal by this point.

"What are you thinking about?" she asked.

He sighed and brought his hand back into the water. "How we're going to get out of this," he said.

"Well, we'll see what's up at the olive mill tomorrow and then go from there."

"And if it turns out to be a dead end? Then what?"

"Then . . . well . . ."

Hmm.

"Exactly."

"What about that guy? The storyteller. Papa Murphy's? Papa Smurf?"

"Papantonis. I told you, it was a story."

A few more beats of silence passed. She thought about what he'd said the night before, about how he wrote the story for fun.

Sucked that she only heard about it now.

"Why didn't you ever tell me about it? Getting it published, I mean," she asked, moving on from his shoulder and grabbing the shampoo bottle.

Theo paused and she waited for a moment to squirt the liquid into her hand.

"You know how my parents are. I . . . I thought people would think it was silly," he finally said after she'd started lathering his oily hair.

"Theodore Galanis," she said with authority, yanking at his hair to turn his head to face her.

"You know my name's not Theodore—" he said.

"Now, when have I ever made fun of you for any of the other

hundred different nerdy things that you do?" She cut him off before he could finish.

"Does this moment count?"

"I'm not making fun of you. I'm stating facts."

She turned his head so he was facing forward, then she dug her fingers into his hair, working the shampoo into his shiny, dark brown tresses. They sat silently for a few minutes as she worked, taking her time massaging his scalp.

"You should have told me," she finally said, barely above a whisper, trying not to let her hurt show through. "You know I would have been happy for you. It's really fucking cool."

"I know."

"And it's really unfair that you let strangers read your work, but not me. I was your first fan, remember?"

"I know."

"And if I find out that Eddie knew about it before me—"

"He doesn't know—"

"Well, if he did, I'd kick your ass. I'd kick *both* of your asses."

"I know."

"Then, good. As long as we're on the same page—"

With his good arm, Theo reached behind his head and wrapped his hand around her wrist before pulling it around to his front, wrapping her arm tightly against his chest.

"I missed you," he whispered.

Dani closed her eyes, taking him in. Feeling his fingers closed around her wrist. Holding her next to him. This was the Theo she remembered. The one who wasn't afraid to show his emotions.

She leaned forward, wrapping her other arm around his chest and burying her face in his neck.

"I missed you, too."

"We've got to get out of here."

"Why? Getting pruney?"

Theo chuckled. "No, out of Greece. I've never wanted to leave Greece so badly."

He held up his hand in front of their faces, spreading his fingers out wide. They *were* starting to prune. "And maybe I need to rinse my hair so I can get out of the tub, too."

She laughed, then pulled away, letting him sink into the tub and under the water to rinse out the shampoo. But as he dunked his head, his *other* head popped up.

¡Ay, Dios mío!

Dani's jaw dropped, and she couldn't turn her gaze away. Theo was fucking packing! She'd always wondered how big his dick was, but she wondered no more. She remembered his mom always talking about how Theo's name meant *gift of God*, and wasn't *that* the truth. A low pulsating pressure started to build in her core.

He lifted his head and torso back out of the water, stealing her attention from his cock, and rubbed the water out of his eyes.

"How's it look?" he asked.

Dani blinked. Fuck, he caught her peeking.

"Umm . . . it's nice."

He turned his head and furrowed his brow at her. "Nice?"

"I mean, come on," she said, cocking her head to the side. "You know it looks . . . good. Really . . . good."

"Good? Juicy, what the fuck are you talking about? Did I get all the shampoo out or what?"

"Ooooooh!" she said, laughing. "The shampoo." She hit herself on the forehead.

"Yes, the shampoo. What did you *think* I was talking about?"

Oh, crap.

"Umm, nothing." She looked every direction except at him.

"Nothing? Juicy?" he said her name like Desi Arnaz calling out Lucille Ball. "Did you sneak a peek?"

She pulled her mouth into a tight line and ducked her head slightly. "I didn't *sneak* a peek, but, well, I told you if it caught my eye . . ." she said with an innocent shrug.

"You're such a pervert," he said, laughing and flicking water back at her.

"What? Like you wouldn't peek if the tables were turned."

"Don't try to justify your perviness," he joked. "At least own it."

"Oh whatever," she said, dunking him back in the tub and trying to sneak *another* peek, but now there were unfortunately too many suds from the shampoo.

Damn.

He popped out of the water, laughing.

"Still miss me?" she asked.

"Absolutely."

An uncontrollable smile formed on her lips.

"Here, let me wash your hair one more time. It still looks a little oily," she said, lathering up her hands once more.

Theo settled back against the tub, allowing her to run her soapy fingers through his hair. Massaging his head. Curling her fingers around his tresses.

"Mmm . . . that feels nice," he hummed.

It did feel nice. Relaxing even. His humming sent a delightful buzzing straight to her nipples.

"It's been weird being alone for so long without human contact," he said.

"I thought you had plenty of contact with Maurice and Louis."

"Not *that* kind of contact. I mean like this. Being touched, not punched in the face."

She could only imagine what that must have been like. Their families were both such affectionate groups. Every gathering started and ended with absurd amounts of hugging that would probably be overwhelming to other people. But to the Guiterrezes and the Galanises, hugs and kisses were normal. To have that taken away and replaced by aggression couldn't have been easy.

She hated thinking about what he must have gone through over the past year. She wanted nothing more than to take care of him. Hold him in her arms and tell him they would be okay. That they would figure a way out of this. How could he ever have thought that she would have abandoned him? Maybe this is all they would ever be, but she'd never leave him. Never again.

Her gaze focused on her fingers swirling through his hair before she finally snapped out of it.

"Okay, time to rinse," she said, leaning back.

Without another word, he dunked again, but this time she looked away so as not to tempt herself with another glance.

"Good?" he said, popping out and wiping his face.

"Good."

"All right, I'm going to get out if you want to turn around."

"I'll grab you a towel," she said, walking over to the drying rack on the wall.

But when she turned back, there Theo was, rising from the tub with his backside to her. Fuck, even his ass looked good. Water clung to every part of his body. What Dani wouldn't do to lick each droplet off.

"Damn, Theo," she said.

"Oh, sorry," he said, starting to squat back into the tub, "I didn't think you'd turn around."

"No, it's fine. I mean, damn, Theo, you've got a nice ass," she said, handing him the towel and *then* turning around.

He laughed. "Thanks, Juicy. I guess it's only fair that you've seen mine now, too."

"Yeah, but you didn't see *all* of my ass."

"Close enough."

His words set fire to her cheeks.

"Well, I . . . uh . . ." Suddenly she was at a loss for words. Her mind jumped all over the place, picturing his ass, his cock, his hand wrapped around her wrist, pulling her closer. Oh God. This was not the time for horniness.

Their night together before he left flashed in her mind again. A fuzzy memory of the two of them on the couch. His hand grazing her cheek, brushing away a tear. Oh fuck. What had she said? What happened that night? Why couldn't she remember it all?

Suddenly the room started spinning around her. Memories from that evening coming at her in bits and pieces. The words on Theo's side flashed in her mind: Πάντα ήσουν εσύ.

"You okay?" he asked, placing his hand on her shoulder.

When had he gotten out of the tub? She scanned him, standing in the middle of the bathroom with the towel wrapped around his waist, and that fucking water still clinging to his skin.

"Yeah . . . yeah, I'm fine," she said, holding her forehead in her hand. "I think I stood up too fast. I'm gonna go lie down," she said, thumbing toward the bedroom.

"Here, let me help you." He wrapped his hand around her waist, guiding her back to the bedroom.

His impossibly wide fingers spread across her stomach as they shuffled into the other room. They moved silently across the floor, placing her on the bed. Once she was settled in, he backed away.

"I'm gonna go finish getting ready for bed," he said.

"Okay."

He started to walk away when she called out for him. "Hey, Theo," she said.

"Yeah?"

She hesitated for a moment, debating her next words. "You . . . you can sleep in the bed. With your shoulder, I mean. You probably shouldn't sleep on the floor."

"Okay, thanks."

He took another step toward the bathroom when she stopped him again. "And I'm sorry I snuck a peek."

He laughed. "It's okay."

"Be honest, though. If the tables had been turned . . ." She let her words fade away like a question. But she had to know if she was the only one.

"Juicy, I never would have made the promise in the first place."

CHAPTER Nine

Theo

WHAT HAD HE BEEN THINKING? TEASING HER. EGGING HER on. Allowing her to fucking *bathe* him.

All night long, he replayed "bath time" in his head. No matter how hard he tried *not* thinking about it, his mind and body wouldn't let him forget the way her fingers felt, massaging his scalp. Or the fact that she'd seen his cock. *And* ass. It didn't help that his shoulder was pulsating with a throbbing pain that kept him up. Though if he was really being honest with himself, his aching cock was more distracting than his shoulder.

The sun was starting to come up, casting an orange glow in the room. A sliver of light sliced through the curtains, casting a radiant beam along Dani's curves as she lay on her side facing away from him. They'd both seemed to dangle as close to the edge of the mattress as possible, leaving a solid two feet between their bodies. But Theo couldn't chance that they might touch.

They'd done enough of that for the evening.

Πάντα ήσουν εσύ.

He let his mind relive Dani's fingers tracing his tattoo, sending a warm tingle along his obliques. How could he explain the words? *Her* words.

It's always been you.

He watched her lying there and thought back to that night. To the way they'd slept together on the couch, her nestled perfectly into his body, holding her hand to that area on his side, mindlessly running her fingers back and forth on his skin in that exact spot. There had been so many things he'd wanted to do, wanted to say, but he couldn't. Not yet. But they had time. They had forever.

At the time, the tattoo had seemed the perfect way to remember that night. Now that he had the words etched on his body, however, he realized he didn't need a reminder of that night. Like he'd ever forget it, even if she had. Her words cycled through his head constantly. With the way he felt about her, the way he'd *always* felt, it didn't seem possible that she hadn't meant it when she said the words.

Now the tattoo seemed foolish. He couldn't tell her what it meant. Not now.

Not ever.

Dani started to stir, and for an instant, Theo thought about pretending he was asleep, but what was the point? She turned her head to look behind her, noticing that he was already awake, then yawned before turning over fully and tucking her forearms under her head.

"Hi," she said with a smile that would melt any man's heart.

"Hi," he responded almost as if he were in a stupor.

Way to play it cool.

"How's your shoulder?" she asked.

"It's okay. I think so long as we're not playing tackle football, I should be fine."

"So you're gonna live?"

"Yes, I'll live." He smiled. "How did you sleep?"

"Well, I can't say it was as comfortable as Vautour's place, but I suppose I slept all right, all things considered. Could have been worse."

"Oh yeah? How so?"

"You could have snored. It's funny. I always pictured you a snorer."

He made an interested face. "And why is that?"

"Because most men snore. I mean, jeez, have you ever heard Eddie? If anything could drive me to murder . . ." She let her voice trail off.

Theo knew exactly what she was talking about. He couldn't count the number of times he had to throw a pillow at Eddie when they had sleepovers. Yet even still, Theo felt the need to vindicate his best friend.

"Well, you were snoring last night," he fibbed.

Dani shot up from the bed, her face absolutely mortified. "No, I wasn't!"

"Oh yeah, totally sawing logs all night long. I had to put a pillow over my head to drown it out," he teased.

"You're joking," she proclaimed. But when he didn't respond, she followed up, "Please tell me you're joking."

"Sorry, Juicy. Like brother, like sister. I always *thought* there was something about you that reminded me of Eddie," he said, putting his finger to his chin and looking up like he was thinking.

"Shut up!" she said, throwing a pillow at him. Theo laughed, catching the pillow before it hit him in the face. "I *knew* I didn't snore."

Theo took the pillow and brought it behind his back, propping himself up.

"Give me back my pillow," she said.

"Nope, sorry. Snore tax." He fluffed up both pillows, making himself more comfortable.

"I wasn't snoring." She glared at him, trying her best to look serious in this rather unserious conversation.

He shrugged, then nestled into the cushions like he was settling back into bed. With a quick movement, Dani reached over to snatch the pillow back from Theo, but he caught her wrist before she was able to take it. They paused, staring at each other for a solid beat, before Dani scrambled for the pillow, sending arms flailing, bodies thrown about the bed. She tried scowling, but their laughter broke through, turning to giggles when he touched the sides of her stomach.

"Don't," she said, still laughing. "You know I'm ticklish."

Oh, Theo knew, all right. Eddie used to tickle her as a form of torture, which satisfyingly resulted in her kicking him in the face once.

"Oh yeah?" he said, his hands shooting to her waist again.

But Dani wasn't having it. She batted his hands away and placed her own on his bare stomach.

Fuck. Theo was ticklish, too.

He struggled to get out from under the bedspread, but once Dani realized what he was doing, she swung her leg over his waist, straddling him while her hands danced all over his body.

Her touch turned from ticklish to sensual. And now with her looming over him with her beautiful black hair cascading over her shoulders and her breasts freely swaying underneath her loose-fitting tank top—fuck—he could feel himself starting to get hard. This was not what he needed.

Her hand ran over his body, touching his tattoo and sending a zap through him, a jolt that startled her and they both froze. She felt it, too.

"Did that hurt?" she asked.

No, it didn't hurt.

It *burned*.

"It's my shoulder," he said, even though she'd been nowhere near his shoulder.

She raised her head then nodded like she understood.

Understood he was full of shit.

"I suppose we should probably start getting ready," she said. "Who knows when Maurice and Louis are going to come knocking."

Right. Maurice and Louis. For a brief moment, he and Dani were the only people who had existed. He'd forgotten where they were and what they were doing. Finally, he experienced a bit of normalcy, of his life back home. Not that he and Dani had ever been in this position—literally—before, but being around her gave him comfort. And made everything else, everything that was bad, fade away.

But only for a moment.

"Yeah," he simply said.

She shifted her weight to dismount him when her ass grazed his now fully hard cock. There was no way she hadn't felt it. She sucked in a quick breath and her eyes widened just a fraction, then she swung her leg wide, presumably to avoid hitting his dick. The instant her body was off him, he coughed and shifted in the bed, trying his best to hide his hard-on by sliding one foot to prop up his knee.

As if she didn't already know it was there.

He tried not to stare at her ass as she bent over her bag, digging out a set of clothes before heading to the bathroom. The instant the door clicked shut, he grabbed his cock to readjust himself and relieve the pressure, then leaned his head back against the headboard.

It's always been you.

• • • • • • • • •

THE ROAD TO DEMETRIOS'S WAS LONG, WINDING, AND BUMPY AS fuck. Theo tried to put the morning out of his mind, focusing on the task at hand. Their little frolic in the bedroom was nothing but a momentary distraction. If they were going to find the eye, he needed to think more about the Minoans and less about how it felt to have Dani straddling him.

"I heard one of the world's oldest olive trees is somewhere on Crete," Dani said, leaning forward to speak with Maurice. "They think it's like three thousand years old." Must have been something she'd learned on her tour.

"We're not stopping," Maurice said as they careened down the dirt road.

Dani sat back in the seat, almost pouting. It was cute that she still wanted to see the sights. Maybe if they got out of this mess, he could take her on a private tour of Greece.

Theo quickly shook the thought away. Like she'd ever want to come back after this. Not to mention her boyfriend.

They pulled up to a giant old stone building with a large medallion with an eye and the μ on the side, most likely the mill. Rows of olive trees with their twisty trunks scattered the hillside across the property behind the building. To the right a bit farther up the driveway was a house. Theo tried picturing the Minoans in this place thousands of years ago. Who knew. Like Dani said, some of these very trees could have been that old.

All four of them got out of the car and walked over to the

building. “No funny business,” Maurice reminded him. “And no Greek.”

Did they really need the warning each and every time they went anywhere?

“What if they don’t speak English?” Theo asked.

“They’ll figure it out.”

Theo internally rolled his eyes. Sure, many locals spoke English, but he hated the entitlement in Maurice’s voice.

He walked up to a man pushing a wheelbarrow full of olives.

“Excuse me, do you speak English?” Theo asked.

“Yes,” the man responded.

“Is the owner here?” Theo asked.

“We don’t do tours at this facility on weekdays,” the man responded.

“Oh, we’re not tourists. We’re . . .”

What? How to explain to this man without setting off alarm bells?

“We’re food writers and we’re writing a book on olive oil. We heard this is one of the oldest olive oil farms in all of Greece.”

That was believable, right?

“Crete,” the man said.

Theo tipped his head, unsure of what he was getting at.

“Oldest in Crete,” the man clarified.

A noteworthy distinction, apparently.

“Er, yes, that’s what I meant. We were hoping, however, to speak to the owner of this farm for a potential feature in our book. Would they happen to be around?”

The man looked around at their group, eyeing them, curiously. “All of you are food writers?”

Theo looked back at Maurice, Louis, and Dani. They didn’t

exactly look the part. Heck, Louis looked like he hadn't read a book in his entire life. "Uh, we are the writers," he said, waving his thumb between himself and Dani.

"What are you saying over there?" Maurice asked, defensively, something the man certainly noticed.

Theo quickly turned and said, "I've got it," and then turned back to the man. "These two are . . . uh . . . with our publisher."

Was that even something publishers did? Theo felt like he'd seen that in movies, so hopefully it was believable.

The man looked at them once more, then said, "Wait here," before heading toward the main house.

They waited for five minutes before the man returned and escorted them to the house, leading them to a stone patio with arbors covered in grape leaves and vines. They sat at a round table, set with water glasses and a pitcher, then an older woman came from the house a few minutes later carrying a wooden tray with bread and dishes of olive oil.

"Καλημέρα," Theo said, standing and extending his hand.

"Good morning. English?" the woman asked.

"Yes, thank you."

"I'm Lydia. Welcome to my home."

"I'm Theo, and this is my frie—my fiancée, Daniela," he stumbled, forgetting for a moment that Maurice and Louis were sitting with them, "and Maurice and Louis. They're with our publisher."

"You look familiar," Lydia said, squinting as she examined him. "Have we met before?"

"No, I don't think so," Theo said, trying to think how they could have possibly met.

Lydia nodded. "Greek?"

"Yes. Greek American. I'm from—"

"New York," Maurice butted in before Theo could unwittingly give themselves away. "We're all from New York."

Lydia tilted her head toward Maurice, studying him like she thought his interruption was unnecessary. Maurice clearly didn't want to chance that she might put two and two together and figure out he was the Greek American from Chicago who'd gone missing a year ago.

"Yes, New York. We're writing about the origins of Greek olive oil for a book," Theo explained.

"All four of you?" Lydia's brow raised, skeptically.

"Well, no. Just me and Daniela. Maurice and Louis do . . . marketing."

What the hell was he even talking about?

"Hmm, I see."

She didn't seem convinced, not that he could blame her. He wasn't doing a great job of selling it.

"So, you want to taste my oil?" she asked.

"Yes, please," Theo said, happy to move on from the lies.

Lydia explained each of the oils as they dipped in tiny pieces of bread. The sharp flavor of olives hit his tongue, coating his mouth with smooth, thick liquid. While the oil swirled around, he used the time to try to think of a way to broach the topic of the Minotaur.

"Why the μ if the name of the company is called Demetrios?" Dani blurted out, pointing to the μ on the bottle.

They really needed to work on their timing and communication. Lydia examined Dani. *Uh-oh.*

"The μ is for Minos, with the act of turning olives into oil dating back to the Minoan civilization."

"And how far back does your family extend into history?" Dani asked.

"Are you asking if we are descendants of the Minoans?"

"No, not exactly. We're curious about your roots and how your family came into this business. For the book."

"We are native Cretans. Our family tree and this farm date back thousands of years. One day when I'm gone, my grandchildren will take over. And then their children. And their children's children. The art of olive oil will never disappear."

"And what's this for?" Dani then asked, pointing to the eye emblem on the bottle of oil. "Any significance?"

Something flashed in Lydia's eye. Dani had been right. Maybe they were onto something.

"Food writers, you say?" Lydia asked.

Theo and Dani glanced at each other, but as Theo was about to open his mouth, Dani beat him to it, reaching her hand across the table and taking Lydia's.

"We're here about the Minotaur," she said.

"I don't know what you're talking about," Lydia said, scooting back in her chair and starting to rise.

"The watchful eye of your ancestors?" Dani continued. "This?" She pointed to the bottle. "This is for the eye of the Minotaur, isn't it?"

Lydia narrowed her eyes. "You are not food writers."

"No, but you want your ancestors to return, right? Maybe we can help you."

"How?"

"He has a theory about the Minotaur," Dani said, "about Papantonis. He was your ancestor, right? Demetrios Papantonis? Is he who the mill is named after?"

They sat silently at the table, waiting for a response from Lydia.

"It's been a long time since I've heard anyone mention Papantonis," Lydia finally said. "I'd assumed people had all but forgotten about him."

"I wrote a story based on his journal," Theo chimed in.

Lydia's head ticked to the side. "What sort of story?"

"An option. A possibility of what might have happened to the Minotaur and the eye."

"I'd like to read that, sometime."

"Would you like to read it now? I have it with me."

"Yes, I think I would. Come inside," she said, standing from the table.

CHAPTER Ten

Dani

And so, while Theseus believed the beast's body held its strength, I saw its true power: its eye. Without his knowing, I cut the bright, fiery eye from the creature. Once extracted from its body, the eye hardened into the most beautiful red gemstone I had ever seen. I took it to my homeland and buried it. There, hidden beneath the ground, its energy seeped into the soil, bringing numerous riches to the earth and prosperity to my family.

Dani and Theo sat on a small couch, bounded on either side by Maurice and Louis, in Lydia's living room. They all sat silently as she read a printout of Theo's story while seated on a chair in the opposite corner. It was a little uncomfortable, not only because they were sitting in silence while she read the five-page story, but also because the couch was much too small for the four of them. Not with Dani's hips, Theo's tall frame, and her desire to sit as far away from Maurice as possible.

It had nothing to do with Theo's magnetism pulling her in.

There was no way they could sit beside each other without touching, especially with all the frilly pillows and the dip in the center that almost forced the two of them together. And with Theo's good arm draped over the back, it forced Dani to fall into him, resting safely under his armpit, like the cute engaged couple that they were pretending to be. Leaning right into the place where that tattoo was etched into his skin.

The tattoo that she *knew* had a meaning and she had every intention of seeing again so she could write down the letters and then look it up.

But as they sat there, with their sides pressed against each other, she fought to keep her attention anywhere but on Theo's crotch. Every time she glanced in that direction, her mind went back to the prior evening and her "peek."

This. This was exactly why she'd tried to avoid seeking it out. Because she knew that if she saw his dick, it would consume her.

Funny thing was, *she* was the one who wanted to do the consuming.

She quickly shook her head, trying to dismiss the thought. Theo looked down at her and shot her a questioning glance.

She waved him off, signaling that it was nothing.

"So," Lydia said, putting the paper down on a coffee table. "This tells me you are an archaeologist."

Theo straightened up a bit, but that made Dani sink only farther into his side. God, he smelled good. Like sun-kissed olives.

"Yes," he responded.

"Why did you tell my employee that you were food writers?" Lydia asked.

"Because we didn't think you'd talk to us about this otherwise," he said.

She nodded as if thinking to herself that he was right about that. "So what do you want to know?"

"Is it real?" Theo asked. "Papantonis's account?"

Lydia leaned back in her chair. "That, I don't know. I know the stories our family has told. The origins of our farm here. But those truths tend to get lost over time, despite how hard we may try to preserve the stories."

"I understand that completely," Dani chimed in. "I'm a librarian and sometimes people come to me for help searching for their family roots. They are often surprised by what is truth versus fiction. I would imagine that's especially true in a culture that's rooted in mythologies."

Lydia nodded, seemingly appreciative of Dani's comments.

"What are the stories your family has told?" Theo asked Lydia.

"Exactly what you have here. Minos hid the Minotaur in the labyrinth, and after Theseus killed it, he intended to take it to Athens. He believed the Minotaur contained the powers of the gods and wanted to worship it. But Demetrios believed the power of the Minotaur was actually contained in its eye. So he cut the eye from its head and brought it here to bring wealth and prosperity to the lands of his family. Our family adopted the crest of the Minotaur as an ode to Demetrios. But ultimately, the eye did not stay here."

"How do you know that if it's buried?" Theo asked.

"Because he said so in his journal."

Dani shot a glance at Theo, who was furrowing his brow. "Have you seen the journal?"

"Not personally. But it's there. At the Acropolis Museum in Athens."

Theo cocked his head. "Are you sure? I've been to the museum countless times, and I've never seen any mention of Papantonis, and certainly no journal."

"That is because you don't know who to ask," Lydia said, proudly. "My grandson, Andreas, is an archaeologist who works at the museum."

"Dr. Andreas Demetrious?" Theo asked.

Lydia's eyes lit up. "You know him?"

She seemed surprised. Dani was surprised, too.

"I know the name," Theo explained.

"Well, Andreas has been studying the Minotaur for many years, trying to solve this very same mystery of whether the eye existed and if so, what happened to it, on behalf of our family. I could connect you if you'd like."

"You would do that?" Theo asked. "Not to discourage you, but why? We're complete strangers."

"Because, for centuries, people have forgotten this legacy of Demetrios. The mythologies omit the eye, like a concerted attempt to conceal history. I want to know why that is. Perhaps you will see something in the manuscripts that others have missed. That, and . . ."

She let her voice trail off and turned her head, staring out the window.

"And what?" Theo asked.

Lydia remained still and quiet for a few moments before blowing out a breath and facing them again. "And there are people who've discounted Demetrios's connection to my family. That is why I was so suspicious of you when you first started asking questions about our history. So I want to know whether there is any truth to my family's lineage, or whether we are carrying this emblem for no reason, and you're the first people in *my* entire lifetime who have come here searching for the answers. Besides . . . I like you. You remind me of someone from my past," she said, squinting her eyes at him as if trying place the familiarity.

Theo's head ticked to the side, clearly wondering whom she could be referring to. From what Dani knew, his family came from the mainland, not Crete.

But maybe it could explain how Theo's papou came about owning the necklace.

"You could work with Andreas to find the eye," Lydia continued, moving past her prior comment, "or, as you said, learn what was truth and what was fiction. Don't you ever want to know the truth? Don't you ever simply want an answer? To find out who you are?"

Her explanation was clear enough, and after spending the last sixteen years being unsure who she was anymore, it was one Dani could understand wholeheartedly.

"I don't know if—" Theo started, but Dani put her hand on his forearm.

"Then we will do our best to help you find that answer," Dani said. "We would love to be in touch with Andreas."

"Perfect. I will call him right now," she said, getting out of her chair and shuffling into the other room.

The moment she was out of earshot, Theo turned to Dani and said, "We can't work with them."

"We have *four* days, Theo. Sorry, but this seems our best bet at the moment, so unless you have any other ideas . . ." She let her voice trail off.

"But we can't involve these innocent people," Theo said under his breath.

"Why not?"

"Because no more people," Maurice snapped, tearing their attention over to him. Dani was shocked by how easy it was for her to forget other people were around when she was with Theo.

"Maurice is right," Theo said. "Besides, they want to know about their family history. Vautour wants to take it from them. If we find out the eye is real and by some luck manage to get our hands on it, he's not going to let them keep it."

"Precisely," Maurice said.

"You're both getting way too ahead of yourselves, here," Dani said, putting her hands up between them as if trying to calm them down. "We don't need to figure that out yet. For now, we need to find as much information as possible about whether the eye existed and what happened to it. What happens if and when we find it is a problem for solving later. And I'm sorry, but we don't have *any* other leads. Andreas getting us access to that journal is our best bet."

Maurice scratched his chin. "Maybe she's right. We see what Andreas has and then we ditch him."

"No," Theo said, grabbing her by the shoulders and turning her body to face him. "I don't think you understand who we're dealing with here, Juicy. Pierre Vautour is not someone who should be messed with. Some of the things he's done—"

"Then maybe you shouldn't tell me," she said, putting up her hand to stop him. "It's easier being foolish when you don't have all the facts to realize how foolish you're being."

Theo laughed incredulously. She hadn't been trying to be funny.

"Why are you laughing?" she asked, scowling.

"Oh, nothing. No wonder my mom always said you were

reckless. I'm thinking of all the times you went into situations half-cocked, and now it all makes sense."

Reckless? Dani's blood started boiling. Is that what his family really thought of her? That she was *reckless*, going into things willy-nilly?

She opened her mouth to protest, when Lydia reentered the room and settled back into her seat, setting a phone on the table beside her.

"I've spoken with Andreas. Would you be able to meet at the ferry terminal tomorrow?"

Dani glanced at a clock hanging on the wall. It was only ten a.m. They needed to get hustling if they were going to meet Vautour's deadline.

"We're a bit pressed for time," Dani said. "Is there any chance we could meet Andreas today?" She could sense Theo's body silently objecting beside her, but she was sorry—his sit-back-and-pray routine wasn't cutting it anymore.

Lydia chuckled. "The sea is very large, and the ferry very slow. But if you want to fly—"

"No airplanes," Maurice chimed in.

Dani shot her head toward Maurice, and then Dani glanced back at Lydia. Her head was tilted slightly to the side and her eyes squinted, wondering *why* no airplanes. Good question.

But Dani already knew the answer. Airplanes meant airports. Airports meant people. Security. Identification. They couldn't exactly hand over Theo's passport to get on the plane. Maybe no one had recognized Theo after all this time—except Dani—but that wouldn't last if they showed up at the airport.

"He lost his passport," Maurice quickly followed up, motioning toward Louis. He must have sensed Lydia's suspicion.

"We're waiting for a replacement from the embassy. But we have a speedboat back in Heraklion. We can drive ourselves."

"That is not an easy journey, traveling all that way by speedboat," Lydia said. "It's quite far."

"Then we'll take a helicopter," Maurice said.

Now *everyone* was looking at Maurice.

"Do you *have* a helicopter?" Lydia asked with her brow raised.

"We do. I'll need to make some arrangements, but if we get moving now, we should be able to get to Athens this afternoon if you want to give Andreas another call," Maurice said almost like a command. He stood up and took a phone out of his pocket, then stepped outside.

Silence fell over the room, aside from the ticking of the clock.

Lydia's gaze danced around from Theo, to Louis, to Dani, and to Maurice pacing outside on the phone before finally picking up her phone and calling someone. Lydia spoke to whomever she was speaking to in Greek, staring at Theo the whole time. He sat straighter, fidgeting with his hands as he listened. With the way the two of them watched each other intently, it was almost as if Lydia were speaking to Theo rather than whoever was on the other end of the phone call.

"Πρέπει να ανησυχώ;" Lydia asked Theo once she hung up the phone.

"Δεν ξέρω, αλλά είμαι. Συγγνώμη," Theo responded.

"English!" Louis barked. He then immediately followed up, calming his tone, "If you don't mind."

Lydia blinked a few times at Louis, questioning him, then said, "Andreas will meet you this evening. Let me know where and when. But for now," she said, reaching for a piece of paper and pen, "I need to get back to work. You can call here when you finalize your plans." She scribbled some numbers on the paper and then stood up, passing the paper to Theo, which Louis instantly snatched out of his hand the moment Lydia looked away.

They all got up from the couch as she escorted them to the door.

"Thank you for your help," Dani said.

"Thank you for not forgetting the forgotten. Good luck," Lydia said, holding the door open for them. "And Theo," she called out after they'd all exited.

He turned around—they all did.

"Yes?"

"Ξέρω ποιος είσαι."

CHAPTER Eleven

Theo

Ξέρω ποιος είσαι.

Lydia's words echoed through his head as they soared through the sky in a private helicopter on their way to Athens. *I know who you are.*

Theo didn't know whether to be worried or hopeful. What did she know? How *much* did she know? And who was this person he reminded her of?

Should I be worried? she'd asked Theo.

I don't know, but I am. I'm sorry.

It was the most direct contact about his situation he'd had with anyone on the outside in months. He wished they'd had more time. An opportunity to give her more information—and to ask for her help not just in finding the eye.

But then again, how did he know if he could trust her?

And could he trust Andreas?

Theo replayed Lydia's half of their phone conversation in his head:

They want to meet today. I don't know who they are, but they have access to a helicopter. They clearly have connections . . .

The archaeologist . . . you may know him . . . American and Greek . . . he knows you.

The couple . . . it seems something is off. Like they don't trust the other two men. See what they know but keep your eye on them . . . and call me if anything happens.

Fortunately, he'd been able to come up with some bullshit excuse about *good luck and safe travels* when Louis had confronted him after they'd left, wanting to know what Lydia had said to him. Unfortunately, Maurice had been able to arrange for a last-minute helicopter pickup in a remote area of western Crete. Vautour certainly did have connections.

And Theo *hated* helicopters.

The helicopter hit a bit of turbulence and bounced in the air. *Fuck*. He held his breath and clutched the seat belt strapped across his chest. His hatred of flying hadn't stopped him from traveling, but it had been a year since he'd flown, and every dip and bump still freaked him out. The maneuverability of the helicopter wasn't helping things. This was why he preferred overnight flights. He would have *much* rather taken the boat even if it took them all goddamn day.

Dani reached over and loosened his death grip on his harness. She then took his hand and placed it in her lap, threading her fingers through his. Theo stared at their hands interlocking with each other. Slowly, she rubbed her thumb over his, calming his nerves. She'd always been good at doing that.

He leaned his head back and closed his eyes, taking in the

steady rhythm of her stroke. God, Dani had a way with her hands.

The events from the last couple of days flooded his thoughts as everything else faded to the background. The pool. The bath. This morning, Dani straddling him in the bed. Flirting. Touching. Her hands making their way all over his body. The same hands that were holding his right now.

He couldn't wait to be alone with her again. To hold her. To comfort her the way she comforted him. He pictured her lying beside him, her palm skating across his abs and diving beneath the waistband of his pants. Those delicate fingers wrapping their way around his cock, stroking him. He swallowed to keep from salivating.

Theo quickly shook the thought away and his eyes shot open. What the fuck was he doing? They weren't on some holiday. He couldn't be over there, fantasizing about Dani jerking him off while they were literally being transported by their captors in a helicopter.

Not to mention the fact that Dani was with someone else. Everything that had been going on between them the last few days was clearly nothing but his imagination running wild. She wasn't coming on to him. She was simply doing what she'd always done: taking care of him like family.

What the hell was wrong with him?

He untwisted his fingers from hers and took back his hand. But not without catching a confused glance from Dani.

What was there to be confused about, though? They were only *pretending* to be a couple. Was holding hands really necessary?

Finally, they neared the mainland and headed to an area on

the outskirts of town where Andreas would be waiting for them. As the pilot hovered for their landing, Theo fought to not reach for Dani again, this time closing his eyes and holding on to the straps at his shoulders. Once they were safely on the ground, they quickly hopped out of the helicopter, grabbed their bags, and hustled away from the aircraft into the wide-open field.

Dani and Theo waited about a hundred feet from the helicopter as Maurice and Louis finished up with the pilot. The sun was high in the sky, beating its rays down on them. Normally at this time of day—the *hottest* part of the day—Theo would have insisted on waiting out the heat inside somewhere. At least on Crete they had the benefit of the sea breeze. Here, the temperatures had to be pushing close to one hundred degrees.

Theo glanced over at Dani, pulling up her hair and fanning her neck. He watched a bead of sweat run down the side of her face, down her neck, and straight into her cleavage below her V-neck. The white T-shirt almost glowed on her honey-colored skin and perfectly molded around her breasts. He'd always liked when she wore white. Sometimes he imagined what she might look like with one of his white tees or button-downs barely covering her ass.

He stared at her chest, her sweat glistening in the sun. When he lifted his eyes and met hers, she was already watching him. She narrowed her gaze, though he tried to look away quickly. But it was too late. He'd been caught.

Fuck. What was *wrong* with him?

"See something you like?" Dani asked, folding her arms, which had the (un)fortunate effect of propping up her boobs even further. There was a hint of attitude in her voice. Like maybe she wasn't too pleased that he'd been looking.

Fuck, fuck, fuck.

"Sorry, I zoned out thinking about something," he said.

"Such as?" she questioned, tilting her head to the side.

He looked past her and blurted out the first thing he saw. "Church!"

Theo winced internally. Church? She caught him looking at her chest and *that's* what he came up with?

"Church?" she repeated, raising her brow.

"Uh . . . yeah," he said, shifting his weight. "It's been a while since I went."

Now Dani scowled. "Theo, you haven't gone to church since you lived with your parents."

"You don't know that."

It was true. "Mm-hmm. Sure, Theo," she said rolling her eyes.

"What's that supposed to mean? 'Mm-hmm'?" he said, mimicking her.

"You're a terrible liar, that's all." She looked at her fingernails almost as if she was bored. But his shame crept in.

"Okay, fine. Look, sorry I looked at your chest. For like a second. But I told you, you're like a sister—"

"Riiiiiiiiight," she said, cutting him off and glancing away. "Your *sister.* Got it."

His face twisted. He didn't like the way she said that, how *irritated* she seemed.

"It's not like it meant anything. That would be messed up, you know?" he said, trying to smooth things over.

And assuage his guilt.

"Great," she scoffed. "Annnnd you're being weird again."

"Weird, how?" he asked, scrunching his face. A horn honking in the distance caught his attention, and he looked over Dani's shoulder to see where the noise was coming from. "What the . . . ?" He craned his neck, searching for the cause of the ruckus.

"My God! I *can't* with you!" She uncrossed her arms and turned to walk away from him, bringing his focus back to her.

"Sorry, I got distracted," he said, rushing up behind her and putting his hand on her biceps, but she snatched it away.

"Juicy—"

"*Don't* call me that," she snapped.

"This again? Fine, Dani—"

"Don't call me that, either."

Her snarl took him aback. "Then what the hell am I supposed to call you?" he asked, bringing his hands to his sides, palms facing out as if asking, *What gives?*

"Daniela," she said, glaring.

He cocked his head. "I haven't called you that . . . I don't know. Maybe ever?"

"You did yesterday." She shot her gaze to him, her eyes like daggers. "Maybe you should make it a habit from now on."

"Okay, what is going on? What did I do? I thought we were good. Is this about this morning?"

Or last night, he thought.

She laughed to herself, crossed her arms again, and looked away. Clearly she had no intention of telling him what he'd done wrong.

The honking was back, this time more erratically. Where the hell was it coming from? Theo looked over, noticing a small, yellow Jeep-like vehicle careening down the road. Something seemed off, but he couldn't make sense of it from that distance.

"Can we talk about this later?" Theo asked, keeping his eye on the car in the distance. The noise caught Maurice's and Louis's attention as well, and they spun around, putting their hands above their eyebrows to shield themselves from the sun.

"What more is there to talk about?" Dani continued, oblivious to what was happening behind her. "You checked out my boobs for a second. I saw your dick. Now we're even and can go back to our normal brother-sister relationship."

He ticked his head to the side. He wouldn't say his full-frontal nudity was *quite* the same as checking out her fully clothed tits, but it didn't seem like the time to argue about semantics.

"Okay, Juic— I mean, Dani . . . ela—" *Damn, that was going to take some getting used to.* "We might want to—"

He didn't finish his thought, though. Not after the approaching vehicle picked up speed and launched off the road . . .

Heading straight toward them.

CHAPTER Twelve

Dani

ONE SECOND, DANI WAS STARING DOWN THEO AND HIS STUPID handsome face, annoyed at herself for having misinterpreted what was going on between them as something more—again—and the next, he was pulling her by the arm out of the way of a bright-ass yellow Jeep-looking car barreling right toward them.

The knobby tires skidded to a halt, blocking them from Maurice and Louis.

"Theo and Daniela?" a thirtysomething-year-old bald man asked. He wore sunglasses, a gold watch, and a crisp yellow T-shirt with white pants.

"Yes," Theo responded, hesitantly.

"Then hop in! We gotta go!" the man said, reaching across the passenger seat to open the door for them. "Hurry up, Andreas sent me!"

They took one look over the hood at Maurice and Louis running down the hill, screaming profanities at them. Her mind raced, contemplating their choices: take their chances with this mystery man or stay with Maurice and Louis. But when Maurice reached around his back and pulled out a gun, their options became clear.

"Get in!" Theo said, guiding Dani toward the vehicle.

She climbed inside with Theo right behind her shoving their bags on the floor, and they were instantly smooshed.

A two-seater.

"Sorry, it's all I've got," the man said, revving the engine and peeling out as Theo buckled the two of them in with Dani on his lap. But not before Louis caught up to them like a motherfucking Terminator.

While running beside the car, he grabbed the door handle and pulled it open. But Dani kicked her legs straight in his chest, and he let go, falling onto the ground as they took off.

Bang! Bang!

All three of them in the car ducked at the sound of gunfire, and the man swerved, knocking Theo and Dani around like a couple of pinballs.

"Μαλάκα!" the man yelled as he carefully peeked in the rearview mirror to see where he was. He drove like a Formula One racer, speeding down the hill until they made it back to the road. He continued at a solid clip, weaving in and out of traffic before he finally reduced their speed once they were a respectable distance from where they'd left Maurice and Louis.

"Who are you?" Dani asked.

"I'm Andreas's cousin, Christos. Other side of the family, though," he clarified. "His yayá called Andreas because she thought you might be in trouble, so he sent me since trouble is my middle name—that's what my girlfriend tells me, at least."

He winked at them. "Plus, now they know who he is. Better for him not to be here."

Theo's arms were wrapped tightly around Dani's waist, as if he was afraid to let go. She twisted on his lap so she could turn to face him. Theo took a deep breath and then buried his face in her chest. But when he finally looked up at her, all she saw was happiness in his eyes.

God, she couldn't stay mad at him. Not when he was looking at her like that.

"Thank you," Theo said, turning to Christos.

"Where are we going?" she asked.

"To my place outside of town. You'll be safe."

Safe. It almost didn't seem possible after the days they had.

"And what about Andreas? Is he going to be okay?" Theo asked.

"Oh yeah," Christos said, waving his hand as if it were nothing. "He figured they might try to find him, but this way, he can play dumb. And hopefully they won't be able to trace you since you're with me."

Maybe Christos should have brought a more inconspicuous car, Dani thought, though she kept her opinions to herself.

Theo rested his head back for a moment and then immediately shot back up. "A phone? Do you have a phone so we can alert our families and the authorities?"

"Sure," Christos said, pulling his phone out of the side pocket of his pants. But when he tried unlocking it, the screen was black. "Shit . . . the battery is dead. Don't worry, we'll find you another one. For now, just try to get comfortable. Err . . ." he murmured, glancing at the two of them in a single seat, "or at least as much as possible."

"What kind of car is this, anyway?" Dani asked.

"This baby is a Keraboss Super K," Christos said, proudly tapping the dashboard. "First car entirely built in Greece. You know, all the best things were born in Greece. The Olympics. Showers. Gyros. Vending machines . . ."

As he continued listing off various Greek inventions, Dani glanced at Theo and smiled. Yeah, all the best things certainly were born in Greece.

• • • • • • • • •

BY THE TIME THEY GOT TO CHRISTOS'S HOUSE, IT WAS ALREADY THE afternoon, but the adrenaline hadn't worn off. The small home sat high on the hill above the rest of the town. Fortunately, the place was quiet and secluded. Unfortunately, there was no cell or internet service. They would have to wait until they drove back to town to call home. At least the chances of Maurice and Louis finding them were slim to none. But Christos parked around back just in case.

Theo and Dani climbed out of the car and stepped over to the patio and looked out at the city in the distance while Christos covered the car with a tarp.

"Can you believe it?" Dani said, staring straight ahead.

"After spending the last thirteen months no more than twenty feet from Maurice and Louis at all times, no, I can't believe it," he responded. "Did that really happen?" he then asked turning his head to look at Dani. "Are we really free?"

"You're free," someone said from behind them.

Dani and Theo spun around to see who, finding a man around Theo's age emerging from the house.

This man was gorgeous with a capital *G*. A Triple G of a different sort: Gorgeous Greek Guy.

He wore dark gray slacks that strained over his thick thighs paired with a loose light blue shirt with the top three buttons undone, revealing his dark chest hair and clearly fit physique. He was a quintessential Greek Adonis: slightly wavy medium-length hair, golden-brown skin, chiseled jaw (and by the looks of it, chiseled everything else), perfect smile with pearly white teeth, and glistening brown eyes staring straight at Dani.

He was looking at her as if she were the Hera to his Zeus. The Persephone to his Hades.

"I'm Dr. Andreas Demetrious," he said, walking up to them and taking Dani's hand first. "You must be Daniela."

He said her name like it was a song. Not the title, but the verse and the chorus, all wrapped into a single word.

"I . . . I am," she managed to eke out.

"And I'm Theo," Theo said, reaching his hand in front of Dani. She noticed a quick glare from him . . . and something else mixed in his voice.

Was he annoyed that she didn't introduce him?

"It is nice to meet you," Andreas said. "I'm sorry for the theatrics earlier. But my yayá was concerned, so we couldn't afford to be leisurely. Seems her instincts were right, Dr. Galanis."

"You know who I am?" Theo asked.

"You're not part of this field and unaware when a fellow explorer goes missing, especially in your own country. After you left, my yayá called back and said she thought you looked familiar. Possibly the Greek American archaeologist who'd disappeared months ago, so I sent her your picture from an online newspaper article and she confirmed it had been you."

Theo nodded his head, taking it all in, but was speechless.

"So, you're an archaeologist, too, right?" Dani jumped in to give time for Theo to process. "That's what your grandmother said."

"Yes. She's very proud of me and loves to tell anyone who will listen about me," Andreas said, putting his hands in his pockets and flashing her what might have been the sexiest smile she'd ever seen.

Oh, this guy was good. Too good. The exact kind of guy Dani would normally chase back home. And the exact kind who would be in and out of her life in less than a month.

Dani glanced at Theo, who was doing a terrible job at pretending not to be bothered. But you didn't spend hours reading beside someone and not pick up on their mannerisms. Such as the way he firmly pressed his lips together. Or how he suddenly snapped to attention.

"And you work at the Acropolis Museum?" Theo asked.

"Yes. When I'm not out in the field."

"Theo works in a museum, too," Dani offered unsolicited.

"The US National Hellenic Museum, right?" Andreas asked, and Theo nodded. "I've been once. It was cute."

Cute? Oh boy.

Theo chuckled, but there was no humor behind it. "You didn't want to join the family olive oil business?" he asked with a bit of snark.

Andreas snickered. "For now, I'm happy here, but maybe someday when I'm ready to settle down with a wife and children," he said, turning his attention back to Dani.

His eyes homed in on hers, and Dani swallowed hard. "I take it you aren't married then?"

He flashed that killer grin again and bashfully hung his head. But Dani could already tell, this man was *not* timid. "No, I'm not married. Painfully single, as my yayá would say."

She could almost feel Theo's glare burning a hole through Andreas.

"Look, if you know who I am, then you'll know that my family thinks I'm dead," Theo said, quickly changing the subject. "Can you help us get home?"

"They'll be looking for you. I think it's most prudent for you to stay put for now," Andreas said.

"For how long?" Theo said. Dani could hear the panic in his voice. With still no communication with the outside world, it must have felt like getting abducted all over again.

"He wasn't just missing. He's been held hostage for months," Dani said before Andreas could respond.

"By whom?"

"Pierre Vautour," Theo said without any further explanation.

Andreas's eyes widened slightly, though he fought to maintain his composure. Guess being in this business also meant knowing all the bad players, too.

"I need to warn my yayá," he said, holding his phone up in the air for a signal even though it was practically useless. "If Pierre Vautour is behind your disappearance, then it's *definitely* not safe for you out there. We need to be careful. He's probably got spies at the embassy, and most certainly with the police."

That tracked.

"I know for a fact he has people working for him within the police on Crete," Theo explained.

"Then we need a plan to get you out of here before we do anything. No one can know you're here," Andreas said.

"What about our families?" Theo asked. "Please, they need to know I'm alive."

"I have a friend at the embassy. Let me talk to her first," Andreas said.

She could feel Theo tense. "It's one more day," she said. "Besides, Pierre might be anticipating we'll contact them. Maybe it's better if we lie low until we figure out our next steps."

"She's right," Andreas jumped in. "How about this? It's probably safer for me to leave than you, at least until we know the coast is clear, so why don't you clean up while I run back into town and make some calls? Christos will make us dinner, and we can all sleep here this evening. And then in the morning, we will figure out next steps."

"How do we know we can trust you?" Theo asked with accusation dripping from his voice. "How do we know you aren't working for him, too?"

Andreas narrowed his eyes at him and pulled his hands out of his pockets, squaring up to Theo. "The only reason you're here is because my yayá had a sixth sense about you. You've put *my* family in danger, so maybe you shouldn't be the one going off about trust."

Theo started to bristle. *Oh no.* But Dani put her hands up in between them. "Okay, okay, emotions are high. Let's not get carried away," she said.

Theo's nostrils flared as he took a few deep breaths, and then he turned and walked away. Dani and Andreas watched Theo pacing about thirty feet away with his hands on his head, before she turned back to Andreas.

"He's not usually like this," she said.

"You mean, a churlish oaf?" he said, crossing his arms.

Andreas's words stung a bit. *Churlish* and *oaf* were two words she'd never use to describe Theo.

"You don't understand," she tried to explain. "Those men? They beat him. Threatened him. They convinced his whole family that he was dead. And the one time he managed to escape, the police brought him right back to them. I'm sure you can see why he might not be the most trusting."

Andreas's face softened, and he relaxed his arms. "I didn't know. I hope you realize, however, that I'm only trying to help. I promised my yayá I would help you. She said she feels like she knows him."

"I do realize that. There's earnestness in your eyes, especially when you mention your yayá." It reminded her of Theo.

He smiled sweetly, took a step forward, and reached for her hand. *Oh God, what is he doing?* "I can see the sincerity in your eyes as well." Her heart pounded, and he gave her hand a squeeze. "I'll be back shortly. Maybe we can talk more then."

He let go and then walked away. What just happened? The heat kicked up a few more degrees, and she started fanning herself again.

And when she turned around, she found Theo staring right at her.

CHAPTER Thirteen

Theo

BEING FRIENDS WITH DANI OVER THE PAST THIRTY YEARS meant learning to cope with jealousy. Theo had watched men come and go. He'd watched her heart get broken and her break hearts in return. He'd witnessed her flirting, and on more than one occasion, he'd been sitting right next to her when someone came up and asked her out.

But it didn't mean he had to like it.

He needed to shake it off. One more night. He could spend one more night with her and then they'd, hopefully, return to the States and get back to their—separate—lives.

Theo grabbed his and Dani's bags and headed down the hall toward the room Christos pointed out. *Please, please, please let there be a couch in this room.* He couldn't spend another night in a bed next to her, and he wasn't sure his shoulder could take a night on the floor.

Dani opened the room and stepped inside. But when Theo went to follow her in, he was greeted (pleasantly) by her backside.

"What are you—" he started, but quickly stopped once he craned his neck around the open door.

He should have wished for more than a couch. This room wasn't much bigger than a tin of sardines.

Dani squeezed the rest of the way into the room with the door only inches from hitting the bed. "I know rooms in Europe are smaller than in the U.S., but this is . . ."

Her voice trailed off, so he finished her sentence. "Puny."

There wasn't a couch. Just a bed. There wasn't even room for him to sleep on the floor, not if he didn't want to be in the way of the door. And the full-size bed didn't look nearly large enough for the two of them.

They closed the door and both stood, staring at the bed.

"Is it me or do the beds keep getting smaller?" she asked.

He couldn't help but snicker, washing away all the frustration and annoyance from earlier.

"Why are you laughing? This is ridiculous!" she said. "What the hell are we supposed to do with this?" she asked.

"I *think* we're supposed to sleep on it."

"Quit joking around! This can't be it," she said, trying not to laugh and gently shoving him.

"And what do you think the alternative is?"

"Argh!" she groaned and face-planted on the bed . . .

Ker-chunk!

The metal bedframe collapsed and bent toward the center, turning the mattress into the shape of a canoe.

"Oh, come on!" she called out to the ether. "My ass isn't *that* big!"

Theo burst out laughing.

"Stop laughing! This isn't funny."

"I mean . . . it's a *little* funny," he said, standing at the edge of the bed and staring down at her.

"No, it's not! I'm caught in a mattress taco! Mattresses should be tostadas, not tacos!"

"Can I please change your nickname from Juicy to Mattress Taco?" he asked, unable to control his laughter.

"No!" she said, rolling over and pointing at him. "I'm *not* a mattress taco!"

"Wait here. I'm going to ask Christos to borrow his phone so I can get a picture," Theo joked.

"Don't you dare! Now help me," she said, reaching her arm out for him.

He leaned over the bed and lent her his arm to pull her out. But with the shape of the bed and the dip in the center, he lost his balance and tumbled into the fold with her. They both burst into laughter as limbs flew everywhere. Body parts pressed against each other. He couldn't be sure, but he thought he'd felt her breasts. Or maybe it was her ass.

But she'd *definitely* just placed her hand high on his thigh, a little too close to his groin. Dangerously close.

"There is no way we can sleep on this," he said.

"That's what I've been saying all along!"

They struggled, wriggling around to get their balance, but it was no use. The bed was fucked. The door suddenly flew open, however, and immediately cut off their laughter.

"What happened?" Christos said with mild exasperation, putting his hands on his head.

"I sat down, and it literally collapsed," Dani tried to explain, propping herself up on top of Theo.

"We can pay for it," Theo said.

"I'm not worried about that," Christos said, waving Theo off. "Come on, I've got another room."

Theo scooted toward the edge of the bed, trying not to put weight on his bad shoulder. Once he was almost out, he reached over to her. "Here," he said, offering his hand and then pulling her the rest of the way.

Theo grabbed their bags again, then they shuffled back down the hall toward another door. Christos stood with his hand on the knob, clearly hesitating.

"I'm sorry, but this is all I've got left," he said, opening the door to a larger room—but with an even *smaller* bed covered in a frilly pink bedspread. They stepped inside and looked around. "It's my girlfriend's daughter's room," Christos explained. "There's another little room with a desk over there." He pointed to another door on the wall opposite the bed.

"It's great, really," Dani said. "Thank you, we appreciate it."

"Well, take your time. My girlfriend will be over for dinner, but it won't be ready for a while still," Christos said. "Bathroom's down the hall. I'll leave you to it."

Once he left and the door clicked shut, Theo and Dani took one look at each other and both burst out laughing.

"Okay, this was *not* what I'd expect from a man who drives a Keraboss Super K," Dani said. "I pictured more discotheque and hanging with the guys from that ride."

No, definitely not. Seemed underneath the flashy car and personality was a softie.

They each turned toward their bags, searching for something to change into, and Dani took a quick shower. Once she returned in a robe she must have found in the bathroom, it was Theo's turn. Without needing to ask, Dani helped him take off his shirt. No words were spoken, but he noticed her inspecting his tattoo once more.

Πάντα ήσουν εσύ.

He sped off to the bathroom before she could ask what it meant again. Fortunately, taking a shower was easier than the bath. By the time he emerged and threw on a pair of fresh navy chinos and a white-and-navy-checkered button-down (much easier than pulling something over his head), Dani was already dressed in the room, wearing a pink and orange wrap dress that hugged in all the right places and opened at a slit on her thigh.

Theo couldn't take his eyes off her. And chances were, other men—like Andreas—wouldn't be able to take their eyes off her, either.

"Do you like it?" she asked after noticing him looking. "I got it from that cute little boutique in downtown Grand Rapids a few months ago." She did a half twirl that revealed way more thigh than should have been legal. Not with the type of scandalous thoughts running through Theo's head.

"Are you sure you won't be cold?" was all Theo could say in response.

Dani frowned. "Theo, it was a million degrees today."

"Yeah, but the evenings get cooler."

"Then I'll ask Andreas or Christos to borrow a jacket," she said, shrugging.

"Do you think that's a good idea?" he asked.

"What on earth are you talking about?" she asked, furrowing her brow.

Okay, now Theo was getting annoyed. It was one thing for her to flirt with the guy. It was another thing to pretend like she wasn't.

"I'm only saying . . . I think maybe you and Andreas were a little too . . . friendly, earlier."

"Friendly?"

Theo rolled his eyes. "Don't be coy, Daniela."

"Oh my God," Dani guffawed. "If you haven't noticed, Theo, Maurice and Louis aren't here anymore. We don't have to keep pretending."

"We told his yayá we were engaged, and there the two of you were, flirting right in front of me. How can we trust someone like that?"

"*I* wasn't flirting. *He* was. And trusting him is easy seeing as we don't have any other choice right now."

Her nonchalance turned his stomach.

"Fine. Look but don't touch," he said.

Where the hell did that come from? The minute the words were out of his mouth, he wished he could suck them back in.

"Look but don't touch?" she repeated with disbelief, craning her neck to glare. "For fuck's sake, you're really taking this big-brother thing a little too far, don't you think?"

"I'm trying to protect you," he growled, standing less than two feet from her.

"Protect me?" She spun around and brought her finger up to his face. "If it wasn't for you, I wouldn't even be in this mess!"

"And if it wasn't for *you*, I wouldn't be, either!" he said, taking a step forward.

Shit.

He hadn't meant to say that.

She cocked her head back, clearly having whiplash from what he'd said.

"What's that supposed to mean?" she asked, her eyes narrowing at him.

He couldn't tell her the truth. That after he'd heard about her *beau* from her dad, he went to the karaoke joint to confirm for himself. That seeing her singing on the stage while staring lovingly at her new man didn't just make him jealous—it crushed him. That the only thing he thought to do about it was to get as far away from her as possible.

So he could forget. So he could finally move on. Maybe he'd even come to Greece and find himself a Good Greek Girl who didn't highlight all the things he liked about Dani.

Because he couldn't watch her with someone else. He couldn't forgive himself for waiting too long to tell her how he felt. Distance was the only answer.

No, he couldn't tell her any of that.

"I mean that if you hadn't been snooping around Knossos, Vautour never would have even known you existed," he said, instead. "And if you hadn't gotten caught, I wouldn't have had to pretend you're my fiancée to keep you safe."

"Oh, so this is my fault?" she asked, now turning her finger inward. "Need I remind you, Theo, that you were the one who came looking for *me* at the museum, not the other way around," she said, pressing her finger into her chest, giving him yet another reason to look at her breasts.

Gutterbrain. Snap out of it.

"Bullshit, Juicy," he said, not giving a shit about calling her Daniela anymore. "You mean to tell me that you saw me at Knossos and weren't going to do anything about it? You never let anything go. You know you would have gone looking for me. Admit it."

"I . . . I . . ."

For once, she was speechless.

It shouldn't have been as satisfying as it was. He smiled. He'd finally gotten to her.

But given the scowl starting to form on her face, it didn't seem like she liked it very much.

"Of course I was going to look for you! I thought you were dead! But the only reason I wanted to find you was so I could tell you off, you pendejo! Did you really expect me to see you at Knossos and be like, 'Oh, there he is. Alive and well. Mystery solved. Time to move on,'" she said, brushing her hands in a *done* motion, "you selfish asshole?!"

Her voice started to quiver. *Shit.* Things were going off the rails now.

"Dani, I'm sor—" he said, bringing his hand up to comfort her, but she backed away.

"I swear, being around you . . . if I'm going to be stuck with a brother, I'd rather be with Eddie. At least Eddie knows better than to meddle in my dating life," she said before retreating from the room.

If she only knew.

. . . .

ONCE THEO TOOK A FEW DEEP BREATHS, HE FINALLY LEFT THE ROOM to join the others in the living room. There were about half a dozen other people who'd come over. Theo's hackles went up until Christos explained that they were trustworthy—other cousins and his girlfriend Phoebe's friends from work. Theo searched the room for Dani. There she was with Phoebe in the kitchen helping pour drinks. She was laughing and having fun.

It reminded him of being at one of their families' gatherings.

So often during those parties, his mother would humblebrag about her cooking, while her mother would overtly boast. Theo and Dani would always find each other from across the room and roll their eyes at their mothers' ridiculousness. He loved how Dani always seemed to be thinking of him at the exact same time that he was thinking about her. It was like their little secret when their gazes would connect. Sometimes it felt like there was no one else in the room as they spoke only through their eyes. God, he missed those parties.

Now, when she caught him looking over and glared back, the only thing her eyes said was *Fuck. Off.*

Theo walked over to the patio doors, staring out at the spectacular view of Athens with the Acropolis far in the distance. The sight of it towering above the city always gave him a rush of adrenaline, picturing the gods looking down on the ancient Greeks, delivering their commands and wielding their powers over the lands. He was lost in a daydream when he felt a hand on his shoulder. He turned to find Andreas.

"I'd like to show you something," he said, motioning for Theo to join him as he walked down the hall, away from the buzz of the party.

Theo glanced over his shoulder, checking on Dani one more time, and then he followed Andreas.

They entered a room, an office with various paintings and pictures depicting Greek life hanging on the wall. And on a desk in the center of the room was a box full of books, maps, and drawings.

"What's this?" Theo asked, looking into the box.

"I brought this from home—my life's work on the eye of the Minotaur."

Theo shot a curious glance at him.

"I think we got off on the wrong foot earlier. Maybe showing you this will show that you can trust me. I have absolutely nothing to gain by helping you."

Fuck. Now Theo felt like an asshole.

"Look, I'm sorry about earlier—" he started, but Andreas put his hand up to stop him.

"You don't have to explain. Daniela helped me to understand," Andreas said with a dreaminess to his eyes.

Hearing her name on his tongue sent a swirl of jealousy and protectiveness roiling through his stomach.

"We're engaged!" Theo blurted out.

Why? Why did he just do that?

Andreas looked taken aback, startling at Theo's words. "Oh, I didn't realize."

"Yeah, we've known each other almost our whole lives," Theo continued. "She's my best friend's sister."

Andreas chuckled. "I assume he had thoughts on the two of you dating."

Oh, Eddie would have more than just thoughts, all right.

But Theo only muttered in agreement.

"Anyway," Theo said, "I just didn't want you to get the wrong idea, is all."

"Of course. I'm sorry if I came across too strongly earlier. Natural habit when there's a pretty woman around, you know, being painfully single and all at this age," he joked, putting his hands up to show no offense.

"Your yayá is like my mom. Always hounding me to settled down with a Good Greek Girl," Theo said with a slight chuckle.

"Yet Daniela is not Greek."

He always wondered what would happen if he told his

mother that he wanted to date Dani. It was a toss-up as to whom he'd need to tell first: Eddie or his mom.

"No, she's not. But if you want to come to America, I'm sure my mom would happily set you up with one of her friends' daughters."

Theo and Andreas laughed, clearly sharing similar experiences even though they lived thousands of miles apart.

"So what all is in here?" Theo said, taking a large book out of the box. Theo flipped a few pages, stopping on a picture of a clay vessel, one he hadn't seen before. Painted on the surface was a man holding up the head of the Minotaur outside a cave. He wore a tunic with a medallion hanging from his neck: the eye with a μ. "Do you know what this is supposed to be a painting of?" Theo asked, pointing at the page in the book.

Andreas craned his neck to see what Theo was looking at. "Ah," he said, relaxing back in place. "Τα Παιδιά του Μινώταυρου."

Theo furrowed his brow. "The Minotaur's Children? What is that?"

Andreas reached into the box and pulled out a leather-bound notebook with various papers and clippings sticking out of it. He thumbed through it before stopping on a page and handing it over to Theo.

It was a sketch of the same symbol that was on the medallion and the same symbol on their family's olive oil bottles and Theo's pendant. He stared at it for a few moments, trying to make sense of what he was looking at, debating whether to show Andreas the medallion around his neck.

"It's a secret society," Andreas said. "A cult that worships the Minotaur. Allegedly, they know the whereabouts of the eye. According to my yayá, they're the ones responsible for the erasure of our family's history."

Theo listened on as he flipped through the book, discovering Andreas's handwritten theories, maps, and drawings about the Minotaur and the eye.

"You can take that with you, if you'd like, so you can read through my notes this evening," Andreas said.

"Are you sure?" Theo asked.

Andreas simply nodded.

"I honestly didn't think people were out there looking for it," Theo said, tucking the book under his arm and then walking around the room, inspecting the various paintings and books lining the shelves. "I always thought it was just a story my papou told me."

"Oh, there will always be people looking for it. Like Atlantis and El Dorado. Explorers will search until they have confirmation. Like that lost Moon City in the Amazon."

"And if there is no confirmation? If those places, those artifacts don't exist?" Theo asked. He was beginning to sound like his parents.

Andreas laughed. "But that's not why we become archaeologists, is it? Because we think the unbelievable might not exist? It's more fun to believe, to wonder, don't you think?"

Of course it was. Hence why Theo took up writing so he could make up his own stories.

"Do you believe in the Minotaur?" Andreas asked.

Believing in the Minotaur went against everything his parents wanted for him. They favored facts, structure, and proven methodologies. While they supported his career, they preferred the stability and prestige that came from working in the museum rather than toiling in the dirt and sun. They also often struggled with his love of mythologies and fantasies. Things they thought of as nothing more than entertainment.

"I didn't before, but now I'm starting to," Theo said.

"You said your papou told you about the eye? How does he know about it?" Andreas asked.

"I'm not sure, exactly," Theo said, recalling one of the many discussions he'd had about it with his grandpa. "He said a friend told him about it when he was visiting Crete as a young man. But he passed away years ago."

"Where was he from?"

"A small fishing village. Perdika."

Andreas stared at him like he'd seen a ghost.

"What? Why are you looking at me like that?" Theo asked, glancing around the room. Had he missed something?

"My yayá . . . she always talks about her first true love from Perdika. I always thought it was just something she said to irritate *my* papou whenever he made her angry. But maybe . . ."

Andreas let his voice trail off as Theo thought back to what Lydia had said to him. How she'd thought he'd looked familiar.

Something about Andreas seemed familiar, too.

"What? Now why are *you* looking at *me* like that?" Andreas asked.

"Lydia. She said I reminded her of someone. And my papou . . . this was his," Theo said, reaching under his collar and pulling out the medallion. Andreas looked at the symbol etched on the pendant and then back at Theo.

"What was your grandfather's name?"

"Zeno."

Now Andreas eyes went wide. "My father, my yayá's firstborn . . . his name is Zeno."

They paused. Did this mean . . . ?

"Wait," Andreas said, walking across the room and pulling

Theo from his thoughts. He scanned the pictures hanging on the wall before settling on one of a large group and then taking it down. He brought the photo over to Theo and pointed at a man. "This is from our latest family reunion. And here's my dad."

Theo gazed into the photo—it was like seeing his papou's ghost. He then looked up and Theo and Andreas stared at each other, both clearly coming to the same conclusion: his papou was Lydia's first love.

And they might be cousins.

That must have been how his papou had come across the medallion. And it explained why their family always celebrated with raki—a Cretan drink—despite his papou growing up on the mainland.

"Do you think . . . do you think maybe your papou wanted you to find us?" Andreas asked. "Maybe that's why he told you the story of the eye and why you have that necklace?"

Every conversation Theo had ever had with his papou whirled through his brain. He racked his mind, trying to remember bits and pieces of his grandfather's life. Where he was from. When he'd visited Crete. Whether he'd ever mentioned anyone named Lydia or another lover before his grandma.

"What if we were to find it together?" Andreas continued.

The book with the photo of the clay pot caught his eye again. What if . . . ?

No, they needed to leave.

"What about your friend at the embassy?" Theo said. "We're supposed to go home."

"I told her that I had American friends in trouble, but I did not say who you were. She said when you are ready, I'm to call and she will arrange an escort to the embassy. The minute your name is out there, however, there is no going back."

Theo didn't need Andreas to spell it out for him. Anyone knowing his whereabouts could put him—and Dani—back in danger.

But leaving would mean putting any further exploration of his ancestry on hold.

"And what if I'm not ready to go?" Theo asked.

Andreas smiled. "Then, ξάδερφε, tomorrow I can show you Demetrios's journal in the museum archives."

Cousin. He liked the sound of that.

"Think about it," Andreas said, placing his hand on Theo's shoulder. "And take your time with this." He tapped the top of the box, and then left Theo in the room.

He took another look at the photo of the clay pot with the man holding the Minotaur's head.

The vessel called to him, though he didn't know why. And without another thought, Theo ripped out the page from the book, folded the paper, and tucked it in his pocket.

CHAPTER Fourteen

Dani

DANI STOOD OUT ON THE PATIO OVERLOOKING THE CITY WITH the Acropolis lit up in the distance. They sure didn't have places like this in Grand Rapids.

She took a deep breath and closed her eyes as she let it out. She'd hated how she left things with Theo earlier. One second, they were laughing and horsing around like old times. The next, she was reminded of the cold hard truth of their predicament.

And now she had to pretend everything about their situation was normal. Laughing. Drinking. Socializing with people who had no clue that she and Theo were still in deep, deep caca.

She sighed and then shuddered. Theo was right, not that she'd ever give him the satisfaction of knowing that—it had gotten a little chilly. But she wouldn't ask for a jacket like she'd proclaimed she'd do earlier. Now that Theo had called her out for flirting with Andreas, well, she felt guilty.

Even though she wasn't even the one who'd been flirting.

"It's beautiful, isn't it?" Theo said, sidling up next to her at the railing.

His presence startled her, and she jumped. How did she not hear him open the patio door?

"It's incredible," she said, pushing the other thoughts out of her head. "Now I *really* see why you come here so often."

Theo smiled, and he had a look in his eye that she couldn't place. He seemed . . . relieved. Happy, even. A glimpse of the Theo she rolled around in bed with this morning. Which only made her feel worse about their argument over Andreas.

"Theo, about earlier—"

"We don't need to talk about that now," he said, holding his hand up to stop her. "Or ever. I was a jerk."

"But I was a brat."

"Yeah, what's new?" he said, grinning.

She brought up her fist to punch him, but he shielded his shoulder and turned away. "I'm injured, remember?"

Oh, she remembered. Her cheeks flushed, picturing him in the bathtub again. But the heat was instantly overtaken by a cool breeze, and she shivered.

"Cold?" he asked her.

"Are you going to say 'I told you so' if I say yes?" she said.

His mouth twisted, clearly in an attempt *not* to tease her for her outfit choice, and then he pulled her into his chest and wrapped his arms around her body. She immediately warmed up, in more ways than one.

"What's gotten into you?" she asked, playfully.

"Andreas. I think he . . . I think we might be related."

Dani furrowed her brow and brought back her head so she could look up at Theo. "How?"

"Remember Lydia saying I reminded her of someone?"

She nodded.

"Well, it turns out she once had a lover from Perdika, where my papou was from. And Andreas's father's name is Zeno."

Her eyes widened as she thought back to Papou Zeno. "So what does that mean?" she asked. "That your papou had an affair with Lydia?"

Theo shrugged. "I don't know. Or he knew Lydia before he met my yayá. It's not like I can ask him. But, it's quite a coincidence, don't you think? And how else would he know about the eye?"

She let that ruminate for a moment, but when she opened her mouth to ask more questions, Theo spoke first. "Juicy, there's something else I want to talk to you about—"

But there wasn't time for that. Phoebe popped open the door, calling out that it was time to eat, and waited for them to enter. Whatever it was that Theo wanted to talk about would have to wait.

They went back into the house and took two places around the long table. As everyone was settling into their seats, Theo leaned in and whispered in Dani's ear, "We'll talk later."

Christos and Phoebe brought out the food—moussaka, salad, lemon potatoes, tzatziki, and gigades—bringing the brightly colored dishes out family style onto the table.

The food got passed around the table, and she initially took small portions. But once they started eating, the food reminded her of home. Or rather, the Galanises' home. God, she'd missed this. This was what she had wanted out of this trip.

Good food. Laughter. Adventure. Life.

Theo.

He'd relaxed since the morning. The news about Andreas

really seemed to loosen him up. For most of the evening, she almost forgot they were still on the run.

After they'd eaten, they sat around the table as Andreas and Theo swapped stories about growing up in Greece versus the United States. It was funny how she'd always thought of Theo as *so* Greek, yet Andreas and Christos teased him for being *so* American. But despite the tension between Andreas and Theo earlier, they joked and ribbed each other like they were old buddies. It reminded her of his relationship with Eddie.

"What about you, Daniela?" Phoebe asked. "What is your family like?"

"Oh, also loud," Dani joked, causing everyone to laugh. "Though not as loud as Theo's family."

"Yeah, but Juicy makes up for it by being the loudest out of all of us," Theo said, earning an elbow to the ribs from Dani.

"Ow, I'm bruised, *remember*?" he said yet again, grabbing his stomach with one hand while the other rested on the back of Dani's chair.

"You're such a baby. How long are you going to milk that one?" she teased.

Christos reentered the room carrying a plate with cake. "Who wants dessert?" he asked, setting the platter on the table.

"What is it?" Theo asked, eyeing it from a few seats down.

"Milopita," Christos responded.

Theo waved his hands. "None for me. I'm allergic to apples."

"Daniela?" Christos asked. "It's an apple cake."

She held her hands over her stomach. "Oh no, thank you. I'm stuffed."

Christos began slicing the cake and passing plates around the table, when Phoebe turned her attention back to Dani.

"Juicy? What's Juicy?" Phoebe asked.

"Oh, it's just a silly nickname he gave me when we were teenagers," Dani responded, wiping her mouth and placing her napkin in her lap.

"But what does it mean?" Christos said.

Dani and Theo looked at each other, and he smiled. Dani covered her face. "Oh God, no. It's so embarrassing."

"Come on! Tell us the story," Andreas said.

"I can't," she said, shaking her head.

"Fine, I'll tell them," Theo said, and Dani reached over, putting her hands over his mouth and laughing as she tried to keep him from telling the tale.

"If you don't tell us now, we'll keep plying you with ouzo so you'll eventually spill later," Christos said.

"Thankfully, I'm not drinking ouzo," Dani said.

"No, but *he* is," Phoebe said.

Theo lifted his glass and took another shot of the clear liquid.

"Traitor," Dani joked.

"Come on, Juicy. Just tell them."

He smiled at her with that smile that would make her do almost anything he asked, despite him being so irritating earlier.

"Gah!" she yelled, throwing her arms in the arm. "Fine. But I will need a shot first."

Phoebe leaned across the table and poured Dani a shot of ouzo. Taking a deep breath, Dani quickly tossed back the drink and shook her hands out to the side. Yuck, she hated the taste of licorice.

"Okay," she said, placing her palms on the table, "so, we had this neighbor growing up. Ma Barker. She was a mean old witch. Always yelling at us if we so much as set a toe on her lawn."

"Whose neighbor was she?" Phoebe asked. "Yours or Theo's?"

"Mine," Dani said.

"And where did you live?" Christos asked Theo.

"I lived a few blocks away," Theo responded.

"Though he might as well have lived with us he was over at my house so often," Dani said, teasingly.

"Oh, whatever. You liked it," Theo said back.

Yeah. She did. Even if she'd never admit it.

Dani playfully sneered at him, then continued her story. "Anyway, Theo and my brother, Eddie, were on the softball team together when we were all in high school. And one day, they were out in our backyard playing catch and one of these idiots threw the ball into an open window at Ma Barker's."

"Accidentally," Theo added.

"Hey, am I telling the story, or are you?" Dani said.

"Sorry," he said, smiling and putting up his hands like he was about to be arrested. "Go ahead."

"Like I said, they threw the ball through the window and wanted to get it back before Ma Barker got home. That's when I caught them trying to climb inside and they got the brilliant idea to have *me* go instead, since I was the smallest. So they hoisted me up to the window, and I barely made it inside because the window was stuck halfway open. I got in the house, grabbed the ball, but when I was heading out, Ma Barker had come home. I was hurrying to get back out, and my shorts got caught on the window."

Everyone was watching her with an intensity she hadn't experienced since back in her high school days. No one was ever this enraptured by her stories anymore, probably because she rarely *had* stories like this nowadays.

She liked it.

"Theo and Eddie pulled and pulled at my arms, but eventually, I had to ditch my shorts. And . . . God, I can't believe I'm telling this story," she said, covering her eyes with her hand and shaking her head. "And the underwear I was wearing said 'Juicy' across the ass."

"Like Juicy Couture?" Phoebe asked.

"Yes, exactly like that. Hot-pink bikini panties with giant white letters spelling 'Juicy.'"

"And it stuck?" Christos asked.

"Yep, just like her shorts in the window," Theo added, taking a bite of the potato still on his plate.

The entire group erupted in laughter, and Dani good-naturedly scowled at Theo. He tossed her a roguish wink, smiling as if he was proud of himself for the nickname.

I hate you, she mouthed at him.

"No, you don't," he said aloud back, smirking.

She rolled her eyes, unable to contain her smile.

"So do you have a nickname for him?" Phoebe asked.

"Of course she does. It's God's Gift, right, babe?" Theo teased.

"Ugh," she said, nudging him in the side, "you're unbearable." Though her laugh said otherwise.

"Babe?" Phoebe asked, tossing them a suggestive look and waggling her finger between them. "Are you two an item?"

"They're engaged," Andreas said very matter-of-factly, casually glancing at Dani and then returning his gaze to his food.

Dani tensed. *What the . . . ?*

She checked out Theo from the corner of her eye. So *that* explains it, the lightness in his mood. Dani opened her mouth, "Actually, we're not—"

But Theo cut her off. "We're not sure when we're going to get married, but hopefully soon."

Theo wrapped his arm around her shoulders. If she didn't know any better, it would have seemed like a possessive move. Little did the rest of them know Theo was just cockblocking her with more of his big-brother protective bullshit.

"I thought you said she was flirting with *you* earlier, ξάδερφε?" Christos said to Andreas, teasingly.

Dani could feel heat rising throughout her body.

"You're no cousin of mine," Andreas said, tossing his napkin across the table at Christos's face. "I'm sorry. I already explained to your fiancé, I meant no offense," he then said to Dani.

"No offense taken," Theo said to Andreas and then turned toward Christos, "but I guarantee we're very much in love."

Dani's cheeks flushed at the words: *in love.*

"Prove it," Christos said.

Theo scoffed. "This is absurd. How are we supposed to prove it?"

"Kiss her."

Dani tensed, trying not to let her panic show on her face. *Oh God. Oh God.*

"We're not kissing in front of all of you," Theo said. Dani couldn't tell if the disgusted look he was making was in response to the demand to prove it or the thought of kissing her.

"Maybe that's enough, Christos," Andreas said.

"Why? It's a kiss. If they're so in love, it shouldn't be a big deal," Christos said.

Dani's gaze shot around the table, taking in everyone's expressions. Confusion. Fascination. Interest.

"Φίλησέ την! Φίλησέ την!" the rest of the group started chanting, joyfully pounding their fists on the table.

It was obvious they wanted to see a kiss. So she turned to Theo and said, "Let's just do it," unsure why she was even going along with it.

"Okay, fine," he said, leaning over and planting a quick, chaste kiss on Dani's lips. "There."

There? Theo's papou kissed better than that. Was this seriously the kiss she'd fantasized about for the last almost two decades? Because talk about a letdown.

"Boooooooo!"

"You call that a kiss?"

I couldn't agree more.

"That's how I kiss my sister!"

That tracks.

"Φίλησέ την! Φίλησέ την!"

Their calls came from all directions.

"All right!" Theo said with a mix of annoyance and amusement.

Theo turned to Dani and placed his hand upon her cheek before pulling her in. Her heart pounded as he scanned her face. Questioning her. Surely wondering what was going on in her head. She closed her eyes, allowing him to bring her face to his. Their lips touched, hesitantly at first, caressing each other with slow, tentative movements. His lips were softer and fuller than she'd imagined, a sharp—and delightful—contrast to the roughness of his beard. His thumb grazed her jaw as he opened his mouth to her, waiting for her to invite him in. And once she did, his tongue glided into her mouth, tangling with her own and sending lightning-like pulses throughout her body.

¡A la verga! She was kissing Theo Galanis.

Suddenly, they were unable to get enough of each other. She sucked in a breath before their lips turned eager. His hand moved from her cheek to the back of her head, holding her to him. Taking her in. She reached her hand to his shirt, twisting it in her fist. She needed him closer.

He tasted of ouzo and lemon, delightful on her taste buds despite her earlier objection to the anise flavor. But on Theo's tongue? She savored it. She wanted *more* of it.

Of him.

This kiss was everything she'd always wanted. The rest of the world faded away. There were only Dani and Theo. Like so many times before, the two of them together even though everyone else carried on in their lives. Always finding their way back to each other, even when every other part of their lives continued to pull them apart.

Always Theo.

It's always been you.

The words came out of nowhere, barreling through her brain like a runaway train. She squeezed her eyes tighter, and a hazy image of him in her apartment last year came into view.

Theo, it's always been you. It's only ever been you.

Dani pulled Theo in deeper, trying desperately to remember more of that night. Her hungry lips needed more, so she took his face in her hands. The harder she pressed, the faster the memories flooded her mind.

The micheladas and fries. Karaoke. Going back to her apartment. Talking on the couch until God knows when. Their knees touching. Fingers twirling together in each other's hands.

Everything finally hit her like a tidal wave.

Have you ever thought about . . . us? she'd asked.

Sure, I have.

Then why haven't you ever tried to kiss me?

I . . . I didn't realize that you wanted me to.

Of course I have. Theo, it's always been you. It's only ever been you.

Suddenly, what had happened that night became crystal clear. She'd placed her hand on the side of his face and scooted closer to him, bringing her face up to his. Their foreheads had touched, the tips of their noses brushing. But when Dani had opened her mouth and leaned in, Theo had stopped her.

Dani . . . I . . . I can't.

Christos's house suddenly snapped into focus, and Dani flung her eyelids open. Somehow during their kiss, she'd crawled practically into Theo's lap. His hands were around her waist, her knee across his thigh. Like she was about to jump him right in front of all these people.

She pulled her lips from Theo's, and he opened his eyes, looking up at her with his beautiful blue irises. Eyes she'd stared into so many times before, but in this moment, there was something else there. Worry? Regret? Apology?

Pity?

She'd seen him make the same face that night. After she told him how she'd felt, and he'd rejected her. Something else had happened that night, though. Why couldn't she remember? Moments before . . . the memory was getting less fuzzy . . . moments before she'd . . . *oh fuck.*

Before she'd vomited on his shirt.

How could she have forgotten?

Their present audience hooted and hollered, clapping at their very open, sensual display. Most of Dani's relationships had been hot, heavy, and brief, so she'd never been one to shy away from public displays of affection, but not like this. Not where she was two seconds away from straddling a man in front of others. And not when in the midst of remembering one of the most mortifying moments of her life.

Her cheeks flushed, almost matching her pinky-peach dress. And when she glanced down, she could see her nipples at full attention.

"Now *that's* what I call a kiss!" someone called out, clearly unaware of her mental anguish.

While the rest of the party seemingly moved on, she quickly removed herself from Theo's lap and tucked a loose strand of hair behind her ear, trying to play down the moment with a bashful smile. And avoiding eye contact with Theo. The last thing she needed was his pity.

But he turned to her and placed his hand on her forearm.

"Dani . . . I . . . I . . ."

Can't.

"I'm sorry," she then said, hurrying from her seat and rushing out of the room with one hand on her lips and the other across her waist. She didn't want to hear that word out of his mouth again. Once had been enough.

Air. She needed air. Her heart pounded as she made a beeline out the door to the patio. Deep breaths. Deep breaths.

She paced with her hands on her hips. This whole time, had Theo remembered that night? Had he been living with that memory each day for the last year? Aware that she'd poured out her heart and that he'd said no?

How could she have been so foolish? And she'd come *here*? To Greece? He must have really thought she was pathetic, still clinging on even after she'd thought he'd died. No wonder he'd been acting weird around her.

A light caught her attention—the glass patio door catching the reflection of the moon as Theo opened it to join her outside.

"Please, Theo. Please not now," she said, walking along the railing to the far end of the patio where hopefully no one else could see her.

But he either didn't hear her or didn't care, because he walked right over to where she was hiding.

"Hey," he said, putting his hand on her shoulder like a football coach trying to console a player off his game.

She closed her eyes, willing herself not to cry. She hadn't cried the first time Theo had rejected her—that she could remember—and she certainly wasn't going to do so now.

"I'm sorry, I don't know what got into me," she said, waving him away and refusing to look at him.

"There's nothing to apologize about. Everyone was egging us on."

"I know. But I didn't mean to get *so* into it," she said, rolling her eyes at herself for acting like a silly, dreamy-eyed teenager.

"Well, I suppose if we're making apologies, then I should be the one apologizing to you."

She furrowed her brow and finally looked his way.

"Apologize for what?"

"For putting you in an awkward position."

She shook her head, still not getting it.

"With your boyfriend," he followed up.

What on earth was he talking about? "Boyfriend? What boyfriend?"

Why did he think . . .

"Oh God, you're not still on this whole thing with Andreas, are you?"

"No, I'm talking about your guy back home. Your . . . your beau."

"My *beau*?" She stared at him incredulously for a moment and then burst out laughing. He didn't actually think Beau was her boyfriend, did he? By the utterly confused look on his face, Theo clearly had no idea what he was talking about.

"But—but your dad said—" Theo sputtered as Dani was trying to control her chuckles.

"And what did he tell you exactly?" She folded her arms.

"He'd said you were out with your beau. We talked about this."

"And that's how he said it? He said I was with *my* beau?"

"Yeah . . . ?" Now Theo was the one who wasn't getting it.

"Well, my *beau* is my coworker who happens to be named Beau. My very *gay* coworker."

Even under the moonlight, Dani could see Theo's face turn white as a sheet. How was he not laughing? This was fucking hilarious.

"Why are you looking at me like that?" Dani asked, pulling him out of his thoughts.

He blinked a few times, seemingly unaware he'd been looking at her in any particular way. "Looking at you like what?"

"Like I told you Beau is an alien."

"Not an alien. Just confused. Your dad . . . he said he was your beau."

Dani rolled her eyes.

"My dad is the one who's confused. It's like he's never heard the name before. Every time I mention Beau, he thinks I'm referring to him as *my* beau instead of that being his name."

"Has your dad ever met him?"

"Yes, which makes it even more baffling. He came over for dinner one time when Eddie was in town, and it was *very* obvious Beau was much more into Eddie than he was me."

Theo put his hands on his hips, tossed his head back, and *then* started laughing. "Wow . . . I . . . I don't even know what to say right now." He ran his hands over his face and then through his silky dark brown hair, shimmering under the moonlight.

"Well, now that we've clarified that I'm not some Jezebel—"

"A fake kiss with your fake fiancé hardly makes you a Jezebel," Theo said.

Fake. Right.

Dani . . . I . . . I can't.

The last thing she needed was to languish over a fake kiss with the man who'd rejected her. Maybe this was her sign that it was finally time to get over him.

"Yeah, okay, well, since that's out of the way, can we please pretend that tonight never happened?" she pleaded. "Like we forget about it forever and never breathe a word about it ever again, assuming we get out of this mess?"

"Forget tonight?"

"The kiss," she clarified.

"Oh. That." His confusion was back. Like her request caught him off guard.

"I seriously don't know what got into me. It must be the situation. Tension is high. My emotions are all over the place. It obviously didn't mean anything."

"Yeah . . . obviously. It's just the situation."

"I don't want things getting weird between us again."

"Yeah, no. I get what you mean," he said, tugging on the

back of his neck. “We’re just two friends who kissed one time. Yeah. It happens.”

“Totally!” she said, excitedly slapping him on the arm. “And we had to make it look convincing.”

“Yeah. Had to.”

“I mean, I almost convinced myself for a second,” she said, nervously laughing. But Theo wasn’t laughing back. Instead, he stared at her almost like it pained him watching her be so pathetic. She needed to make things less awkward. She didn’t want him thinking she was over there pining for him.

“Don’t get me wrong, I wasn’t like *into* it, into it,” she continued as his gaze steadfastly focused. “Sure, it was a good kiss. But, like, I’ve kissed lots of guys where it meant nothing. This was like a silly dare. And you know I can’t say no to a dare. Like, oh! Remember that one time when—”

“Juicy, please stop.”

His strained words shut her up instantaneously.

“I’m sorry,” she said, biting her lip. “I’m making it weird, aren’t I?”

“Yes, but it’s fine. We’re in a weird situation. But seriously, we don’t ever need to mention it again. It never happened.”

“Really?”

“Yes. Not another word about it. Promise.” He crossed his heart and put up his hand.

Yet for some reason, disappointment rippled through her instead of relief. She quickly shook the thought away.

They stood silently for a few moments, not looking at each other.

“I suppose now’s the time to tell you, I’m not leaving tomorrow,” Theo said, like a needle scratching a record.

"What?!"

"Don't worry, Andreas can still arrange for you to get to the embassy. You'll be safe. But I'm going to stay and help him search for the eye."

Anger boiled over inside her.

"The hell you are! Theo, we're getting the fuck out of here. End of discussion."

"I can't leave. Not without seeing the pages from Demetrios's journal. I'll regret it if I leave before then," he said with a genuineness in his eye.

"You've got to be joking," Dani said, folding her arms. "Do you not remember being held hostage *for a year*?"

"And now I'm free."

She laughed. Unbelievable. "You're not *free*, Theo. You won't be free until you are back home."

He placed his hands on her shoulders. "I have to do this. I have to know why my grandfather told me those stories. Why me? Why tell me at all? I need to know, Juicy. Can't you understand that?"

"Then I'm staying with you."

He frowned and dropped his arms. "No, absolutely not."

"Oh, so what, you can put yourself in danger, but I can't do the same? Well, I'm not asking for your permission, Theo. If you're staying, then so am I. Don't try to talk me out of it."

As always, Theo put everything on his shoulders. His responsibility. His duty. The weight of everyone else's expectations weighing him down.

She needed him to understand that he wasn't alone in this. He never was.

"We'll find it together," she said, taking his hand and squeezing.

He then pulled her in for a hug, wrapping his long arms around her body. Her mind floated back to that kiss, but she quickly pushed it to the back of her brain.

"Don't tell Eddie," he said, his voice reverberating through his chest, "but I think *you* might actually be my best friend."

Dani smiled and pressed her cheek into his pecs. Even if she couldn't have Theo in the way she wanted, at least she still had this.

"You're right. Eddie would have jumped ship back at the museum," she joked.

"Eddie wouldn't have been in a museum in the first place," Theo retorted, and they both started laughing.

Dani looked up at Theo, still with his arms wrapped around her, as he looked down. Her heart pounded. She wished things were different. That he was feeling what she was feeling because, damn, she wanted to kiss him again.

"I'm glad you're here," he whispered.

"I can't say I'm glad I'm here," she said, and they both chuckled again, "but I'm glad I'm with you."

He scanned her face, his eyes jumping from her gaze to her lips. For a moment, she thought maybe . . . just maybe . . . he might kiss her again. But instead, he rested his chin on the top of her head, and the silence returned.

Sigh. This would have to do.

CHAPTER Fifteen

Theo

THE SUN STARTED TO CREEP INTO THE ROOM, BUT IT DIDN'T matter. Theo was already awake. Wide awake.

It was quickly becoming a habit for him.

And it didn't have anything to do with the fact that Theo's mind raced, trying to remember everything his papou had ever said about Crete and the eye, and calculating their next moves. His thoughts were just a distraction from the fact that Dani was sleeping beside him on the tiny twin bed, her body curled up into his side. Her hand rested on his bare stomach. He wasn't sure when she'd snuggled into him, but when he woke up an hour ago with his arm already completely numb from being wrapped around her, he became increasingly aware that it must have been a long time.

That kiss. That fucking kiss. It replayed in his mind all night. The way she pulled at his shirt. How she repositioned her body over his lap. The way her impossibly soft lips played with his.

It was everything he'd wanted out of a kiss with Dani—except that it wasn't real.

Like she'd said, they'd been caught up in the moment and playing their parts. It didn't mean anything. She didn't feel that way about him anymore. If she ever had.

It's always been you.

God, he felt like an idiot getting that tattoo. The ink burned, searing against her skin pressed against him.

Dani sucked in a breath, stirring. Theo tipped his head, watching her through his eyelashes as Dani rose into consciousness and realized where she was positioned. Slowly, she pulled away from his body, clearly thinking he was still asleep and not wanting to wake him. But as she separated their bodies, she stopped and studied his tattoo. Her fingers grazed over the letters, sending a warm buzz across his skin. He fought to keep from reacting to her touch, not wanting her to stop. But his body couldn't be controlled, and he impulsively flinched.

She shot her gaze up to his and pulled her hand away.

"Good morning," he whispered.

"How long have you been awake?" she asked, not even bothering with the morning pleasantries.

It was obvious why. She wanted to know if he'd noticed her touching his tattoo.

"Long enough," he simply responded.

"What does it mean?"

It didn't take a rocket scientist to figure out what she was talking about.

"It means 'know thyself.'" He said the first thing that came to his mind.

Seeing as Dani couldn't read Greek, she'd have no idea that

he'd recited the words over the entrance of the Temple of Apollo at Delphi—Γνῶθι σεαυτόν—rather than the actual meaning of *her* words inscribed on his body.

"Interesting," she said. "Why did you get it?"

"Seemed appropriate at the time."

She nodded, seeming to buy his bullshit.

"So, I was thinking about last night," she said out of nowhere, rolling onto her stomach and looking straight at him.

Speaking of interesting.

He shifted, lifting his body up slightly onto the pillow, careful not to make too much noise, and bringing one hand behind his head while the other rested across his stomach.

"Yeah? What about it?" he asked as casually as he could muster.

She looked down, playing with the fringe on the bedding. "I couldn't sleep. There was just this clamoring in my head," she said, bringing her hands up to her temples and demonstrating the raucousness.

"What was the clamoring saying?"

"It was saying, 'He's right there.' 'Don't touch him.' 'Don't be weird.'"

Theo snickered. "Funny, because when I woke up you were right here," he said, bringing the hand on his stomach across his body to show her where he'd found her.

"Yeah . . . I know. That's how I could finally fall asleep. I scooted back over this morning."

Hmm . . . he'd assumed it had been unintentional.

"Theo," she said suddenly, "what if I don't want to forget what happened last night anymore? What if I don't want to pretend?" She looked at his mouth and then back to his eyes. "I've been thinking about that kiss all night."

Theo swallowed. Was that a good thing or a bad thing? He wasn't sure where this was going.

"I lied," she continued speaking in hushed tones.

He raised an eyebrow, and his stomach sank. What on earth could she have possibly lied about?

"I wasn't *not* into it," she said, then instantly scrunched her face. "I'm sorry, that didn't make any sense. You'd think a librarian would be better with words," she said, nervously laughing. "I guess I lied when I acted like it was any old kiss. And I thought you should know."

Relief washed through his body, which was quickly replaced by an all-over feeling of elation.

She flashed a quick glance at him, catching his gaze for a moment to gauge his reaction, and then immediately turned her attention back to the bedspread. God, it was cute.

"I was into it, too," he said, putting her out of her misery.

Dani let out a breath and buried her head in her pillow, then lifted it again with the most beautiful smile he'd ever seen. Just that one look sent a delightful prickling sensation dancing across his skin, and he couldn't help but smile in return. Her giddiness was contagious.

"Oh good," she said. "I was worried it was just me."

He laughed, trying his damnedest not to wake the rest of the house and have the moment ruined. "No, Juicy, it wasn't just you. So what changed? Because last night, you seemed very much like you wanted to forget it ever happened."

"I realized that I didn't want you thinking you were like any other random guy I've kissed. *You* make it different. And you're right. We're adults. I think we can handle that we've kissed. And that it was . . . good. Like, really good, right?" she asked, wrinkling her nose.

Acting like it had been no big deal last night had hurt. They'd known each other for almost their entire lives. Of course it was a big fucking deal!

But it was so much more than that, and hearing her admit it felt . . . nice.

He snickered. "Yeah, it was a good kiss."

"I know things are complicated right now, and getting out of this mess needs to be our top priority. But I don't know what's going to happen here, and if we die—"

"Juicy, we're not going to die," Theo said, smiling and brushing a loose tendril of her hair from her face. "We're safe. He doesn't know where we are."

"Okay, but what if he finds us again? And what if we *do* die here? What if we help Andreas and we fall off a cliff? Or a temple collapses on us?"

"We're going to a museum. I think we'll be fine," he said with a slight chuckle.

"You don't know that. You certainly didn't leave the States thinking you were going to lose a year of your life. So what if that kiss last night was the last kiss either of us ever has?"

"What are you trying to say?" he asked, cocking his head to the side.

"I'm . . . I'm trying to say that all I could think about last night is how I really want to kiss you again."

"You know, you could have led with that." He smiled, then reached his hand for her. "Come here."

She scooted up toward him, and he wrapped one of his hands around her waist, the other cupping her cheek. A pleasant buzz swirled through his stomach as she started to lean in, but then stopped herself, bringing the swirling to an abrupt halt.

"This doesn't have to change anything, right?" she asked.

He let out the breath he didn't realize he'd been holding and grinned. "No, not a thing."

She leaned in, then again pulled back. "It's only a kiss."

"Yep. Only a kiss."

She nearly closed the gap, but once more, stopped herself, "And I—"

But he didn't let her finish. He pulled her face to his, enveloping her mouth with his own. Reminding himself of what it had felt like to kiss her last night for the first time.

The second time was just as good.

Their tongues tangled together as her fingers tangled through his hair. His hands held her body against his as their mouths melded. Lying beside her, every inch of his body felt her presence, from the top of his head to the tips of his toes. Her lips moved away from his mouth and planted soft, delicate kisses along his jawline and neck.

Theo let each of her kisses sink in, implanting their etch along his skin like the tattoo on his side. He licked his own lips and closed his eyes, allowing himself to be immersed in her touch. She took his hand, lowered it beneath the blanket and placed it on her ass. This ass he'd fantasized about. Pictured in his dreams. It was now in his hands, and it was even more tender than he'd imagined as he kneaded his fingers into her. Their bodies twisted as he groped her, and slowly, she started rocking against him with her apex grinding against his thigh.

This *wasn't* only a kiss.

His cock ached to relieve some of the pressure, and he pulled her body atop his, placing their cores against each other's. The hardness of his cock couldn't be mistaken, and for a moment, he'd considered that he'd gone too far too fast. But Dani's hips rolled against him with firm, slow circles.

A low groan escaped his lips, and she lifted her head from his neck and looked him straight in his eyes.

"I feel dirty doing this in Phoebe's daughter's bed," Dani said, though she made no effort to stop.

"Doing what? It's just a kiss," he said with a smirk.

Without taking her eyes from him, she picked up the speed in her hips, and he could feel the slippery wetness between her legs soaking through the fabric of their underwear. There was an intensity to her stare. A hunger in her eyes that wiped his smirk away and replaced it with a ravishing desire. The pressure built as he fought not to roll her over, strip her of her clothes, and bury his cock deep inside her.

A loud rapping on the bedroom door startled them. Dani gasped and quickly rolled off Theo, pulling the blanket up over her chest, as he shifted to hopefully conceal what they'd been doing.

"Theo? Daniela?" Andreas called from the other side of the door.

Theo and Dani looked at each other. Her hair was a mess. Her cheeks flushed. But damn, was she beautiful.

"You okay?" he asked. Once she nodded, Theo called out to Andreas, "Come in."

Andreas opened the door and immediately laughed upon seeing the two of them in the tiny bed. "I didn't realize this was where Christos had put you up."

"Yeah, well, we broke the bed in the other room," Theo said.

Andreas's eyebrow raised and he gave them a suggestive look.

"Not like that," Dani said, laughing.

"Okay," he said, still smiling. "Well, I thought we might head to the museum early this morning so you can see Papatonis's journal. Get there before it opens to lessen our chances of Vautour's men lurking around waiting for you."

"Good idea," Theo said.

"Great. Well, Christos is making breakfast if you want to get ready and then come out to eat. I'll leave you to it," Andreas said, giving them a quick nod and then closing the door.

For a split second, Theo thought maybe they'd resume what they were doing before the interruption, but the moment had passed.

"You can go first this time," Dani said.

He looked down at his groin and, no, he certainly could *not* go first. "No I can't, Juicy."

"Why not?"

Theo lifted the blanket to show her his rock-hard dick.

"Oh." Her eyes went wide, and she licked her lips. "Well, I can't go first, either."

"Why not?"

She took Theo's hand and placed it between her legs.

Against her very. Wet. Panties.

Oh, fuck me.

He didn't remove his hand, though. Maybe the moment hadn't passed. Theo cupped her mound, letting the slick wetness soak through the fabric and coat his fingers. She closed her eyes and bit her bottom lip as a sinful moan escaped her mouth. God, he wanted to fuck her.

Another knock came at the door, and Theo took back his hand faster than a bolt of lightning from Zeus himself.

"Christos wants to make sure you don't have any other allergies," Andreas said through the door.

Theo opened his mouth to respond, but just a garbled mess

came out. He quickly cleared his throat and said, "No, just apples."

Dani got up from the bed, officially ending the moment. He strained to keep himself from putting his fingers in his mouth and tasting her. Though maybe he'd get another opportunity later.

"We'd better get moving," she said. "I'll go first."

Theo watched as she bounded out of the room. But as she was about to shut the door, she looked back at him one more time.

And he put his fingers in his mouth.

CHAPTER Sixteen

Dani

THEY ALL CLIMBED OUT OF THE CAR AND FOLLOWED ANDREAS through the already-bustling tourist area toward the Acropolis Museum. The modern glass building sat directly next to the southern entrance to the Acropolis but was a separate attraction all to itself. Her original tour group had planned to make both stops. She wondered how it was going.

Maybe she could find a way to say goodbye to Harold after all.

It was before opening hours, but Andreas swiped a badge to let them in. He casually strode over to speak with the security guard, telling him they were his prearranged guests, then motioned for them to continue following him to the elevators.

Ding!

The elevator doors opened, letting them out into the basement.

"This is where we keep some of our archives and storage," Andreas explained, leading the way once again.

The basement was cold and dry—probably temperature

controlled—but Dani's body was still on fire from her and Theo's little rendezvous that morning. Things had heated up fast. One second they were kissing, and the next, well, if they hadn't been interrupted, who knew what would have happened. She couldn't wait to be alone together again.

Finally they made it to a locked room, and Andreas swiped his badge again. At the front of the room were a few large tables. He told them to wait there for a moment, and then he finally returned with a box.

"Here, put these on," he said, handing white gloves to each of them.

As they put on the gloves, he pulled out some old documents, sealed in plastic sleeves.

"These are pages from Papantonis's journal," Andreas said as he lined them up in front of Theo and Dani. "They were discovered over one hundred years ago at some ruins on the west side of Crete."

Dani bent over to read the documents, but she couldn't understand a thing since they were written in Greek. But Theo quickly became engrossed in the pages.

"May I?" Theo asked Andreas, motioning toward the small notebook in his satchel, asking for permission to take notes.

"Please," Andreas said, nodding for him to proceed. While Theo scoured the documents, Dani turned toward Andreas.

"Why aren't these on display in the museum?" she asked.

"For many reasons," Andreas said, folding his arms and resting against a counter behind him, "primarily that we only exhibit a fraction of the museum's collection at one time. But for this item in particular—the journal? Because its authenticity has been questioned," he explained.

"By who?"

"Truthfully, I don't know. But I suspect it has something to do with Τα Παιδιά του Μινώταυρου."

"What's that?" Dani asked, furrowing her brow.

"The Minotaur's Children. A cult that protects the secrets of the Minotaur."

The hairs raised on Dani's arms. Cult? She didn't like the sound of that. Seriously, what were they getting themselves into?

"Are they dangerous?" she asked.

He shrugged. "I don't know. I haven't found any evidence of their existence. Just rumors, whispers, and dead ends."

"Did your papou ever talk about this cult, Theo?" Dani asked.

He looked up from the pages, glancing around as if he hadn't heard a thing they'd been talking about. She loved when he got so focused on something that the rest of the world almost seemed to stop around him.

She loved it because that's how she felt whenever they were together.

"I'm sorry, what were you saying?" he asked.

"The cult. Did Papou Zeno ever talk about it?" she repeated.

He shook his head. "Never. First I'd heard of it was yesterday when Andreas showed me this." Theo reached into his satchel and pulled out a small leather-bound book with clippings and other papers sticking out of it. He handed it across the table to Andreas, who then flipped through the pages and stopped on a drawing of the eye and μ symbol.

Dani wrinkled her brow. "This is your family's crest," she said.

"Yes, we changed it many years ago, trying to draw attention to the Minotaur's Children."

"Has it worked?"

He tipped his head to the side and laughed. "Would we be here if it did?"

Well, at least it didn't get their attention in a *bad* way.

"Oh, this is interesting," Theo said.

He picked up one of the letters encased in plastic and placed it in the center of the table so everyone could read it. Again, not that Dani could read anything.

They leaned in, staring at the document before Dani shrugged her shoulders and said, "It's all Greek to me."

Andreas laughed. "I'll read it to you then. This one says, 'We've reached the gateway to the sea with the eye of the Minotaur, it no longer being safe in its original burial place. Its power grows restless and must be released from confinement. Now its true potential will be realized, and it will be free.

"'From here, we will travel back to my home. There, below where Helios rises in the east, I will put the eye to rest, accessible only to those who recognize its power. Despite his quarrels, Poseidon himself could not have picked a better place for this beast to spend eternity. It is here that the eye will sleep and blend into the dirt itself, watching over the land of my ancestors and bringing strength and fertility to my people.'"

They stood in silence, waiting for Theo to explain.

"Don't you see?" Theo asked. "This might be a clue."

Andreas and Dani both raised skeptical eyebrows.

"Papantonis talks about traveling *back* to his home," Theo said as if that explained anything.

"I can see that. But we already know where Demetrios is from. You've been there already," Andreas said. "My yayá's mill?"

He said it as if saying, *Remember?*

"Right, and she told us that the eye was moved. Maybe it was somewhere else on Crete at first and *then* he took it to your yayá's property. Have you already searched the grounds at the mill?" Theo asked.

"Of course, we've looked all over there."

Theo and Andreas stared at each other, racking their brains as to where else on Crete the eye could be.

"Near Knossos?"

"What about Rethymno?"

"Or Sitia?"

They continued calling out the names of various locations in Crete with no rhyme or reason, while Dani sifted through the pages of Papantonis's journal. There had to be something there. Some clue as to where he was from.

She thought of all the people who'd come to the local library in Grand Rapids, searching for information on their own families. So often people came to realize that their family histories were not what they'd been led to believe.

Perhaps the same could be said of Papantonis.

"What if it's not in Crete?" Dani blurted out, interrupting Theo and Andreas's friendly debate.

"What do you mean?" Theo asked, tilting his head to the side.

"The eye. What if it's not in Crete because Papantonis was from somewhere else?" she said.

"And you're basing that on what?" Andreas asked, folding his arms.

A swarm of nerves buzzed through her body. She brought her hands to a steeple at the bridge of her nose, closed her eyes, and took a deep breath. *Think. Think.*

She allowed her brain to wander, pulling out pieces of Papantonis's letter and letting them ruminate in her mind.

Blend into the dirt.

"The dirt!" she exclaimed.

"Daniela, I'm not following," Theo said, clearly wanting to understand her but frustrated that he didn't.

"What do you know about the soils in Greece?" she asked no one in particular.

Not that it mattered, because no one answered. They all looked around at one another, waiting for someone else to respond.

"Look, Papantonis said the eye would blend into the dirt. What if he meant that literally, as in the soil was the same color as the gemstone? I've seen red soil before. Not here, of course, but in other parts of the world," she said, as if she'd *been* to other parts of the world. But that was beside the point. "Maybe we need to dissect each word of this letter and analyze what it could mean."

She had to admit, she wasn't basing it on much more than a hunch. But what other options did they have?

"So, where do you think he was from, then?" Andreas asked.

"I . . . that, I don't know," she said. "But I'm a librarian. Let me help find an answer."

"And how do you presume to do that?" he asked.

"Got any libraries?"

Andreas laughed. "Well, Greece is *home* to the library, didn't you know?"

"I did know that, actually," she responded. The question was borderline insulting, although she was sure Andreas hadn't meant it to be. A person didn't love books as much as Dani did and not know where libraries came from.

"Then you may also know that Athens has many wonderful libraries," he said. "Though I'm afraid, I've probably searched every book in this city for answers, and I've come up empty-handed."

"Even the rare collections?" she asked.

"*Especially* the rare collections," he said.

"When was the last time?" Theo asked. "What building?"

"It was in the Vallianeio Megaron," Andreas responded, clearly wondering what he was getting it. "But I'm telling you, there was nothing."

"Did you know that when the library was moved to its current location at the SNFCC, they discovered a whole collection of old texts in a room that had been blocked for decades by a bookshelf?" Theo asked.

Andreas straightened his stance. "No, I . . . I didn't know that. How did *you* know that?"

"Libraries are a special interest of mine," Theo said, giving Dani a wink.

Dani could barely hold back her smile. Her mind took her right back to that morning.

"To the National Library, then?" Andreas asked, pulling her out of her thoughts.

"To the library," Dani said, staring straight into Theo's eyes.

CHAPTER

Seventeen

Theo

THEO HAD ALWAYS WANTED TO BRING DANI TO THE STAVROS Niarchos Foundation Cultural Center. The walls of books were truly a librarian's dream. He couldn't say this was exactly how he imagined their visit would be, but now as he walked beside Dani hand in hand past the canal toward the sharp-angled modern-glass-and-concrete building, he didn't want it any other way.

"The National Library recently moved its entire collection to this new building," Theo explained to Dani as they walked up to the library entrance with a wall made of dozens of windowpanes. "This library houses the largest collection of Greek historical texts in the world."

"If we can't find the answer here," Andreas added, "then it doesn't exist."

When Theo opened the door, Dani's eyes lit up like Belle

opening the doors to the library in *Beauty and the Beast*. Floors and floors of books filled the large, open room. Light filled the area, casting a glow upon the shelves. Dani entered the space and looked up while slowly turning in a circle. Never mind that most, if not all, of the books were likely in a language she couldn't read. It didn't matter. She was like a kid in a candy store, staring at the collection in awe.

And Theo was staring at her, unable to hold back his smile.

Dani was in her element. The wide grin on her face brought out the sparkle in her eye. He wished she could spend the next week in this building, scouring the shelves. The Main Library in the old Ryerson Building back in Grand Rapids where she worked was a cool building and all, but this?

This was like working in a zoo and then finally visiting the Sahara. Like eating at Olive Garden and then finally traveling to Italy.

The urge to take her to every library in the entire world came over him to see this wonderment in her eyes again.

"I . . . I don't even know where to start," Dani said, giddy as a schoolgirl.

"I will see if we can get access to their rare Greek collections room," Andreas said. "That's going to be the best place to find evidence of Papantonis's birthplace."

"What should we do while you're doing that?" Dani asked.

"Here," Theo said, pointing to a chair in front of a computer. "Let's search the catalog."

Dani sat in front of the computer, but her face instantly dropped. "It's in Greek."

"I'll help you, babe," Theo said as he reached for another chair and sidled up to her.

"If you see anything that looks interesting, wait here for me," Andreas said.

Andreas and Theo gave each other the subtlest of nods and then Andreas took off in the direction of the main desk. Theo watched him as he walked away, trying to see where he was going. But Theo could feel Dani's eyes on him.

"What?" he finally asked, looking her way.

"You're watching him like a hawk," she said.

"I just want to make sure we know where he's going," Theo said, turning his attention to the computer.

"Oh, don't worry, I've got my eye on him," Dani said, suggestively.

Theo snapped his gaze to Dani. She wasn't still interested in him, was she? Not after everything that happened last night—and this morning?

"I'm kidding," she said, laughing. But Theo didn't laugh in return. "What? Still jealous?" she asked, smirking.

"No, Juicy, I'm not jealous," he said with a scoff. *Please.*

"You sure? Maybe we weren't convincing last night."

"We were convincing," he said point-blank. "I mean, what? Should we be making out in the library? Because if that's what we need to do, I'm game."

Dani gasped. "That's sacrilege!" she said with a playful gasp.

"What? Making out in the library?"

"Yes! You can't desecrate such a holy place."

Theo laughed. "Please. Like you've never made out in a library," he said, tossing her an *I don't believe you* look.

"Never."

Hmm. For some reason, this was surprising.

Well, not for *some* reason. For lots of reasons. Dani was never one to shy away from public displays of affection.

"How is that possible?" he asked. "You spend more time in the library than anyone else I know."

"Okay, first off, I *have* to spend my time in the library because it's my job. But even still, just because I spend a lot of time in the library doesn't mean I *make out* with people in it. I mean, I've never known someone who spent so much time playing in the dirt on archaeological digs—"

"I've done more than make out with someone on a dig, Juicy," he said, giving her a sly eye.

Her jaw dropped and she covered her mouth. "No, you haven't," she said, almost giggling.

"I have."

He didn't know why he was telling her this, but it was sort of fun.

"How many times?" she asked.

He ducked his head. "Are you really asking me how many times I've had sex on an archaeological dig?"

She nodded like she really wanted to know, and, damn, it sent a quick jolt to his cock.

"Twice."

"*Only* twice?" she asked, scrunching her face almost like she was disappointed in his answer.

"Oh, okay," he said with a laugh. "How many times have you had sex in a library?"

"Never. I told you. That's sacrilege."

"No, you said you'd never made out with someone."

"Right. Same thing."

"No, Juicy," he said, hanging his head and laughing. "That's not the same thing."

She made a face. "How do you expect me to have sex with someone without making out with them?"

"It's easy."

She stared at him like she was waiting for an explanation. A tutorial, perhaps?

"It's called fucking," he said.

Dani's mouth dropped into a devilish O. What the hell had come over him? Clearly their little morning rendezvous gave him a boost of sexual confidence.

"My God, Theo, are you a bad boy?" she asked waggling her brow.

"I don't think the knowledge of fucking immediately gets someone classified as a bad boy," Theo said, tossing her a telling glance.

"So then, what are you? When it comes to women?"

Theo glanced down at her lap, noticing her twisting her hands together, before returning his gaze to her face. Was she nervous?

"What do you mean?"

She shrugged. "Are you an alpha? A teddy bear? Do you treat your woman like a queen? Are you aloof? It's kind of hard to tell by girlfriends you've had. They're all so . . . well-behaved. Good Greek Girls, right?"

Theo laughed. "In comparison to you, maybe."

Dani waved her hand over her shoulder. "Sorry that I like a little fun, unlike your boring exes."

"Hey, they weren't boring. They were intimidated."

"By who? *Me?*"

Shit. He hadn't meant to say that.

"By the whole situation," he said, trying to play it off. "I mean, you have to admit—Thanksgiving with the Galanis and Guiterrez clans is *a lot.*"

He'd never actually realized how extra their family gatherings were until he spent one Christmas Eve with his college girlfriend's family. It was so quiet. Civil. There were no arguments over whose sugar-dusted nut cookies were better, his sister's kourambiedes cookies, or Dani's Mexican wedding cookies (Theo always voted for Dani). And the food on their plates was so . . . brown. Not a dolma or a bowl of salsa in sight.

He missed his and Dani's families' amalgamation of cuisine: Grexican, they liked to call it. There was nothing like his mother's pork stew with a heaping spoonful of Mrs. Guiterrez's Mexican rice on top. Or a shot of raki followed by Carlos's spicy, cinnamony hot chocolate. But from the minute you walked in the door until the last good-night of the evening, there was laughter and clatter.

Giorgina hadn't particularly enjoyed her experience at the Galanis-Guiterrez holidays. Even though she was a Triple G, a few times she'd mentioned she expected that future holidays would be more . . . conventional, as she called it. *When we start our own traditions*, she'd said. Theo figured Giorgina needed to warm up to their families, that was all. Eventually she'd see that what they had was special, and she'd be one of them. Three years into their relationship, and she still didn't seem to understand.

Too bad it took Theo three years to realize it himself.

"Well, you're the one brave enough to bring a guest in the first place," Dani said. "I'd never bring a guy into that chaos."

"Ever?"

"Uh-uh," Dani said, shaking her head.

"You know, I don't think I've ever met a guy that you've dated other than the randos you've picked up at Palmer's," Theo said. "I don't even know what's your type."

"Why would you?"

Theo furrowed his brow. "Why *wouldn't* I?"

"Um, well, for starters, they usually aren't around long enough for it to make a difference. Besides, you live two hundred miles away. I'm not going to waste your limited time in town introducing you to some guy who probably won't even be around by the next weekend. So there you go. That's my type."

"What is?"

"Guys who don't stick around."

There was a sadness to her voice. Like maybe she didn't particularly like the fact that they didn't stick around.

"You never answered my question, by the way," she said.

"Which one?"

"About what kind of guy *you* are."

Theo watched her for a moment, considering her body language. She didn't look at him when she said it, opting instead to stare straight at the computer screen, her finger scrolling slowly on the mouse even though they'd yet to type anything into the computer.

"I'm not sure," he finally said.

"Well, what would Giorgina say?"

Giorgina would probably say he was an asshole, but he wasn't about to tell Dani that. Last thing he needed was for her to ask *why* Giorgina felt that way.

"I'm not sure my ex is the best person to ask," he said.

"What? No way, your ex is the *perfect* person to ask."

"Fine. She'd probably say I'm . . ." He thought of the first word that came to mind and said, "attentive."

"Oh."

Another *oh*. He *really* needed to start learning what those *oh*s meant. Dani stared at him blankly, clearly trying to figure out exactly what he meant by that. He could have explained that Giorgina always appreciated how he took care of her and met her needs, especially in the bedroom. But in reality, the night they broke up, Giorgina called him out on his attentiveness to Dani, rather than to herself. And Theo did nothing to deny it.

Because he knew that even when he was with Giorgina, his mind was often on Dani. And that wasn't fair to her. To either of them.

"We should probably get to work," Dani said, changing the subject and scooting her chair closer to the table.

She may have been done with the conversation, but he wasn't. She couldn't ask all those questions about him and then not answer any about herself.

"So you really haven't, then, have you?" he asked. "Made out with someone in the library?"

"No, I haven't." She stared at the screen, almost as if trying to pretend he wasn't talking.

"But would you?"

She pulled her lower lip between her teeth, considering his question.

"I mean . . ."

Her voice trailed off and that was all the answer he needed. *Sacrilege, my ass.*

"Go on," he said. He wanted to know. Needed to know.

"I mean . . . I suppose it's always been a fantasy of mine to get railed between the stacks," she said, finally looking his way and giving him a devilish grin.

Theo choked and then coughed. That was *not* what he was expecting.

And now his dick was getting hard, picturing himself plunging into Dani's tight, wet pussy as she held on to a shelf behind her. Dani, muffling her moans. Gotta keep quiet in the library, after all.

Suddenly, Theo found himself with a new library fantasy, too.

"Shhh!" someone shushed them from another computer, causing both of them to jump and then duck their heads like teenagers.

"You know I've never been good at . . . well, you know . . . being good," Dani whispered, lifting her brow as she sat back in her seat and glanced at his lap. Fuck, she really needed to stop looking at him like that. Theo adjusted his pants to conceal his hard-on, but not without catching Dani biting her bottom lip.

She looked down once more, noticing the straining fabric that he so desperately tried to hide under the computer table, and she smiled, finally turning her attention to the computer. She stared at it for a moment before again realizing that everything was in Greek.

"Here," he said, "scooch over."

She moved her chair a fraction of an inch, and he scooted closer, their thighs grazing each other's slightly. Thankfully, his dick wasn't at *full* attention anymore. But that touch did something else to him, sending a prickling sensation all along his forearms, making the hair on his arms raise.

All this talk with Dani about sex and libraries and getting railed was getting to his head.

"Okay, what am I searching for?" he asked, trying to take his focus off the proximity of Dani's legs.

"Type in 'Demetrios Papantonis,'" she said.

He typed in "Papantonis," and a number of results came up in the search.

"Do you want to give me something more specific?" he asked.

"How about 'Demetrios Papantonis, birthplace'?"

Zero results

"Let's try this again," she said. "This time go with 'Demetrios Papantonis, biography.'"

Still nothing.

"Maybe we should try a different angle. What about 'native soils of Greece'?"

It was worth a shot. Theo typed in a few different combinations and finally got a hit.

"It looks like they're all upstairs in the stacks," he said.

"What's in the stacks?" Andreas said, standing behind them.

Where had he come from? So much for keeping their eye on him.

"Books on soils," Dani said.

"Well, I got passes to the rare collections room," Andreas said, holding up two badges. "Unfortunately, there's a limit of two at a time."

"Great," Theo said. "How about the two of you go there, and I'll look into the soils?"

Dani put her hand on his forearm. "No, I don't want to leave you." The fear in her voice could not be missed.

He didn't want to leave her, either.

"That's okay," Andreas said. "You two go to the rare collections. I'll look for the soils."

"Are you sure?" Theo asked.

Andreas smiled. "Of course. I'll meet you outside the room once I'm finished. But just in case, here," he said, handing Theo a piece of paper with an address and phone number. "This is the address to Christos's house and our phone numbers."

Hopefully, they wouldn't need it.

"Then shall we go check it out?" Theo asked Dani.

She smiled.

"What's that for?" he asked.

"You know I've been dying to check out the books since we got in here." Even with everything else going on around them, her excitement couldn't be contained. Her passion was something he'd always admired about her.

He stood up and held out his hand. "Let's do it."

CHAPTER Eighteen

Dani

AS DANI CLIMBED THE BACK STAIRWELL TO THE THIRD FLOOR of the library, the only thing she could think about was whether her ass looked good or not. Theo followed her, at eye level with her behind. After the morning in bed and all their talk of getting railed in the stacks at the library, the only thing on her mind was fucking.

The library had so many places to fuck. The reading tables. The shelves. The ladders. Bend her over a card catalog and file it away under "best places to fuck in the library." There was also something about the forbiddenness of it all. Keep quiet. Don't talk above a whisper. Don't make any noise. Life as a straitlaced librarian was never something she had on her bingo card. But getting fucked in the library? Now, *that* was definitely a box Dani wanted to check off her sexual bucket list.

And she'd told Theo that she wanted that.

Given the circumstances, she was almost a little embarrassed at how horny she was for Theo. Prior to this . . . trip . . . she and Theo had never talked about sex before. Ever. But now it was at the forefront of her mind.

Dani glanced behind her, catching Theo staring at her ass, as suspected.

"Stop looking at my ass," she said with a smirk.

"Juicy, if you don't want me looking at your ass, don't walk in front of me."

"Fine, then you go first." She paused on the stairs and stepped to the side for him to pass her.

"Uh-uh," he said, shaking his head. "I don't want you looking at my ass."

She playfully rolled her eyes and then resumed climbing up the stairs. But this time she sashayed her hips, taking each step slowly.

"Okay, now you're fucking with me," he said. She could hear the playfulness in his voice. Man, this was fun.

"Why, whatever do you mean, Dr. Galanis?" she said, turning her head ever so slightly and placing her index finger on her bottom lip, using her silliest sexy voice like she was Marilyn Monroe climbing out of a birthday cake. She turned around to face him, but Theo wasn't laughing at her silly voice like she'd anticipated. Instead, there was a fire burning in his eyes. Tension that he was holding back.

"Don't call me that," he said, his voice hoarse as he took the last stair and stood facing her. He towered over her as she sank back against the wall. "Not unless you want me to turn your library fantasy into reality right here."

Holy fuck. Heat spread over Dani's entire body. She didn't know nerdy, good boy Theo had such ferocity in him.

She liked it.

"I didn't realize you had a name kink, Dr. . . . Galanis," she exaggerated.

"I didn't either . . . Daniela."

He stared at her with hooded eyes, and for a moment she thought he might legitimately hoist her against his waist and plop her down on a table in the research hall.

"You are making it *very* hard to focus," he said, leaning into her ear. He grabbed her by the hips and pressed his groin into her.

"Seems your focus isn't the only thing of yours I'm making hard," she said, pressing back to satisfy her own tension building in her core.

"You have no idea."

"I dunno . . . I think I have a pretty good idea," she said, allowing her lips to graze his ear and then pulling it into her mouth, sucking on his tender lobe like she wished she could do to his cock.

She grabbed him by his belt loops, pulling him closer to her, when a child came jumping down the stairs onto the landing right above them. They quickly broke apart and straightened themselves up before the child's parents rounded the corner. Dani tossed the mom a bashful smile, and then Theo took her by the hand and guided her the rest of the way up the stairs.

"We should probably be a little more discreet," Theo whispered. "I don't want to get arrested for public indecency."

"Hey, that's an option to get us out of here without having to worry about Pierre intervening with the police. Your face would probably be plastered all over if you got arrested," she joked.

"Perhaps. Though I'm not sure I want the very first photo for my mom to see of me alive to be a mugshot because I got caught with a hard-on in the library," Theo said, smiling.

"Then perhaps we'd better behave," she said. "I don't think I can handle having to explain that situation to your mom."

To be honest, Mrs. Galanis semi-terrified her. Not that she didn't love her, but she had high expectations for her son, and Dani was *pretty* sure getting Theo arrested wouldn't exactly help her "reckless" image no matter the circumstances.

They finally made it to the rare collections room and swiped their badges. It was like Candy Land for librarians. One-of-a-kind texts that only a limited number of people could get their hands on. She walked around the roughly five-hundred-square-foot room bordered on two sides by shelves and shelves of books in all shapes and sizes, scanning the bindings of the various titles while Theo went over the list of instructions and handed her a pair of gloves. The wall of windows on the other two sides of the room looked out into the library atrium. Another area had books in protective cases, and in the center sat two large wooden tables with felt tops to review the materials.

"I wish I could read these," she said, running her white-gloved finger along the spines. "I feel like I'm not going to be much help other than watching you read." Which was sexy and all, and, honestly, it was one of her favorite things to do when he'd come over and they'd literally spend an afternoon reading in silence, but not a great use of time under the current circumstances.

"Then, here," he said, grabbing a piece of scrap paper and a pen on the table and scribbling a few words. "Why don't you go through the books, check the indexes, and look for this." He held out the paper, which said "Παπατώνης, Δημητρίου." "This is Demetrios's name in Greek. If it's there, then find that spot in the text and I'll take a look."

"This is going to take forever."

"Do you have other plans?"

"Well, no, but aren't you getting hungry?"

"Let's go through this shelf and once we're done, we'll find Andreas so we can get something to eat."

"Oh!" she said, grabbing his arm. "There's this place I wanted to check out in Athens. It's supposed to have the *best* kebabs . . ."

Dani's voice trailed off as Theo tipped his head at her and raised his brows.

"No time for Fodor's best-of list?" she said, scrunching her face.

Theo laughed. "Look, once we make it out of this mess, I promise you, I'll bring you back for a real vacation and we'll go see all the sights, eat all the kebabs, and drink all the ouzo. But for now, let's figure out whatever we can about the eye of the Minotaur, and then get the hell home."

"You actually want to come back here after this?" she asked, wrinkling her forehead.

"I mean, I assumed I would eventually. I love it here. You don't?"

"I . . . I don't know. I love being here with *you*," she said, almost surprised by her honesty. And judging by the way he smiled at her tenderly, it seemed her honesty surprised him, as well. "But," she continued, "I'm worried I might have PTSD. And that makes a big assumption that there even will be an 'after this.'"

He took a step closer and placed his hands on her shoulders. "There *will* be an after, I promise. One way or another, we *will* get home, okay?"

She stared up at him, wanting to believe him, but she couldn't help the doubt creeping in. "What if Pierre finds us before we can get out of here?" she asked.

"Then, my sweetie pie babycakes," he said, taking a step

back and grabbing a book from the shelf, placing it in her hands, "you'd better start reading."

He winked and smiled, trying his damnedest not to let her spiral into despair.

"Sweetie pie babycakes?" she asked, casting him a skeptical look.

"Too much?"

She laughed and rolled her eyes before nudging him out of the way and grabbing a stack of books that she promptly set on the table before plopping down beside them.

Hours. They spent hours reading through various texts. Flipping through pages. Reshelving books that had nothing to do with Papantonis other than a brief mention of his existence. Every now and then, Andreas would come to check on them to see if they'd made any progress. But progress was fleeting.

Reading beside Theo was usually one of Dani's favorite activities. Other guys would prefer not to waste their time together fingering pages of a book rather than fingering her. But with Theo, she'd never been more content than when they were sitting next to each other on her couch, engrossed in books. She'd never felt more . . . *connected* to someone.

But not now. He'd written out the words she was supposed to be looking for—Παπατώνης, Δημητρίου—but it didn't matter. She'd never get the hang of Greek. She really should have spent more time trying to learn the language before her trip.

She laughed to herself at the thought of this still being a trip. Figures that her first international excursion would turn out to be a disaster. It was like the universe telling her she belonged in Grand Rapids and nowhere else.

Why had she even bothered leaving?

"What's that face for?" Theo asked.

Dani looked up and blinked. "Face? What face?"

"You look annoyed."

"Oh, that's me thinking about how I'm never leaving Grand Rapids ever again."

She closed another book and placed it on the stack to return to the shelf, making sure to keep things orderly to make it as easy as possible for the librarians. People who pulled dozens of library books and jumbled them out of order were the bane of her existence.

"See, I leave Grand Rapids and bad things happen," she said, taking another book and flipping straight to the back. Παπατώνης, Δημητρίου? Παπατώνης, Δημητρίου? Nothing.

Slam.

"You don't actually believe that, do you?" Theo asked, sounding somewhat concerned.

"How can I not? Move away for college? Dad gets in an accident. Go to Europe? I get kidnapped. The cards are stacked against me."

"You know your dad's accident had nothing to do with you leaving. And this?" he said, putting his arms up and motioning to their situation, "This is pure dumb luck."

"You mean bad luck," she grumbled.

"Maybe the problem isn't that you left Grand Rapids. The problem might be that you haven't left enough."

Dani stopped what she was doing to look at him. She was surprised by the sincerity in his eyes. The worry that she might actually believe the things that were coming out of her mouth. She'd never told anyone how she'd felt about sticking around Grand Rapids. She wasn't sure *she* could trust the words coming out of her mouth, either.

"I thought . . . I thought I'd be doing something different

with my life, is all. I look at you, and you're the director of . . . of . . ." Damn it, she couldn't remember what exactly Theo did. "Director of fancy shit," she said, and he laughed. "Adulting. Traveling the world. Going to *fancy* charity auctions with your well-behaved Triple G girlfriends who've got their shit together. Living in your *fancy* row house. And here I am, living in my parents' garage. No wait . . . I'm sorry. I *was* living in my parents' garage until they decided to sell it."

"Juicy," he said, scooting closer to her, "first off, I don't think I've ever described a single aspect of my life as 'fancy.' Second, don't whittle your life down to your living arrangements. You're so fucking smart—you got your master's degree while working full-time in a year. You're brave and don't put up with anyone's bullshit, mine included. And you're the most caring person I've ever met, putting your family first when they needed help."

"Only because I was scared," she said, her voice quivering. "And they didn't . . . they didn't even need me. That's what my parents told me before I left on this trip. I feel like no one needs me. Watch, I'm going to become an old cat lady librarian."

"*I* need you."

His words caught her off guard—and seemed to catch him off guard, too.

Theo cleared his throat and stood up, running his hand through his hair before setting the book he'd been holding on to the stack with the others.

"Maybe we should find Andreas and go get those kebabs," he said.

"You sure?"

"Yeah, I'm beginning to think Papantonis didn't actually exist," Theo said, obviously trying to change the subject.

"You saw his journal this morning. How can you say he didn't exist?"

"I'm not saying the journal wasn't real. But the person? There's so little about him outside of his own texts. Maybe he was the alter ego of some other person. Maybe Theseus. Like he didn't want people to know it was him."

"Or maybe that's what Papantonis wanted people to think," Dani said, excited by the prospect.

"Huh?" Theo's confusion couldn't be masked. "That doesn't make any sense."

Dani's shoulders deflated. No, it didn't.

"I *must* be getting hungry. And all these Greek letters are turning my brain into Greek alphabet soup."

Theo snickered. "Yeah, it's time for food."

He turned his back to put the room back in order, but as Dani got up from the chair, something caught her eye. The corner of a book peeking out from the top of the shelf. Something pulled Dani toward that book. It beckoned her. Teased her with its teensy little corner peeking out over the edge. Daring her to go for it.

Dani was never one to pick truth when it came to truth or dare. Besides, that book would niggle at her mind if she left it now. Murphy's Law, and all that.

She brushed past Theo and placed both her hands on the shelf, tugging at it to check its stability.

"Juicy, what are you doing?" he asked in a hushed, cautioning tone, glancing over his shoulder at her to make sure no one could see them from out the window.

"I see something," she said, placing her hand on the shelves.

"Leave it," he commanded.

"It will take two seconds," she said, lifting herself up the shelving like it was a ladder.

The wood creaked as her weight shifted. *Steady. Steady.*

Her shoe slipped and a tiny "ope" slipped out of her mouth as she braced herself to crash on her ass. But instead of the feel of the hard floor, two large hands propped up her butt. She glanced behind her, seeing Theo holding her up.

"Hey, watch where you're putting those things," she said, smiling.

"I can let go if you want." He winked.

No, she didn't want. She liked the way his hands molded around her curves. How strong they were as he cupped her. Or how they might feel without this barrier of clothing. How dangerously close they were to the other sensitive spots of her body. But now wasn't the time for her imagination to run wild, despite how badly her body wanted to run buck wild.

"Give me a boost," she said.

He raised her up as she climbed the shelving. Only a few more inches. She stretched to reach the book, her fingers grazing the edge so that they accidentally pushed the book back farther onto the shelf. She didn't need the help anymore, but Theo held her by the hips now, steadying her body as she reached.

"Juicy . . ." he said, his voice low and warning.

"Just a sec," she said, grunting and biting on her lip as she stretched.

Almost. There.

"Juicy . . . they're here."

"Who's what?" she said, looking down to find Theo staring out the window at something.

She glanced toward the direction of his gaze down the hallway outside of the room. No, not something.

Maurice.

Th-crack!

The shelf beneath her feet gave way, breaking under the weight of her body. Dani screamed, struggling to grab something, anything, to keep her from tumbling down. But it was no use. She clung to the bookcase as best she could when suddenly, the entire thing started to topple over.

"No, no, no!" she cried out, more afraid of getting pancaked by a five-hundred-pound bookcase than getting caught by Maurice. Before her mind had time to process it, however, her body was shoved to the side, missing the crashing bookshelf by mere inches. She held her eyes shut, clenching every part of her as she stiffened for impact as the clatter of the falling wood and books crashed through the cavernous room. But her body remained upright, finally coming to a stop with her back pressed against the shelves next to the ones that had fallen. Yet despite the shelves digging into her back, the only thing she felt was warmth.

Hard, verbena-scented warmth.

Slowly, she opened her eyes, peeking in case dust and debris still fell through the air. Curled on top of her, however, was Theo. His arms and head created a protective barrier around her own, tucking her into him rather than protecting himself. He was . . . solid. Firm.

Delightful.

But they didn't have time for delightful.

Theo unfurled himself from her and the two of them looked toward Maurice, now barreling toward the room. He wrenched the doorknob, but it didn't budge. Unfortunately, it was Dani and Theo's only way out. Maurice yelled at the top of his lungs as he slammed his body into the door, trying to bash it down. In the distance, Dani saw a library employee rushing up the stairs, yelling at Maurice in Greek, with Louis right behind them. Dani and Theo looked all around the room, trying to figure out another option, when the doorjamb started to give way. Theo slung his bag over his shoulder and then grabbed a chair, raising it above his head.

"What are you doing?" Dani said.

"Getting us the hell out of here."

Theo threw the chair at one of the windows on the wall away from Maurice, shattering the internal window right at the same moment Maurice busted through the door. A piercing alarm reverberated throughout the building, sending the entire library to a halt.

Without a second of indecision, Theo climbed through the window and reached back to pull Dani along as Maurice rushed at them. But Dani grabbed a book and threw it at his head and then took off in the opposite direction of Maurice and Louis.

Dani glanced behind them for a second, only to see Maurice and Louis climbing atop the pile of books, screaming for them to stop.

"Don't look back," Theo said.

She snapped her attention toward him as they weaved through the collections, making their way down the stairs toward the exit. The other patrons had pulled out their phones and began filming, calling out to them words Dani didn't understand. The once-quiet library was now as loud as a bustling train station with everyone gathering to see the action.

"Βοήθεια! Μας κυνηγούν!" Theo shouted to the onlookers. "They're chasing us!"

People started moving out of their way, and then promptly got *in* the way of Maurice and Louis.

"Get back here!" Maurice screamed. But it was no use. Theo

and Dani were already to the revolving door. As they spun through the turnstile, Dani got one more look, seeing Maurice and Louis swinging their fists at the crowd.

Once outside, they turned toward the canal. *Fuck*. Andreas. Where was he? Right then, Maurice came busting out of the main entrance.

"Quick, he can't swim," Theo said, pulling Dani toward the canal.

The narrow waterway was at least four hundred meters long. But as they approached the water and despite it being full of kayakers, they realized it was only a few feet deep. Maybe deeper toward the center. Dani looked behind them, and Maurice was closing in fast. By that point, they had no other choice. So without further delay, they ran into the water until it was deep enough to swim and then swam as fast as they could toward the opposite end. But Maurice had other plans. He ran into the water and yanked a passerby out of their kayak, then paddled quickly toward Dani and Theo. Once they could stand again, they ran through the water, but Maurice swiped at Theo's legs with the paddle, causing him to fall with a big splash.

Maurice launched out of the boat onto Theo, pinning him under the water, trying to drown him. His arms flailed as he gasped for breath. It was like watching a film in slow motion, watching him die. But she'd thought she lost him once. She wasn't going to lose him again.

Dani grabbed the paddle and swung it at Maurice, but he noticed just in time to release Theo and turned to catch it before impact. As Theo struggled to get away from him and recover his breath, Maurice jerked the paddle, bringing Dani to her knees in front of him. He then wrenched her wrist, and she screamed out. A revolting grin stretched across his face.

"I told your fiancé I wasn't above hitting a woman," Maurice said, clearly getting pleasure out of hurting her as he twisted.

But as he raised his fist, Theo called out from behind him, "And I told you to keep your fucking hands off her."

Maurice looked up at Theo standing over him right as Theo side-kicked him in the face, instantly knocking him out. Dani stared in awe. Where had Theo learned how to do that? Maurice fell into the water face first with a *ker-splat*, and Theo rushed over to her.

"Are you okay?" he asked, checking her for injuries.

"Yes, I'm fine."

"Well, good, because Louis just came out of the building," Theo said, helping lift Dani to her feet and then moving over to drag Maurice from the water.

"What are you doing? Leave him," she said.

"I can't let him drown," Theo said.

After they got Maurice's unconscious body back on dry land, they took off on foot, running along the pedestrian path that crossed over the roadway toward the sea.

"Don't stop," Theo said.

The adrenaline must have kicked in because her legs weren't tired, even though it was hard work keeping up with Theo's long limbs. They were at least two hundred feet in front of Louis, but she remembered how fast he was, so she didn't allow herself to let off the gas for even an instant. Sweat dripped down her face, but she didn't care. There wasn't time to worry about wiping it away.

They made their way across the bridge over to a marina, and Theo pointed.

"There!"

A man was at the end of the dock, untying a speedboat.

She wasn't sure what the plan was, but she kept running toward the boat.

"Get in, get in!" Theo shouted at her as he swiped past the man and took the keys straight out of his hand.

The man started screaming as Theo launched off into the boat, which had the effect of pushing it away from the dock.

"Συγγνώμη!" Theo said, placing his hands together in an apology and starting the boat just as Louis made his way down the pier. But he was too late. The engine roared to life, and Theo pushed the throttle all the way forward.

And only once they were out of the marina and into the harbor did Dani finally take a breath.

CHAPTER Nineteen

Theo

"HOW DID THEY FIND US?" DANI ASKED AFTER THEO SLOWED down the boat.

He meandered along a wharf, looking for a spot to ditch it.

"I have no idea. Maybe they saw us at the Acropolis Museum and followed us here?" Theo said.

"But it's been hours. Why would they have waited so long?"

Good question.

"Maybe they wanted to see if we found anything."

It was the only explanation he could come up with. Otherwise, how *did* they find them?

Finally, Theo found a slip, far on the outskirts of the marina so hopefully no one would notice the boat for a while. The last thing he needed was to get arrested for theft. He maneuvered the boat into the spot and then cut the engine. But before they got out, he searched the compartments for the owner's contact information.

"What are you looking for?" Dani asked.

He found the registration and copied the name and address. "So I can send an apology and directions to their boat," Theo said, tucking the information in his bag. "Come on, let's go."

They left the port and started walking in silence. Tired. Beat. Wet. Good thing Andreas had given them Christos's address. Hopefully they could catch a cab that would take them there and then Christos could pay. It was the only option they had, at the moment.

He spotted a cab from down the street, and Theo put up his hand to wave him over, but Dani immediately grabbed it and pulled it down.

"What are you doing?" Dani asked.

"We need a cab so we can get back to Christos's," he said.

"No, we *need* to go home. We're not safe here," she said, worry all over her face.

"We lost them. I don't think Maurice and Louis are suddenly going to drive up on the side of the road here."

"You almost died, Theo!" Dani yelled. "He had you pinned under the water, gasping for air. You could have drowned."

Her words stopped him in his tracks.

"What happens the next time? Huh?" she continued as cars whizzed by them. "Do you think they're just going to let you go? You may not know where the eye is, but you have *something* they want. Your loyalty? Your silence? I'd say your intelligence, but you're being pretty stupid right now."

He winced internally. It felt like a stab through the heart. But he had no retort.

Because she was right.

He thought of all the times she took risks back when they were kids. She'd always been so stubborn, never listening to anyone when they told her *no* or said she was being foolish.

And now there he was, the foolish one.

"I know you think this means something. That your papou told you those stories because he wanted you to make this discovery someday, but you said it yourself—it was just a story."

Her voice pleaded with him to understand. Pleaded with him to believe his own words, the very words he said to Vautour to convince him of his ignorance.

"I thought you were dead, Theo. Please don't make me *watch* you die, too. I don't think I could take it."

Theo stared at her, picturing himself in her shoes. If he had to witness her death, he would never be able to live with himself.

"You're right," he finally said. "We'll go home."

She closed her eyes, let out a long breath, and smiled.

"We still need to get to Christos's, though," he said, and her eyelids flung open, but he tamped his hands to calm her down. "Just so we can go through Andreas's connection at the embassy."

"And then we go home?" She looked at him with those eyes that could make him do anything.

Even give up his search for answers.

"And then we go home. I promise."

. . . .

BY THE TIME THEY MADE IT BACK TO CHRISTOS'S, ANDREAS HAD AL-ready beaten them there. The relief on his face when they pulled up in the cab told Theo all the answers he needed: they were cousins, regardless of whether by blood or not.

They spent the evening making arrangements for Theo and Dani to meet Andreas's contact at the embassy in the morning, and then after another one of Christos's meals that they would most certainly miss, and Andreas agreeing to send some money to the boat owner on Theo's behalf, Dani went to bed. Theo and Andreas stayed up a bit longer, telling stories about their grandparents and becoming surer of their blood relation with each similar mannerism. Theo said he'd send a photo of his papou as soon as he got back to the States so Andreas could compare. Though they still weren't sure how—or even *if*—they'd bring it up to Lydia or their parents. Truthfully, Theo didn't want to leave. He wanted to verify Papantonis's existence. He wanted to explore his roots.

But he'd made a promise.

Theo snuck into the bedroom a little after midnight, but Dani was already sleeping on her side. Even with the windows open, the room was hot. So he stripped down to his boxers and snuggled up behind her, careful not to rouse her. It had been a long day, and tomorrow would likely be just as grueling, even if not physically. Her vanilla scent soothed him quickly to sleep, however. And as he dozed off, he wondered if he'd ever sleep the same without her again.

He'd been asleep for a few hours before eventually needing to relieve the pressure on his shoulder. Throwing the chair at the window in the library earlier in the day definitely didn't help with his healing. Plus, it was hot as fuck in that room. Theo turned onto his back, trying not to displace the mattress and disturb Dani too much, but where he expected their bodies to dip toward each other in the center of the bed, Theo felt nothing.

His hand darted over to her side of the bed. Empty. Theo flung his eyes open, ready to fly out of the room to search for her, but when he shot up, he saw a light coming from underneath the door of the adjacent study. With the slightest, slowest of movements, Theo climbed off the bed and crept over to the other room.

He twisted the doorknob and opened the door a crack. And there she was, sitting at a tiny desk in the corner of the room with one leg pulled up to her chest and the other dangling below her as she hunched over a couple of books, a pencil in her hand.

His movement in the doorway caught her attention, and she spun the chair in his direction. The light cast a halo around her, and Theo lifted his hand to shield his eyes as he quickly slid into the room.

"Oh, sorry. I didn't mean to wake you," she said, angling the light away from the door. But now that he could see her, he almost wished she'd turn it back.

Because seeing Dani sitting there in the world's shortest black shorts and a hot-pink low-cut tank top sans bra wasn't going to help when and if he tried going back to sleep. How did he not notice that's what she was wearing when he got into the bed?

"You didn't wake me," Theo finally said. "It's . . . it's too hot to sleep."

"Yeah, I got up a few hours ago. You're like a furnace."

You should feel me now.

"Sorry," he said.

She laughed and ducked her head. "You don't need to apologize. I swear, it's like another part of Vautour's evil plan. Torture us with this heat."

Oh, it was torture, all right.

"What are you doing?" Theo asked, trying to take his mind off how hot he was.

"Translating."

"Translating what?"

"This?" she said with a wince, holding up a book—*the* book that had been peeking out over the top of the bookshelf in the library.

"You stole a library book?" Theo said, folding his arms and

leaning against the doorjamb. "Tsk, tsk, Juicy. That's very un-librarian-like."

She twisted her pretty face with a devilish grin. "Look, you know I've never been one for rules. A leopard doesn't change its spots."

He had to admit that he never pictured her as the straitlaced-librarian type. Theo always thought Dani would be some sort of recreation guide or a travel writer. Something that gave her independence and adventure. Sitting behind the counter at their hometown library wasn't something he ever imagined for her. Not Dani, high school daredevil.

"I'm glad to see library sciences didn't change you," he said.

"You're one to talk. You literally stole a boat today. But don't worry. I'll always be a muchacha mala at heart," she said, waggling her brow.

And sending a jolt straight to his cock. He hadn't heard that phrase in years. Not since they were kids and Dani's parents chastised her whenever she got in trouble. But he didn't want to think about Dani being a bad girl. It hit differently now.

He needed to change the subject. Fast.

"You know you could have asked me to translate that," he said.

"You were sleeping."

"Once I got up, smart-ass."

"Yeah, well, *I* couldn't sleep, so I figured I might as well make myself useful. Maybe something that would help Andreas after we leave. Though Duolingo apparently didn't teach me shit. Seriously, did I *really* need to know how to say 'carrot' in Greek?"

Theo snickered. "I think you'd be surprised."

"Well, actually . . . I think *you'll* be the one who is surprised."

He furrowed his brow and ticked his head to the side. "How so?"

"Papantonis. I found a mention." She smiled wide.

His eyes lit up. "Really?!" he asked. "Where? What did you find?" he asked.

"Here's what I have so far," she said, handing over a piece of paper.

Theo reached over for the paper, but it was too dark to read, so he walked the three feet over to the lamp, resting his backside on the desk beside Dani. He read over her translation:

> *Demetrios Papantonis birthplace unknown.*
> *Born fishing village Attica coast. Lived Crete*
> *years return mainland Athens.*

"Is this it?" he asked, flipping the page over to double-check she hadn't written anything on the back side.

Dani snatched the paper. "Yes, that's it. You try translating a book in a language you can't speak with nothing but this," she said, waving a pocket-size Greek phrase book in his face and tossing it back on the table.

"And you were able to get all this from that book?" he asked.

"Well"—she shrugged—"I took a few liberties."

"Show me where you got this," he said, pointing to the handwritten words.

She flipped the pages in the library book, then handed it to him. The pages were still damp from their swim through the canal. He read through the passage she'd translated, and she hadn't done a bad job.

"God, this room is seriously like an oven," she said, reaching her arms up and twisting her long, black hair into a messy bun on the top of her head, magically securing it with a pencil.

He thought that was something they did only in movies. How could a pencil, after all, manage to hold all that hair in one place?

Man, it was hot.

"Is that a prerequisite for all librarians and teachers?" he asked.

"Is what?"

"The pencil-in-the-hair updo? How does it even manage to stay in place?"

"Oh this?" she asked, pointing to her head. "It's easy. See?"

She pulled the pencil out of the bun like a knight unsheathing his blade, then shook her head, letting her shiny, silky hair cascade to her shoulders. It was hands down the sexiest thing Theo had ever witnessed.

Fuck me now.

She repeated the motions to twist her hair back into a bun, leaving wispy tendrils of hair floating on her neck. He glanced over at her face, noticing her eyes focused on his boxer briefs.

So maybe her mind was elsewhere, too.

"How was my translation?" she asked.

He blinked a few times to get back to reality and cleared his throat.

"Pretty close. The whole thing says, 'The exact birthplace of Demetrios Papantonis is unknown. It is believed he was born in a fishing village off the Attica coast. He lived on Crete for many years before returning to the mainland and living out his days in present-day Athens.' So the name of the fishing village wasn't Attica—it is referring to the entire coast."

"Well, that could be any number of villages," Dani pointed out. "Here, let me grab a map."

He went back into the main room and grabbed his satchel, then made his way back.

Theo unfolded the map on the desk, smoothing it out with his hand and leaning over as she sat on the chair beside him.

"Here's the coastline," he said, running his finger along an area on the map about two inches long, pinpointing the Attica coast.

"Well, that really narrows it down," Dani said, sarcastically. "Shall we stop house by house and ask if anyone knows where Demetrios Papantonis was born?"

"Fuck," Theo said, standing straight and pacing in the small open area with his hands resting atop his head. "This is impossible."

"No, we're just missing something," Dani said. "Do you have that translation from the Papantonis journal? The one about the resting place of the Minotaur?"

"Yeah, let me grab it," he said, reaching down and digging his notebook out of his satchel. "Here," he said, handing it to her.

She took the notebook and read through his scribblings, running her finger along his handwriting. He'd always loved watching her read. It was like he could see the wheels turning in her mind.

Her brow started to wrinkle, and she pulled the notebook closer to her face.

"Need to borrow my glasses?" he joked.

But she waved him off, then grabbed the map, bringing it up to her face, trading her attention back and forth between the notebook and the map, before setting the notebook down and giving her full attention to the map.

"What do you see—" he started, but she reached out her hand to stop him, placing it on his stomach mere inches above the waistband of his boxer briefs.

He flinched at her touch, and she quickly pulled her hand away.

"Sorry," she said.

He wasn't. He wanted to take her palm and place it back on his stomach. Let her explore his body. Climb atop her and slide between her legs, planting soft kisses along her neck.

"I didn't mean to startle you. But I think I may have an idea. Listen," she said, sitting up. "Papantonis said: 'We've reached the gateway to the sea with the eye of the Minotaur . . . From here, we will travel back to my home. There, below where Helios rises in the east, I will put the eye to rest, accessible only to those who recognize its power. Despite his quarrels, Poseidon himself could not have picked a better place for this beast to spend eternity. It is here that the eye will sleep and blend into the dirt itself, watching over the land of my ancestors and bringing strength and fertility to my people.'"

"Yeah, I remember," Theo said. "We already knew that, but it doesn't say *where* his home was."

"No, but what about this?" she said, pointing to a place on the map.

He looked at her finger, then up at her face. "I don't get it."

"The Temple of Poseidon. It's right here along the coast. 'Poseidon himself could not have picked a better place'? What if the resting place is there? At the temple?"

Theo furrowed his brow. "Someone would have found it by now if it was there," he said.

Dani frowned. "Really? Then how do you explain that Lost Moon City they found last year, or whatever it was called?

Discoveries have been made in the last five years. There are still so many places left out there to find. Why not this?"

She was right. Even some of his own discoveries had been there for hundreds of years before being unearthed. The eye of the Minotaur could be no different.

"All right, you might be onto something," he said. "I can't believe you found this. Pretty badass, Juicy."

"Thanks," she said, clearly proud of herself. "I guess we can let Andreas know in the morning before we leave in case he wants to check it out." With that, she refolded the map and closed the book.

Right. In case *Andreas* wants to check it out.

Damn, how he wished he could explore it himself. Unless . . .

Dani shifted in the chair to get up, and then noticed Theo not moving. "What?" she asked, though she quickly caught on. "No, Theo. We can't go with him. We're going to the embassy tomorrow. You promised."

"I know, I know," he said, waving his hands. "We're going home."

She stared at him, and then it hit her. "You don't *want* to leave," she said.

He flashed his eyes to hers, then quickly made a face. "Don't be ridiculous. Of course I want to leave."

"No, you don't. You want to find the eye. That's it, isn't it? Now that we've got a lead, you're curious. You actually think it's out there."

He stared at her, fighting for the right words, when he finally blurted out, "Fine. Yes, I think you might be onto something. Maybe there *is* something at Poseidon's temple," he said. "Do you know what a discovery like this could mean? This is the kind of shit archaeologists dream of."

She looked at her translation again, considering their options, then back at Theo.

"Okay, but what if there isn't anything up there? Then what?" she asked.

"You *just* spent five minutes convincing me that it could be there, and *now* you're trying to convince me that you're wrong?"

"Yeah, but that doesn't mean it's there for *us* to discover," she said, motioning her hands back and forth between their bodies. "Do I need to remind you about Maurice and Louis? They're still out there. And if you don't remember, you kicked Maurice in the face. Something tells me he's not going to let that slide."

"Don't you think they would have found us by now? For all we know, them finding us at the library might have been a coincidence."

"Oh, so now *you're* all about the coincidences." She crossed her arms and looked away from him.

He kneeled in front of her and spun the chair so she faced him. "Aren't you even just a *little* curious?" he asked.

"What are you doing? Are you literally begging me?" She scowled at him.

"No, Juicy. I made a promise, and I will keep it if that's what you want. But I'm asking, aren't you curious?"

Her mouth twisted as if biting back the words. "Of course I'm curious. But I also like being alive."

"So do I. And I never feel more alive than when I'm with you."

Her lips opened to form a large O, and she shook her head while smiling incredulously. "Oh, you're good."

"It's the truth."

And it was. Dani literally brought him back to life.

"Do you say things like that to all the girls, Dr. Galanis?"

A guttural sound unwillingly escaped his throat upon hearing her say his name like that again. "Only you."

A delightfully devious sense of satisfaction washed over her face. He swallowed.

"You're not just saying sweet things like that trying to get into my panties, are you, Dr. Galanis?" She opened her legs wider, and with those short shorts, he could see said panties.

"I don't think I've been keeping any secret about wanting to get in your panties today," he said, trying to stay focused on her eyes despite her apex being at *his* eye level, "but no, I'm not only saying those things for that reason. I meant what I said."

She bit her lip and stared at him, the wheels clearly turning in her brain. But he didn't move. He stayed in his position of worship, because that was what she deserved.

"Fine, we'll check out the temple," she said, but then put up her finger, "but under one condition."

"And what's that?"

"If at any time I get a bad feeling, we leave. No questions. No more promises. No more getting on your knees and *not* begging. And if we have any other encounters with Maurice and Louis, we're out of here."

"That sounds to me like *five* conditions, Juicy," he said, taking her hand in his and lifting up the rest of her fingers. He then threaded his fingers through hers, and they each stared at their hands weaving together. God, he wanted to touch her.

"Then we have a deal," she said.

There wasn't nearly enough space between the two of them. Especially with the way his cock started to expand.

"You know, I might not be a Good Greek Girl, but I can be a good girl," she said.

Fuck me now.

"I thought you were a muchacha mala," he said, suggestively.

"I can be whatever you like, Dr. Galanis," she said with hooded eyes.

He swallowed hard.

"Do you like it when I call you that?" she asked, wrapping her legs around his shoulders and pulling herself closer.

"Ye . . . yes." The words came out in a garbled, choking sound.

"Do you want me to be a good girl or a bad girl?"

She relaxed her legs and brought one in between them, grazing his crotch with the top of her foot, and he licked his lips.

"What's the difference?" he asked.

"Well," she said, slowly leaning over and reaching down. Her hand cupped his cock, stroking it over the fabric of his boxers as her other hand reached up to his neck, pulling him closer as she placed kisses along his skin.

"A good girl will do whatever you want," she said in between kisses. "A *bad* girl will do whatever *I* want."

"I want . . ." he said, panting, "I want my face between your legs."

She pushed the chair back, stood up, and gave him a devilish smile. "Then I guess I'm going to have to be a bad girl, because *I* want your cock in my mouth. Stand up."

He did as he was told. Once he was at her level, she pulled down his boxers, springing free his erection. She then took his length firmly in her hand, stroking him several times before lowering to the floor.

"Wait," he said, stopping her before she put him in her mouth.

Her eyes widened, like she was worried. "What's wrong?"

"Nothing's wrong. I want to kiss you first," he said while smiling. Because, God, he wanted to kiss her so fucking badly.

"Please tell me you're not one of those guys who gets weird about kissing a girl after she goes down on him, are you?"

He laughed, cupping her face in his hands. "No. I'll kiss you anytime, anywhere. But I've been thinking about kissing you again all day, and it's going to kill me if I need to wait, even if that's in exchange for a blow job."

"Interesting," she said, smirking, "I've never met a guy who'd exchange a blow job for a kiss."

"I mean, to be clear, Juicy, I'd still like both," he said, smiling. "But I *really* want to kiss you. So are you going to be a good girl for me?"

Dani smiled, then rose to her feet and stood on her tippytoes with both of her hands on his pecs.

"Good girl," he said before crashing his lips to hers and pulling her body against him by grabbing hold of her ass. He took her in his mouth, unable to get enough. These kisses that he'd imagined for so many years more than lived up to the hype created in his head.

His hands skimmed along her body as his mouth worked its way around her lips, skating between her skin and her waistband, diving beneath her panties and right in between her legs. She sucked in a breath as his fingers found her clit, already slippery and begging to be touched.

"My God, Juicy, your nickname certainly carries a whole new meaning now," he said against her mouth, twisting her lips between his.

"You'll never be able to look at me the same again," she said with humor in her voice.

"That was already going to be questionable after this morning. Fuck, I want to taste you."

"Uh-uh," she said, backing away and kneeling again to grasp his erection. "Me first."

She ran her tongue along the length of the underside of his cock, and he had to lean back and grip the desk so as not to fall over. Once she reached the tip, she circled the cockhead with her tongue, tasting his precum, and pressing her lips together.

"Mmm."

Then, without any hesitation, she took him fully in her mouth. Theo sucked in a deep breath, fighting not to let out the world's loudest moan. She wrapped one hand around his dick, moving it in sync with her mouth, as her other hand cupped his balls.

"Oh fuck."

She reached up and pulled out the pencil, letting her locks cascade around her shoulders while staring up at him with those big, beautiful brown eyes. He brushed both of his hands through her hair, careful not to restrict her movements. As he looked at her, his mind ran through all the times that he'd envisioned this exact experience.

Real life was better.

A thousand tiny goose bumps spread over his body, and she increased her speed. With it, he edged closer to orgasming. For a fraction of a second, he thought to apologize for coming so quickly, but fuck that. She felt so fucking good. There was nothing to apologize for.

"I'm going to come," he said. But she didn't stop, letting him come in her mouth as he shuddered with pleasure.

She then stood up and smiled, and he pulled her in for a kiss, tasting himself on her.

But he wasn't done.

He pushed off the desk and spun her around, his mouth still on hers. Then, he picked her up, placing her ass on the desk, and then he backed away. First, he lifted her tank top, revealing her perfectly round breasts, which for an instant made him reconsider whether the side-boob was the best part or if the entire thing was perfection. It didn't matter, so long as they were Dani's, he was obsessed.

He lowered his mouth to her chest, taking in each of her nipples one at a time, popping them out of his mouth as he moved from one to the next. He twirled his tongue around her hard buds as she dug her fingernails into his hair and wrapped her legs around his back.

"It's too bad the bed is so tiny," he said.

"Why is that?"

"Because I desperately want to fuck you," he said against her taut nipple.

"We don't need a big bed for that."

"No, but the first time I fuck you isn't going to be in a bed that's going to remind me of my parents' house or pressed against a rickety old desk. It's either going to be the proper way in a proper bed or in a library."

She grinned and playfully pushed his abdomen. "I told you, Theo, that's sacrilege."

"No," he said, bringing his hands to her booty shorts and lifting her ass to pull them off, "you said you wanted to get railed in a library. And I'm going to make that happen."

"You're quite confident, aren't you, Dr. Galanis?"

He smirked then brought his index finger up to her lips. "Suck," he commanded.

With her eyes wide open, she put his finger in her mouth then took her time, drawing it out. He then did the same, and then brought his finger down to her opening, sliding his wet finger along the slit. She whimpered as he teased her.

"Tell me what you want," he said.

"I . . . I . . ." she strained, "I want you to put your finger in me."

He did as she said, and she clenched around his digit.

"And what else?" he asked as he pumped his finger in and out of her.

"I want you to lick my pussy."

"We'll get to that in a moment," he said, picking up speed. "And what else?"

"And . . . and . . ." She was breathless, her body trembling as he plunged another finger into her and massaged her clit with his thumb.

"Say it. What do you want?"

"I . . . I want you to fuck me in a library."

"Say it again."

"I want you to fuck me in a library, Dr. Galanis."

He almost came again hearing those greedy, desirous words coming from her lips. But instead, he removed his fingers and kneeled in front of the desk, pulling her core to the edge.

"So then to answer your earlier question," he said, planting kisses on the insides of her thighs, continuing to tease her, "yes. I'm *extremely* confident."

His mouth dove to her opening, drawing his wet, hot tongue across her length in one long drag. She tossed her head back and moaned, sweet, delicious moans that he'd never forget. It satisfied him to satisfy her. Hearing her calling his name while she ground her pussy against his face. He took her clit between his lips, sucking on her tender nub, then rapidly flicked it with his tongue over and over before thrusting his fingers back in.

Her sweet, juicy liquid ran down his arm, but he didn't stop. She was close. He could feel it as she clenched around him.

"Oh God, Theo. You're going to make me come. Don't stop! Don't stop!"

As if he had any intention of doing so.

Her entire body convulsed around him, and she traded her hands from digging into his hair to holding herself against the wall behind her. Once her body stopped shuddering, he removed his fingers and planted one final kiss inside her thigh and then he sat back, resting his back against the wall as she stared down at him from the desk.

"That was . . ." she said, breathless.

"Yeah."

"We've got to get out of this mess."

"Yeah, we do."

"Because I'm not going to die here without you fucking me in a library."

CHAPTER Twenty

Dani

DR. THEO GALANIS WAS GOD'S GIFT.

When the fuck did he learn how to do *that*? To know she'd spent countless hours with a man that talented and wasn't on the receiving end of his *extremely* skilled mouth every day was really a damn shame. But she didn't intend to miss out on it ever again.

Dani studied Theo from across the table as he went over the plan with Andreas and Christos, pointing out the locations on the map the next morning. It was originally her plan, so she probably should have been participating, but after everything that happened last night, she couldn't focus on anything but Theo's dick.

Once they'd made it back to the twin bed, it took all her efforts to keep from saying to hell with the library-fucking plan and fuck right there. But instead, they stayed up most of the night kissing and getting each other off in other ways. Over and over.

And over.

Her body couldn't be satiated. Not that her orgasms weren't mind-blowing. Each one felt as intense as the last and incredibly satisfying. But she still wanted more. She wanted Theo. She knew she wouldn't be sated until she felt him inside her. All of him.

She sipped on her coffee, unable to take her eyes off Theo.

So fucking hot.

"What was that?" Andreas asked her.

Dani's attention came into focus, and she found all three men staring at her. *Oh shit. Did I say that out loud?*

"Nothing," she said. "Sorry, I didn't get much sleep last night. It was so fucking hot."

She glanced at Theo, and he shifted in his seat, giving her the most sinful of looks. He then took a bite of his cream-and-phyllo breakfast pastry and licked his finger, his eyes not looking away for even a second.

"Great. Let me go make a few calls to see if I can get special access to the temple. Wait here," Andreas said, getting up from the table and walking away.

"Andreas really knows everyone, doesn't he?" Dani asked Christos.

He laughed. "You have no idea. You can't go anywhere with him without him seeing at least one person he knows. And *everyone* who's anybody in Greek archaeology knows his name, especially in Athens."

"He sounds like you, but in Greece," Dani said, nudging Theo in the side.

"I don't know, I doubt I have the same kind of sway that Andreas seems to have," Theo said.

"Don't sell yourself short. Hey, remember that time you got us into that early screening of the *Clash of the Titans* remake?" she asked.

Theo laughed and then shook his head. "My uncle owned that theater, you know," he said. "You teasing me?"

"I swear I'm not," Dani said. "I'm being a *good* girl, I promise."

Theo smirked and mouthed, *You're bad.*

She shouldn't be so turned on with Christos sitting right there, but, fuck, she couldn't wait until they were alone again.

Andreas returned. "Good news," he announced, putting his hands on the back of the chair and leaning over. "I've arranged for us to stay after sunset once the site is closed to the public."

"Why don't we go now?" Dani asked.

"Because if we go now, we'll be limited to the public areas. But I have a friend who owes me a favor and will let us into the roped-off areas once the tourists have gone," Andreas explained.

Christos looked at his watch. "What should we do until then?"

"Well, we could go to Sounio Beach. Have some lunch. Enjoy the crystal-blue waters of the gulf. It's located down the hill from the temple," Andreas said.

"We don't have swimming suits," Dani said.

"Then we'll stop on the way and get some. We need to pick up some flashlights, anyway," Andreas said. "Come on, let's go."

They drove a few hours out of town, heading south toward Sounio, making a quick pit stop at a touristy beach shop to pick up swimsuits and a few other items for the evening. Eventually, the Temple of Poseidon appeared in the distance on Cape Sounion, sitting atop a cliff a few hundred feet above the sea, a stone's throw from the beach. A row of columns, similar to that of the Parthenon but smaller, made up the structure, although it was clear that part of it had collapsed over the years.

"So what was the purpose of this temple?" Dani asked as they drove through the town, winding down the hill toward the beach.

Theo and Andreas started speaking at the same time. Dani noticed the two of them looking at each other in the rearview mirror.

"Go ahead," Theo said.

"No, after you. I insist," Andreas responded.

How things had changed over the last two days.

"Poseidon, the god of the sea, was Zeus's brother," Theo explained. "In ancient times, many believed that storms and trouble at sea were displays of Poseidon's wrath and ire, so the temple was built to honor him."

"They said this is where Theseus's ship sailed to after his return from Crete and his slaying of the Minotaur," Andreas then called out. "Have you heard the story?"

"I'm not sure," Dani said, assuming he was speaking to her since Theo would have clearly known the story.

"Well, Theseus, son of Aegeus, king of Athens, was returning home and was supposed to display a white sail on his ship to signify his safe return. But when he forgot to change the sail, Aegeus thought Theseus had died and flung himself into the sea in despair. It's how the Aegean Sea got its name."

"He killed himself without confirming the truth? Doesn't sound like a very wise king. Maybe the Athenians were better off without him," Dani said.

"Brutal, Juicy," Theo said.

"Sorry," she said, shrugging with a smile.

"It's also thought that this was a place for cult worship," Andreas said.

"Well, that would make sense, then, if there were people who worshiped the Minotaur," Dani said. "Perhaps this is where they came."

She thought back to the clay vessel she saw in the museum in

Crete of the man holding the Minotaur's head outside a cave. Though in that piece, the structure with columns perched above the cave.

"Are there any caves around here?" Dani asked.

"No, I don't think so," Andreas answered. "Why do you ask?"

Hmm.

"Just curious."

"Well, we're here," Andreas said, parking the car.

They grabbed their bags and headed toward the beach where Andreas had already made reservations for sunbeds right at the edge of the water. They changed into their swimsuits and settled in for the day, sitting side by side. Thankfully, the swimsuit she found at the shop was much more modest than the one she'd worn at Vautour's, despite this one being an actual two-piece. The white bikini wasn't anything special, but it provided full coverage. And she certainly wasn't mad about the option Theo had picked out—*very* short board shorts that did little to hide the size of his cock.

Dani stared out at the clear water, listening to the waves and people laughing and enjoying their day. Christos sat nearby, working on his tan. Andreas was somewhere at the bar, trying to woo some chick. Theo sat beside Dani, reading out of Andreas's leather journal. If you didn't know any better, they would seem like regular people having an ordinary day at the beach. The whole thing was surreal.

"What are you reading about?" she asked, turning over on her side to look at him.

"More about the Minotaur's Children."

"Anything interesting?"

"Not much. Mostly that whenever Andreas found a lead, such as a marking or a reference, the next time he would go to the same place, it would be gone. They clearly don't want to be found . . . or the eye, for that matter."

"Kind of a gross name—the Minotaur's Children. You know, with the whole bestiality component, don't you think?"

Theo laughed. "I suppose so. Hadn't really thought of it, to be honest."

"Are you serious?" Dani said, making a face. "That was the first thing I thought when I heard the name."

"That's because you've got a dirty mind."

"You like it," Dani said, sticking her tongue out at him.

"Yeah, I do," he said, grinning.

Dani leaned back, satisfied with herself.

"You don't think people were having sex with the Minotaur, do you?" she asked. Because if they were, yuck.

"I doubt it. Greek myths don't really shy away from talking about sex, and there's no mention of people having sex with the Minotaur."

"Unless," Dani said, excitedly rolling over on the daybed, "the Minotaur's Children had those references erased!"

He chuckled. "Unless that. Who knows? You could be right."

She settled onto her side again and tucked her hands under her head as she stared at Theo. He looked so sexy lying there, reading. Watching him was one of her favorite pastimes, though it was much better with him in beach attire sans shirt.

She missed this. She missed *him*. Just being with him.

"Tell me the story of the Minotaur," she said.

"You've heard it."

"I know. But I like hearing you tell it."

"Well," he said, closing the book and turning slightly to face her, "King Minos had prayed to Poseidon for a beautiful white bull, which Minos was then supposed to sacrifice to Poseidon.

But he didn't. So as a punishment, Poseidon and Aphrodite arranged for Minos's wife, Pasiphae, to fall in love with the bull. Pasiphae then had Daedalus, Minos's craftsman, build a wooden cow contraption so she could have sex with the bull."

Dani's eyebrow raised. "You're joking! I don't remember him building a Trojan *bull*!"

Theo shook his head. "I'm afraid not. After she gave birth to the half man, half bull, Minos had Daedalus construct a labyrinth beneath the palace to keep the Minotaur. Later, after the death of Minos's son in Athens, King Aegeus would send seven young men and seven young women to Crete to be sacrificed to the Minotaur. If they made it out of the labyrinth, they would be free. But no one made it out. Not until Theseus came around."

"And who was Theseus again? The guy with the sail?"

"Right. King Aegeus's son. Theseus had set out on a mission to complete a series of dangerous tasks. The defeat of the Minotaur was his final task. And when he arrived on Crete, Minos's daughter, Ariadne, fell in love with him at first sight, and she offered to help him through the labyrinth by giving him a spool of thread that he could use to find his way back out of the maze after slaughtering the Minotaur."

"What happened to her?"

"He abandoned her on the island of Naxos when she was sleeping."

"Wow, Theseus was a dick."

"Or a prince used to being admired and adored."

Funny, because Dani was admiring Theo as he talked. He knew these stories as if he'd written them himself. Knowing all the ins and outs. All of the people involved. It was cute.

"What?" he asked. "Why are you looking at me like that?"

"I think it's sexy when you turn into a Greek geek."

"Oh yeah?"

"Mm-hmm. I'm thinking we might need to get into the water so I can get you hard and then get myself off by rubbing my clit on your cock."

"Fuck, Juicy," he said, sitting up and immediately crossing his hands over his crotch. "You can't say shit like that in public."

"Why not?"

"Because in about ten seconds I'm not going to be able to stand up without an obvious erection."

"Then you'd better catch me!"

Dani hopped up and ran toward the water. Theo wasn't far behind her, though. She screamed playfully as she swam to keep him from catching her too soon, but he tackled her in the water, spinning her around so she straddled his waist. They bobbed up and down in the chest-deep water. She kissed him, already feeling him go hard below her ass. God, what she wouldn't give to fuck him in the ocean right now.

"I bought condoms," she said, wrapping her arms around his shoulders and feeling very proud of herself for thinking ahead when they were at the beach shop.

He laughed. "Where did you get condoms?"

"From the gift shop."

"How? Did you steal them?"

"Hey, I may not follow the rules all the time, but I'm no thief!" she said. "Aside from that library book."

"Then how did you get them with Andreas paying?"

"I stood behind him and then flashed the box at the cashier, pointing and mouthing 'These, too.'"

Now Theo was laughing so hard his voice echoed throughout the beach area.

"Don't blame me. You Greeks are a horny bunch. I mean, did you see all the wooden dick keychains and whatnot?"

"You have *no* idea how horny we are," he said in that low, gravelly voice that made it sound like he was ready to rip her clothes off at any minute.

She fucking loved that voice.

She ground her hips against his erection. "I don't know. I think I have a pretty good idea of how horny you are."

He closed his eyes and then buried his face in her neck. "Juicy, you have no idea how fucking badly I want you right now."

"Again, I think I have a pretty good idea," she said, wiggling her hips.

"No. You have *no* idea how long I've wanted this."

What was he saying? He pulled back his face to look at her, scanning her face. Waiting for her to say something. Anything.

But after he rejected her before, she wasn't going to be the one to put herself out there first. Not this time.

"So what's the plan, here?" she asked, changing the subject. "Like Pierre told us. Always have a plan B. What happens if we get up there and it's a bust?"

"Then that's it," he continued. "We head home."

"That's only because you want to check fucking in the library off of your sexual bucket list, too."

He smiled. "Not gonna lie, Juicy, that's a huge motivating factor."

Good.

"So that's the plan, then. If we get up there and can't find anything, we're on the first plane out of here. Deal?"

"You forgot library fucking," she said.

"That goes without saying," he said, winking.

"Theo! Daniela!" Andreas called from the beach, waving them back. "We've got food!"

"This is so weird, isn't it?" Dani asked as they started wading back to the chairs. "Like days ago we were being held hostage by criminals who were forcing us to search for the eye, and now we're at a beach resort chilling and eating with someone who *might* be your cousin, and willingly still on a quest for that same artifact."

"Well, if you hadn't come along, I'd still be playing in the sandbox at Knossos. Andreas and I may be the archaeologists, but you're the one who's piecing together the puzzle."

She blushed. "Guess you can say I'm the better half."

"Juicy, you've always been my better half."

He pulled her in for a quick kiss, then released her body and started swimming to the beach.

CHAPTER Twenty-One

Theo

HE WANTED *HER*. THAT'S WHAT HE SHOULD HAVE SAID.

But after opening the door only for her to so quickly shut it, he froze. She didn't seem interested in talking about it. So as they drove up to the Temple of Poseidon he decided any discussion about what was going on between them would have to wait for another day.

He'd been to the temple before. He'd been many times, actually. And each time was as intriguing as the last. Though this would be the first time that he'd be staying after it closed.

The sun had started to set, casting an orange-yellow glow over the entire sea. They walked up to the ticket booth, and the man sitting at the desk leaned out the window to give Andreas a hug.

Seriously. He knew *everyone*.

"Go on and head in," the man said. "I'll be around shortly to tell people that they need to leave. But you can stay when I do that. Wait to cross any of the ropes until everyone else is gone, though. I don't want to get fired."

"Of course," Andreas said.

They walked up the path toward the temple. There were still many visitors, all hoping to catch sunset at the temple. A must-see for any Greek tourist. A must-see for Theo, as well. In all his many visits to Greece, Theo tried to make a sunset stop at the Temple of Poseidon a habit. And on more than one occasion when he made this stop, he thought about Dani while he did so, wondering what she was doing, where she was, what it would be like if she were there with him. Never in his life would he have imagined that she would finally be here with him in this very spot.

He didn't know what they'd be looking for. He'd skimmed through Andreas's diary, but he hadn't found any more clues. They'd have to hunt for it.

They scoured the temple. Looking at the stones from the public side of the ropes. Checking to see if there were any markings or other differentiations that would tell them that there was something there. They walked across all the grounds. Inspecting each spot in case there was something that they'd missed. But there was nothing.

Theo started to worry. They needed these people to leave so they could cross the ropes and look around the marble temple.

Eventually, the sun had set, and the remaining visitors made their way to the exit. Once the coast was clear, they turned on their flashlights and broke past the barrier.

"Let's split up. Everyone take a side, and I'll take the top," Theo instructed. "Take your time. Look for anything out of the ordinary."

Slowly, they walked the length of the temple, shining their

lights on the stone. As Dani, Christos, and Andreas each took an edge of the temple, Theo scoured the platform on top inch by inch. He poked and prodded the stones, searching for trap doors or stones out of place. The wind picked up, casting a chilly breeze over the site. But after an hour . . . two hours . . . three . . . the likelihood that the site would prove fruitful was starting to fade.

What was he thinking? Dani had been right. They'd had a chance to leave, and they should have taken it. But there he was, dreaming of fairy tales and myths, all the things that his parents had told him to let go of. It was time to grow up.

He'd been writing these stories for so long that he started to think that maybe, maybe those stories could be real. Maybe that could be his life, the Indiana Jones type. The hero. Saving the damsel in distress from bad guys. Searching for lost treasures. Confirming myths were actual realities.

It sounded pretty childish when he thought about it. The worst part about it was that he had chastised Dani earlier because she hadn't left when she had the opportunity to do so. Yet there he was putting both of their lives at risk. Sure, he may have meant it when he said that he didn't want to put her at risk anymore, but actions spoke louder than words.

The truth of the matter was that he wasn't Indiana Jones. And this wasn't a fun search for lost treasure. This was dangerous.

God, what Dani must think of him right now.

"Hey, what's wrong?" Dani asked.

Shit, where did she come from? "What do you mean?"

"You look worried. You walked off and have been pacing in the same spot for the last fifteen minutes."

Theo looked up at his surroundings, not having realized that he'd stepped away from the temple.

"I've been thinking."

"Obviously," she said, playfully rolling her eyes. "Thinking about what?"

"That maybe you were right," he said. "I was being stupid." He kicked a rock at his feet.

"Hey, don't do that," she said, placing her hands on his shoulders and forcing him to look at her. "We *both* thought something might be here. And don't you go trying to steal credit. I'm the one who suggested Poseidon's temple, remember?" She flashed him an unfairly endearing smile.

"I know, I just wanted to do something really cool for once. Show everyone that myths and fairy tales aren't dead."

"You mean, show your parents."

"I suppose them, too. But, I don't know, it was cool thinking there might actually be the eye of the Minotaur buried somewhere on this site."

"Well, we don't know yet that it isn't."

He tilted his head and gave her a skeptical look. "We've been here for hours."

"We're also searching in the dark. Come on, read me the entry from Papantonis's journal again."

They walked over to his bag, and he pulled out his notebook where he'd transcribed the letters, flipping through the pages until he found the right one. Andreas and Christos joined them as he looked.

"Here it is," he said. "'We've reached the gateway to the sea with the eye of the Minotaur, it no longer being safe in its original burial place. Its power grows restless and must be released from confinement. Now its true potential will be realized, and it will be free.

"'From here, we will travel back to my home. There, below

where Helios rises in the east, I will put the eye to rest, accessible only to those who recognize its power. Despite his quarrels, Poseidon himself could not have picked a better place for this beast to spend eternity. It is here that the eye will sleep and blend into the dirt itself, watching over the land of my ancestors and bringing strength and fertility to my people.'"

"Hmm . . ." Dani murmured, folding her arms and pacing. The moonlight cast a glow across her skin. Theo loved when she made this face, her deep-in-thought face.

"So we're here because this is near Papantonis's birthplace and the reference to Poseidon," she said, tapping her finger on her chin. "But we must be missing something. What about the reference to Helios? Who is Helios—like the sun?"

"Basically. He's the god of the sun."

"Well, that's weird, because doesn't the sun rise in the east everywhere? What about this place would be unique to that?"

"Do you think it could have something to do with where the sun rises and where the light hits the temple?"

"Possibly? It would mean we'd have to come back in the morning."

"Unless we have his birthplace wrong."

"But then what about Poseidon?"

He opened his mouth to say something about the possible birthplace when suddenly he was blinded by a bright white light. The four of them shielded their eyes as a dark figure moved toward them.

"What the . . . ?" he said, taking Dani's hand and pulling her back from the figure. But when they turned around to run, there were more figures in hooded black cloaks, closing in on them.

"Fuck, fuck, fuck," Christos said. "What have you gotten us into, Andreas?"

"Me?" Andreas said, putting his hand to his chest.

Theo's heart pounded as Dani clung to his arm. The four of them were ushered up the stairs to the top of the temple while the cloaked figures surrounded them, shining lights on them from all directions.

"Who are you?" Dani called out with a shaky voice.

"Τα Παιδιά του Μινώταυρου."

The Minotaur's Children.

• • • • • • • • • •

THE NEXT HOUR WAS A BLUR. THE FOUR OF THEM CRAMMED INTO A van without windows with two cloaked figures guarding the door. Despite a barrage of demands and questions from Christos and Andreas, the figures didn't speak. Theo didn't even bother trying to get answers. His only focus was on Dani.

He wrapped one arm around her, and with his other hand he held her hands. He could feel her trembling, though she kept a stony face. He wanted to tell her it would be okay, but being ushered into a windowless van didn't exactly instill confidence.

Finally, the van stopped, and the engine turned off. Theo's heart pounded, but he tried to stay strong for Dani. When the doors finally opened, the cloaked figures ushered them out. And there, right in front of them, was one of the grandest estates he'd ever seen in all of Greece.

All four of them lined up in a row, staring at the house, a modern multilevel estate spanning what felt like the length of an entire football field. The building was all clean lines and angles, something he'd picture in a Sotheby's International luxury real estate magazine. The large windows at the entrance allowed them to see through the center of the house to a view of the sea. They were perched somewhere high above the Aegean, but Theo couldn't quite place it. If he had to guess, they were somewhere between Poseidon's temple and Athens.

"I wonder who lives here," Christos said.

"Something tells me we're about to find out," Theo said.

One of the cloaked figures led the way, taking them through a maze of rooms and winding their way downstairs until they finally came to a large set of double doors with an emblem of the eye and the μ. They all looked at one another, unsure of what lay before them on the other side.

Theo was both frightened and fascinated as one of the cloaked figures pushed open the doors in the center and motioned for them to enter.

On the other side of the doors was a large room overlooking the sea with a swimming pool outside. There were low meandering walls built into the floor, twisting and winding in random patterns with benches and chaises at various dead ends and one larger open area in the center with a single bench. Sitting atop the center bench was another cloaked figure, though this one a man with the hood off.

"Welcome," he said, motioning for them to come closer.

Dani held on to Theo's hand tight as they all made their way toward the center of the room like Dorothy and her friends in *The Wizard of Oz*.

"What is this place?" Andreas asked, looking around the room, running his hand along the walls.

"This is the Labyrinth. I take it, you have not heard of it, Dr. Demetrious?"

"You know who I am?" Andreas asked.

"I know who all of you are. An interesting cast of characters.

Dr. Andreas Demetrious, archaeologist at the National Archaeological Museum. Christos Samara, food purveyor and cousin to Dr. Demetrious. Daniela Guiterrez, American librarian. And Dr. Theo Galanis, the dead Greek American archaeologist. Except it seems, maybe not *all* dead."

"But *how* do you know who we are?" Andreas asked.

"I make it my business to know who might be searching for the eye of the Minotaur," the man said.

"And who are you, exactly?" Theo interrupted. "You seem to know all about us, but you haven't introduced yourself."

"You can call me ιερέας."

"Priest," Theo said.

"That is correct."

"And what are we doing here? Where are we even?"

"Like I said, I make it my business to know who might be searching for the eye. I'd heard about your incident yesterday at the National Library. We, the Minotaur's Children, are very protective of our father. We can't have anyone searching the grounds at Poseidon's temple after hours."

"So then you know where it is?" Andreas asked.

"Where what is?"

"The eye."

The priest laughed. "Oh no. That's a myth."

Dani and Theo looked at each other, confused, and then looked back at the priest.

"I'm sorry, what is it exactly that the Minotaur's Children are worshiping then?" Dani asked.

"We celebrate the strength and virility of the Minotaur," the priest said, smiling almost with adoration.

The *virility* of the Minotaur? They were celebrating the lovemaking between Pasiphae and the bull? Theo scanned the room, and the benches and chaises took on a whole new light.

"The Minotaur's Children . . . is a *sex* cult?" Theo asked.

The priest looked mortified. "Oh goodness, no," he said, holding his hand to his chest as he started laughing. "Is that what you were thinking?"

"Um . . . yeah. You haven't exactly told us who you are or what we're doing here," Theo said. "Virility? I mean, come on. Did the Minotaur even *have* any children? Not to mention this place. This is like a swingers' paradise," he said, motioning to the furnishings.

He'd heard some far-fetched ideas in his years, but most of those remained in the mythology books.

"We are a society who seeks to protect the truth of the Minotaur. Descendants of Theseus, who harnessed its true strength."

Andreas laughed. "So, in other words, you can't have Demetrios Papantonis taking the glory from Theseus, is that right?"

"Demetrios Papantonis was nothing but a storyteller," the priest said.

"Cool," Dani chimed in. "I'm sorry, but why did you bring us here?"

Leave it to her to cut out the bullshit.

"There's nothing out there," the priest said, standing from the bench. "I'm saving you the trouble of wasting more time than you already have searching for a nonexistent relic. Trust me, we've looked. The library upstairs is full of just about every writing that even *mentions* the Minotaur. Over the years, the Minotaur's Children have followed every lead. And it seems we eventually came to the same conclusion after studying

Demetrios Papantonis's writings as you did about the Temple of Poseidon. But after countless days and hours searching the temple over the course of years, we've determined that Papantonis's words were nothing but a metaphor. The temple is merely a place for us to worship the *spirit* of the Minotaur."

"Then why remove all evidence that he existed?" Andreas asked.

"Because we needed to protect the sanctity of Theseus. If people thought Theseus had been fooled into letting a powerful gemstone like the eye out of his grasp, he would have lost credibility," the priest explained.

"You were worried about his *credibility*? The man lied and deserted the woman who saved him *on a beach*!" Dani said. "Unbelievable. You could have told us all this back at the temple. You didn't need to scare the shit out of us by tossing us in a shady-ass van and driving us to this house."

"Well, if I'm being honest—" the priest started.

"Please," Dani interrupted. "Honesty would be lovely."

Theo snickered. He hoped she never got rid of that sass.

The priest paused, twisting his mouth. He clearly didn't like it as much. "As I was saying, the way the Minotaur's Children have thrived all these years is by recruiting members. And who better to join our ranks than other Minotaur hunters, men who've found their way to the Temple of Poseidon, searching the grounds for the Minotaur's remains?"

"So, let me get this straight," Andreas said, bringing his hands into a steeple in front of his face and placing his index fingers on the bridge of his nose. "You brought us here to . . . become members?"

"Well, not all of you," the priest said, looking at Dani.

"Why? Because I'm not Greek?"

"No, not that," the priest said.

Dani rolled her eyes. "I bet they don't even acknowledge that Theseus only succeeded because of Ariadne," she said under her breath. Theo couldn't help but chuckle.

"What if we don't want to join your . . ." *Cult*, Theo thought to himself. "Society?"

"The choice is yours. No harm will come to you if you decline."

"What *will* happen to us if we decline?" Theo asked. "Aren't you afraid that we'll tell others what we saw here?"

"Who would believe you? There are few mentions of Demetrios Papantonis in history. Aside from his journal, which has questionable origins, there are *no* mentions of the eye of the Minotaur in *any* historical writings. And no member of the Minotaur's Children will reveal their association, if you're able to discover their identity in the first place. But as a show of good faith, my name is Lysander Stavrou, and I am a member of the Hellenic Parliament.

"To be clear, we gain nothing by letting you go. But you, on the other hand, have much to lose if you reveal what you've learned here today. The Minotaur's Children is full of many powerful people who don't take threats lightly.

"Either way, you are welcome to stay here tonight. I promise, you will be safe. And if you choose to leave, tomorrow, Dr. Galanis, we will arrange for you and Ms. Guiterrez to go back to the United States. I know there are many people who would be delighted to see that you are alive and well," Lysander said.

"I have a connection at the embassy," Andreas said, proudly.

"I know," Lysander said, causing all of them to glance at one another, "but your friend can only speed up the process. Dr. Galanis, Ms. Guiterrez, you'll be *on* the plane tomorrow if you so decide."

A rush of emotions swelled in Theo's chest, and he needed to sit down. Dani helped him to a bench and sat next to him.

"Are you okay?" she asked, putting one hand on his back, the other on his forearm.

Theo let out a breath. "Yeah. It . . . it doesn't feel real."

"Well, we're not home yet, but soon," she said, taking his hand and kissing the back of it.

Thirteen months. It had been thirteen months since he'd left Michigan. And now? Now he'd finally be going home.

"So, have you made a decision?" Lysander asked.

Theo looked at Dani and put his hand on her cheek. "I made a promise," he said to her, and then he turned to Lysander. "We'd like to go home."

Dani squeezed his hand, sending another surge of emotions through him.

Lysander nodded. "And you two?" he asked Andreas and Christos.

Andreas crossed his arms, and Christos confusingly looked him up and down then quickly did the same. "You've spent a lifetime discrediting my family," Andreas said. "Perhaps Demetrios was merely a storyteller, but he was real. You have my word that I won't reveal anything we've heard here, but I also won't pretend he didn't exist. I will keep searching for proof of his life until the day I die. So, no, I will not become a member of the Minotaur's Children."

"What he said," Christos followed up.

"Fair enough. We will show you to your rooms. Please, you are welcome to explore. Do whatever you'd like while you are our guests," Lysander said.

"Do you have a phone we could use?" Theo asked.

"No phones. What happens at the Labyrinth stays at the Labyrinth. But I assure you, in the morning we will plan your reappearance into society. We can go to the press first. Or the embassy. Or take you straight to a telephone. Whatever you prefer."

A man showed up in the doorway to take them to their rooms. They walked down the hall silently, Dani holding on to Theo's arm with her head on his shoulder. One by one, the man dropped them off at their rooms—Andreas, then Christos, and finally Dani and Theo.

"Think we've downgraded to a cot?" Dani asked outside the door.

Theo smiled and thought, *I hope so.* Because he wanted to be as close to Dani as possible.

The door opened, and inside was a sleek, modern bedroom with a low king-size bed, acacia nightstands and dresser, sitting area with a fireplace and mahogany-colored leather chairs, and floor-to-ceiling windows.

Sure beat his living arrangements at the farm with Maurice and Louis.

"If you push this button, the windows will tint, and no one will be able to see in," the man explained, standing at a switch panel on the wall. "And this button lowers the shades. There's a similar panel in the bathroom."

Dani walked around the room, running her hands along the furnishings.

"Are there any clothes we could borrow to sleep in?" she asked. "All we have are these." She held up a bag with her stuff from the beach and pointed at Theo's satchel.

"Of course. You'll find sets of sleeping attire in the bathroom.

They might be a little large for you. We don't often have visitors of your . . . size," the man said.

Read: women.

"If there is anything else you need, please do not hesitate to ask. I'll leave you for now," the man said, giving them a little bow and exiting the room.

Theo blew out a long breath and ran his fingers through his hair.

"How are you feeling?" Dani asked, coming up to him and wrapping her arms around his waist.

"Honestly, I'm still in shock. This is happening, right? I'm not imagining this?"

"No, you're not imagining it," she said, smiling.

"I guess I'm wondering, what if this is all a ruse, too?"

"I suppose we won't really know until the morning. But this feels different than before, no?"

"It feels different," he said. He then smiled and leaned down to kiss her, pulling her up into his arms as she wrapped hers around his neck.

Finally, things felt . . . good.

"Mmm . . ." she murmured once her lips parted from his, "I never get tired of kissing you."

"Yeah?"

"Yeah." She planted another quick kiss on his lips. "I've still got beach on me. Shall we go get clean so that we can get dirty again? That bed is definitely a mattress tostada, not a taco."

"Sure," he said, smiling. "You know what's funny?"

"What's that?" she asked, linking her fingers with his and guiding him to the bathroom.

"I've been in Greece for over a year, sleeping on a mattress on the floor in a one-room cottage with Maurice and Louis, yet in the last week since you got here, I've stayed the night in the two nicest houses I've ever set foot in. Of course, I was being held hostage both times, but still. I mean, have you ever seen a place like this before?"

They entered the bathroom with a wall of windows on two sides and a large bathtub big enough for two in the corner facing out.

"Theo, you seem to forget I haven't seen *anything* before this excursion," she said with a bit of a chuckle. "Um, do you really think no one can see in?" she then asked, motioning toward the windows.

"Here, let's try the switch." He flipped the switch, and the tint of the windows changed slightly, but they could still see out perfectly well.

"I'm not sure I believe people can't see in. What if they're only saying that so they can spy on us when we're naked?"

"Why don't I go down there and see?" he said, wrapping his arms around her from behind and nodding toward the outside area below their room. "I'll give you a thumbs-up if it's opaque and come back."

"Okay. I'll start the water."

He gave her another quick kiss, then left her alone in the bathroom and closed the door. As he was about to exit the bedroom, however, he stopped by her beach bag and dug around for the condoms. There they were. He loved that she was thinking about that when they were in the store. He grabbed a few, putting two in his pocket just in case and another couple in the nightstand so they'd be prepared for later.

Once that was all settled, he made his way outside to the

gardens. He looked up at their room. If Dani was standing there, he couldn't see her. So he gave a thumbs-up and waved, hoping that she saw him. He then turned around, staring out at the sea, feeling a sense of relief for the first time in months. No, it wasn't that. It was something else.

Happiness.

CHAPTER

Twenty-Two

Dani

ONCE THEO GAVE HER THE THUMBS-UP AND SHE'D NEEDLESSLY waved back, Dani stripped off her clothes and climbed into the tub. She wanted to be ready and waiting by the time he returned.

She closed her eyes as she settled into the bath, releasing all the tension and burdens from the last few days. There may still have been danger lurking, but at least they were no longer directly under Pierre's watch.

The warm water enveloped her body, soothing her soul. What a trip. Dani couldn't say her first time out of the country was the *best* experience, but if she'd been given the choice to do it all again with option A being that things would happen exactly as they had—with Vautour, the kidnapping, and all—and option B being what she'd originally planned—a group tour of all the sites with nothing eventful—she'd choose option A every time.

She'd choose Theo.

Speaking of . . .

Dani opened her eyes and sat up. Where was he?

"Theo? Are you out there?" she called out.

Silence.

What was taking him so long?

She had no concept of time or knowing how long she'd been waiting, but based on the pruning of her fingers and the now-lukewarm temperature of the water, it had to have been a while.

They'd planned that he'd come right back and join her, hadn't they?

Oh, whatever. He'd be back soon.

She leaned back and let her hands dance along the surface of the water, keeping her mind occupied as she waited. But another five or so minutes passed and still no Theo.

Maybe he'd come back and fallen asleep? He *had* seemed really tired.

Her pruney fingers couldn't take much more, so she got out of the tub and dried off, then grabbed a set of white linen pajamas from a shelf. The man who'd shown them to their room was right—these weren't made for someone her size. The sleeves were at least four inches too long, and the pants at least six. She rolled them up, then headed into the bedroom.

The empty bedroom.

"Theo?" she said again, even though he obviously wasn't there.

A sick, sinking ache formed in the pit of her stomach, and her heart rate picked up. She needed to find him.

Dani rushed to the door, her hands shaking as she turned the doorknob. The house was silent. Too quiet. She tiptoed down the hall, making her way downstairs and peering into each room she came upon. No one was there.

Her jaw started to tremble. *No, no, no.* They'd taken him. How could she have been so foolish? So trusting? These men gave them no reason to believe them, and she and Theo were so exhausted that they would have believed anything.

And did.

Before she knew it, she was full-on running, calling his name as she searched the house. Looking for him. Looking for anyone.

How could she let this happen? How could she have lost him again?

Tears streamed down her face.

"Juicy?"

Dani spun around, finding Theo peering out a doorway.

"Theo!" She ran over to him and right into his arms.

"Hey, hey, what's wrong?" he said, trying to pull her back to look at her face.

"Where *were* you? I thought someone had taken you again," she said through her tears.

"I'm sorry. I was heading back, and then I got lost. But then I found the kitchen so I wanted to bring you something to eat, and I'm sorry. I should have gone back sooner."

"Don't leave me ever again," she cried into his chest.

"I'll never leave you."

She finally pulled back upon hearing his words. "Do you mean that?"

"Yes, Juicy. I promise," he said, cupping her face in his hands and wiping away her tears with his thumbs. "God, you're beautiful."

"Even when I'm crying?"

"Even when you're crying." He pulled her closer and kissed her forehead. "I want to show you something."

Right then, her stomach growled.

"Is it a sandwich?" she joked, wiping away an errant tear.

He laughed. "No, it's not a sandwich."

"Is it a gyro?"

"A gyro *is* a sandwich."

"Hard disagree."

"Disagree? What exactly is your definition of a sandwich?" he asked, raising his brow.

"An assortment of fillings between two pieces of bread."

"How does a gyro not meet that definition?"

"Gyros are either in a pita pocket or wrapped in a pita, not two pieces of bread."

"What if the pita is cut in two?"

"Nuh-uh. That's cheating."

"Cheating?! It's a sandwich!"

"Let me guess. You think a *hot dog* is a sandwich?"

"Okay, well, do you want to keep debating the definition of the sandwich, or do you want me to show you what it is I found?" he asked with a laugh. His smile finally put her at ease.

"How about you show me."

Theo took her hand and led her through the doorway to a dining room, then through the room and into another.

"I like your jammies," he said as they walked.

"They're only ten sizes too big."

"They look cute on you."

He pushed open a door and they entered an industrial-grade kitchen with Andreas and Christos standing at a stainless steel counter dunking pita bread into some sort of dip.

"Oh, hey," Andreas said, setting the bread down as Christos waved midbite.

"Look who I found," Theo said. Or, you know, who was crying like a lost child in the mall. "This one is ours," he said, pointing to a plate with an assortment of vegetables, olives, fruit, pita, and dollops of dips.

"You made this?" Dani asked.

"Well, I didn't *make* it, but I compiled this arrangement," Theo explained.

"It's so good," Christos said with a mouthful.

"Well, I still have something I wanted to show Dani," Theo said, picking up the tray and taking her hand again, "so we're going to get going."

Andreas and Christos gave them a little wave and then they headed out of the room.

"Now where are we going? Back to the room to the mattress tostada?" she asked.

"Not yet. Come on."

They weaved through the house, finally seeing other people up and about. Dani suddenly felt a little silly thinking that Theo had disappeared when they were so clearly not alone in the house. But that was almost a distant memory now that Theo's hand enveloped hers.

Finally, they came upon a door and Theo let go of her hand for an instant to turn the knob before taking her hand again and leading her inside.

And once there, Dani let go of *his* hand and walked toward the center of the room. No, not just any room.

A two-floor library.

"This is amazing," she said, turning her head every which way to take everything in. The simple wrought iron railing and spiral staircase. The bookcases full of books of all sizes and colors. The large reading table and reading chairs. Even the deep-seated sectional looked like the perfect place to curl up and read a book.

"How did you find this room?" she asked.

Theo made his way farther into the room and set down the plate on the reading table.

"I asked Lysander. He'd mentioned the library earlier, so I found him and asked where it was."

"Well, it's truly remarkable," she said, making her way over to Theo—and more important, the food—though not taking her eyes off the beauty of the room.

"I thought you'd like it."

She looked at him and smiled, then sat on the table with the plate between the two of them. Her feet dangled in the air as they ate, and she talked about what her home library would look like if she ever got one. Hers would obviously be much smaller—the public library didn't pay *that* well—but it would be full of all her favorite books. Organized by vibe and with a special section for those gifted by Theo (her favorites).

Theo also described his perfect home library. One with a ladder to reach books near the ceiling. Obviously, his books would be organized by subject matter.

"Think there's anything to drink in here?" she wondered, hopping off the table.

"Maybe over there," he said, tipping up his head toward a bar cart in the corner.

She checked it out, removing the tops on a few bottles of various alcohol and sniffing for identification since she couldn't read the labels. *Hmm . . . this one smells okay.*

She poured a couple of fingers in a glass and made her way back to Theo, resting against the table with his ankles crossed.

"Bad news," she said.

"What's that?"

"No clam juice. Only whiskey, or whatever this is," she said, holding out the bottle to show him and then taking a sip. The intense fruity, spicy liquor hit her taste buds. She offered it to Theo, and he took a sip.

"It's Metaxa," he said. "It's like a brandy."

"Well, it's delicious. Why don't we ever have this at Christmas?"

"Maybe next time we will."

She took another sip, and then he took the glass from her and set it on the table beside him, then pulled her closer.

"You know, Juicy, I didn't just bring you here for snacks and brandy."

"Oh no?" She smiled, loving the way it felt with his arms around her.

"No. If you haven't noticed, we're in a library."

"That we are."

"And you know what I've been wanting to do to you in a library." His hand glided underneath her nightshirt, and he lightly grazed her skin just above the waistband. She could feel her body turning to goo.

"You say that as if this isn't something that you only added to your sex bingo card two days ago."

"Maybe," he said, leaning in to kiss her neck. "Doesn't change the fact that it's burning a hole on my bingo card."

"Wrong metaphor," she said, closing her eyes and succumbing to his kisses. She could already smell the Metaxa trail he was planting on her neck.

"It doesn't matter. It's been on your sexual bucket list, so your wish is my command."

"We'd better lock the door."

"Already did."

"And tint the windows."

"Done."

"Oh, and we need a condom!"

He pulled away then reached into his pocket and held up one of the condoms she'd gotten from the tourist shop earlier that day.

"My, my, Theo, you certainly are prepared."

"I know it's not exactly the library you had in mind, but we can consider this a partial fulfilment of your wish. I'll fully make it up to you when we return to the States."

He said it with such confidence. This wouldn't be the last time they made love.

Dani pressed her lips to his, letting him explore her body with his hands as hers rested against his pecs. He gripped her ass, tilting her pelvis toward his already-erect cock. Feeling how hard he already was for her gave her sweet satisfaction. He wanted this as much as she did.

Without removing his mouth from hers, his hand snaked around to the front of her pajama shirt and started unbuttoning from the top down. Once he reached the bottom, he released their lips and leaned back as he opened the shirt to reveal her breasts. A light whisper of cold air danced over her, sending goose bumps across her chest. But as he molded his hands over her breasts, those goose bumps were replaced by his warmth inside and out. It was like his hands were made for holding her.

He pulled her back toward him, kissing her again while his hand massaged her breast, every so often taking her nipple between his thumb and index finger and giving her a light pinch that sent a pleasurable zap straight to her core. When he removed his hand from her breast entirely, she let out a disappointed whimper.

Until his hand skated down her body and dove underneath the waistband of her pajama bottoms and went in between her legs. His fingers grazed back and forth along her opening, his teasing only making her wetter for him. Each time he pressed against her clit, she moaned into his mouth. She could feel him smile against her lips, particularly when his fingers circled around her most sensitive spot.

"What?" she asked against his mouth, unable to stop smiling herself.

"Nothing," he said, taking his lips from her and kissing along her neck without stopping his hands. "I love all your sounds."

"Well, I love the way your hands feel on me."

"Would you like to feel my mouth on you?"

"Oh God, yes, please."

He took his hand out from her pants and walked her over to the reading chairs in the corner of the room, pulling off her pants before settling her in the chair and kneeling on the floor in front of her.

"I don't like how many clothes you still have on," she said, pouting and gazing at his still-fully-clothed body.

"Don't worry. I'll remedy that soon."

"Well, I want to see you touch yourself while your mouth is on me. I want to see how hard you are for me. Please."

He smiled. "Okay, Juicy, since you asked so nicely."

He stood and reached his hands over behind his head and pulled off his shirt. Hot. Then, he kicked off his shoes while unbuttoning his pants. His cock sprang free as he peeled off his pants and tossed them to the side. Now, standing in front of her stark-naked save for the gold pendant around his neck, she could admire him in all his glory.

"Damn, Theo. Had I known what you had hiding underneath your clothes all these years . . ." She let her voice trail off as she admired his body.

"What? What would you have done?" he asked, taking his cock in his hand and starting to stroke. *So fucking hot.*

She bit her lip and moved her own hands down her body, one on her breast and the other between her legs.

"I definitely would have been doing *this* a little bit more while thinking about you," she said, putting her fingers inside her and writhing in the seat.

He smirked and lowered to her level, not stopping his hand from pumping on his shaft. "Funny, because I was doing this *a lot* while thinking about you."

She didn't have time to wrap her head around his statement before his mouth dove between her legs. But once his hot mouth covered her opening, everything else around her ceased to exist. She tried keeping her eyes open so she could watch what he was doing to her and watch him touch himself, but her eyes kept rolling into the back of her head as he alternated between sucking and flicking her clit with his tongue. To think that she'd been missing out on his magical tongue all those years. Without taking his tongue away, he added a finger, then two, curling them inside her to hit the right spot.

The pressure increased, and every part of her body swelled with growing pleasure.

"Oh God, Theo, you're going to make me come. I'm not ready . . . I'm not ready."

"Tell me. Walk me through it," he said, taking his mouth away and staring up at her.

"I want to feel your cock inside me," she begged.

"We'll still have time. But I want you to come for me now, and then I'll make you come again. Can you do that?" he asked, his fingers pumping inside her, faster and faster.

"Yes," she breathed out.

"Say it again."

"Yes!"

"Come for me, baby. Be a good girl."

She clenched around his fingers as an orgasmic wave crashed through her body, a wave she could ride all day and all night long. Every part of her body filled with pleasure. And every inch of her craved more.

"I need you," she said.

"You have me," he said, slowly taking his fingers from inside her and putting them in his mouth, sucking her juices.

So. Fucking. Hot.

"You know what I mean."

"Where do you want me?" he asked.

"I don't care. Right here. No, over there," she said, pointing to the wall of bookshelves. "Everywhere."

Seriously. If she didn't have him inside her soon, she was going to resort to begging. Which she wasn't above doing.

"Demanding. I like it," he said, reaching for his pants and into the pockets for a condom. He tore open the square and sheathed his cock, making it look sexy. Her core ached as she watched him, almost in pain as she waited. She might come again in anticipation.

He stood in front of her, and for a moment she wished he hadn't put on the condom yet so she could suck him off, but he held out his hand for hers, and in one quick movement, he pulled her up from her seat and straight into his arms. Her ass rested with his dick grazing her underside, teasing her being so close to her entrance.

Theo stared into her eyes as he carried her over to the bookshelves, pressing her back against the shelving. He let go of her with one hand, which he brought down between them and gripped his shaft, positioning it outside her opening. He rubbed his head on her clit, sending more pleasure bombs firing in all directions.

"My God, Theo, are you *trying* to kill me?" she asked, breathless.

"No," he said, laughing, "I'm trying to make sure I last more than five seconds."

She smiled. "I suppose it's probably been a while. Guessing you haven't been with anyone in over a year?"

"Oh yeah, but that's not why."

She eyed him curiously. "Then what is it?"

"You."

Without further hesitation, he plunged into her, filling her completely, stopping once they were fully connected.

Dani and Theo. Theo and Dani. They'd always been a pair. But never more so than now.

"Oh fuck," he said, bringing his hand over her head and gripping the bookshelf.

Slowly, she rolled her hips, grinding herself on his cock. As if her movements gave him permission, he rocked back then plunged into her again, this time firmer. Harder. And again. And again.

She held on to him tightly, afraid that if she let go he would vanish and she'd never feel this again. His hands gripped her thighs below her butt as he thrust into her.

"God, you feel so good," he said.

"So do you."

She tightened her pussy around him, and he grunted. "Fuck, don't do that," he said. "You're going to make me come too fast."

"Then let me do some of the work. Take me to the couch."

Without pulling out, he carried her to the couch. But once there, she brought her feet to the floor and dismounted him.

"Sit down," she commanded.

He did as she said, and then she turned around, climbing on top of him and then lowering onto his erection. Each of them let out a low moan at their reconnection. She bobbed up and down on his length, twirling her hips each time she lowered so she could grind on his base.

She reclined so her back was flush against his chest, and he kissed her neck. With one of his hands on her breast, the other reached around and massaged her clit, moving faster to keep up with the rolling of her hips.

"I want to see you," he said into her ear.

She spun around and climbed on top of him again. He brought his hands up on either side of her face, below her jaw, staring into her eyes as they moved together.

"I'm going to come," he said.

"Me, too."

A few more thrusts, and he cried out in pleasure. He continued to plunge into her as he rode out the wave moments before she did the same. They were both out of breath, panting, and staring into each other's eyes. And when Theo kissed her once more, Dani knew things would never be the same between them.

Because Dani was in love.

As she'd always been.

CHAPTER

Twenty-Three

Theo

THE FAMILIAR SOUND OF PAGES TURNING WOKE THEO FROM HIS sleep. He slowly opened his eyes, finding Dani sitting opposite him on the library sofa, thumbing through a book in those ridiculously large pajamas. He watched her for a moment, taking her in before she noticed that he was awake. He wasn't sure how long he'd been out—after they'd had sex, they'd fallen asleep on the sofa in heavenly bliss.

Making love to Dani was more incredible than he'd ever imagined it would be. The way they moved in sync. How they talked. Their ability to know what each other wanted and to fulfill those desires. Dani made him feel special, like his lovemaking was extraordinary. It wasn't that he didn't know what he was doing in the bedroom (or rather, the library), and he thought he looked pretty good naked, but somehow, everything clicked with Dani.

And he wasn't done with her. If he had things his way, he'd never be.

He just needed to figure out a way to tell her that.

After they were home. He'd tell her how he felt after they were safe once and for all, and all this was over.

Dani turned another page and looked up, catching Theo's eye. She then smiled and closed the book in her lap.

"Are you spying on me?" she asked.

"Maybe. Looks like perhaps you were creeping on me, too, though," he said, sitting up and reaching for her, pulling her into his lap. "Hey, beautiful."

"Hey," she said, letting the book she was holding fall beside her on the couch.

He kissed her delicately, no longer needing to rush as if it might be the only opportunity.

"I love watching you read," he said. "It's so fucking sexy."

"Oh yeah?"

"I've always found it *very* hot. You make this face when you're reading, and then you twist your bottom lip with your thumb and index finger, like this," he said, demonstrating.

She playfully slapped his hand away. "Oh my God, that is *not* hot!"

"It is when you do it."

"Well," she said, brushing his hair out of his face, "I think it's sexy when *you* read."

He couldn't help smiling. "How so?"

"Well, first, I like how relaxed you get. Like when you lean back like this," she said, sliding off his lap and sinking deep into the couch, "and then you put your bare feet up on the coffee table and cross your ankles."

"I didn't know you had a foot fetish."

"No, I have a *Theo* fetish," she said, giving him a sexy wink that sent warm fuzzies fluttering in his stomach. "Anyway, I like seeing you let yourself get lost in a book. It's like you're finally free of all the other bullshit around you."

"What are you trying to say?" he said with a slight chuckle as he propped his elbow up on the back of the couch and rested his head.

She shrugged. "I dunno. Sometimes you're a little uptight, that's all."

He tensed and cocked back his head. Uptight.

Her comment somewhat took him aback, though not because it upset him. More because he knew it was true, and she'd never called him out on it before. All his life, he'd been moving toward his parents' vision of their American dream for him. He'd never really talked about it with Dani, or anyone else, for that matter. Instead, he did what they'd wanted. Lived the *life* they'd wanted. *Dated* whom they wanted. The only time he truly felt like he could be himself was around Dani. So to hear her call him uptight . . .

"Yeah, well," he said, turning away from her and wanting to go back to talking about something else. "We should probably head back up to the bedroom in case someone needs this room."

He searched through the pile of clothes on the floor for his shirt, but right as he was about to pull it on over his head, Dani stopped him, touching him on the side. Her fingers traced over the tattoo.

Πάντα ήσουν εσύ.

"Why won't you tell me what it means, Theo?" she asked.

Not now.

"I told you what it means."

Her eyebrows knit together, and then she took a deep breath and sighed. She then crawled over to the other side of the couch, grabbed a piece of paper, and handed it to him:

Πάντα = Always
ήσουν = ~~you were~~ been
εσύ = you

His stomach swirled with a dozen emotions he couldn't differentiate.

"I figured it out," she said. "What I can't figure out, however, is why you keep lying to me about it. Or I guess maybe I can. I don't remember much about that night, but I think I remember the highlights. Specifically you telling me you couldn't do"—she gestured between them—"this. Which I suppose begs the question. What *is* it that we're doing?"

"I . . . I don't know."

She laughed, incredulously. "Great," she said, snatching the paper away and crumpling it in her hands. "Just great. Okay, I guess it's time to go upstairs."

She started to get off the couch, but he stopped her, taking her by the wrist and looking up at her.

"What do you *want* it to be, Juicy?"

"What do I want it to be?" she asked, exasperated. "Theo, I told you that it's always been you, that I wanted to *be* with you, and you rejected me! And now we're here, and we're fucking, and I . . . I guess it doesn't really matter what I want."

Her eyes started to well with tears, and he couldn't have that. He couldn't have her thinking that this was only about sex.

"I didn't reject you," he said.

"Um, yes, you did," she said, taking her hand back, folding

her arms across her chest. "I was drunk, but I remember that much. You said, 'Dani, I can't.' Pretty hard to forget that part." She rolled her eyes.

"You're right. Dani, you *were* drunk," he said, staring up at her. "Wasted even. Slurring your words. I've been in love with you for half my life, and I wasn't going to take advantage of you like some douchebag opportunist. And I was still with Giorgina. Regardless of my feelings for you, I couldn't take things further until I broke things off with her. I know you—you never would have respected me if I'd done that. I wouldn't have respected *myself.* And to be completely honest, I wasn't sure you even meant those words. I'm not sure if you recall, but seconds later, you literally threw up on me."

She recoiled a bit, seeming to remember that part.

"Look," he continued, "I'm not saying that to make you feel bad—" But she cut him off.

"If all that is true—"

"It *is* true," he interrupted.

But she furrowed her brow and kept going. "If all that is true, then why did you leave?"

He sighed. He'd asked himself the same question so many times. "Because I'm an idiot."

"What's that supposed to mean?"

"I know it was shitty to leave you there without saying goodbye, but I didn't sleep all night. I couldn't stop thinking about it. So I immediately drove back to Chicago and broke up with Giorgina. I told her that I didn't think we were looking for the same thing, but she knew it was because of you. I didn't deny it.

"But I couldn't come right back to you. We needed time. *I* needed time. I wanted things to be right—to be perfect. I'd been waiting for this my entire adult life, and I didn't want to fuck it up. So then what did I do? I fucked it up."

"How did *you* fuck it up?" she asked, finally sitting next to him again.

"Fries and micheladas, remember? I'd made a plan. I was going to come home and tell you everything. But then your dad mentioned Beau, and I saw you out with him, doing the *same* things we'd done a few weeks before, and I thought you'd already moved on. Instead of asking you about it like a grown-up, I left. Instead of meeting up for fries and micheladas, I hopped on a plane like all I had to do was get some distance to get you out of my system. I wanted to be irresponsible. To go back on a dig, exactly what my parents wanted me to *stop* doing, so I could forget about you. And now look at me," he said, motioning to himself. "I've lost a year of my life because I was too scared to tell you how I felt."

"When did you get this?" she asked, putting her hand on the tattoo.

"The weekend before I came home that last time. I had this whole speech planned out. To tell you how it had always been *you.* I felt foolish about it once I thought you were with someone else. But in the moment, when you spoke those words? I felt like it was real."

"It *was* real."

"Was it?" he asked, not really sure what to think anymore.

"Yes, Theo," she said, scooting closer. "My God, I was lost without you. After they . . . after they announced your presumed death," she said, barely able to choke out the words, "I felt like a piece of me had been ripped out of my soul. Why do you think I'm even here?"

He tilted his head to the side, trying to figure out what she was talking about. "I thought you were here on vacation?"

"Right, but I could have gone to any number of places. Thailand, New Zealand, Chile . . . or any of the other countries that I'd always talked about visiting. But out of all the places in the world, I came here because . . ." She paused and bit her lip, fighting to keep the truth inside. "Because I . . . I . . . I wanted to be close to you, as close as I could get even if you were no longer here. I missed you so fucking much."

He crashed his lips against hers, pulling her body flush with his. Years of tension and longing unraveled between their lips. Words that had gone unspoken for far too long. They wanted this. Both of them wanted this.

He pulled his mouth away, holding her beautiful face in his hands. Never wanting to be without her ever again. But he needed his intentions to be clear.

"Juicy, I don't want there to be any question. I don't want my fear to get in the way ever again. I love you. I've always loved you. I'm sorry it took me so long to say that. But if we're going to do this, I need you to know that I'm all in. I don't want to half-ass this."

"I love you, too. It's *always* been you. One hundred percent." She wrapped her arms around his neck.

"This isn't the emotions talking, is it? This crazy situation?"

"Theo, I'm in *fucking* Greece because of you. And as you very well know, I had multiple opportunities to escape on my own. But I didn't. Because I didn't want to leave you. It's not the situation for you, is it?"

"Daniela, I got a *fucking* tattoo of the last words you spoke to me."

She smiled. "You never call me 'Daniela.' It feels weird."

"Yeah, it did feel a little weird," he said, laughing. "Why didn't you ever tell me how you felt?"

"Well, I suppose it's not the main reason, but in large part because you always had a Triple G waiting for you back in Chicago."

It was a fair criticism.

"I'm not going to lie, Theo," she continued, "sometimes it was hard being friends. I didn't *want* to have feelings for you, because I thought it would fuck everything up. And I really tried not to cross that line because you're right—had you reciprocated that evening, I probably would have hated *myself* for coming on to you when you were unavailable."

"I know," he said, hanging his head a bit. "You know, though, that Triple Gs were something my parents wanted."

"And you happily obliged."

"Happily? I wouldn't say that. More like it was easy. It made my parents happy. Most of the time, my relationships were pretty mundane and drama-free. And not to shine the light away from my own unavailability, but you didn't seem interested in guys like me, despite my one, single tattoo."

She sighed. "I guess guys like that—reckless men—made me feel like I was still that rebellious teenager who did all the things we weren't supposed to do. It's like I've been resisting becoming boring, which is pretty silly when I think about it because I actually *like* my life working as a librarian. I *like* spending my weekends getting lost in books."

"You are anything but boring, Juicy," he said, smiling and tucking a hair behind her ear.

"Really? Because I put my life on hold, Theo. All my plans, all my dreams to travel the world, everything got placed on the back burner after my dad's accident, which I didn't even need to do. But I'd convinced myself that my parents needed me because I was too scared that I wouldn't live up to the hype I'd built. And then you were out there living your best life. You got out. You'd moved on. I was . . . I was embarrassed that I never did. So I guess that's it. That's the main reason I never told you how I felt. I mean, don't get me wrong, as much as I like the life I've made for myself in Grand Rapids, I still can't shake those feelings of inadequacy. And who was I to suck you back?"

"Dani, I wanted to be there because you were there. And for what it's worth, I think you have so much going for you. Getting out doesn't equal success and happiness. You have so much more peace knowing who you are than I do living my parents' vision for me. The only time I truly feel content is when I'm with you."

"Then why didn't *you* say anything?"

"For starters, Eddie."

"Oh, fuck Eddie."

"I'd rather not," he said with a smile.

Dani punched him playfully in the arm. "Seriously. Eddie doesn't get a say on who I date."

"Well, in all fairness, it was a pact we made when we were seventeen. It's been so long since we talked about it that I don't even know what he'd think at this point."

"You made a *pact*?!"

He nodded. "Yeah. That summer after Operation Juicy-Gate."

Dani scrunched her face. "For real?"

Theo nodded. "He said he saw me checking out your ass."

"I knew it!" She punched him again.

"Hey," he said, smiling and holding his arm. "I mean, it was *right* there in front of my face. How was I supposed to avoid checking it out?"

"Did it turn you on?" She waggled her brow.

"I was a seventeen-year-old virgin. *Everything* turned me on. But I agreed to Eddie's stupid pact. To be totally honest, I didn't think it would be an issue because I *wasn't* into you. Not like that. Not back then. You were my best friend's little sister. Not even my innate bodily functions could impact that."

"So when did it change?" She readjusted herself on the couch and brought her legs up to her chest, turning to the side to listen.

He turned to square up their shoulders, and he propped his arm on the back of the sofa, then rested his head in his hand. Never in a million years did he picture having this conversation with her in a swank house in Greece. He took a moment to take everything in, the surrealness of it all. Of finally telling Dani how he felt.

"The first time the thought crossed my mind, as in more than in a teenage-boner sort of way, was your prom. I didn't understand how that guy stood you up. You're such an awesome chick. I hated seeing how hurt you were. But I remember dancing with you and this thought popped into my mind: 'I wonder if she'd feel better if I kissed her.' And it scared the shit out of me."

"Scared you?"

"Yeah, because it was the first time I'd thought about doing anything like it. I *wanted* to kiss you. And once it had crossed my mind, it was like it opened the floodgates. I couldn't *stop* thinking about kissing you. I couldn't stop looking at you. I was sure you'd noticed over the years."

"Well, did you happen to notice that I was always looking at you, too?"

"A few times. Though I thought it was simply bad timing on my part, that you'd caught me staring."

She leaned forward and grabbed his arm. "I thought you caught *me* staring! Oh my God, like at your mom and dad's anniversary party? I thought *for sure* you knew."

"Oh, I knew," he said, lifting his hand to her face and brushing her cheek. "When you know, you know, right?"

She put her hand on his and brought it to her mouth, kissing his palm before holding it in place against her face with her eyes closed.

He may not have been aware of how she'd felt at the time, but by then, at twenty-seven years old at his parents' thirtieth wedding anniversary, he'd recognized that he was in love with Dani.

"So we knew we knew ten years ago, and now, here we are," she said, opening her eyes and burying her face in his hand.

"Yeah." He hated the pain that he felt for all those lost years, especially this last one. She was too far away. "Come here," he said, pulling her across his lap so she was straddling him.

He stared up at her as she stared into his eyes, brushing his hair from his forehead and studying every feature of his face. She planted her soft lips upon him, so tender and caring.

"Do you think this will work? I'm not a Triple G," she said.

"Sure you are. You're a Good Guiterrez Girl," he said, smiling.

"Uh-uh. I'm a muchacha mala, remember?"

He pulled her closer and whispered in her ear. "You were a good girl earlier."

"You're naughty," she said, leaning back and waggling her

brow. "But seriously, Theo. Your mom called me 'reckless.' Can this work?"

"I think we already know that it can. And you know my mom loves you. Even if you *do* get me into trouble sometimes," he said, winking at her.

"Right, but I just want to remind you one more time of Giorgina, and Daphne, and Evangeline, and—"

He put his finger on her lips to stop her.

"Look, Juicy, we could talk about all the reasons it took this long for us to admit our feelings, or we can stop making excuses and allow ourselves to be with each other now. I'm done doing things because it's what I think my parents want. *I* want this. I want *you*."

"And I'm done being scared. As my dad would say, it's time to get busy living my life. And I want to do it with you."

He smiled and then kissed her again. He'd never get tired of kissing her.

"I can't wait to get home so we can start living that life together," he said, unable to stop smiling. "Too bad we can't go back having made a really fucking awesome discovery, though. I would have loved to show my parents that it wasn't for nothing. That I'm actually good at what I do."

But instead of smiling back, Dani pulled her bottom lip into her mouth. She looked sheepish. Like she had some secret she'd been keeping.

"So, about that," she said. "How badly do you really want to go home?"

CHAPTER Twenty-Four

Dani

DANI WATCHED AS ALL THE COLOR DRAINED FROM THEO'S FACE. "Juicy, no."

"Wait, hear me out," she said, putting her hands on his shoulders.

"Whatever it is you're going to say isn't going to change things," he said, putting his hand up to stop her from proceeding. "I convinced you to check out Poseidon's temple, but then we made a deal. And now I want to go home. Badly. Preferably alive."

"But I think I may be onto something!"

"No, I don't want to hear it," he said, rolling her off his hips, standing up, and waving his hands. "We already tried. It's time to pack up and go. Cut our losses."

"It's at the Parthenon!" she blurted out and then quickly covered her mouth.

Her proclamation stopped Theo in his tracks.

Yes! When she'd been reading various books in the library

and come up with her most recent theory as he'd slept beside her, she'd almost woken him up. Yet the very idea of sticking around Greece after everything he'd already gone through was absolutely ludicrous—but . . . then hearing him talk about proving himself to his parents gave her other ideas.

And based on his apparent interest in hearing her out, maybe he was having second thoughts, as well.

Slowly, he turned around. "Okay, I'm not saying I'm changing my mind," he said, "but I want to know what led you to that conclusion."

She knew he wouldn't be able to ignore the intrigue.

"Remember what Papantonis said about the sun? 'There, below where Helios rises in the east, I will put the eye to rest . . . Despite his quarrels, Poseidon himself could not have picked a better place for this beast to spend eternity'?" she recited.

"Yeah? The sun rises in the east."

"Right, but where does *Helios* rise in the east?" She waited a beat before following up, "The east pediment of the Parthenon. Look," she said, grabbing a large book from the coffee table in front of the couch.

Theo walked back to the sofa and sat beside her. She opened the book and flipped to a diagram of the Parthenon, showing two sets of statues on either side of the marble structure, each side containing twenty or so individual pieces. The pediments had been damaged over the years through a combination of skirmishes, fires, natural disasters, and weather. But through reconstructions and artist renderings, various experts had come up with an idea of what the original pediments once looked like.

The east pediment depicted the birth of Athena with other gods watching nearby: Zeus, Demeter, Dionysus, Artemis, Hephaestus, Hera.

And Helios rising with his chariot from the far end.

Theo studied the page as Dani chewed on her thumbnail, watching him impatiently. She hadn't necessarily been trying to continue looking for the Minotaur. But when she was flipping through books as Theo slept, the mention of Helios caught her attention. Her research then led her to the Parthenon. But it wasn't only that.

"I don't know. This could simply be happenstance," he said.

She knew he'd say that.

"Okay, but now what about this?" she said, turning to the page covering the west pediment.

And standing in the center fighting over the region with Athena was Poseidon. *Despite his quarrels.*

Theo pulled the book into his lap, flipping back and forth between the pages. Studying the diagrams. Reading the descriptive text. Finally, he set the book on the coffee table and leaned back on the couch, running his fingers through his hair before resting his hands behind his head. He blew out a long breath and then looked over at Dani.

"Well, if that's not a clue, then that's one hell of a coincidence," he said. "But there's no way it can be at the Parthenon. Someone would have found it already."

"That's what I was thinking, too. But then I remembered this clay pot I saw at the museum in Heraklion. A man wearing the eye medallion, holding the Minotaur's head. He was emerging from a cave with some sort of temple atop a land mass. I've been searching through these books to see if I could find a picture, but what if that's it? What if it's not at the Parthenon itself, but instead in a cave below it at the Acropolis? On the east side where Helios rises? And look—"

She grabbed another book that, from what she could tell,

talked about excavations at the Acropolis. And there was a photo of red soil.

"'It is here that the eye will sleep and blend into the dirt itself,'" she recited.

"Wait," Theo said, putting his hand on her forearm and pausing to think. "Come with me!"

He quickly gathered up his clothes, and then they bolted out of the room, running through the halls of the house and up the stairs back to their bedroom. He dove for his bag and pulled out that leather notebook, flipped to the page in the center where a piece of paper was neatly folded. He then brought the paper to the bed and unfolded it atop the bedspread.

It was a page from a book with a picture of the clay vessel Dani had seen at the museum.

"This is it! The clay pot I saw at the museum. Where did you get this?" she asked.

"From Andreas's stuff. I tore it out of a book."

"Why?"

"It seemed important at the time."

They both stared at the painting on the vessel. Nothing about it gave any actual indication that it was of the Acropolis and the Parthenon, but in light of Dani's discovery, it seemed that maybe, just maybe, the thing they were searching for was somewhere on the east side of the Acropolis.

"So, let me ask again. How badly do you want to go home?" she asked.

"Ask me after we go to the Acropolis."

• • • • • • • • • •

LYSANDER HAD KEPT HIS PROMISE. WHEN THEY WOKE IN THE MORNING, they'd learned that he'd already arranged for flights to take them back home late that evening. He'd also seemingly pulled some strings and was able to get copies of their passports expedited from the embassy.

Now all they had to do was wait until midnight. Or, as Dani put it: they had until midnight to find the eye of the Minotaur.

Lysander had offered to arrange transportation for them to the airport, but Theo and Dani declined. They didn't need the Minotaur's Children to know what they were up to. So instead, they simply asked for a ride back to Athens so they could "sightsee" before their flight home. Now, without Maurice and Louis looking over their shoulders and watching their every move, they were free to travel as they pleased. If anyone recognized him at this point, it wouldn't matter. Because soon, they'd be on a plane back to the United States. So after saying their goodbyes to Andreas and Christos, and vowing to keep in touch, Dani and Theo made their way into Athens.

The Acropolis was known for having multiple cave openings dedicated for the cult worship of various gods. The odds there was an additional undiscovered cave were a bit unlikely, but excavations within the last one hundred years weren't unheard of. After everything they'd gone through, what harm was there in at least a peek?

They had to be strategic. Poking around the Acropolis was a quick way to earn a one-way ticket to the slammer. So they decided to wait until the crowds thinned out later in the day, hopefully limiting the number of tattletales who might be watching them.

"You ready?" Theo said as they stood outside the southern entrance.

Dani nodded, and he took her hand.

They didn't know exactly what they were looking for, given

that the painting was the only reference they had to go on. They circled the lower eastern slopes, holding up the page Theo had torn out of Andreas's book and searching for a perspective that matched the painting. Even though they'd gone later in the day, however, there were still a few too many people to get a proper look.

Dani and Theo stepped back as a tour group came up behind them, looking to pass.

"And here," the tour guide announced, "is the Aglaureion, one of the largest caves at the Acropolis. This cave was to honor Aglauros, the daughter of King Cecrops. It is said she flung herself off the Acropolis to save the city from invasion."

The group slowly moved past them as the tour guide continued to talk, his voice somewhat familiar, when Dani finally recognized the voice: it was Cosmo.

"Daniela?" another voice asked to her right.

Dani turned, and standing there was Harold, her travel companion from her first few days in Greece.

"Harold!" she said, flinging her arms around the old man.

"Well, well, well, never thought I'd see you again," Harold said. "I gotta admit—I was a little disappointed when I'd heard that you'd left. All these old fogeys are more ancient than the ruins we've been touring. None of them stay up past six p.m."

"Yeah . . . the last few days have been . . . unexpected."

Harold took one look at Theo standing beside her, and then he said with a smile, "I'd say so."

"Oh, Harold, this is Theo," she said.

They shook hands and exchanged pleasantries, when Harold then turned to Dani and said, "As in your Theo?"

Dani blushed and ducked her head a bit.

"Yes, her Theo," he answered for her, tipping up her chin and gazing at her lovingly.

If Harold wasn't standing there, she would have kissed him. Her Theo. She liked the sound of that.

"So, you're not dead," Harold said. "Or am I starting to see things, too?"

Theo gave a nervous laugh.

"It's a long story," Dani offered, "but, no, you're not seeing things. He's alive."

"Oh, good. Because I thought I saw a rock over there that looked like a sideways eye," he said, tossing a thumb over his shoulder, "and I really thought it was maybe time to get my eyes checked again."

Dani and Theo snapped their heads toward each other.

"Where exactly did you see that rock?" Dani asked.

"Back thataway, up above the pathway a bit," he said, turning around and pointing. Then he eyed her, suspiciously. "Why? You're not up to something no good, are you?"

Dani's mouth gaped like a fish out of water. *Shit.*

"Cuz if you need a lookout . . ." Harold then added.

Now Theo and Dani were the ones eyeing him suspiciously. "What are you getting at, Harold?" Dani asked.

"I'm only sayin' . . . I'm an old man who needs a little break once in a while. So, I dunno . . . I might just sit right here," he said, grunting as he lowered himself to a boulder, "and, oh, you know, if someone comes walking that way, I might have a bit of a coughing fit from the dust. One loud enough so that anyone on this side of the Acropolis might hear me."

"You'd do that?" Dani asked.

"I ain't got nothing better to do," he said, "but it seems you do." He gave her a suggestive look.

Did he think they were sneaking off to have sex? Not that she wasn't very much looking forward to doing it again, but now was not the time or the place.

"Harold, we're not—"

But he held up his hand to stop her. "Plausible deniability," he said. "I'm simply an old man catching his breath."

She smiled, and then leaned down and kissed his cheek. "You were one of the best parts about this trip, so you know."

He then looked up at Theo and said, "Don't worry. I already told her, she's not my type."

They all laughed, and he shooed them away as he stood watch. Theo and Dani wound their way along the path, focusing their attention on the rocks above them. For a moment, Dani thought maybe Harold's eyesight *had* been playing tricks on him. Everything looked the same. Plain. Jagged. Rocks.

But there, beyond the end of the pathway, was something else. High above the path, like Harold had said, was what appeared to be an eye carved into the rock, the carving slightly worn away by weather.

Dani pointed. "There," she said.

Theo narrowed his gaze, following the line of sight from her finger toward the hillside. Once it seemed he'd connected with the spot, he took out the page with the pot and held it up in the air.

"This looks like it could be the spot. It's the right angle, but I don't see a cave," he said.

Other than the rock, there wasn't anything unusual about the spot. There was no indication of a cave. No indentation in the stone. Just a pile of rocks.

"Maybe we need a closer look," she said.

Theo turned around to gauge their surroundings, his hands

on his hips. The spot was exposed to the area outside the Acropolis's fence. There was no way they'd be able to get up there without someone seeing. Even with Harold standing guard, there were far too many people.

"I don't think we can get up there," he said.

"What if we wait?" Dani said.

"Wait for what?"

"Until dark."

Theo frowned. "It won't be dark until at least eight p.m. Our flight is at midnight. We can't stay here, Juicy. This is our chance to leave."

"No, *this* is our chance. What if this is it? Are you going to be satisfied going home knowing that we didn't even check? What happened to the Theo who's always ready for an adventure?"

"You realize that I would do anything that you asked me to, right?"

"Okay, then I'm asking you to do this. Come on, Theo. You said you never feel more alive than when we're together. So let's live. One more adventure."

CHAPTER

Twenty-Five

Theo

ONE MORE ADVENTURE.

Somehow, sneaking around the Acropolis after closing wasn't the kind of adventure Theo ever imagined he'd partake in.

Nor did he ever imagine he'd be paying an old man like Harold in moussaka and spanakopita to keep watch for them at a restaurant outside the gates once the sun went down. But Dani trusted him, so Theo did, too.

The plan was simple: After heading out to get flashlights, gloves, a foldable shovel, and rope, they'd return to the Acropolis right before closing and hide out behind some rocks until the coast was clear. Then, once the site was empty, they'd travel up to the spot with the eye rock and investigate further. If Harold noticed anything from beyond the gates, he'd create a commotion, hopefully one loud enough to get their attention.

It was a real crapshoot. But Dani had been right—if they didn't at least check, it would gnaw at him for the rest of his life.

"What do you think?" Dani said, whispering. "It's almost nine. Should we go ahead and try?"

"Let's do it."

They got up from their hiding place and crept up the hillside, avoiding use of the flashlights as best they could. Fortunately, the full moon helped illuminate their path. Slowly, they made their way up the rocks, careful not to make too much noise. Once they got to the spot with the eye rock, they hunkered down and turned on the flashlights to inspect the rock.

"What do you think?" Dani asked.

Theo ran his hand over the carving. "This is definitely man-made," he said. "And look."

He ran his hand over another spot on the rock, even more faint and worn away from erosion. But even with the weathering, he could still make it out.

The µ.

"Is that . . . ?" Dani asked.

"I'm pretty sure."

"This has to be it."

Theo nodded. What *it* was, remained to be seen. But it was definitely something.

He turned around again to see their vantage point and determine whether they'd be caught if he illuminated the grounds. It was risky, but after the risks they'd already taken, what were a few more. With a quick wave of his hand, he scanned the flashlight over the area, trying to see if there was any opening for a cave. But it looked like nothing more than a pile of rocks that had crumbled over time and ended up in this exact spot.

He tried nudging the rock, but it was no use. There were too many other rocks atop it for it to budge.

"I wonder if these rocks are blocking the entrance," Theo said. "It looks like maybe they collapsed."

"That would explain why the eye rock is cocked on its side."

True.

"Unfortunately, I don't think these rocks are moving without any heavy equipment," Theo said.

"So that's it?" Dani asked.

She seemed deflated.

"I don't see how else to get around it."

"What if there's something up here?" Dani said, climbing a little higher.

"Just be careful, will you?" he said. "Last thing we need is for one of us to break an ankle up here."

"Theo, when have you known me to break anything?"

"Aside from my heart?" he joked.

"Don't worry, I'm remedying that. Besides, you know what they say?"

"What's that?"

"The key to mending a broken heart is a magical puss—eeeeeee!" Dani cried as she disappeared into a hole.

"Dani!" Theo yelled, no longer caring about someone seeing or hearing them. He scrambled up the rocks toward the area where she'd disappeared. At the top there was an almost perfectly round hole. He shined the flashlight in, and there, resting about fifteen feet down covered in dirt and dust, was Dani.

"Juicy! Are you okay?!" he called down to her.

She groaned and sat up. "Yeah, I'm okay."

"Hold on, I'm going to secure the rope, and I'll come down to you."

Once he found a solid rock to tie the rope around, he lowered it into the hole before climbing down to her. The moment his boots hit the ground, he dropped to his knees to check on Dani.

"Sure you're okay? You didn't break anything, did you?" he asked.

"No, but it knocked the wind out of me," she said. "What is this place?"

Theo scanned the flashlight around the cavern. It was pitch-dark save for their flashlights. The area was about double the size of his office at the museum, but empty. As he waved the light around the area, though, something caught his eye.

"Look," he said, pointing his flashlight at a round slab against the rock about twenty feet from them.

Dani grabbed her flashlight and shined it in the same spot, illuminating a semiround stone that didn't look natural. Without speaking, they stood and walked over to the stone. Upon further inspection, it became clear that it was a doorway of sorts. With all their might, they pushed the rock, rolling it on its side and revealing another entry cut deep into the side of the Acropolis.

Once the stone was out of the way, they shined their lights down the opening into a tunnel that was at least another fifty feet long.

"Here goes nothing," Theo said, taking her hand.

Slowly, they walked through the rock tunnel, continuing to scan their flashlights in every direction. At the end of the tunnel, they came upon another room.

This one was even larger than the area where Dani had fallen, about the size of a grade school gym. In the middle of the room sat an altar-like stone slab. And atop the altar, a larnax.

"¡Ay, Dios mío!" Dani said at the same time Theo said, "Ho-ly shit."

"What is that?" Dani asked.

"It's a larnax, a type of coffin used by the Minoans."

It wasn't very large compared to coffins of the present day. It appeared to be ceramic made to look like wood. The box was covered with drawings and pictures.

"It doesn't look big enough for a Minotaur," Dani said.

"Have you known many Minotaurs?" Theo asked jokingly.

"Have you?"

"Fair. Shall we take a closer look?"

Dani nodded and they moved toward the chest, stepping up the altar until they were face-to-face with the box. Other than in a museum, Theo hadn't come across a larnax in real life. The piece was painted with intricate designs. An eye. A squiggly pattern reminiscent of water. And, most interestingly, a man slaughtering a bull. Theseus.

Whatever lay inside, this was a discovery of discoveries.

"What now?" Dani said. "I'm sort of thinking we shouldn't open it. Like, what if *this* is Pandora's box?"

Pandora's box. Originally a jar containing all the evils and terrors of the world.

Dani was right. It didn't feel right opening the box, not like this. Not under cover of night after breaking into the Acropolis. It was a coffin, after all.

"I agree."

"What do you think we should do with it?" she asked.

"Maybe we alert Andreas and see if he can help?" Theo said.

Out of nowhere, a bright light pointed directly at them. Both Theo and Dani shielded their eyes.

Fuck. They'd been caught.

Theo had the urge to curse Harold, until the spotlight was

replaced by a lantern that illuminated the entire cavern and revealed their guests.

Pierre Vautour, Maurice, and Louis.

How? No one knew where they were except Harold. And the chance that he'd somehow been connected to Vautour seemed even more far-fetched than the likelihood that a Minotaur lay in that larnax.

Maurice held the lantern high above his shoulders as Vautour stepped into the room and clapped.

"Bravo, Dr. Galanis. I knew you'd succeed," Vautour said.

As much as he wanted to give Dani the credit for the find, now wasn't the time.

"How did you find us?" Theo asked, in fighting stance.

"You didn't think I'd let my most important asset travel around Greece without some security, did you? Maurice and Louis could only do so much," Vautour said, like that provided *any* sort of explanation. "Your medallion," he then offered, motioning to the gold chain that hung around Theo's neck.

Theo's hand shot to the necklace that he'd worn for almost the entirety of his adult life, feeling the pendant between his fingers.

"I replaced it with a new one with tracking inside it some months ago," Vautour explain. "I've kept tabs on you since day one, though we lost you a few times when the signal was a bit spotty."

Since day one? So Theo never had a chance. He never would have been able to get away, not as long as he wore the necklace. The necklace his papou had left to him after he'd died.

Theo's arm jerked forcefully, ripping the chain from his neck and tossing it in the dirt.

"Where is mine?" he asked, trying to hold himself together.

"Oh, I don't know. I think we got rid of it, didn't we, Maurice?" Vautour asked.

"Probably," Maurice said.

"That was my grandfather's," Theo said.

"Oops." Vautour shrugged.

Theo clenched his fists. God, he wanted to punch him. Both of them.

"Anyway," Vautour continued, clearly not giving one shit about Theo's papou, "we saw you seemed to be spending an inordinate amount of time at the Acropolis today and figured we might as well see what you were up to. Maurice always suspected that you knew more than what you were telling him. Now, open it."

Vautour pointed to the larnax.

"No," Theo said.

Vautour sighed. "I'm getting really tired of you thinking you have the upper hand here."

"What makes you think *you* do?" Dani called out.

"How about this?" Maurice said, pulling a gun out from behind his back.

Theo's stomach plummeted.

They should have left.

They should be at the airport right now.

"And I thought you weren't a murderer?" Theo said, trying to maintain an even tone, but he knew it was futile.

"I'm not. But I can't say the same about Maurice. Open it," Vautour commanded again.

Theo's shoulders slumped. There weren't any other options. No olive oil displays to knock over. No bathroom windows to climb out of. No Keraboss Super Ks to hop into. The only choice left was to comply.

"Okay," Theo said, reaching around for his bag so he could get his gloves.

But Maurice shuffled forward, brandishing the gun. "Stop what you're doing!"

Theo threw up his hands. "I'm getting my gloves to handle the piece," he explained.

"Leave the backpack alone!"

"But it's an important archaeological artifact. I shouldn't handle it without gloves," Theo tried to reason.

"Leave it," Maurice said again.

"Quit wasting time, Dr. Galanis, and open the box," Vautour said.

"I need her help," he said, motioning to Dani. "It's probably heavy and I don't want to damage the piece."

"Fine, fine," Vautour said, waving his hands in front of him like he was bored. "But hurry up."

Theo looked at Dani and tossed her a sympathetic glance.

I love you, she mouthed.

As impossible as it seemed, Theo smiled. "I love you, too."

They turned their backs to Vautour and Maurice, and each took a deep breath before placing their hands on the lid of the larnax.

"Lift on the count of three," Theo said. "One. Two. Three."

They lifted the heavy ceramic lid and carefully lowered it to the ground. Having watched *Raiders of the Lost Ark* one too many times, Theo was almost afraid to look inside, as if soul-sucking demons were going to fly out and melt the skin off his face.

He'd always believed in myths and fairy tales, but this box tested the extent of his beliefs. His heart pounded as he and Dani stood back up and peered into the box.

But they didn't find the skull of a bull's head. Or the body of a half man, half beast. Instead, the only thing inside the three-by-four-foot box was a single gemstone the color of blood. An unrefined ruby the size of a football with jagged edges.

The eye of the Minotaur.

"Fuck me," Dani said under her breath.

Theo had never seen a ruby this size. Especially in Greece. It couldn't have originated here.

"What is it?" Vautour called out from behind them. "Show it to me!"

Theo reached into the box, lifted the heavy ruby from its resting place, and turned around.

"Yes! Yes!" Vautour cried out.

"This is it. This is all that's in there," Theo said.

"Then bring it to me," Vautour said, waving him forward.

Theo took a step but then stopped. "And then what? What happens after I hand this to you?"

"Do not be an imbecile. Bring it to me and I won't leave you trapped down here for the rest of your miserable existence," Vautour said.

"How do we know you won't do that anyway?" Dani asked.

"I suppose you'll have to trust me."

Theo wanted to laugh. Trust a wanted criminal. Sure, sounded like a great idea.

"Hey, Theo," Dani said, tearing his attention from Vautour. "Remember Bobby."

Theo furrowed his brow for a minute. Why the fuck would she bring up that time he almost got his ass kicked by Bobby Thomas in the seventh grade?

Then Theo looked down at that football-shaped ruby. This was a bad idea. A *very* bad idea. But like so many of Dani's pranks and antics, there wasn't time to think. So without further hesitation, Theo called out, "Hey, Maurice! Catch!"

Theo tossed the ruby in the air at Maurice. In that split second, Theo watched Maurice make a decision between the gun and the lantern, or the ruby. Unsurprisingly, he chose the ruby.

Dani reached down and picked up a clump of dirt in her hand, tossing it in Vautour's and Louis's distracted faces. They each yelled out and dropped their flashlights to reach up for their eyes. Maurice's lantern hit the ground, bursting into a million pieces at the same time the gun hit and went off. But now, with only a few light beams from their flashlights, it was almost impossible to see who was where or if anyone had been hit. Theo grabbed Dani's hand, and they headed toward the flashlights Vautour and Louis had dropped to pick them up and then they ran. They ran faster than he'd ever run before, thankful that Dani's strong thighs gave her power that should have been impossible for a person of her stature. Vautour's, Louis's, and Maurice's yells came from behind them. Their lack of flashlights would slow them down, but it wouldn't stop them for good.

Dani and Theo made it to the rope.

"You first," Dani said, handing the rope to him.

"No! You go!" he insisted. He wasn't leaving her down there.

"You'll be faster. Get up there and then pull me out."

"Juicy—"

"We don't have time for this! Go!"

Despite the struggle in his heart, Theo did as she said. He climbed the rope faster than any high school gym test and as soon as he made it out, he called down for her.

"I'm ready!" she called out.

Pure adrenaline rushed through his body as he pulled up the

rope. With all his strength, one hand over the other, he pulled, bracing his feet against another rock at the top of the hole. Once Dani's head finally poked out the top and her arms crested the opening, Theo finally felt as though he could breathe again.

He reached down to pull her out the rest of the way by her armpits, heaving her body on top of him. They lay there for a moment with panting breaths, unable to move, and holding each other tight. Finally, Theo released his hold and then grabbed her face and inspected her.

"Are you hurt?" he asked. "Did you get shot?"

She shook her head in his hands. "I'm fine. You?"

"I'm not sure I'd describe what I'm feeling as fine, but I'm alive. Though more important, so are you."

A gunshot fired out of the hole, startling them.

"Get us the hell out of here, you son of a bitch!" Maurice shouted.

Theo and Dani scooted away from the opening to avoid any stray bullets as Maurice, Louis, and Vautour continued to yell profanities.

"What do you think we should do?" Dani asked.

"Well, if he keeps shooting, I don't know that we'll have to do much of anything. Maybe we get the hell out of here and let the police find them?"

"Then we'd better hustle," Dani said, climbing off him and offering her hand to help him up.

Right as they turned to flee, however, a group of uniformed men came running up the path shining flashlights on them.

"Ψηλά τα χέρια! Hands up!"

Theo and Dani raised their hands in the air as the men circled them, pointing guns at them. The ΕΛ.ΑΣ., the Hellenic Police force.

"Μην κινείστε!" one of the men yelled at them to stay put.

As if they had any intention of trying to flee when surrounded by a dozen armed men.

Theo called out they were innocent, speaking in Greek. As quickly as he could, he blurted out that he was Dr. Theo Galanis, the Greek American archaeologist who'd gone missing, but that he'd been captured by the notorious smuggler Pierre Vautour, who was down in the hole below them.

When an officer peered over the edge and Maurice fired a shot, the officers all swarmed the hole. While the men yelled back and forth with Maurice, Louis, and Vautour in Greek and French—clearly not being paid on the side by Vautour—a police sergeant approached Theo and Dani.

"Ελληνικά?" the sergeant asked.

"No, English, please," Theo said.

"I'm Sergeant Diakos. This man here alerted us to some unusual activity at the Acropolis," he said, motioning to Harold at his side. "Said he saw some people sneaking around with flashlights after closing time."

"Yep, saw some rather suspicious-looking gentlemen who were up to no good," Harold said. "I suspect the ones down in that hole there." He pointed to the opening. When Sergeant Diakos turned his head to look, Harold gave Dani a wink, and she reached for his hand and squeezed it quickly, letting go before the sergeant saw them.

"And who did you say you were?" Sergeant Diakos asked, turning his attention back to them.

"Dr. Theo Galanis and Daniela Guiterrez. We were abducted by Pierre Vautour and forced to search for artifacts," Theo explained.

"What sort of artifacts?"

"Would you believe me if I told you the eye of the Minotaur?"

Sergeant Diakos laughed. "You mean the eye of the mythological bull at Knossos?"

But Theo and Dani didn't laugh.

"You're serious?" Sergeant Diakos said, his face turning solemn. "Did you find it?"

"We did," Theo said. "We need to call Dr. Andreas Demetrious from the National Museum as soon as possible. Once those men are removed from down below, this area needs to be cordoned off and fully excavated by professionals. No one else should go down there until Dr. Demetrious arrives."

Sergeant Diakos stared at them for a few moments, and then he took a phone out of his pocket. "We have a situation here at the Acropolis."

Theo and Dani stood there, waiting while the sergeant explained what was going on to whoever was on the other end of the call. Once he was off the phone, he turned back to them and said, "You will need to stay here until this gets sorted out."

"We understand," Theo said.

Sergeant Diakos nodded, and then joined the officers arguing at the cave opening with Vautour, Louis, and Maurice. Dani then turned to Harold.

"I'm sorry I called the police, but I saw those men creeping around and it seemed like you might be in some trouble," Harold explained. "And if any of what you said is true, seems like I was right."

"No, it's a good thing you did," Dani said. "Those men have been holding Theo captive for the last year. That's why he went missing."

"Thank you," Theo said, shaking Harold's hand. "You have no idea how incredibly grateful we are."

"Well, I may have only known Daniela for a few days," Harold explained, "but I could tell she was a special person the minute I met her."

Theo wrapped his arm around Dani's waist and looked down at her. "Yeah, she is."

CHAPTER Twenty-Six

Dani

A LIGHT SEA BREEZE BLEW THE WHITE CURTAINS ON THE BALcony into a billowy wave. Beyond the door, she could see the deep blue waters of the Mediterranean sparkling under Helios's rays as she lay in bed. She'd never truly believed in Greek myths before this trip, but as she stared at her own Greek god sitting shirtless out on the balcony railing, she'd come around on the whole idea.

Theo truly was God's gift.

It had been a week since they'd discovered the eye of the Minotaur. Fortunately, the piece remained intact despite Theo tossing it at Maurice. For now, the gem was being held in a vault at the police station, but eventually it would make its way to one of Athens's many museums. Theo's gut initially told him the ruby likely came from some other land, given that rubies weren't typically found in Greece. As he'd explained to the police, it may have made its way to Greece during the Persian ruler Xerxes I's invasion. What that meant for Papantonis's account remained to be seen. Perhaps his stories had been true. Perhaps the Persians found the beast's remains and traded it for the ruby. They would probably never learn the truth.

As Dani and Theo had come to understand, like most Greek tales, the lines between fact and mythology sometimes blurred.

Which had given Theo a great idea for his next story. And when she'd teasingly asked him to make sure he described Xerxes in his story to look like that hot guy who played him in the movies, the one from *Love Actually*, Theo had simply responded, "Whatever you want, babe." She almost liked it when he called her "babe" more than when he called her "Juicy." Almost.

The first few days after the discovery had been hectic, full of police interviews and questionings, consultations with the Greek Archaeological Service, and meetings with the US Embassy. Thankfully, due to Vautour's notoriety, no one had questioned Theo's and Dani's presence at the Acropolis nor believed Vautour's, Louis's, and Maurice's claims that they'd merely followed them there.

At long, long last, Pierre Vautour was in jail.

Theo and Dani had presented enough evidence to support their claims, including Theo's medallion, which gave the police location data for his movements over the last year. Such as Pierre's Aegean island villa.

And the estate of the Minotaur's Children.

Even though the GPS had been spotty, it still managed to capture a brief ping at the estate.

Not wanting to break their agreement with Lysander, they lied and said the estate was another of Vautour's. But when the police went to check it out, it was suddenly empty. All the books in the library, gone. The eye emblem on the door to the Labyrinth, missing. The only indication that the house had been connected to the secret society was the intricate maze pattern built into the floor. Even the property records pointed to shell companies and off-shore accounts that would likely take ages to untangle.

In the eyes of the law, the Minotaur's Children didn't exist. But Theo and Dani were okay with that. After all, if it wasn't for Lysander, who knew where they might be right now.

Certainly not where she was currently relaxing in a cliffside luxury resort on Santorini—all-inclusive, courtesy of some unknown benefactor.

Or, more likely, Lysander.

Dani stared at Theo as he sipped on his coffee, unaware of her gaze. She caught a glimpse of his tattoo as he lifted his arm—*It's always been you.* Truer words had never been spoken.

God, she loved him. She couldn't stand watching him any longer without touching him.

She climbed out of bed and headed to the balcony. The instant he noticed her movement out of the corner of his eye, he startled. It probably would take a while for his nerves to relax. Even with Vautour, Louis, and Maurice in jail and the police on their side, Theo hadn't quite gotten used to his freedom. But just as quickly as he'd startled, he smiled, seeing it was only her.

"Good morning," he said.

"Καλημέρα," she replied, planting a quick kiss on his lips.

"Been working on your Greek?" he asked, reaching out for her as she approached and immediately wrapping his arms around her waist.

"I figured if we're going to be here for a while, I need to put in a little more effort to learn the language."

"Sounds good coming from your lips."

"Yeah?"

"Mm-hmm. I love everything that comes from those lips." He kissed her again, this time giving her a taste of his coffee-soaked tongue.

"Is that an invitation?" she asked, pressing her hips against his cock and waggling her brows.

"That depends on how you're feeling about *how* we're going to tell our families about us today. If you want to make the announcement obvious because my dick is hard, then sure. Because they landed at the airport a little while ago, and they're on their way here right now."

"What?!" Dani shouted. "Theo! What time is it? Why didn't you wake me up?"

She started to pull away from his arms so she could get ready. After Andreas had asked Theo and Dani to stay for a few more weeks to help with the research and excavation, their families had insisted that they fly out to Greece to see them. All of them. Dani's parents and Eddie. Theo's parents, sister, and her husband and kids. They'd made a few video calls over the last couple of days, but they'd yet to tell their families about their relationship. Partly because after spending the last year fighting for his life, Theo didn't want to put himself in danger again right away by telling Eddie he was fucking his sister.

But mainly, they wanted to focus on them. Learning about each other in these new capacities. Loving each other without family distractions.

Andreas and Theo still weren't sure how to handle the potential that they were cousins. For now, they decided to keep it to themselves. They figured Theo's reunion with his family and catching them up on his year in captivity was probably all the excitement they needed for now. But they already made plans for Andreas (and Christos) to visit them in the US. Because all of them, blood relatives or not, were now family.

"Not so fast," Theo said, pulling her back in his arms. "They still need to drive from the airport and check into the hotel. It's not like they're going to arrive and immediately come knocking on our door. I told them we could meet for lunch once they got settled in."

"Do you not remember your mom? She *will* come to your room immediately. You're her baby. She literally hugged the laptop when you called that first time."

Dani laughed, thinking about Mrs. Galanis's boobs pressed against the laptop camera.

"It will be fine. Though I suppose we probably should have thought about what we're going to say," Theo said, brushing a strand of her hair behind her ear.

Dani pulled her lips into a tight line. Yes, they probably should have talked about it, but Dani had been avoiding this conversation for the last week. Not because she didn't know how she felt about Theo. She loved him, unequivocally, fully, and deeply. She'd never loved anyone the way she loved him. She wanted to spend the rest of her life with him, traveling the world, going on all the adventures, reading together on the couch, and eating all the fries and drinking all the micheladas until they grew old together. If she didn't have what Harold and Patricia had, then she didn't want it.

But what if that's not what his family wanted? Or rather, what if he couldn't stand up to them? She wasn't a Triple G. The ability to disappoint his parents wasn't in Theo's blood.

"I can see those wheels spinning in your head," Theo said, stealing her from her thoughts. "Tell me, what are you thinking?"

"What if . . . what if they're upset?"

"They'll get over it. And do you *really* think it'll be all that surprising to them? We haven't exactly been hiding it on the phone calls. We just haven't *told* them. Besides, I'm sure they all always wondered. I visit you more than I visit my parents."

"That's only because it's patently uncool to say you're heading home to see your mom and dad."

"And you know me, the epitome of coolness," he said, flashing her his dorkiest cool smile.

"What if . . . what if it doesn't work out between us?"

"Impossible. I already know all your flaws, and I'm perfect," he said, smiling.

She buried her head in his chest, laughing.

"And you're sure this is what you really want?" she asked.

"Juicy," he said, taking her chin in his hand and tipping her face up to meet his, "I imprinted your words on my body. It has *always* been you. It *will* always be you. And now that I've had this time with you, there will never be anyone else. I love you. Nothing will ever change that."

She put both of her hands on his face and kissed him. Every unspoken moment, every questioning glance, went into that kiss. They already had what Harold and Patricia had had, and no one could take that away from them.

"You pinche cabron!"

Eddie's voice bellowed over the sound of the waves crashing below.

Dani and Theo released their mouths from each other and spun every which way, searching for Eddie. There he was, looking up from a balcony below them and one over. *Crap.*

"What happened?!" Dani's mother's voice called out seconds before peering up at them from the balcony neighboring Eddie's. "Daniela?! What are you doing? Is that . . . is that

Theo?" Her mother squinted, trying to figure out if the bearded man holding her was Theo.

"Daniela?!" Great, now Theo's parents were out there on the balcony above Dani and Theo's, and moments later, Ophelia, her husband, and their kids joined them.

"Oooooh!" Theo's seven-year-old niece cooed. "Unckie Theo and Auntie Cochina are kissing!"

"Ewww!" his ten-year-old nephew called out, making a barfing face.

Heads were popping up all over the place, giving Dani whiplash trying to figure out where everyone's voices were coming from.

"Theo?" his mom said, staring down at them with her hands on her hips while Dani was still in his arms and both of them were half-undressed. "What is going on?"

Theo and Dani looked at each other. "Well?" he said to her.

"Here goes nothing, I suppose. Love you no matter what happens?" she asked.

He smiled. "Always."

Acknowledgments

I wrote this book during the hardest year of my life—the year I filed for divorce. I didn't know that was how things were going to turn out when I signed the contract for this book, yet mere days later, my entire world got flipped upside down. Writing a romance novel, and even just being a romance author, while going through a divorce is something. You question everything: your belief in love, your passion to continue, whether you're even qualified to write about romance anymore. The cursor on my manuscript didn't budge for months (and that's when I bothered to open the file in the first place), and as the time ticked by, I worried I might not make my deadline.

For the record, I turned it in early.

Because ultimately, I believed in myself. And I *do* believe in love. From my parents, who've been married for over fifty years, to my friends and family, who showed me all the different ways to love a person during the time I needed it most, I saw and experienced love all around me. It's why I love this genre and this community—because we believe in HEAs, even when life throws us curveballs or doesn't turn out the way we'd envisioned.

I'm proud of me, and I'm prouder of this book, more than anything else I've ever written. I'm not embarrassed to say so. Honestly, we don't outwardly acknowledge when we're proud of ourselves enough. But I accomplished something that was damn hard, and not only that, I love what came together in these pages. And I want to recognize that and not shy away from all the pain and heartache that it took to get here, because, well, to do so would be to ignore reality. I'm not going to do that anymore.

None of this would have happened, however, without the support of my family, friends, publishing team, and the romance community.

First, to my pub team at Berkley. To my editor, Sarah Blumenstock, and assistant editor, Liz Sellers: I live for your feedback in the margins, especially like the comments during the bathtub scene! You manage to pull things out of me that I didn't know were there, always helping me deliver a better book. To my publicist, Kristin Cipolla, and marketers, Jessica Plummer and Hillary Tacuri: Thank you truly for everything you do. You are all rock stars!! Thank you to the editing team—Michelle Kasper, production editor; Christine Legon, managing editor; Randie Lipkin, copyeditor—Penguin Random House Audio, and the foreign rights teams and publishers. And of course, to cover artist and designer Camila Gray for working her magic yet AGAIN and art director Emily Osborne. The covers for this series are nothing short of amazing. They say not to judge a book by its cover, but with covers like these, please do!

To my agent, Jill Marsal: Thank you for your support and willingness to hop on a call at any time. I'm so happy to have you in my corner.

To all the readers who've read my books and said hi at signings and cons, and who love this genre as much as I do: You make this all worth it. Your stories and our interactions genuinely touch me. Thank you for loving love.

To Jen Comfort: What would I do without you? Thank you for keeping me on task and reading my drivel before it's ready for public consumption. I will follow you to the river, and I'll stay with you forever—off-key and all.

To all the author friends I've made over the years, the Ponies (Jas, Elle, Kate, Jen, Lin, Mel, Kelly, and Alexis), the Complicated Cats (Rachel, Ava, Alicia, Jen, and Rosie), the Berkletes (far too many to name), and so, so many more: You are all amazing. The joy I get from being around all of you, whether in person or virtually, fills my heart *and* my creative well in a way nothing else can. Perhaps it's cheesy, but you inspire me.

To Jasmine: It's been a year. You made it better. I can't thank you enough for being such an awesome friend, and now that we're on the other side of it all, I can't wait to travel the world with you.

To all my friends and family who were there for me this past year, gave me strength, showed me patience, and gave me grace, especially Meredith, Cindy, Anna, Heather, Mary, Kim, David, and Eileen: I'm so fortunate to have you in my life.

To Mommo and Daddo: Oops, I did it again. I'm sorry I can't help but write the spicy ones. 😇 You should have known when you nicknamed me Pickle Juice that I'd be trouble. (I guess there's a reason Dad always called me Cochina.) But you love me just the way I am, and I love you both more than I can ever express.

To Natalia: Thank you for listening to me just about every day, even when I'm obsessing over / complaining about the same things day in and day out. And thank you for being there and for saving up your spit.

To my sister: As they say, there were never such devoted sisters, and you've shown me that ten thousand times over. Thank you for giving me courage, for giving the best hugs, and for telling me you love me every time we talk. Let the YOLO tour continue!

To Henrik: I know you can't read, but your furry presence at my feet helped me get this book done (though your snores are truly distracting—in a cute way).

Finally, I want to thank Rachel and Brandon. Words will NEVER be able to capture the gratitude I have for the two of you. I love you both, especially you, Rachel. (Don't worry, everyone, B already knows this.) You are the real deal.

Jo Segura

READERS GUIDE

Discussion Questions

1. The story begins with Dani discovering that Theo has been captured, leading to her capture, too. He tries numerous times to get her to safety, but Dani is too stubborn. What would you do if you were Dani? Would you leave and get help? Stay with Theo? What do you think the outcome would have been had Dani left Theo when she first had the chance?

2. Dani struggles with not living up to her high school dreams and expectations. Do you think Dani would be a different person had she never returned to Grand Rapids? Are you living the life you imagined when you were in high school? If not, how has your life differed from your expectations?

3. One of the things Dani laments is how she's never traveled the world like she always thought she would. When was

the first time you traveled away from home, and where did you go? Was the experience scary, exciting, or something else? What places are on your travel bucket list and why?

4. The miscommunication trope is one of those love-it-or-hate-it tropes. Had Theo just talked to Dani before taking off to Greece, perhaps none of the events in the book would have happened. When do you think Theo should have confronted Dani about his feelings? Right away? After he saw her with Beau? Their first night together after they reunited? Some other time? Are there ever times when you think *not* confronting someone is warranted? What are your thoughts on the miscommunication trope?

5. Theo grapples with wanting to make his parents proud while also living his own life. Do you think there is a way for Theo to accomplish both? How? Have you ever struggled with adhering to family expectations versus wanting to live your own life? In what ways?

6. Dani and Theo take turns being the hero of the story, each saving the day and each other in different ways. What do you think makes someone a hero? Who do you think is the hero of the story and why? (And don't forget side characters—some may say it's Harold.)

7. What is your favorite Greek myth? If you were a Greek god (one already in the books or completely new), who would you be and why?

8. Food plays a huge role in Dani's and Theo's family gatherings. Do you have a go-to dish? What sort of food traditions does your family have?

9. Theo gives Dani the nickname "Juicy" after an embarrassing wardrobe malfunction. Do you have any embarrassing nicknames? If you were to earn a nickname based on what you're wearing right now (doesn't have to be your underwear, LOL), what would it be?

Author photo copyright © Sean Hoyt

USA Today bestselling author **JO SEGURA** lives in the Pacific Northwest with her doggo, who vies for her attention with his sweet puppy-dog eyes whenever she's trying to write. Her stories feature strong, passionate heroines and draw upon aspects of her life, such as her love of good food, her Mexican heritage, and her fascination with archaeology. When she's not writing, you can find her practicing law, perusing the aisles of Trader Joe's, or sitting outside doing BuzzFeed quizzes (though she doesn't care what the chicken nugget quiz said—her favorite fruit is *not* banana).

VISIT JO SEGURA ONLINE

JoSegura.com
JoSeguraBooks
JoSeguraBooks.substack.com